BRIDE TAKES A WARRIOR

Highland Vows & Vengeance
Book 4

by Kara Griffin

ARE YOU SIGNED UP FOR DRAGONBLADE'S BLOG?

You'll get the latest news and information on exclusive giveaways, exclusive excerpts, coming releases, sales, free books, cover reveals and more.

Check out our complete list of authors, too!

No spam, no junk. That's a promise!

Sign Up Here

www.dragonbladepublishing.com

Dearest Reader;

Thank you for your support of a small press. At Dragonblade Publishing, we strive to bring you the highest quality Historical Romance from some of the best authors in the business. Without your support, there is no 'us', so we sincerely hope you adore these stories and find some new favorite authors along the way.

Happy Reading!

CEO, Dragonblade Publishing

**Additional Dragonblade books by
Author Kara Griffin**

Highland Vows & Vengeance Series
Bride Takes a Scot (Book 1)
Bride Takes a Laird (Book 2)
Bride Takes a Charmer (Book 3)
Bride Takes a Warrior (Book 4)

About the Book

Breckin Buchanan, a renowned warrior, is in no mood to placate the king, especially when he is commanded to take a border baron's daughter as his wife. As he gives himself to the pursuit of protecting weakened Highland clans and finding out the truth behind his sister's death, he has no patience to woo a wife, especially a coddled, willful lass. But at the first sight of Eva Scott's beauty, he might reconsider that.

Eva's life drastically changes when she's forced to marry the utterly handsome and stubborn warrior. She is used to an extravagant life where she's doted upon and tended to by servants, but now, she must learn to fend for herself. Born to a life of opulence, Eva quickly realizes that wealth has little meaning to the Highlanders. As she tries to adapt to the Highland way of life, she is determined to prove that she doesn't need Breckin, his clan, or anyone. But that becomes most difficult when his ardent attention awakens a longing for his touch, acceptance, and love.

From the moment they meet, neither can deny their intense desire and stormy passion. Breckin finds himself drawn home more often and discovers Eva has turned into a determined woman. Eva hopes Breckin will reveal his heart but doing that might take drastic measures on her part, especially when he is reticent about his life.

As Breckin gets closer to discovering the truth behind his sister's death, his vengeance ignites his need to destroy his enemy. His purpose wavers when Eva's life is in peril and he is unable to rescue her. Eva's courage and resilience enriches him and gives Breckin hope that there is more to life than war. Will his bittersweet revenge force him to accept Eva and give her a place within his clan and his heart?

Will these Highland vows and vengeance hold the promise of love and redemption for Breckin and Eva?

Character List

BUCHANAN CLAN
Breckin Buchanan – Hero
Conner Buchanan and Caden Buchanan – Twin brothers
Clare – Aunt
Gideon – Comrade / Commander-in-arms
Deena – Gideon's wife
Hamish – Gideon's son
Willa – Gideon's mother / Healer
Ise-Olcan (she-wolf) – Willa's pet
Aymer – Gate watchman
Alton – Stablemaster
Father Murphy – Clan clergyman
Lawrence – Clan builder

HOUSE OF SCOTT
Eva – Heroine
Michael – Father
Anne – Mother (deceased)
Richard Scott, Stephen Scott, Howard Scott – Brothers
Luella – Maidservant

OTHER NOTABLES
King Alexander of Scotland
Queen Margaret of Scotland
Edmund – Edinburgh Chamberlain

Campbells – Allied Clan

Grahams – Allied Clan

John MacLaren – Rival

Danella MacLaren – Hero's Ex-Betrothed

William Stewart – Rival

Garreth – Alderman in the woods

Harriet – Young woman in the woods

Master Amos – Merchant

CHAPTER ONE

Dryhope Tower, Selkirk
Border of Scotland
Early February, 1260

A RUSTLING SOUND alerted Eva that someone was inside her bed chamber. She kept her eyes closed, knowing who had entered. Surely, morning hadn't come already. She only wanted a moment more of rest before her maidservant rousted her from the warmth of her bed. The creak of the floorboards and hearth gate came with noises from Luella as she moved about the chamber. Crackling in the hearth signaled that soon Eva would have to leave her bed.

"Good morn, Mistress. You must awaken. Your father has returned and has bid that you attend him in all possible haste in the great hall," Luella said as she stood by the bedside. "Come, now, arise. You must roust yourself. 'Tis time to begin your day."

"Must I?" Eva fisted her eyes to remove sleep from them and then peered above at the crimson velvet canopy that covered the wooden poster bed. She threw her legs over the edge of the bedside and sat up. Grateful for the warmth of the hearth, she didn't bother to pull on a wrap. Then she remembered this was the day that she was supposed to meet Brother Abram at the village church for her lessons.

With a gasp of excitement, she hurried to the basin, washed, and by the time she'd finished her morning ablutions, Luella had an underdress ready. Eva stripped out of her nightdress, stepped close to her, and allowed Luella to garb her. The soft, warm material of the underdress was set over her and instantly chased away the slight chill.

"Choose a simple gown for this day, Luella. I am off to church this morn."

"Very well, Mistress." Luella left her and approached the wardrobe. She returned holding a beige, long-sleeved linen dress with a rounded neckline.

It was one of Eva's favorite gowns because it was warm enough without being cumbersome or heavy. She slipped it over her head and Luella tugged it into place, pulled the twisted fabric belt around her waist, and tied it.

"There, Mistress, you are ready for the day. I must say how fetching you look."

Eva smiled at her maidservant because she always complimented her appearance. Not that it turned Eva's head or induced her vanity. "My thanks, Luella. Did I hear you say that Da is home?"

"He is, and he told me to hasten you. There must be some urgent news, for he seemed intent on seeing you immediately. He said to send you to the hall right away and not let you fob me off."

Eva chuckled lightly at her maid's jest. "Then let us not delay and take overlong with my hair. A simple tie at the nape will do," she suggested.

Luella agreed and combed her hair, which took a long moment but finally the strands were tied in place.

As the maid arranged her hair, Eva wondered why her father had returned earlier than expected. He'd visited Edinburgh to meet with other border lords and she thought that he'd take a least a fortnight or more to return. She couldn't reason it.

Now, she slipped on her warm boots and snatched her cloak from the peg inside the door for her planned walk to the church, after she met with her da.

"My thanks, Luella, for your aid. I shall see you later."

"I will come with you, Mistress."

Eva snickered with a soft breath. "You just want to know the news. Well, come along then and we shall find out together." She left the chamber and didn't wait for Luella as she trailed her.

On her walk through the manor, Eva eyed the opulent décor and furnishings of her home, much of which she had purchased with her household allowance. Her dear da always noticed when she'd purchased something new and it always pleased him. Fortunately, her da's wealth enabled her to spend to her heart's content. If she found something she wanted, she bought it—from elaborate candleholders to rich fabrics and expensive carpets from abroad—nothing was too costly to acquire.

She passed the long stretch of hallway that led to the stairs. How she loved her home, especially this ornate railing, carved from the wood of the oldest tree on her father's land. The poor tree had been felled during a storm, but its beautiful wood lived on. Her hand glided over the smooth, polished railing as she descended the stairs. She'd paid the carpenter a fortune to have it made, but it was well worth the cost.

At the landing, she turned and headed for the hall where her father often held audiences. She rarely ate there and preferred to eat in the cozy solar adjacent to the overlarge room. The hall's starkness seemed to match her father's mood.

He usually greeted her with a smile but as she took him in, she noticed how the hair on his head and in his trimmed beard had begun to hold more gray streaks than dark brown. He wasn't a large man, but not lanky either. Still, he took up most of the space in the seat that he occupied. Strangely enough, he hadn't bothered to remove the cloak that he'd worn during his travel and sat at the table as if he was about to leave. More intriguing was that his breath was raspy and instead of looking up to greet her, his eyes remained on the parchment he held.

She glided across the gleaming floorboards and stood next to a broad, ornately carved wooden chair she'd recently acquired.

After setting her cloak over the back of the chair, she clutched the top of it.

"Da, you are home. I did not expect you so soon. I am gladdened to see you but I have not much time. Father Abrams is awaiting me for my lesson." She rounded the chair and stood beside him and placed a light kiss on his whiskered cheek. He hadn't glanced up at her yet and kept his gaze on the parchment in front of him.

He acknowledged her with a grunt. Lord Michael Scott, her dear da, finally set aside the parchment and his face was most staid when he lifted his chin to look at her. "I am afraid that your singing lesson has been canceled."

"Canceled? But Brother Abrams told me that we would start a new song today. I looked forward to it," she said with a small pout to her lips. Singing was perhaps the only thing in recent days that brought her joy, well, besides visiting the merchants. After all, she had a propensity to spend her da's coins. "Did he say why?"

"It was not he that canceled it, but me, lass. Your lessons have come to an end, sprig."

Eva's displeasure had to show on her face but instead of being angry with her father, she smiled and took the seat next to him. That he called her "sprig", his endearment for her, softened her reaction to his dreadful news. "An end? Why would you end my lessons? You know how fond I am of singing."

"We must leave for Edinburgh this day."

"Leave? Did you not only return? And why would I go with you? You never take me on your travels, especially to Edinburgh. I detest riding in the carriage and never travel."

"I made haste to get here at the king's behest. You see…" her father's voice trailed off and his shoulders rose and fell with a heavy sigh. That's when she noticed his breath labored a little.

"Da, are you ailing?"

"I must have picked up a chill on my trek, but I am well enough. We have much to discuss."

She was slightly concerned for his well-being, but he didn't seem to be. "What is it?" Eva was disheartened at his tone because it alluded to bad tidings which she was certain would displease her.

Her da reached across the table and took hold of her hand. "The king has betrothed you. I was told to bring you posthaste for the wedding. We must hurry and return to Edinburgh."

"Betrothed? To who? Surely you could have told him some falsity to get out of it."

His brows rose, showing he was aghast at such a suggestion. "You would have me speak falsely to the king? No, sprig, I could not do that. Several men are being offered as grooms and we will find out who the king has named as your husband when we arrive." He broke into a coughing fit and she hurried to pat his back.

He flapped his hand at her and she ceased trying to give him aid. Words couldn't form as her mind reeled with his news. She was being forced to marry and by the king no less? *Sweet Mary.* She had no retort to his news and if she had, it would dismay her dear da.

He continued with a softening to his eyes after clearing his throat, "Ah, you, sprig, are so akin to your mother, a beauty that would make any man happy. With your long brown locks and pretty blue eyes… I see so much of Anne in you and I miss her terribly. Every time I look at you, I am reminded of her."

Eva's heart twinged at her da's somber words. Her father rarely spoke about her mother and the mention of her brought on a little melancholy too. Her mother died birthing her and Eva was said to take after her in likeness. Still, she knew little about the woman and often held guilt because if not for her, her mother would not have died. That he spoke of her now seemed unaccountable. Eva always thought her father blamed her for his loss, yet he never said so outright.

Her father sighed wistfully and continued, "She would have been proud to have you as a daughter. I should have taken better care to have you trained in wifely duties, alas, I spoiled you. But 'tis time you married. You need to be settled with a husband and begin your life as a woman should, not here taking care of an old man."

"Oh, Da, you are not old and I do not mind taking care of you." Eva could have laughed at that because she did little to care for him.

They had a manor full of maids and servants who tended to their every need. Being the baby and only daughter, her father had indulged her with gifts when she was young and an abundant allowance when she grew to womanhood. Now the thought of having to leave him and her home tightened her chest.

"But I like my life here with you, Da, and do not want a husband." Eva tried to think of any excuse to delay or to object to the king's decree. As she pressed the wavy locks of her hair behind her shoulder, she muttered, "Could we not tell him that I am ailing or am unable to travel? Surely the king would believe you." Eva lowered her chin, dejected at what her father told her. Of all the news he could have imparted, that she was to be betrothed was the last thing she expected.

"I cannot tell a falsity to my king, lass. We must reach Edinburgh before month's end. The weddings are taking place then. We have no time to dally and must be on the road by midday. Now, ready yourself and be quick. Pack your things and be sure to bring something appropriate to wear for the feast and celebration. The king says it will be quite an enjoyable affair with many in attendance."

"Can I at least eat my morning fare before I am hied off to this wedding?" Her tone was light yet curt.

"Aye, let us partake of our morning feast. Tell me about your lessons with Brother Abram. When I told him that you would no longer be coming for lessons, he was somewhat relieved."

Eva chuckled and leaned forward to snatch a sweet roll from the basket on the table. Though she wasn't hungry after receiving such dreadful news, she forced herself to eat. The ride to

Edinburgh was long and would take at least two days. Her stomach fluttered with nervousness as it was and it would do well to put something in it.

She then poured a cup of mead for them both. "Brother Abrams probably was relieved. Each time I met with him, he swore that the Bishop would have his hide if he found out he was teaching me the chants. Your alms to the church certainly persuaded him to take the risk."

Her father scoffed a laugh. "Yet he was still willing to teach you. I fear he may have been besotted by you. He says you have the sweetest voice he's ever heard. That he was willing to risk the Bishop's punishments says much, even if my alms were substantial."

She knew that to be true. Brother Abram was kind to take the time to help her vocalize the songs she wanted to learn. He spent a good amount of time helping her to get the pitch and ranges right, teaching her in both English and Latin. She'd miss the man and was sad that she would no longer get to sing in church.

As she ate, she questioned her father further about his trip to Edinburgh. "I thought you were going to Edinburgh to meet with the lords. How did the king know that you were there?"

"Many of the men that I met with are the king's council. They told him that I would attend the meeting, which sadly reminded him of you, and Alexander called me forth. Sprig, I know that you are distressed to marry and that you want to stay here but that cannot be. The king has put forth a plan that involves others in these marriage pacts and we must accept his courtesy. I want you to be happy, lass, and to make the most of your marriage. I shall be deeply distraught if you do not. Promise me that you will make the effort to be content."

Eva patted his hand in an attempt to placate him. He seemed rather anxious about the matter. "Of course, Da, I promise. I am not pleased by it, but as you said, I have no choice. It will take me a short time to pack. I will worry for you. Who will take care of you if I am not here? You shall have no family about the manor."

"There are plenty of servants and your eldest brother, Richard, is meeting us in Edinburgh as well. He will bear witness to your wedding and then he shall return here with me." Her father picked up the cup she'd placed before him and drank. Then he rose and gave her an affectionate gaze. "It pleases me to know that you will be looked after..."

Eva tried not to frown at her father's words because there was something more he wasn't telling her. Still, she could never get her father to reveal what he wished to withhold. "Why is Richard returning with you? Does he not have service left in the king's army? And what of Stephen and Howard?"

She hadn't seen her brothers in over a year or more. When Richard went to serve the king, he was full of pride. Stephen left shortly after Richard and sought to find his fortune, whatever that was. Their father and her middle brother, Stephen, had fought and harsh words were spoken. How she missed Stephen. Of her three brothers, she was closest to him because he had always included her and never ignored her. Though he was older, Stephen never minded her constant questions. Richard never had time for her and Howard always had his nose in a book of scripture. She wasn't disheartened that her youngest brother was put in service to the church. With her brothers gone though, life had been somewhat lonely.

Eva wondered if that was why her father had indulged her now by giving her an unending supply of coins. Was guilt for his absence the reason for his generosity? Her family had left her on her own but she never lacked for anything, except, of course, for companionship and family.

"Your wedding will give me great favor with the king. I was able to convince Alexander to release Richard from his duty. Your brother will return with me and will stay on. I shall be gladdened to hand over the reins of keeping this manor and travel to him for he is the eldest."

"But you like to travel and shall miss it, will you not?" She disbelieved he would so easily give up his profession of trading across the channel. "Ah, so you took advantage of my departure?"

"Departure, sprig? With your marriage, you will find a new home and life. Your wedding is coveted by the king and queen. You will be married to a worthy man and I cannot allow my emotions to interfere with my sire's command or what is best for you."

Her shoulders sagged a little and she sighed. "Very well, I will go then and make ready. I shall meet you outside shortly."

She took the last bite of her sweet roll, drank the rest of the mead in her cup, and set it gently on the table. Eva hoped whomever she married wasn't a staunch lord who forbade her from her pursuits—not that she had many interests. She liked to shop at the merchant's stalls and purchase exquisite fabrics and other items, sing in the church, walk about the land, and look after her da when he was home. She lived a simple but fulfilled life.

Being in such an isolated area, she hadn't had many friendships but that hadn't mattered because she kept herself busy. The women in the area were brash and seemed envious of her, although she couldn't imagine why. Eva thought herself to be friendly, kind, and steadfast.

Hopefully, she would be the lady of a grand manor, married to a lord who entertained and would spoil her as much as her da had. Her life was about to be uprooted but she didn't think it would change all that much, especially if she married a man who held lands, wealth, and was influential with other lords.

She almost bumped into Luella on the way to her chamber. Eva passed by her and rushed up the steps, keeping her emotions steeled. As much as she wanted to shout or cry at the injustice of the travesty, she wouldn't show such sentiments.

Inside her chamber, she grabbed the largest satchel she owned and peered at her wardrobe. She was hopeless when it came to dressing herself and relied on Luella when it came to choosing the appropriate garments each day.

"Mistress, I am sorry and shall miss you. All the servants shall be saddened to see you go."

When she craned her neck to look at Luella, she noticed the girl's tears. It made it even harder to hold onto her emotions. "Come, help me choose what garments to take on my journey. You always know what looks best on me and cease your weeping. It will do no good for either of us because you shall make me cry too."

Luella practically skipped to the wardrobe and removed a beautiful velvet blue gown with golden trim. She took care to fold it so it wouldn't be entirely wrinkled. Then her maid chose another elaborate cream gown with brown lace. "Will these do? You should wear the cream gown for your wedding, Mistress."

Sweet Mary, her wedding. She would be given to a man. Gone was the freedom of being a young maiden with no responsibilities or burdens. Eva hoped with all her heart that whoever she was bound to wasn't a complete knave. She shook the horrid thought away and smiled at Luella as she packed the trunk and satchel with her clothing.

"Perfect choices, Luella. Now I need some garments for everyday wear. Nothing too extravagant but perhaps modest and warm. The weather is still chilly since spring has yet to appear."

As she left the rest of the selections to Luella, Eva collected a few pairs of slippers, some jewelry, hair coverings, and toiletries she'd need. She slipped her feet out of the worn boots she'd chosen to wear that day and replaced them with warmer boots sufficient enough to travel in. Then she grabbed a heavier cloak because the journey would be cold.

"Mistress, you are not going to return, are you?" Luella sniffled her tears.

"Probably not. But I beg you to pack my belongings because I am certain Da will have them sent to me, or perhaps I can have my husband bring me so I might collect them after the wedding." Eva's chest tightened at the thought of leaving her precious belongings behind. She cherished every item she'd bought, down to the smallest candleholder but she'd make sure to receive them wherever she was going.

She hefted the heavy satchel and ambled to the doorway of her bedchamber. With sadness welling inside her, she turned back and peered at the place that held much solace for her. It was where she spent much of her time. "Luella, my thanks for…for your help and kindness."

Luella scrambled forward and took the satchel from her. "Let me carry that, Mistress, and you do not need to thank me. I was gladdened to serve you. I shall have men come and collect your trunk."

The maid was such a sweet girl, only a year or two younger than Eva. She tried never to overtax her with chores and gave her time to relax and pursue her own pleasures. Since only her father and she resided at their home, there wasn't much to do. But she wasn't privy to what the servants did in the manor, only what they did directly for her.

Outside, she walked toward the awaiting carriage. Her da stood next to the horseman, giving him direction. Suddenly, her father pitched forward and fell face-first to the ground. The men standing near the horses shouted and dashed to him.

"Da!" Eva yelled and sprinted forth. When she reached her da, she knelt next to him and pressed her hand on his face. "Da, what happened? Are you hurt?"

He wheezed and gasped for breath so much so that he couldn't answer.

"Da, you cannot travel in this condition. Let us get you back inside. When you are better, we shall leave for Edinburgh. Perhaps in a day or two." Eva motioned to her father's men and they helped him from the ground and supported him as they led him back inside.

"Mistress, what can I do?" Luella asked.

"Send someone to fetch the healer from the village, as hastily as you can. Tell him that my da is in peril and needs immediate aid."

Luella lifted the hem of her skirt and hurried off.

Eva lowered her head and walked toward the entrance of the manor. Concern tightened her chest and shoulders at her father's ailment. That he hadn't argued with her told her that he was in far more serious distress than she realized. Not that she wanted to have her da ill, but she was thankful for a day or two respite from having to go to her wedding.

With a little over a fortnight until month's end, they had to leave soon. It took only two day's ride by horse to reach the town of Edinburgh. If they left within a sennight before their anticipated arrival, the carriage would reach the castle in plenty of time—enough for her to be given away in matrimony to a stranger. *Sweet Mary.*

Eventually, Eva would have to face her future and new life. For now, she would ensure her father didn't meet his end and care for him as he deserved.

CHAPTER TWO

Clairinch Island, Stirlingshire
Highlands of Scotland
Late February, 1260

THE DECORATIVE WOODEN torch mounted in the ground stood erect before the waters of Loch Lomond. Its elaborate brass scrolls and flower etching in the wooden stand was an ill-fated reminder of who had once lain there. Now the torch's flame danced in the breeze and shone its brightness in the dusk of the early evening, a beacon for Breckin, Laird of the Buchanan Clan, and a remembrance of his sister who had died on that very spot a year before, almost to the day.

Breckin lowered his head in prayer, a plea that had crossed his lips many times as he worshipped at the torch. He hoped that Marian had entered Heaven but he knew it was probable that she did not. Taking your life was a grievous sin and one not easily forgiven by God Himself.

He had ridden ahead so he might ensure the torch's flame remained lit. He'd given his sentry the duty of keeping the fire alight throughout the day and night. When he raised his head, he pressed back the long strands of his blond hair and tucked it behind his ears. The wind easily dislodged his locks as he drew a deep breath and allowed the waters over the loch and the hale breeze to allay his restlessness of returning from war.

Horses tromped over the wooden bridge of the loch and

crossed onto the wooded island of Clairinch. The small tree-covered island, home to the Buchanans, provided them safety and a place to come together. Before the bridge, Buchanan land stretched as far as five leagues from north to south and was as wide as five leagues in parts. It was a good amount of territory to protect but none would dare to trespass on his property. Even his most notorious enemies made a wide berth around his land for they knew they would suffer the wrath of his warriors.

His men returned from their fracas with the MacGregors who had stolen some of the Grahams' winter stores. They'd given their ally, the Grahams, aid when they needed strong arms against their foes. Their quest to regain the Grahams' stores was easy enough, and even though swords were raised, the MacGregors put up little fight and hastily returned the stolen goods.

Most of his men continued to move across the bridge except for his most trusted friend. His commander-in-arms, Gideon, approached with heavy steps. "Och, there ye are. I thought ye would find your way here. Ye always do." The torch's firelight shone on the auburn locks of his friend's hair and brightened his beard-covered face.

"Aye, I needed to take a moment to—"

"Laird, ye still mourn but she's been gone so long. Why do ye not put it behind ye? Douse the flame and be done with it. Ye chastise yourself for naught," Gideon's voice came low and he faced the water.

Breckin raised his voice in retort, "I cannot put it behind me…not until I learn the truth. Marian would not have taken her life. I am certain of that. Until I find out the reason for her death, this torch will stay lit." He couldn't fathom why his bonny sister would kill herself. She had had much to live for and had just been betrothed to a man to whom she had given her heart. Marian looked forward to her wedding and life—and then suddenly, she was gone.

"Ye are a stubborn man. She's condemned to Purgatory or Hell. Might as well accept that and release yourself from the misery."

Breckin's chest tensed at his friend's words. "Good deeds will pave the way for her."

Gideon scoffed and pressed his hands over his reddish beard. "Ye think your deeds will aid her? She took her life, my friend, and there is naught ye can do to save her soul."

"If I do enough good deeds, God will accept her." Breckin wouldn't desist in trying. And until he learned the truth of her death, he would go forth to aid other clans against their foes. Helping those less fortunate or unable to defend themselves might be favorable in God's eyes. Surely his Lord and Savior would take that into consideration.

"Ye fool yourself and hold guilt for naught."

"I should have known what was going on in her life, should have protected her. Of course, I hold guilt, Gideon, as I should."

Gideon shook his head adamantly. "Nay, that is not so but I will cease haranguing ye about it. One day ye will accept that she is gone and what she'd done. Regardless of how many clans ye save, it will not change what happened. Come, let us return to the keep."

Breckin followed Gideon across the bridge and on the lane that led to the middle of the island where they'd occupied cottages, work buildings, and a large stable that housed their steeds. On the approach to the small garrison, he saw Aymer, the gate watchman, and his brother, Alton, the stablemaster. They seemed to be awaiting him. The brothers resembled pine trees, for they had thick dark-shaded bodies, black hair and eyes, and prickly natures. Both held serious miens on their faces. Unsmiling and unwelcoming, they waited until he reached them.

Breckin hoped there was no trouble because all he wanted to do was find a good hearty meal and maybe get some well-needed sleep. "What goes? Given the look on your faces, it must be dire."

Alton pressed his brother back a step. "I should be the one to tell him."

"Go on then," Aymer said.

"Your brothers… They are atop the stable's roof. I tried to get them to come down but they will not listen to me. By God, they will fall to their death if they're not careful."

Breckin drew a weary sigh and had hoped on his return he wouldn't gain any ill-favored reports of his younger brothers' misdeeds. The two of them were always finding new ways to irritate or scare the hell out of him. Indeed, as he walked into the stableyard, he spotted Connor and Caden, twins who looked so much alike that no one could tell them apart. But that never mattered because his brothers were inseparable. Where there was one—there was the other.

"What are ye doing up there?" Breckin called and shifted his eyes to peer above.

"Laird, ye returned. Await us, we will be right down," one of his brothers shouted.

Breckin flinched when one of his brothers hopped from one beam to the next. Before the boys could retreat from the roof, a crack came, and one of the upper beams folded in on the stable. He heard one of his brothers shout and then a loud bang.

Everyone within hearing distance sprinted inside the building. In the center of the lane between the stalls, his brother lay upon a heaping pile of manure. Fortunately, the pile of cosh was large enough to break his fall and save him from breaking his neck. A beam was prevented from falling completely to the ground when another beam blocked it. The roof continued to creak, and Breckin hoped his other brother made it safely down.

"Caden, are ye hurt?" This apparently came from Connor who peered through the gaping hole of the stable roof above.

"Christ Almighty, save me from these two dimwits," Breckin said as he stared at his younger brother covered with reeking horse droppings. Even Caden's light strands of hair were soiled with the mucky manure and bits of straw. He groaned.

Aymer stepped forward and tossed his hand down to help his brother out of the mess. "Are ye hurt, wee Caden?"

He shook his head. "Laird, we did not expect ye…"

"Apparently not. Connor, get down here, and for God's sake, do not fall through the roof." As he waited for the other twin, Breckin considered what their penalty would be. He was tired of coming up with appropriate punishments for them. This time though, they had gone too far. His brothers, not even half a score in age, tested his patience time and again. Breckin hoped they'd mature, but even with arms training, his brothers still reveled in causing havoc and performing "daring feats," as they'd called it.

Connor arrived and hurried to see if their brother was hurt. "Why, ye are not even bleeding. Ye cannot claim that as a brave feat, Caden." He chortled but ceased when he noticed Breckin's glare.

The two of them had long, light hair that much resembled Breckin's in color. Though Breckin had their father's green eyes, his brothers' eyes were as blue as an afternoon summer sky, akin to their mother's. Their grubby faces were dirty, and likewise, their garments had seen better days. Their clothing and bodies needed a long washing in the loch. How he wanted to be the one to dunk them in the water, if only to cause them discomfort.

"Everyone, return to your posts." Breckin stood with his hands fisted at his waist, trying to come up with a reasonable, or hell, even an unreasonable punishment for them. His wee brothers tried to bypass him, but he stepped in front of them before they could abscond. "Not ye two. Halt. Stay where ye are."

They stopped abruptly and lowered their heads.

"I will not even ask why ye would risk your lives by climbing on the stable roof. Lord, Caden, ye stink to high heaven. Go, both of ye, and get cleaned up and meet me at Aunt Clare's. We will have our supper and I will dole out your punishment then. Be quick about it and do not make me come to find ye." Before he could speak further, his brothers dashed from the stables. He'd have to scour his mind for some unpleasant task for them to do—but he doubted they'd learn their lesson. They hadn't so far.

Breckin reached the outside of the stable and approached

Aymer. "Those two are going to force me to an early grave."

Aymer bellowed. "Aye, aye. I kept watch on them all day but they disappeared, and then I found them hopping from one beam to another atop the roof. They have a death wish, aye?"

"Seems so. Now I have to think of how to reprimand them."

"Something will come to ye, Laird, it always does," Aymer said. "Since ye are here, I would give ye my report now. The sentry reported no trespassers whilst ye were gone except that they met the king's messenger at the border by the blackened trees. He gave them a missive for ye." His guardsman handed him the sealed parchment and bowed. "If that be all?"

"Aye, go on, Aymer, seek your rest." Breckin held the parchment and walked toward his aunt's cottage. When he returned from war or travel, he usually stayed in the soldiers' barracks. But this night, he wanted a comfortable, warm bed, and his aunt's good cooking. He reached her door in quick time and entered.

Breckin breathed deeply when he entered. Clare was likely the best cook in the clan and she'd made something delicious. Its scent wafted throughout the cottage and reminded him that he hadn't eaten a decent meal in days since he'd been on the move. On the approach to the kitchen area, he spotted his aunt who bent over and stirred a small cauldron atop a fire in the hearth.

When she heard a noise behind her, she gasped and dropped the spoon. It ended up sinking in the stew. "Bloody hell, Breckin, ye frightened me half to death. Care to give a warning when ye enter?" His aunt, a thin-bodied woman, wore a wimple over the reddish-brown locks of her shoulder-length hair. Deep blue eyes, the same as his mother's, glared at him.

"My apologies, Clare, I did not mean to scare ye. I'll be staying here this night. Is there enough stew for me?" He flashed a big smile in hopes that it would appease her.

"Of course, ye can stay, and aye, there is plenty for ye. Sit ye down at the table. Your brothers should come soon, for they haven't eaten since early this morn. Their stomachs will coax them home." Clare got another spoon and used it to retrieve the one that had fallen in the stew.

"I saw them. They will be here soon." Breckin sat at the worn table nearby and allowed his tension to ease from him.

His aunt had been a godsend since his parents had passed to the hereafter almost two years before. Clare aided him in caring for his siblings when his laird duties became more demanding. With his sister Marian gone, that only left him and his two younger brothers. Still, he had a good-sized clan to rule and oversee. He tried to be a fair and just laird, training his brethren to become warriors renowned for their force and unwavering triumphs.

Try as he might, he had yet to think of a way to reprimand his brothers. Their chastisement needed to be harsh and instill caution the next time they decided to perform addled feats. He placed the parchment Aymer had given him on the table and heard the door open behind him with a creak. His brothers stepped lightly until they reached the table.

"I did not. 'Twas your fault. Ye should have listened to me," Connor groused.

"If ye did not push me, I would not have fallen through the—" Caden said.

"Shush, both of ye. Sit ye down and remain quiet," Breckin said in a no-nonsense tone. His younger brothers somewhat feared him. That might well be a good thing since they bloody likely didn't fear anyone else. Now, how to punish them? "I will hear no excuses about your behavior this day. How many times have I told ye not to endanger yourselves? Ye risk your necks when ye do such things. Have ye no God-given sense? Nay, do not answer."

Clare rushed forth and placed filled bowls of stew before them. Then she placed a basket of bread on the table and smiled. "Go on, eat your fill, lads."

Breckin took a breath before he sentenced his brothers, knowing he had to be strict. "On the morrow, ye will rise at dawn and retrieve water for the barracks and kitchen. Then report for arms training and stay there until midday. When ye are finished, ye will come here, eat your supper, and then go to the stables. Ye will clean every stall until your job is done, and Alton will tell me if ye did a fair job of it too. This is your sentence for the next fortnight."

His brothers groaned but didn't retort or make a complaint. They knew that it was futile. If they made a single grievance, he would make the punishment longer and more taxing.

Clare set before him a cup of ale and took a seat near his. "'Tis good to have ye home, Breckin. The lads missed ye. Oh, they will not tell ye so, but they did. And I am pleased ye are here because I have had my hands full of looking after them."

"Ye should have accepted the maid's aid when I offered it, Clare. She hoped to serve us."

Clare snorted a laugh. "Oh? She hoped to serve ye, not me. I tell ye the lass is smitten with ye, Breckin, but ye are blind to it."

"Amara's attention was unwanted; besides, she is too young for me. I am much too busy to be distracted by such unimportant matters. Ye have only to say the word and I shall get ye help." Breckin suspected his brothers were too much for his aunt to handle, but she refused any support, even if the lassies had other motives in mind.

"I will not have other women in my home." Clare glanced at him, shook her head, and returned her attention to her meal.

Breckin pressed the parchment open that he'd set on the table and read the lines. His lips tightened at the words scrawled across the page. The king had written the summons himself and bade him to make the journey to Edinburgh. It was an odd request. Alexander had his fealty, for he'd sworn it before his entire court when the king had married Queen Margaret. The matter must be important but it gave no indication of the situation or need.

He had only just returned home and had no wish to travel so soon. With his younger brothers' misdeeds, trying to find out how Marian died, and handling the minor scuffles of other clans, he had no time to make such a tiresome journey. Yet no one refused the king and he had no choice but to go.

"I will be leaving on the morrow for Edinburgh, Clare. The king calls me. Whilst I am gone, I will have the lads stay with Gideon. He'll reform these two." With that settled, Breckin picked up a spoon and ate the heavenly stew before him. He abated his hunger with a large piece of bread and smeared it with a good amount of creamy spread. After, he washed his meal down with the oversized cup of ale his aunt had poured for him.

"Well, I am gladdened to hear it. I could use a break from those two," Clare said.

His brothers spooned up the stew, unspeaking, with their heads practically in their bowls.

He turned his gaze on them. "When ye are finished your supper, ye will go to bed. I will hear no noise from either of ye for the rest of the night."

His brothers kept their mouths closed but they nodded to indicate they understood.

As soon as he finished his meal, Breckin left the cottage and ambled toward Gideon's home to inform him of his departure. When he reached the large, stone house, he knocked at the door. It was opened by Hamish, Gideon's wee lad. He had his father's likeness with his reddish hair and freckled face, and was a sweet lad, not one bent on giving his father heart pains with daring feats like his brothers did to Breckin.

"Get your da, Hamish."

The lad disappeared and Gideon pulled the door open wider. "Oh, Laird, I did not expect to see ye again this night. I thought ye'd be at slumber by now."

"Aye, I will seek my bed soon enough. I wanted to let ye know that I will leave for Edinburgh in the morn and bid ye to watch over my brothers whilst I am gone. They will stay here at night." Breckin turned away and his commander followed him, rushing to catch up.

"Hold on, Laird… My wife might not be agreeable to that," Gideon said.

"Since when do ye let your wife's agreement dictate your duty?" Breckin wanted to laugh at his challenge but remained somber. "Clare needs a break from them. My brothers have caused a wee bit of hell since I've been gone and I need someone who can keep them in hand. They have been duly punished and will only be in your cottage at night for sleep. But I want ye to keep watch on them throughout the day. See that they do not kill themselves."

"I suppose it will not be much of a hardship. Och, one day, Laird, ye will have a bonny wife who will grumble at ye as mine does to me," Gideon said with a bellow.

"Well, fortunately for me, I do not have a wife. That is the last thing I need."

"Aye, ye could already be wedded if the lass did not call it off. Do ye ever think of her?"

Breckin felt the pull of his brows as he scowled at his comrade. "Who? Danella MacLaren? To tell ye the truth, I was gladdened when her family ended our betrothal. I was not ready to marry anyone at that time..." He hadn't thought about his betrothal to the MacLaren woman for a while. His parents had only died a year before and he was still trying to figure out how to be a father to his siblings and leader to his clan.

His betrothed had broken their clan's pact with his, over a year before with no excuse. Since then, the MacLarens feared the Buchanans as well, as they should. With the ended treaty, there was no cause to support them, leaving them open to a rival's havoc on their lands and against their clan. Breckin had no sympathy for them because the MacLarens caused their own grief.

"Ye do not fool me, Breckin. I thought her the perfect wife for ye. Ye really should think about finding a wife soon to help ye rear your brothers. Aye, before ye get too old to satisfy a woman as well." Gideon chortled and shoved his shoulder in jest.

"I satisfy plenty of women."

Gideon scoffed and then bellowed with a laugh. "Aye, when?

How long has it been since ye been with a woman?"

He wanted to use his fist to answer his comrade, but instead ignored his friend's banter. "I have been somewhat busy with clan matters and... Hell, a wife or a woman is the last thing on my mind right now. There are more important matters to attend to."

Gideon sighed with a moan. "A woman can aid ye more than ye know and mayhap help ye rid that angst ye carry around on your shoulders."

"Perhaps that is so." Breckin nodded. "Och, but when I must do my duty and marry, I will. Until then, ye will have to deal with my angst. I will keep my brothers in line and see that our clan prospers. No wife is necessary for that."

"Aye, so we all hold hope. 'Tis odd, though, that the MacLarens have not tried to make amends for their withdrawal or affront. Do ye think they consider themselves our rival?"

He shrugged in answer to Gideon's question. "Probably, but I have had no time to deal with their pettiness. I was too accepting at the time when they withdrew their daughter's hand and might have spoken of a rivalry. Now, I am gladdened that I did not have to marry her. The MacLarens are a needy clan and there are too many other needful clans hereabouts."

"She was a sweet lass who would've taken care of ye. That is what ye need. A woman who would see to matters of home and hearth." Gideon flashed a smile. "My wife takes good care of me and our son. Without her, I do not know how I would fare."

"One day, my friend, I will marry and shall find a woman as worthy as your Deena."

"Ye should be so fortunate," Gideon said and chuckled. "Why are ye going to Edinburgh?"

"I wish I did not have to go because there is much to do here. The MacNabs still await word from me on when I will meet with them. Then—as you know—there are my brothers. I fear that they need a guiding hand and mine are tied right now. If only I could find out the truth about Marian's death, I could put that behind me and settle the matter. But och, I'm off to do the king's bidding, whatever that is…" Breckin hadn't realized he'd walked so far and ended up passing the stable. He turned around and headed back so he could have Alton have his horse ready in the morning.

"Ye do not know why the king calls ye to meet?"

Breckin threw up his hands because he hadn't the faintest notion. "Nay, och, I will find out when I get there. Look after my brothers and see that they do not kill themselves on your watch. I shall return with as much haste as I can and relieve ye of the duty."

He walked away from his comrade and entered the stable. The beam that had fallen had been removed and the roof had been repaired. That his brother fell through the roof certainly gave forewarning that the wood needed to be replaced. At least his brothers hadn't been killed in their pursuit of an escapade. Near the back, he heard Alton's voice and headed in that direction. Peering over the door of an empty stall, he could see his stablemaster carrying on with a woman in an empty stall and Breckin hastily swung the gate open. He meant to startle the couple and indeed, his clansman stood hastily.

"Ah, Laird… I…did not expect ye back…"

Breckin heard the woman's gasp as she hid behind the wall. He didn't acknowledge her and hoped not to cause her embarrassment. "Alton, have my horse ready at dawn."

"Oh, aye, will do, Laird." Alton bowed to him and waited for him to turn away.

Breckin chuckled under his breath. He wasn't aware that his stablemaster had a woman. The man notoriously stank of horses and manure. Surely no woman wanted to sport with him. But what did he know? He left the stable and continued home, letting the night air ease him.

In the last days, he'd gotten only a few hours of rest, and little sleep. He was tired and needed a respite before he'd make the long trek to Edinburgh. When he entered his aunt's cottage, it was quiet. She sat beside the hearth in a chair, sewing something.

He bade her a good night and strolled toward the bedchamber he used whenever he stayed in the cottage. With the door firmly closed behind him, he disrobed, lay on the cot in the corner with its straw-filled tick and pulled back the heavy tartan blanket.

Breckin closed his eyes, but sleep evaded him as his mind turned over the fact that he would be in Edinburgh soon, and the banter that Gideon had thrown at him.

A wife, ha. He'd be the worst sort of husband, surely unacceptable for any woman at this time. With all that weighed upon him, he wasn't ready to settle down. There was too much to do before he'd take a wife. The distant future loomed as if he'd never achieve such an aspiration. Still, the thought of having a sweet, willing woman to warm his bed at night and caring for him during the day wasn't too displeasing.

Maybe one day his life would be settled enough and he'd have an adoring woman caring for him. Breckin scoffed lightly at that thought. What woman would want to marry a warrior who only knew about battles? He vowed then that he would take a wife before he reached two scores in age. That was if the senseless wars he participated in didn't kill him first.

CHAPTER THREE

Edinburgh, Scotland
Late February, 1260

EDINBURGH WAS A crowded, busy town. On the lane that meandered toward the great castle, merchants and shopkeepers lined the way. It was market day and Eva was thrilled to see the many shops: a tailor, a cordwainer, and an apothecary. Many people came from surrounding villages to attend and make purchases even though the rain had soaked the stalls, lanes, and items for sale.

Their carriage slowed on the muddy thoroughfare when men in knee-length tunics drove their cattle in front of them. Women bustled their children to clear the lane and some wealthier women wearing rich garments and tall-heeled shoes to avoid the muck, made no move to hurry out of the way.

People stood about, some in groups, prattling and catching up on the latest news, unmindful of the rain that dampened their garments. A company of performers pulled a cart that held their costumes and stage, much to the children's delight. Eva couldn't see enough of all the excitement. There was so much to take in, she didn't know where to look. When the town crier rang his bell, many of the people scurried forth to hear his message. She wondered what news he would announce.

How she adored market day. At home, their market couldn't compare to the extensive sellers here in Edinburgh. Their town's stalls barely stretched down one side of a short lane. This town's shops and stalls seemed to go on to the end of the road. If she had time, she would venture out from the castle and perhaps visit the tailor or purchase a new pair of shoes from the cordwainer.

Their carriage was pulled up the incline of the hill adjacent to the stone trestle bridge that led to the gatehouse. Guards stood ready to intercept them, but her father's men gave their family name and they were waved onward. Over the cobbled stones, the carriage rocked and rolled forward until it finally came to a stop near the edge of the courtyard.

Eva's eyes took in everything, from the flapping of the pennons atop the fortress to the large pen that kept horses secure, to the scurry of men and women attending to their tasks. It was so thrilling and she wondered why she had prevented herself from the experience previously. She should have traveled with her father to Edinburgh when he'd offered. There seemed to be a liveliness to the town as if there was a buzz of anticipation in the air.

The only apprehension she had was that she'd soon be married. Even that dreadful farce and the heavy rainfall they'd contended with during their travel couldn't put a damper on the sights and sounds of Edinburgh.

One of her father's men opened the carriage door and set a wooden crate for her to step upon. Eva disembarked and awaited her father. Throughout the journey, he'd continued to ail but he had improved a little before they had left for the trek. His wheezing lessened but she could still hear it and see his chest labor with his breath. Eva worried for him, and even more so because once she married, she'd be unable to care for him.

As they walked toward the entrance of the castle, they were met by a burly man. He hastened forward and bowed. "Lord Michael, you have arrived. And this must be your fair daughter, Mistress Eva." He bowed again and when he straightened, he wore a smile.

"Eva, this is Chamberlain Edmund, the king's man." Her

father staggered a bit as he bowed in return.

"Sir," she said and curtseyed to him before taking her father's arm to support him without letting him appear frail. Still, he somewhat leaned against her as they entered the castle with the chamberlain who walked quickly ahead of them without waiting for them to catch up.

"Welcome. I am sure you must want to take a respite from your journey and get dry from this horrid rain. Hopefully, it will cease soon. It seems to be lightening. The king will greet everyone on the morrow but the queen has asked that Mistress Eva attend her later in the evening. Follow me and we shall get you settled," the chamberlain spoke rapidly.

Her father's steps were sluggish and she continued to hold on to him as they crept along. The chamberlain waited for them at the end of a hallway and peered at them as if he was inconvenienced by their slow progress.

"Sir, my da is ailing and cannot walk so fast."

"Oh, Mistress Eva, I...did not realize." The man's face fell, and he appeared embarrassed. "We shall take care then to go slow. Shall I have a healer fetched? I can have one of the king's physicians attend to him."

"He was checked over before we left for Edinburgh. My da just needs to rest."

Her father moaned and rasped as he kept his footing. "I do not need a...healer, Edmund. Just show us to our chamber."

She noted the concern in the chamberlain's eyes but nodded so he would continue. Their progression through the castle led them through a myriad of corridors and past many doorways.

Eva couldn't keep her gaze on one thing longer than a moment. The grandness of the castle made her a little envious because not only was it furnished with exquisite items, but it had regalness and elegance her own home had never attained.

Through the hallways, they continued until the chamberlain stopped at a door and motioned to the men who had trailed behind to enter. They carried their baggage and hurried to deliver it inside.

"This will be your chamber whilst you are here. There are two adjoining rooms. I deem you will be comfortable but if there is anything you need, I am here to serve you."

Her father finally found his voice. "Our thanks, Edmund. I will rest, and daughter, you should change and make ready to visit with the queen."

They entered and Edmund bid them farewell and closed the door. Her father pulled off his heavy cloak and moved to stand near the hearth where flames sent heat permeating through the chamber.

Eva rushed forward and took his cloak. "Why do you not take a respite here for a while? The fire will warm you." She set his cloak on the chair opposite his before going to the door to her room.

Her antechamber was richly furnished with a wooden bed, covered with heavy tartan blankets and pillows. On one side sat a table with a pitcher and a pewter cup. There was a large heavily draped window that faced the gardens beyond with one chair to sit on to enjoy the view. But a dampness swarmed the room with a musty, stale scent. The heavily stoned walls were probably inundated with moisture from the rain.

"I am going to get ready and might visit the market—" She was interrupted when someone knocked on the door. With quick steps, she hurried to open it. Servants strolled in, one after another, carrying buckets of steaming water for the tub which she'd only just noticed behind a screen. They filled the tub as a woman stopped and bowed before her.

The woman had her hair worn completely hidden by a wimple but her brows were a deep brown color that matched her eyes. Her smile was sincere and it reached those eyes. "Milady, I am Brenda. I am assigned as your attendant whilst you are here. I thought you might like a bath to warm yourself from your travel. Do you need my help?"

She nodded and walked toward the screen. "I would like your assistance."

"Come, Mistress. Let us get you clean and ready to meet the queen."

Eva undressed and stepped into the warm water. She relaxed back but really, her stomach was in a mass of knots. She was nervous about meeting the queen and the rest of the events to come—especially finding out who she would marry. But she would try her best to remain calm. It would do well for her not to panic and cause her father great embarrassment.

She didn't take long to bathe and once she was dried, she chose the plain, dark green gown Luella had packed for her. The maid—Brenda—assisted in pulling back her hair and twisting it in an elaborate coif. Eva didn't much care to have her hair braided or tied up. She preferred it to hang loose and when necessary, be covered by a head wrap.

"There, Mistress, you do look fetching," Brenda said as she finished.

"My thanks." Eva dipped her head and watched the maid leave the chamber. As soon as she had closed the door, Eva pulled the ties and braids free from her hair and fingered her tresses so they hung loosely over her back. Then she slipped her feet into her boots and shook out her cloak to settle around her shoulders.

Eva had hoped to have a little time before meeting with the queen so she could venture out and visit the market. By the time she finished readying, her father had fallen asleep. She placed a woolen blanket over him and tucked it by his sides so it wouldn't dislodge. With a gentle kiss on his forehead, she whispered goodbye.

On her way out, she grabbed a pouch of coins from her satchel, tied it to her belt, and covered it with the fabric of her cloak. Atop one of the trunks in the chamber, there was an empty basket that she would make use of to carry whatever she purchased at the market. Quietly, she closed the door and walked lightly toward the castle's exit. When she reached the doors of the castle, she came across the chamberlain who greeted her with a smile.

"Mistress Eva, I see you ventured from your chamber. Are you leaving the castle?"

"I am…that is… Do I have enough time to visit the market?"

The chamberlain's chin bobbed. "The queen will meet with you after the late meal. So you have plenty of time. I should send an escort with you." He twitched a finger at a page.

"That is not necessary, sir. I like to visit the market by myself and take my time browsing the stalls. I shall return soon." She quickly curtseyed to him and hurried off.

Eva didn't think she needed protection and the market was close to the castle, so she couldn't get lost. Apparently, the chamberlain didn't agree and sent the page to trail her anyway. The lad, whose hair covered his eyes, had tidy garments, and he appeared apt at his duty. He kept a few paces behind her and so she ignored him and continued.

Eva strolled along with her basket tucked in the fold of her arm and reached the costermonger's cart. In rows of five, barrels sat filled with various fruits and vegetables. She purchased her father's favorite apples, three of them, and placed them in the basket. They would do well for a light meal in between their mid-day fare and supper. After she paid for the fruit, she noticed the baker's stall next, filled with loaves of bread, covered with cloth to protect them from the rain. She bought two loaves.

She stopped to stand by a tree to situate the items she'd purchased when she noticed a man staring at her from across the lane. Her breath caught in her throat as she peered at him. He was a tall Highlander and a handsome one at that. With long, light locks, he certainly portrayed the wild man image that she likened to the men from the north.

The man's muscular body was garbed in a red plaid tartan with a thick leather belt at his hips. A scabbard crossed his back and held a massive sword. She lowered her eyes when he caught her looking. Eva's cheeks heated at her embarrassment and when she chanced to take another peek at him, she caught him watching her with vivid green eyes. He had the most attractive face she'd ever seen on a man, lightly whiskered and shaded in the same lightness of his locks.

Hastily, she walked away, completely abashed by her forwardness. That's when she noticed the page was gone and must've left her. She approached the apothecary's stall and intended to buy something to help her father's wheezing.

"I need a remedy for my father. He is having trouble breathing and wheezes," she told the man who stood in front of the stall.

"I am sorry to hear that, Mistress." The seller was an aged man who quickly gave her a medicinal for her father's ailment. "This tincture, Mistress, should aid him. 'Tis just spices mixed with a wee bit of plant oil. Have him add some drops to his ale twice each day. And take this wad of jimsonweed. Burn it in your hearth so it fills the chamber with its curative smoke. He shall be eased in no time."

Eva took the jar and reddish-purple stems from him, paid the man, and thanked him. Then she realized she hadn't brought anything for herself. She grabbed a jar from his stall table, opened it, lifted it to her nose, and took a whiff. The mixture wafted to her and reminded her of spring when flowers bloomed. "This smells nice."

"Oh, aye, Mistress. 'Tis a cream to soften your face, made from rose petal oil and a scoop of beeswax. Just rub it on after a wash and your skin shall be as soft as a bairn's."

"I shall take it."

After paying for her purchases, she secured them in the basket and walked along the lane, admiring the many stalls she passed. Someone startled her when they shouted behind her. Eva turned abruptly and found the Highlander she'd seen earlier. He stood close, holding onto the arm of a lad. The man appeared angry as his brows furrowed and he gripped the lad as if he was about to give him a thrashing.

"Leave him be! What is the trouble…?" Before she could finish her question, the lad dislodged his arm from the man and sprinted off.

"Come back here, ye wee thief," the Highlander shouted. But the lad disappeared beyond a group of people standing on the lane. "Ye should guard yourself, lass, against thieves," he said huskily and handed her coin pouch back.

Eva took the pouch from him, and frowned at it. She'd been unaware that the lad had picked it from her. When she lifted her gaze to the Highlander, his becoming green eyes stayed on hers and caused heat to wind its way through her. What held her spellbound was his lightly whiskered face. He had the beginnings of a beard but it didn't overtake the skin of his hard jaws. His manly brows furrowed slightly as he stared back at her.

She craned her neck to look at his face and uttered, "My thanks, but I was in no need of your aid. There were only a handful of coins in the pouch, not much of a loss."

"I was only trying to save ye from losing your coin," he said, stepping closer.

He was intimidating not only with his height but also with the strength he portrayed. His bared arms bulged at the biceps and even his forearms were thick with muscle.

The man made no further rebuke for her carelessness.

"'Tis no wonder the lad ran off. You frightened him and should have a care how you speak to those of a tender age." Eva likely insulted him given his hard stare and slack-jawed expression. She hurried away and tucked the pouch inside her overdress seam to keep it safe. After ensuring that the Highlander hadn't followed her, she tried to find the lad.

At the end of the lane, she spotted him. The dark-haired lad stood with a woman and he appeared to be upset. Likely the Highlander had scared the wits from him. She approached slowly so she wouldn't cause him to flee. When she stood beside them, she overheard the lad.

"I swear, Ma, I tried but was caught," the lad said to the woman.

Eva stepped in front of the lad. "You tried to thieve from me."

"Oh, Mistress, I am sorry. My son…he was just trying to help me. Pray, do not call the sheriff's men. We meant no harm." The woman looked as if she'd weep. Her tattered garments, as well as the lad's, indicated that they were vagrants. She realized that they were an impoverished family who were probably hungry.

Eva took pity on her. "I am not here to cause trouble, ma'am. I just…" With a glance nearby, she hastened to a cart and purchased another basket. Then she removed the items she'd bought except for the bread and the apples. She returned to the woman and handed the basket to her. "Here, take this."

The woman's eyes widened at her with disbelief. "I…I cannot take that, Mistress."

"Please, take it. And here, a few coins to help you get through the next day or two." Eva collected four coins in her palm and placed them in the woman's hand.

The woman sobbed and clutched the coins. "I do not know how to thank you, Mistress."

"Have you no husband? Home?"

She shook her head. "My husband died fighting for the king and we were ousted from our home when I could not pay the owner. We have been in the cold for months."

Eva commiserated with the woman. "I am sorry to hear that. Make sure your lad doesn't thieve though. The last thing you need is for him to end up jailed. If your son needs employment, have him come to the castle. I shall tell the chamberlain to give him a job. He can earn coins to help you."

"You would do that for us, Mistress?"

Eva nodded and turned. "Of course, I would be glad to. What is his name?"

"Thomas, Mistress."

"Very well. Have Thomas come to the castle on the morrow. I must go now." Eva hurried away and returned to buy more apples for her father, and bread.

After she took care of replenishing the items she'd given away, she rushed back to the castle. The sky had dimmed and surely the late meal had been served. Eva didn't want to be late for her meeting with the queen, so she would find the chamberlain later to tell him about the lad. She left the items she'd purchased in her chamber, checked on her da who continued to sleep, fixed her appearance, and rushed back to the great hall where she presumed the meeting with the queen would be held. Unfortunately, she hadn't noticed the muddy edge of her gown.

"Mistress Eva," Chamberlain Edmund called from down the hallway.

"Sir," she said and curtseyed. "I am not late, am I?"

"The queen has not come yet so nay, not late at all. Come, I will show you where to go," he said and held out his arm. "Queen Margaret is taking an audience in her private solar with some of her ladies in attendance and shall arrive momentarily." He eyed the edge of her gown and smiled. "Did ye enjoy your outing?"

"I did until… Yes, the market is wonderful." Apprehensively, Eva held onto his arm and walked next to him. She took advantage of the moment and told him about the lad and the family's position. "They are in dire need. There must be something we can do to help them."

"What a dreadful situation for you, Mistress. That you would offer such aid to the lad after he tried to thieve from you…"

"His father died while serving the king. Surely there is something you can do to help Thomas and his mother. Is there not a job he can do…perhaps in the stables or helping the kitchen servants? Surely the king cares about that family and their loss." She implored him with hopeful eyes.

"I suppose so, Mistress. I could find something for the lad to do and shall look for him on the morrow," he said and stopped. "You are a tenderhearted lass to think of them, and aye, we should do something to aid them. Here we are." He opened a door and waved her inside.

She pulled away, thanked him, and hurriedly entered. Inside the small but cozy solar stood a few women who whispered amongst themselves. They glanced at her but when they realized she wasn't the queen, they returned to their conversations, ignoring her. Eva felt awkward because she was unfamiliar with the women and wasn't one to converse easily with people she didn't know, so she slunk back toward the wall and waited.

A short while later, the queen finally arrived. Margaret was thin with long brown hair and long limbs. Her hair was covered with a short wimple. She smiled at them, nodding her head as she looked at each of the women. "Ladies, welcome. Come and sit with me." She seemed to glide across the floor until she reached the plush chair by the hearth.

There were several chairs situated near her seat. Eva was the last to join them. She took the last unoccupied chair and sat back, content to watch and listen. The queen made small talk with the women until she finally raised her hand.

"My husband means to give the hands of some women to the Highlanders. I hope to abate their fears, but alas, I am certain nothing shall be of a comfort. Alexander means well and has selected the most courageous and noble Highlanders to wed them to. They shall not be disappointed with the selection. When they meet them, they will see how fortunate they are."

Several of the queen's attendants agreed with nods. Conversations rose as the women talked with each other and put their views forth about the coming marriages. As she watched the women, Eva realized that she was the only "bride" present and that none of the others had attended the queen's gathering.

Eva looked away from the queen and moved her gaze around the chamber to note the queen's taste for furnishings and other decorative items: elegant tapestries, golden candlesticks, small statues of religious figures, and other unknown objects. She hadn't realized the queen had given the ladies their leave until Margaret stood before her.

"Mistress Eva, come with me." She quickly turned and moved to the other side of the room.

Eva hurried to follow and the queen stopped at the one window casement in the solar. "Your Grace, I am honored to be here."

"Are you?" Margaret chuckled. "It appears to me that perhaps you speak falsely. Were you listening? I doubt you were." Even though she appeared affronted by Eva's aloofness, Margaret's empathy came with a small smile. "I understand why you would be apprehensive. I was myself a betrothed bride and had not met Alexander long before our wedding."

Eva nodded but kept quiet. She didn't want to say anything to offend the queen.

"Now, I had my hopes set that you would find Laird Buchanan to your liking. He is rather handsome, and has a serious demeanor, but would do well for a husband."

She felt her chest constrict when Margaret mentioned a laird. It made her situation more real to her. There was a husband at the end of this. "Ah, Laird Buchanan, Your Grace? Are you saying that we shall marry Highlanders?"

"Were you not listening at all, lass? Aye, Highlanders. I am certain that Laird Buchanan shall find you exceedingly beautiful and you will make a good match. I do believe that you may have more than one man vying for your hand, Mistress Eva, which is why I want to whisper Buchanan's name in your ear. And before you speak your reasons against such a match, I should tell you that Laird Buchanan needs a good woman. Are you such a woman?"

Eva almost groaned aloud but she managed to keep her distress hidden. *Grace and decorum*, she reminded herself. No one refused the king or queen and if they wanted her to accept Buchanan, then she had to make an effort to show her eagerness. *Sweet Mary.* "I hope so, My Lady. At least, I shall try."

"I doubt you need to try at all. He will be overcome by your beauty." At the moment, Eva's supposed beauty seemed less of a blessing and more of a curse. Margaret's smile widened and her eyes shone as if she wanted to say more but didn't. Eventually, she led Eva away from the window casement and toward the door. "Now that is settled, we shall see what you think of him at your first meeting."

"I am certain, My Lady, that I will find him acceptable."

The queen opened the door. Before she could flee, Margaret blocked her from leaving. "Mistress Eva, you may be used to being coddled, for I heard that your dear father holds you in great esteem… But I suggest that you do not expect to be treated so affectionately by a Highlander. Highland men have no time for tenderness or to indulge their wives. Best remember that and save yourself a little bit of heartache."

She bowed to the queen and turned to leave. Along the way to her chamber, Eva almost laughed at this dreadful farce and her conversation with the queen. It wasn't that she found it comical, quite the opposite. It seemed that she'd be doomed to a life of hardship and a husband who cared not about her wants or needs. Eva didn't like the sound of that and prayed that wasn't so. She didn't know much about the Highlanders and had spent all of her life by the border. Most of the people she'd met appeared more English than Scottish.

With hope, Laird Buchanan would be an amiable husband and treat her with as much care and tenderness as her father had.

CHAPTER FOUR

THE LASS HAD left before he could ask her name. Breckin was taken aback by her beauty when he'd first spotted her on the lane. She was lovely with long, glorious brown hair that curled at the edges. It was when he was close enough to see her eyes, though, that she thoroughly captivated him. She had eyes as blue as the sea, so rich in color that they seemed to shimmer with excitement. He could lose himself in the depth of them and wondered what she found so enthralling. She fascinated him even from afar and when he noticed a lad getting too close to her, he had to step in when he suspected the lad was going to snatch her coin pouch.

Breckin detested Edinburgh with its crowds and thieves. He couldn't stand aside and allow the woman to be filched of her coins. Yet she wasn't as appreciative as he thought she would be when he foiled the lad's attempt to rob her. He shook his head at the absurdity of her carelessness and continued to walk toward the castle.

Rain soaked him thoroughly from his hair to his boots. He wanted to get dry, eat a hot meal, and get a night's rest. All of which had to wait until after he met with Alexander. Most people moved out of his way as he progressed through the market. The gate was just ahead and he hastened his steps. He hoped to get his meeting with the king over with quickly so he could find lodging at an inn close by and on the morrow be on his way home.

He reached the heavily iron gates and stepped close. "Buchanan to see the king." Breckin needn't say more.

The guards sprang forth, opened the gate, and moved to the wall to allow him to pass. He marched through and kept walking until he was stopped again at the entrance to the castle. More guards were posted and a man made his way past them. He seemed affable and wore a greeting smile.

"You must be Laird Buchanan? I could tell right off what with Alexander's description of you." To the guards, the man said, "Allow him to enter."

Breckin nodded. "Aye, I am Buchanan. The king called for my attendance."

"Come, he has been awaiting you." The man mumbled as he walked ahead, "I am Edmund, our fair king's chamberlain. I am at your service, Laird Buchanan, if you have any needs."

He didn't retort to the overzealous man but followed silently behind him.

"The king is within his private solar." Edmund knocked and opened the door slightly. "Laird Buchanan has arrived, sire."

"Well, show him inside," came a voice.

Breckin entered the chamber and noticed Alexander standing near a window casement. He seemed to be deep in thought. The small chamber was furnished with a few tables with chairs scattered about. A larger table was situated on one side and was flanked by an oversized chair. Although the room was small, it afforded a coziness with tapestries set on the walls and a hearth that had dimmed with its fire long extinguished.

He hadn't seen the king in recent years. Not only had he clan troubles and the death of his parents to contend with but there hadn't been a need to visit Edinburgh or the king. Breckin took in the sight of his longtime friend and bowed his head in greeting. His comrade had aged somewhat and was no longer the lanky lad with whom he had visited frequently and sparred.

"Sire." He bowed.

When he straightened, he discovered that Alexander grinned in greeting. "Breckin, you are here at last. Edmund, bring some food and drink for us. Have someone stoke the fire and light some candles," the king directed.

Edmund practically bounced on his step and shouted for a page who entered and quickly saw to the task of lighting the many candles in the chamber as well as stoking the fire. The chamberlain disappeared and the page followed.

Alexander neared the door and closed it. "Come, sit with me near the fire. I suspect you were soaked through on the journey and need to get warm."

Breckin meandered his way past the chairs and tables until he reached the hearth. "Aye, I was, and the journey was longer than I remembered."

"It has been a while, has it not? It is good to see you, Breckin." Alexander sat in a chair by the hearth and rubbed his hands together.

"It has indeed. Why have you called me, sire?"

"I have much to discuss with you but before we get to that... I wanted to tell you that I was sorry to hear about your parents' deaths. It has been a while since they passed, aye, I know, but I haven't seen you since... My father was fond of your da and they were comrades long before my father was named king. Do you remember when we were forced to go along on their many hunting treks?"

Breckin chuckled lightly. "I recall swimming bare-arsed in the loch whilst our das fished or foraged in the woods. You always got me in trouble too."

Alexander laughed with a scoff and raised his hands. "Me? It was you who always got us in trouble. You were older and therefore responsible for our plights. As I recall, I always followed you around."

"Perhaps." Fond memories came and Breckin recollected the times he'd spent with Alexander when they were lads, the adventure, and their misbehavior. That brought a smile to him as he thought about his brothers who were just as adventurous and misbehaved. Maybe it was just a lad's nature to be so and he shouldn't be so hard on his brothers.

"You were always the one who disappeared, and of course, I followed you. Those times hold a great fondness for me and the freedom that we had. How I wish times were as easy now, but alas, life is about to get complicated."

He frowned slightly at the king's words. "Is there trouble, sire?"

Alexander shook his head. "Not presently but soon enough, there will be difficult times and strife ahead for us all."

"What do you mean? Since you are now joined to England what with your marriage, surely there are no difficulties betwixt us? Is there?" Breckin sat forward and studied the king's face. His sovereign didn't seem overly concerned.

The king fingered his red beard and then slid his hands down his tunic. "For now, England gives us no trouble. Who knows how long that shall last? I have called you here because—" Alexander ceased in midsentence when a knock came at the door.

The king called "enter" and servants bustled in, carrying trays of foodstuff and a pitcher of ale with cups situated on a smaller tray. Once everything was set on the table between them, the servants quickly left the chamber.

"Let us drink to our good health and success." The king shifted forward and poured them each a cup of ale. He handed a cup to him and Breckin accepted it. "*Slàinte*," Alexander said and raised his cup.

As Breckin lifted the drink to his mouth, he kept his gaze on the king. Before they were interrupted, the king was going to reveal why he'd called him. His curiosity was more than piqued and he was impatient to learn the reason he'd been sent for. "You were saying…"

"Aye, I called you here because you have the fiercest soldiers in Scotland."

"Are we to war?"

Alexander nodded. "Soon enough, but not until I return from England. I am taking Margaret to visit her family because she intends to have our bairn there. I shall be gone for months but upon my return, I shall call many boots to serve in my army."

Breckin set his cup on the table and clasped his hands, settling them between his knees. "That is joyous news, sire. About your bairn, I mean, not about the oncoming war."

Alexander chuckled. "I am certain you are just as pleased by the news of an oncoming war as you are about the news of my child. You Buchanans do have one of the fiercest armies in all of Scotland. My thanks, though, for the sentiment. Finally, the woman does her duty and Margaret is giving me an heir. All of Scotland shall rejoice when the time comes."

"Indeed we shall, sire. Who are you planning to invade?"

"Norway. I mean to stretch our lands as far north and west, ousting Haakon once and for all. Haakon cares more for religion than he does for his followers. He leaves his brethren open for attack and we shall do everything within our power to make that happen. When the time comes, I shall need your warriors."

Breckin nodded without hesitation. "Of course, sire. My men are at your disposal whenever ye need them. Ye have only to call on us."

"Good. Now, there is another matter that we need to remedy. The land you occupy, which, from my understanding, belongs to the Buchanans given to your grandfather by Lord Lennox. Yet no tax has been submitted...ever. It amounts to a hefty sum since no levy has been paid since your family was given the land and took control of the territory."

Breckin tilted his head to the side and considered what the king had told him. "Sire, the land was given to us by Lord Lennox, and in return, we were to supply him with a pound of wax each year. We have kept to our arrangement and have never been late with our payment."

Alexander folded one of his legs over the other and leaned back. "Aye, so you have and so Lord Lennox has told me. I have not received a complaint from Lord Lennox about your payment arrangement with him. Your accord with him has nothing to do with the fact that you were still beholden to pay the tithe on the land to the sovereignty, namely, me. Lennox has not paid it since he is no longer in possession of said land, and your family has not put forth what is owed."

"We are not in the position at this time, sire, to make such reparations. Perhaps if you give us until the end of the year, our harvest might yield enough to make a small payment."

The king shook his head. "I doubt that, Breckin, and we cannot accept a small payment. But there is a solution, one which might be coveted by you."

"And that is?"

"I mean to unite border clans with some of the Highland clans. To do so, I have offered brides to your brethren and do so to you. These marriages will instill my plan to unite our nation. I want Scotland to be united from the southern border to the far reaches of the north, especially before I seek to invade Haakon's lands."

"Brides?" Breckin swallowed and tried not to sound outraged.

"Aye, brides. You will be offered a bonny bride. All you need to do to win her hand is defeat your brethren in a hand-to-hand battle and all levy shall be forgiven. Before you speak your objection, the clans involved are the MacKendricks, Camerons, and Mackintoshes. There are four brides in all and are the bonniest women in the land."

Breckin swallowed his angst before he gave his reasons for rejecting the king's offer. "I have no time for a wife right now, Alexander. What with the scuffles in the north, I have been trying to win alliances and helping lesser clans secure their lands. We Buchanans have been protecting weaker clans and with spring on our heels, the situation is sure to become pressing."

"Aye, so I have heard of your altruism for the northern clans. They are fortunate, are they not, that you aid them? But it matters not because I will have your agreement."

Breckin pressed his fingers on his nape and tried to remain calm. "Along with that, sire, I am trying to find out what happened to my sister and I'm trying to be a father to my younger brothers. Lord knows they challenge me at every turn. Nay, there is no time for a wife right now. I thank ye for the offer though."

Laughter bellowed from Alexander and his eyes shone with his mirth. "'Tis not an offer, Breckin, but a command, unless you wish to be detained. Can you make payment now for the owed tax?"

Detained? Did Alexander intend to imprison him if he couldn't pay the levy? Breckin fisted his hands and took a breath. "I told ye nay and that I need time…"

Alexander shook his head. "I cannot give you the time you ask for. Either you pay now, marry one of the lasses, or you can take residence in one of the castle cells. Which is it to be, Breckin?"

Bollocks, the king practically put a noose around his neck. He wanted to shout his objection but Alexander forced his hand. Breckin had no option but to accept the offered bride. He was damned irked about it though. "Very well, sire, since ye give me no choice, I will marry as ye bade. Will the entire tax be forgiven? If I am going to accept a bride, then I will not be paying the past debt." Then a smile twitched at his lips because fighting with Cameron, Mackintosh, and MacKendrick was going to help rid his frustration at this deplorable misfortune.

"Aye, the entire amount owed will be wiped away. Now before you run off to lick your wounds and soothe your pride, Breckin, there are some stipulations. For one, you cannot marry the woman and drop her off on your land. You will be married in all sense of the word and there will be no annulment sought on your behalf or hers. Do not try to intimidate the lass. The marriage will afford you happiness. Accept that for once in your life."

Breckin grunted. *Happiness?* All that marriage would do was saddle him with an unwanted bride for whom he had no time, who would likely be displeased with him as a husband, and cause him endless troubles.

"I will hear your vow to take this woman as your wife and to do everything within your power to enrich *your* and her life with this marriage. You see, comrade, I do you a great honor and service. You might not be pleased right now, but eventually, you will see the merit of it."

He grunted again and fisted his hands but kept them between his legs as he leaned his forearms on his thighs. "You give me no choice, sire, but to affirm this vow."

"Good, good." Alexander stood and waited for him to join him.

Breckin rose from his seat and stood before the king. "Whatever trickery this is, I better not be saddled with a hellion or, God forbid, a shrew."

Alexander bellowed with laughter. "Trust in me, Breckin, you will be more than pleased with your wife. On the morrow, there will be a feast at the evening meal where you will meet the ladies. The bouts will be discussed and we shall move forward quickly. I intend to have the marriages solidified before I leave for England. You will stay here in the castle until after the sacraments are performed by the priest. Now, leave me."

He walked to the door and when he closed it behind him, Breckin stood by the wall in complete despair at what had just passed between him and the king. Nowhere was it written that they had to pay the tithe on their land to the king but that did not mean it wasn't true. Perhaps he should seek Lord Lennox and find out exactly what had been stipulated when his grandfather had been given the land. He'd always ensured a pound of wax was delivered to Lord Lennox right after Saint Stephen's Day as was agreed upon when his grandfather had purchased the land, but he never considered that they also owed tax to the king.

"Laird Buchanan?" Edmund approached. "Are you finished with your meeting with the king?"

"Aye." He couldn't bring himself to speak of what transpired, but he was certain that the king's chamberlain was probably privy to what the king demanded.

"Come, let us get you settled in the chamber with the other lairds. You shall be here for at least a sennight or possibly longer." Edmund motioned him forward.

Before they reached the chamber where the men stayed, Breckin stopped him. "I need to collect my belongings and see that my horse is settled at the hostelry. This night, I will return to stay in the chamber."

"Very well, Milord." Edmund bowed to him and when he straightened, he chuckled. "There is a fine inn down the lane where you might find a stronger drink than ale. I suspect you might need a good stiff dram…"

Breckin agreed. He wanted to dull his senses a wee bit and to forget even momentarily what the king demanded. He hastened to the exit of the castle and passed the gate without so much as a glance at the guardsmen.

Outside, the early evening air placated his angst and affront. Breckin did not appreciate being put in such a position—having to take a wife—to make reparations for something unknown to him. He supposed, though, that taking a wife in lieu of having to pay a hefty tax was somewhat of a blessing. Recent harvests had barely sustained them throughout the winters. He only hoped that the woman he'd marry was worthy and that they were well-matched.

THE KING'S ANTECHAMBER was a flurry of activity. Breckin stood just inside the door and awaited the night's revelry, not that he wanted to celebrate the thought of his marriage. Try as he might to be enthusiastic about the brides or sparring with the lairds, he was bored and anxious to get back on the road to Buchanan land. Twice now he refrained from yawning. Breckin wasn't one to spend the night mingling with lords or being entertained. He hoped the night would end early enough to afford him a good night's sleep.

Then he noticed *her*—the woman he'd seen in the village the day before—the woman he'd tried to rescue from the thief. She appeared even more beautiful than she had at the market. In a long, flowing, cream-colored gown that fit her to perfection, she walked with such an elegance he'd never seen in a woman before. He wasn't the sort of man who shied away from women, but since their run-in, he wanted to make a good impression. As he approached, he stood aside when she helped an older man whom he assumed was her father, setting him in a chair near the buttery.

She stepped forward and fetched a drink for the man; her eyes widened when she took him in. "*You.* What are *you* doing here?"

He bowed but kept his expression devoid of mirth. She didn't sound pleased to see him again. "Mistress, 'tis good to see ye here. I hope ye did not go after that lad, the one who thieved your coins."

"Indeed I did. If you had only taken a moment to ask him why he tried to thieve from me, you would have realized that the poor lad was only hungry."

"Ye ask for trouble with that brashness, lass." He couldn't keep the irritation from his tone because she put herself in peril. "Hungry or not, 'tis unlawful to thieve."

"So you uphold the law at all times? Cast the first stone, sir—"

"I cast no stones, only truth and honor." Breckin wanted to laugh at her absurd view of thievery but instead, he grunted at her insult. He wasn't sure if he wanted to wring her bonny neck or kiss her. She irked him but at the same time charmed him. "Aye, I sin, as I am certain ye do as well. If ye like, we could sin together." He flashed a grin to her but she seemed not to get the hint of his jest. A maiden, then. He continued, "I am gladdened ye are unharmed. Ye could have been more grateful and offered courtesy for my assistance and—"

She busied herself in pouring a cup of ale for the older man and turned her back to him. Still, he heard her say, "Your intrusion. No one asked you to save me."

"I could not stand aside and not give aid to a fair maiden such as yourself." Breckin watched her walk away. How such a bonny woman irritated him, and yet, captivated him at the same time, he couldn't reason. If only she didn't speak, he could gaze upon her loveliness and be content. He appreciated the sultry cadence of her voice, but it was the words with the slight bite to them that he disliked.

The side door panel opened and Alexander entered. He almost had to duck beneath the threshold as tall as he stood. The queen followed him to the dais. Breckin shuffled back and leaned against the window casement ledge, thankful that finally, the evening diversion had begun so he could get it over with.

Alexander cleared his throat and motioned to all. "This is a day of import, and I am pleased to see you here. This evening, we shall have a feast with dancing and merriment. I will give you this time to greet each other and become familiar. Before the night ends, the selections will be discussed and finalized on the morrow. I bid you to eat and drink."

Breckin stayed near the window and watched the bustle of servants open the doors to the great hall. Almost everyone in the antechamber made their way toward the large adjacent room. It was lit with large candelabras and the glow shone on the faces of those already making for the dance. The plucking of the harpist sent a melodic ambiance through the chamber but did nothing to allay his mood.

A servant passed by and Breckin snatched a cup of ale from him. He wasn't about to join in the revelry and considered the night a complete waste of time. Still, he would partake of the king's ale and dull every single one of his senses.

"Why are you standing here by yourself?"

He glanced up to find the queen standing nearby. "Your Grace..." Breckin bowed. "Ah, I was but sipping my ale. How are ye? Alexander tells me that ye are expecting a bairn. On behalf of all the Buchanans, we are delighted to welcome our future king."

Margaret giggled. "How presumptuous of you, Laird Buchanan. Perhaps we shall have a princess. Now tell me, was it my imagination or did I see you and Mistress Eva rowing by the buttery earlier?"

Eva? The market woman's name was Eva. It was a lovely name, not that he wanted to care about it. "Nay, Milady, not rowing but simply having a difference of opinion."

The queen stepped beside him, out of the way of the dancers on the floor. "Alexander tells me that you are against this marriage. Is this true?"

He raised his eyes to look into the queen's. She was audacious and direct. "Matters at home are pressing, Milady, which prevents me from rejoicing at such a union."

Margaret shifted forward and lowered her voice, "Laird Buchanan, I would like to share something with you but it must remain betwixt us… A dragon sits on a high cliff with her bright shimmering scales for all to see. All bask in her beauty and she appeals to all but most fear to get too near. On the outside, she might seem unapproachable, but as you are a renowned warrior, I am sure that you have the intelligence to uncover the beauty within." She craned her neck and appeared to be gazing at the market woman, Mistress Eva.

"Is this a riddle, Milady? Do ye wish me to solve it?"

"What I wish, Buchanan, is that you see not with your eyes but perhaps with your heart. I shall leave you with that." Margaret chuckled as she walked away.

Breckin shook his head with consternation because he wasn't sure what the queen wanted of him. Whatever she meant, he was sure she was talking about Mistress Eva. With that, his eyes roamed the large chamber for her but he didn't see her. He strolled toward the exit and crossed the hall. A balcony afforded an escape for him and he intended to take in some night air until he heard a familiar voice and then he glimpsed her before shifting behind the wall. Breckin couldn't help but overhear them.

"I tell you, da, they are all barbarians. You saw them. How am I supposed to marry one of them? I doubt they have sufficient homes. Why, I will probably be living in a dirt-floor cottage somewhere on a hill in the middle of nowhere. I am sure I shall perish."

"Ah, sprig, you are being a little overwrought. Surely these men have homes and you will not perish." The man laughed. "You are a rational woman and will find a way to make the best of your situation."

"Being married to a Highlander? I doubt that, Da."

Breckin stepped back until he was well away from the entrance of the balcony. He shook his head at hearing her view of him and his brethren. Yet she might be right. They were somewhat barbaric but they needed to be. It was fight and triumph or be defeated in the north. Obviously, the woman was used to extravagance of which he had none. She definitely wouldn't do as his wife.

He'd strike her from the running. But it was a damnable shame because he was attracted to her. Nay, he was completely enthralled by her. She was a beauty even if she irked him and that would have made the marriage bed a pleasurable place to be.

CHAPTER FIVE

THE DAY OF the battles began well enough and at least the rain had ceased. Breckin wasn't chosen to fight in the first two battles much to his disappointment. He'd hoped to put his fist in a face or two to rid him of his angst. If he had to choose a bride, he wanted the first, or at the very least, the second selection. Alas, he wasn't chosen for the bouts. Now, in studying his opponents, he recognized their flaws and could have easily defeated either of them in the hand-to-hand battle.

As he watched Declan MacKendrick thrash Shaw Mackintosh, he considered his opponents' moves and fighting stances. Breckin paced alongside the square, wishing he was brawling. Since Declan had won the first bout and selected Milady Isabella for his wife, she was out of the running. Isabella would have made a good selection for his wife.

Breckin grew frustrated when Cameron and Mackintosh were selected for the second fight. As he watched, he grew weary at the thought that he'd be left to accept the last bride. He only hoped it wasn't Mistress Eva. Cameron was intent to win and wouldn't let up on his punches to Mackintosh. When Cameron was finally declared the winner of round two, Magnus chose Milady Kendra for his bride. She was a beautiful woman and seemed amiable to marriage with Cameron.

He noticed Mackintosh's ire at losing and the swelling of his face. Cameron had done a job in distorting the man's appearance, for Shaw had a black eye and a wee bit of blood on his lip. It seemed to Breckin that he might have thrown the fight to his opponent. But why would Shaw do such a reprehensible thing? No Highlander would purposely lose unless… Before the bout, he'd seen the queen speaking to Shaw and the man hadn't seemed pleased with whatever the queen imparted.

Damnation, the meddlesome woman is fixing the fights.

Breckin ambled toward Shaw Mackintosh, intent to ask him that question when the queen approached. She marched forward and stepped in front of him, purposely blocking his path.

"Have you thought about what I told you, Laird Buchanan?"

He stopped short and bowed to Margaret. "Thought about what, Your Grace?"

"The dragon and her shiny scales?"

Breckin chuckled and recalled her strange riddle. "'Tis the truth, Your Grace, I did not give it much thought."

"You should," she whispered and walked away.

He shook his head in complete astonishment that the queen was trying to tell him something but she wouldn't just come out and say what that was. Breckin watched Lady Sorsha rush after Mackintosh and they disappeared inside the castle. Dejected, he surmised that Sorsha was interested in gaining Shaw for her husband.

He walked slowly toward the keep and considered the queen's riddle. Two brides remained—Lady Sorsha and Mistress Eva. With a chuckle, he scoffed as he thought about which lady he'd liken to a dragon with shiny scales. Of the two remaining brides, Lady Sorsha was sweet and had an amiable demeanor. He could still win her hand if he won the bout against Shaw. Then he realized that Margaret had meant Mistress Eva—she was the dragon with the shiny scales. He tried to recall what else Margaret had said. She alluded to the fact that Eva had beauty within as well as without. He had yet to witness such appeal in her.

"Laird Buchanan…"

He turned around when someone called him. Breckin waited for Mackintosh's comrade to reach him. "Aye?"

"Shaw asked that you come to him. He wants to speak with you privately."

He nodded and followed the soldier. Near the wall, he spotted Mackintosh in wait for him. When he got closer, the soldier walked away and left them alone. Shaw paced before the wall and stopped before him.

"Ye know, Breckin, that we are being used for our king and queen's entertainment."

Breckin pressed the long locks of his hair back from his forehead and grunted. "Aye, I suspect that is so as well but what can we do about it?"

"I say we forsake the last bout and decide right now which brides we will choose." Shaw peered at him as if he waited for his accord but Breckin wasn't about to let the man choose his bride.

"If I agree to this farce, how do we know the king and queen will allow us to forgo the fight? I do not wish to spar with ye even though I could take ye." Breckin stood close enough to Shaw to assert his ability to win any bout they would undertake.

"If the king wants us to accept his terms, he will permit us to marry without the last fracas."

Breckin grunted because, unlike Shaw, he had to go along with the king's demand. He couldn't afford to pay the tithe that he owed. The king promised to forgive his debt if he went along with the so-called entertainment. But he wasn't about to deny Shaw the ability to get out of fighting in the last battle since he'd already fought in the first two fracases. "Lady Sorsha is sweet and would make a good wife."

Shaw flinched when he named Sorsha. "Aye, she is sweet, but she was recently widowed, and lest ye forget, Lady Sorsha bore a child for her husband, my own now deceased cousin. We hope to keep the child amongst the family. I heard that she was a willful minx who oft causes discord in the home, although I had not witnessed such when I visited the Chattans."

"She's a widow? Her child is a wee terror?" Breckin moaned. "Ye know that I have younger brothers who try my patience and I have enough trouble keeping them in line…" He stopped pacing and turned to him.

Shaw ceased his steps and set his fisted hands on his hips. "Mistress Eva might be willful as well, but she's young and ye won't have to get her with child right away. Besides, she is beautiful. Have ye ever seen such a face or such bonny hair on a woman?"

"She is comely and bedding her would not be too much of a hardship," Breckin said and chuckled at his jest. It was her disdain for Highlanders that put him off. If he took Eva as his bride, he would need to convince her that he and his brethren were civilized and noble, a feat to be sure, since she obviously scorned the northerners.

"Mistress Eva draws every man's eye and every woman's ire. If ye take her, ye would be the envy of every man in Scotland and the women in your clan most envious."

Breckin grunted at Shaw's attempt at convincing him to agree. "She's young enough to train to my tastes, I suppose. If ye want Sorsha, then I am not too put out to take Eva's hand. Och, how will we sway the king and queen to accept our chosen brides?"

Shaw dipped his head as the queen approached. They turned to her and bowed slightly. Margaret walked regally toward them but did not smile and seemed intent on speaking to them.

"Your Grace," they both greeted her at the same time.

"Lairds Mackintosh and Buchanan, I would have a word with you. As you know, there are but two brides left. Unfortunately, my dear Alexander was called away to meet with his council and the last bout is no longer necessary."

"All is well?" Shaw asked.

"Oh, all is well. Worry not. The lords only wish to ensure Alexander's visit to England will not put them in jeopardy. They deem he might be easily persuaded by my father to concede to matters in which the lords hold interest."

Shaw lowered his head as she explained. "I understand ye will soon visit your family. Are ye pleased by this, Your Grace?"

"Our nation is humbly looking forward to the birth of your bairn," Breckin said.

"I shall be gladdened to see my family. The news of Scotland's successor will reach you within days, I am certain." Margaret waved off the chamberlain who stood nearby. "Now, we should settle the matter of the brides. This night we will hold the weddings after the late meal and then have a bit of a celebration. Since you were amiable and conceded to my interference in the first two bouts, Mackintosh, what say you? Who do you choose?"

Breckin felt the tug of his brows when she confessed to meddling in the bouts. Only Margaret would have the bollocks to force their hands and interfere with the king's plan. He should hold a little angst toward his queen but couldn't. Whatever her motive, he was sure she intended to do good and not harm to any of them.

Shaw glanced at Breckin who gave a slight nod. "I choose Lady Sorsha."

Margaret clapped her hands together and squealed. "Oh, this is marvelous. She was hoping you'd choose her. Of course, there always was something betwixt you two, was there not? Since the others have already spoken their vows, we shall commence with your weddings shortly. Make your way to the hall in a short time and I'll have the chancellor fetched."

"Aye, Your Grace. I'll be off then so I might tell Sorsha the news." Shaw bowed to her and gave a nod to Breckin before he turned and marched away.

"And you, Laird Buchanan, remember what I said. Just because you are faced with a dragon does not mean you cannot appreciate her. She might have a tender heart within."

Might? He could have laughed at the queen's reminder. If

Mistress Eva was tenderhearted, he'd be a dragon himself—which he supposed wasn't too far off the mark. Those he'd fought against in recent months could attest to that because he had not relented in his attack or protection of clans he'd intended to defend. A warrior never backed down and he wouldn't retreat now, even when faced with a dragon.

Breckin decided to get the telling over with. He searched the grounds for Eva Scott and saw her standing with her father near the entrance of the castle. With hastened steps, he reached her and called out, "Mistress Eva, I need to speak to ye."

Her father nodded to her, then turned and walked away.

He was left with the woman. She eyed him suspiciously. Lord, she was lovely. How could such a beauty hold such disdain for him and his brethren? She had an unfavorable view of him and that irritated him. But why should he care what she thought of him? Did he even want her approval? Breckin hadn't ever needed anyone's acceptance but for some reason, he wanted it now.

"What is it you want, Laird Buchanan?"

"I spoke with the queen and she told me that the king has cancelled the last bout. Mackintosh chose Lady Sorsha for his bride and I was given…" He waited to see if she realized her fate before he'd utter the words.

"Are you saying we are to marry, Laird Buchanan?" She frowned and her shoulders sagged. Her obvious distress had to cause her bonny head to spin with the thought of being married to him. She seemed to swallow a lump of gutted emotion, but then she took a breath and sounded composed when she said, "Well, neither of us has a choice in this matter. I cannot say that I am pleased to be offered as your wife but what can I do? I suppose that I shall accept you and you must accept me. That is what you are saying, is it not?"

He wanted to laugh at her disgruntlement but wouldn't be so crass. "That is exactly what I am saying, lass. We shall be wed this eve."

"I would not celebrate if I were you, Laird Buchanan. I will not celebrate either. This marriage will be unpleasant for us both unless…" The press of her white teeth against her pink bottom lip made him wonder what her mouth tasted like. He shook himself. Now was not the time to think about bedding his wife to be. Not yet. Not if she was unwilling.

"Unless what, lass?"

Her demeanor changed in an instant from appalled to acceptance, given that the fire in her eyes changed to a smoulder as she set a winsome smile on her face. "We make the best of it. I am not afeared of a challenge, Buchanan. Are you?"

Breckin chuckled under his breath and shook his head. She'd be a challenge all right, and one that he'd face head-on. The lass had gumption. She might make a good Buchanan wife after all. "My heart is set on ye, lass."

"If you intend to make a wretched husband, you shall regret it." She turned and walked away, her steps almost a march as she hurried to get away from him.

Breckin laughed then. She was ireful and most displeased that she'd have to marry him. It mattered not because, as she'd said, neither of them had a choice. He would make the best of it, though, and perhaps they could reach a truce. The last thing he wanted was an unwilling, ireful bride. Maybe he could even get her to sheath her claws before he took her to their marriage bed. Then he scoffed. That was highly unlikely. Besides, he wasn't opposed to a woman with claws in bed.

Breckin returned to the chamber that he shared with the other Highlanders. He collected his belongings and stuffed them into his satchel. Later that night, he intended to leave. He'd be on his way home before the sun rose on the morrow—with a wife. Cosh, it was enough to turn his stomach.

Shaw Mackintosh entered the chamber and seemed to be collecting garments. "How did Mistress Scott take your news?"

"Ah, well, let us say she was none too pleased. I might take a screeching bride to my bed this night," Breckin jested. "Och, it would not be the first time I had to soothe a nervous virgin. We shall do our duty."

"Well, she is young and will accept ye given time. I'm headed to the stream to wash if ye want to join me."

Breckin grabbed his satchel, followed him, and they left the castle grounds. Along the short walk, neither spoke. Surrounding the still waters of the loch, the rocky slope pitched toward the waterway. Except for a few yew bushes, there were no evergreens or crags. The land was almost barren and the view went on for leagues.

In the grayish expanse of the sky, high above, birds flew, soaring effortlessly. Such a sight allayed and calmed his ire at the situation he'd found himself in. He wished he was as free but alas, he was now shackled with marital misery. Breckin didn't like being away from the Highlands either and the sooner he returned to his lands, the better. He needed the solace that only the pristine lochs and invigorating air could bring. Soon enough, he would return to where he belonged, and that lightened him a little.

The stream was cold and he used his hands to scoop water to wash. He wasn't about to disrobe and douse himself with it. Once he was clean enough, he redressed and fastened the scabbard that held his sword over his back. He rolled up his clothing and shoved it inside the satchel.

Mackintosh finished bathing and stood beside him on the stream's bank. "We should return. Let us go and face our fate."

Breckin belted his tartan and grunted. "Aye, to my ill-fated destiny."

Mackintosh cuffed his shoulder with force. "Do not be so surly, my friend. Even if Mistress Scott is a terrible wife, she'll give ye handsome bairns. And lest ye forget, ye can always spend time away from your fief."

Breckin bellowed a laugh. "At least there is that." Then he remembered what the king had told him—he couldn't just leave her on his land and spend time away.

Since spring was oncoming, he would be about his land more

often and would rarely spend time at home. She'd have to understand that he had duties to see to, those which did not include a willful wife. He thought about what Shaw said and that Eva would give him handsome bairns. If anything, he would at least enjoy that part of marriage.

Then he pressed his hands over his face as he considered what she'd think of his home. She'd called him a barbarian. He hadn't paid much attention to matters of home in recent years and had no dwelling to speak of. That sank his shoulders a little because he had naught to offer the woman in the way of home or wealth.

Along the ride home, Breckin needed to give thought as to where she'd live. Since he usually stayed in the barracks with his soldiers, he couldn't put her there. Then he considered housing her with his aunt, but he couldn't foist another mouth to feed on Clare. She'd done enough already to help him. He'd have to find an unused cottage, one that afforded them privacy. She might appreciate being left on her own since she declared her aversion to him.

Breckin's shoulders tensed at that thought. He didn't want Eva to loathe him—he wanted her to be fond of him, to want to be with him, or at the very least suffer his presence without being chagrined. If he could induce such a miracle, marriage to her might not be half bad.

CHAPTER SIX

THE LIGHT MELODY of a harpist sounded as Eva entered the great hall for the night's festivity—namely her wedding to the Highlander. Breckin, from what she'd discerned of him, was that he turned a deaf ear to her, was unkind to children, and arrogant. But he was also handsome—Lord, was he pleasant to look at—and he was the leader of his clan. Hopefully, when he got to know her better, he'd be softer, kinder, and more courteous.

As much as she pleaded with her father, there was little either of them could do to refute the marriage. Eva wore her best gown, the blue velvet with golden embellishments. She always felt regal in it but this night, nothing brought her joy. Her end waved before her as if she was drowning in a vast sea with nothing to hold on to. Even gulps of breath did little to ease her apprehension. She despaired at the thought of her future—an impending destiny without her father, her home, and the opulence to which she'd become accustomed.

The queen entered the chamber and walked quickly to the dais. She held up a hand and all silenced. "Lords, Ladies, and Gentlefolk, we are privileged to bear witness this day the marriage betwixt Laird Mackintosh and Lady Sorsha, and Laird Buchanan and Mistress Eva. The chancellor has come down with a malady and so we asked Father Benedict to perform the ceremonies. If the brides and grooms would step forward."

Eva walked ahead of her father and stopped at the base of the dais. Laird Buchanan reached her side and stood silently next to her. She kept her gaze averted because she didn't want him to see how dismayed she was. But that was short-lived because he smelled so nice. She took a moment to gaze at him, at the way his hair hung past his shoulders unbound. He hadn't removed the short-trimmed beard that covered part of his face. He appeared manly, warrior-like, and strong. If anything, that gave her a little comfort because he certainly would protect her.

A young priest strolled forward and stepped onto the dais next to the queen. He cleared his throat and peered at them. "My good Lords, Ladies, and Gentlefolk, I am pleased by her Grace's request to perform the Sacrament of Marriage ..."

Eva's mind roamed and she thought about all the reasons why she'd object. Yet even if she wanted to balk at the marriage, she couldn't. She had to agree and give her consent to marry the Highlander. The priest continued his flowery description about what marriage meant but she barely heard a word. Beside them, Laird Mackintosh and Lady Sorsha spoke their vows and all in the great hall rejoiced. They seemed amiable to the marriage and smiled at the revelry of those who cheered.

Father Benedict turned and whispered something to the queen to which she responded. Their words were so softly spoken that none heard them. After, he motioned to her and Eva thought she'd be overcome with faintness. Her hands shook and heat rose within her. She managed to stay on her feet as the priest spoke to her. All eyes in the chamber fastened on her and her face burned with coyness.

"Mistress Eva, do you freely give yourself to this man—?"

"Freely?" she asked with an almost-croak to her voice.

The priest bobbed his head. "Freely. Will you take to be your husband, the handsome Laird Buchanan, and pledge to him before all gathered here, to be his love and his defender in unrest? Will you stand by him in all things fair and foul? Will you cherish him, forsaking all others, keeping only unto him, so as long as you both shall live?"

Eva swallowed hard and stared at her feet when she answered, "I freely do, Father."

The priest smiled and then motioned to Laird Buchanan. "Laird Buchanan, will you take to be your wife, the beautiful Mistress Eva, and pledge to her before all gathered here, to be her love and her defender in unrest? Will you stand by her in all things fair and foul? Will you cherish her, forsaking all others, keeping only unto her, for as long as you both shall live?"

Breckin stepped forward and nodded. "I will, Father."

Eva raised her face at the sound of his deep voice. He didn't falter in his answer but sounded resigned to his fate. Should that give her hope that they would do well together? *Sweet Mary*, she hoped so.

The priest made the Sign of the Cross. "May life's challenges be met together with courage and optimism, and may your days be filled with laughter, trust, friendship, and love. You once walked alone, but now you walk with each other, hand in hand. You now have someone to share life with, to offer refuge and sheltering love at the end of each day. With God's blessing, I pronounce you married, husband and wife from this day forward. You may now seal your vows with a kiss if you so wish."

Father Benedict's words did little to make her feel so not alone. Buchanan drew near and lightly brushed his lips over hers. Eva was surprised by the pleasantness of his kiss. At least he was noble and hadn't tried to maul her. She was grateful for that. As everyone disassembled, he clutched her hand and drew her away from the dais.

"Milady, we should talk…"

"I must see to my father. Can we speak later?" She curtseyed to him and tried to get away. She needed time to accept what had just happened—that she married him—a man likened to a warrior. Eva turned away but he snatched her arm and forced her back.

"Nay, we need to speak now. I mean to leave this night for my home. There is no time to dawdle. If ye will get your things and meet me by the entrance of the castle, we can be on our way." His voice took on a stern tone and she closed her eyes briefly to settle herself.

"Laird Buchanan—"

"Ye are my wife now and may call me Breckin. I do not mean to rush ye, Milady, but there are pressing matters to which I need to return."

"You wish not to join in the celebration?" Eva was astounded that he reasoned with her and even more so when he shook his head. She thought he'd just command and she would have no say in any matter. "I thank you for explaining, Breckin, and I detest asking you for a boon since we are newly married."

"A boon?" He scowled hard and gazed over the top of her head.

"A boon, ah, your favor. My father ails and should not travel in the night. The air is not good for his breathing or ailment. I was hoping that we could escort him home on the morrow so he wouldn't be alone. My brother was supposed to be here but he hasn't arrived. Can we take my father home and settle him and then leave for your home?" Eva had voiced her wish with politeness.

He seemed to be considering her request and finally returned his eyes to hers. "We will take your da home on the morrow, at first light, and then leave for my land. This night, though, Milady, ye will be spending it with me."

Eva's breath hitched but she tried to appear unaffected by his request. "I...should stay with my da. He will need someone to look after him."

He shook his head. "Nay, my wife stays with me. Have a maidservant stay with your da. If she needs ye, she will fetch ye. Otherwise, ye will be in my chamber where ye belong."

"Will you not see reason...?" Eva lowered her head in defeat.

"I am reasonable, lass, but ye ask too much. The king demanded that we honor this marriage with reverence and give ourselves to it in every sense. I gave in to your request to take your da home and ye should be content with that. I will not allow ye more than that." He walked off and left her.

Eva stood there for a moment and tried to regain her composure. He wanted to spend the night with her. *Sweet Mary.* And he called that being reasonable? She would have laughed if it wasn't so absurd. With haste, she crossed the great hall and found her father enjoying a conversation with another older man.

"Da, I must join my husband but want to get you settled for the night."

Her father grunted. "Go on, sprig, I know the way to our chamber. Collect your belongings and join your husband. Shall I see you on the morrow?"

She nodded and a tremble seemed to reverberate through her. There was no getting out of the marriage, the wifely duty, or her cowardice. "Since Richard has not yet arrived, I asked Laird Buchanan to escort you home on the morrow, Da. So we shall see each other then. I will make sure you are settled at home before I leave for...for the Highlands." Eva could barely bring herself to say the words. She'd leave her beloved father and home forever. At least she had a few more days before she was on her own.

As she left the great hall, she searched for Laird Buchanan. He was nowhere to be found. So she retreated to her chamber and collected her garments and possessions. She shoved them in her satchel with vigor and once she was ready, she stood near the door, hesitant to leave. With determination, she shook herself and pulled the door open. When she marched down the hallway to find out where her husband was staying, she found the chamberlain speaking with a maid.

"Milady Buchanan," the chamberlain called.

She flinched at being called Buchanan but she supposed she probably should get used to it. "Sir, do you know where I might find Laird Buchanan?"

He bowed and rose with a splendid smile. "You mean your husband? Aye, he asked me to escort you to your chamber. Follow me." As usual, Edmund didn't wait for her to acknowledge him but turned on his heel and headed down the hallway.

At the end of a vestibule, he stopped at a door. "Your chamber, Milady." He motioned to her to enter and turned away.

Eva pushed open the door and stepped inside. She set her satchel next to the entrance, closed the door, and stood there in a mesh of quivering nerves. Every part of her shook with apprehension at the thought of what she'd do this night with her so-called husband. She wasn't completely ignorant of what a man and woman did in bed and had witnessed some of the servants in precarious situations. Still, she never dreamed she would do such things, and with a man like Breckin.

Breckin stood by the window casement with his chin leaning on his fist. He turned and lowered his arms. He didn't smile, but then she surmised he never did. Or, at least, she'd never seen him do so. Was he always so severe?

"Laird Buchanan... Ah, I mean, *Breckin*, I am here as you requested."

He twitched a finger at her and his lips broadened in what she might consider a grin. *Sweet Mary*, he was handsome even with the set of his brows. The thought that she was now married to him instilled even more apprehension within her. It wasn't that she was afraid of him but more that she didn't know how to be. Should she try to appease him? Should she object if he insisted on taking his husbandly rights? Such matters caused her heart to thrum in her chest and ears.

Eva walked with slow steps toward him. When she reached him, she stopped in front of him and folded her hands. "We should probably talk about what is expected..."

"What I expect, lass, is a wife who obeys me. I will try to be a good husband to ye. We should take this night to... Ye are afeared," he said when he took her hands. "Ye tremble. I do not intend to harm ye. There is no need to be afraid."

"There is every reason to be. I have never been with a man and I expect that I…" Eva felt heat flushing her cheeks at her admission. "I will be inept at this."

"I should hope ye have not been with another, lass. Worry not, because I will try to be gentle." He set his hands on her shoulders and leaned forward.

When his lips touched hers, Eva's first instinct was to pull away but she stayed still and allowed him to kiss her. He brushed his mouth against hers; his harsh scruff scratched against her soft skin like nothing she'd ever experienced. Then he used his warm tongue to get her to respond to the desirous way he kissed her. Timidly, she touched her own tongue to his but then something overcame her, urging her to do more, experience more. She stepped into his embrace and he put his arms around her body, pulling her close. Her breasts pressed against his chest and something instigated her to want and need more. She wrapped her arms around his hard body and moaned softly at the fervent kiss they shared.

Breckin pulled back and his breath was raspy from their desirous kiss. "Lass, I…we should probably get ready for bed."

Eva nodded absently and turned away from him. Her nerves jumped to her throat. She couldn't voice her fear but stood facing the bed. He approached from behind her and set his hands on her shoulders. Breckin placed his lips on her neck and kissed her as his hands worked to remove her gown. When he pressed the garment down her arms, the chilled air in the chamber caused her to tremble from cold and the night to come.

She stood in her undergarments, a thin chemise that ended above her knees. Never had she felt so exposed. Breckin continued to stand behind her and pulled her back against him. The heat of his chest warmed her as his large hand pressed against the flesh of her stomach and he caressed her.

"I desire ye, lass." The passionate way he spoke sent heat through her.

Eva closed her eyes and felt his desire pressing against her buttocks. As she waited to see what he'd do, he turned her around.

"Will ye disrobe me?" he asked huskily.

"I am astounded that you were able to wear this within the castle," she said, as she took hold of the strap that held his sword on his back.

"The king knows better than to take my weapon away, and if he wants the use of it, he wouldst not offend me."

"The king wants you to use your sword for him…to war?"

"Aye, in the future, lass, not this night."

She sighed at that and wished for the reprieve, even if it meant war, but it wasn't to be. With shaky hands, she unfastened the scabbard across his chest and set it on a nearby chair. The sword was heavy and large. It was a hefty war instrument; broad and unembellished by any ornament. Afterward, she returned to him and removed his layers of tartans, and finally his tunic. He wore absolutely nothing beneath his lower tartan and the sight of his manhood forced a light gasp from her.

Eva wanted to avert her eyes but was intrigued by his body, and she stared at him until he cleared his throat. She fixed her gaze on his naked chest. The expanse had no hair but was smooth and muscular. If she had any brazenness within her, she'd reach out and touch him but she wouldn't be so forward.

He must've read her mind because he took her hands and set them on his chest. Eva drew in a breath at the sensation of his hot, hard skin. She raised her chin and found him watching her. Breckin dipped his head and set his mouth back on hers. Never had she expected to be moved by a man's touch but her body reacted to his caresses. She was uncertain what was happening to her but she enjoyed the sensations.

Breckin lifted her in his arms and carried her to the side of the bed. He gently set her on the bedding and watched her with hooded eyes. Even in the dimly-lit bed chamber, she could see the greenness of his eyes. His gaze captivated her and somehow alleviated the need to panic. Then he caressed her thighs and shifted them upward until he reached the top of her chemise.

He settled his head next to hers and whispered, "I want to see ye, your bonny body." Breckin hurriedly yanked her chemise down her body until he was able to remove it completely.

Eva lay back and covered her breasts with her hands. She'd never been on display before and tried to shift away from him. He took her hands in his and pushed them to the sides of her body. His gaze lingered on her and she shivered from the intensity of his beautiful eyes.

"Ye are bonny, aye, and should not hide yourself, lass." He pressed his hands upward on her arms until he cuddled her face in his palms. Breckin set his mouth back on hers and kissed her passionately but gently.

Eva tried to respond in kind but was overwhelmed by his desire. His hands seemed to be everywhere on her body and then she felt his fingers at her womanhood. She yanked her head back and gasped. "I am not sure I like this."

"Ye will, lass, I vow ye will. We will go slow and easy."

He returned his hand to her center and pressed his fingers inside her. She tried to focus on what he was doing but something within her twinged like a small pulse that reverberated through her. Eva closed her eyes, abashed at what he was doing. With a light sigh, she tried to focus on his touch and to find pleasure in it and being with him.

The bed shifted and he lay beside her. Breckin kept up the pleasurable torment with his hands and mouth on her neck and shoulder and sent her reeling with desire. Eva's body stiffened when he moved atop her and she felt his need at the core of her womanhood. She gasped and tried to push him away but he was too solid to move.

"Easy, lass. Relax and accept me," he said gruffly.

As he entered her, Eva scrunched her eyes closed and kept herself from crying out. She huffed at his invasion and wanted to enjoy it but couldn't. The unfamiliar sensations heightened her fear and prevented her from giving herself to the sensuality.

"Please, cease… I do not like this."

Breckin moaned and leaned his head against hers. His breath rasped against her cheek. "I would stop, but cannot, lass. We should get it done." With a thrust of his body, he fully entered her. It was as if she was being invaded, somehow. He tried to kiss her but she turned her head.

She didn't want to be humiliated but felt on the verge of tears. Eva refused to be a coward and she grabbed hold of his arms, hoping to endure the act without crying. "Hasten then and be done with it."

As he moved within her, Eva's body gave over to the pleasurable torment. A twinge began in the center of her being and spread outwardly as if it would completely overtake her. She kept hold of his muscular arms as he thrust against her. The way his body moved against hers spurred her to meet him. The sounds from his throat gave her the realization that he was tormented too. After a long moment and a final, deep plunge, he finally ceased moving. Breckin trembled and gasped, and then fell against her.

She lay back and was completely amazed at what happened between them. Eva had to wonder if that was how it would be— what couples experienced together. If so, she wasn't sure she wanted to perform her wifely duty. Yet there had been moments of possible pleasure and she'd hoped he would prove her wrong.

"Are ye all right, lass? Did I hurt ye?" He shifted to her side, pressed a hand on her face, and lifted her chin so she would look at him.

Eva shook her head and grabbed the bed cover to shield herself from his view. "I am well enough, and no, you did not hurt me. I am stronger than I look."

Breckin chuckled and raised a brow. "Good, because ye need to be strong to survive in the Highlands." He left the bed and lit a candle on the bedside table. Then he stoked the fire with the poker and added a log to the hearth. When he returned to her, he sat on the side of the bed and eyed her. "It always hurts the first time, Eva, but the next time it will not be so—"

"*Next* time? We have to do that again? I do not want there to be a next time," she said, cutting him off.

"There will be a next time...plenty more times. 'Tis what husbands and wives do. And we must join so that we shall have bairns." He snatched up her hand and clasped it. "But worry not because when we get to my land, ye will not see me often. I am rarely at home. Ye will have freedom."

Eva tugged her hand back from his grasp and felt the pull of her brows at his words. "Freedom? So you plan to abandon me?"

"As the laird, I am often called away. Ye should understand that. Was your da not called away to handle his lordly matters? Surely ye understand."

She pressed her lips together as she thought about his explanation. "I suppose that is true. Well, I appreciate you enlightening me. That might be a good thing since I do not think I even like you, Laird Buchanan."

He raised his brows, then lowered them over the bridge of his nose. She didn't like him? Well, she had a little gumption and he was surprised by her confession. Why that bothered him, he couldn't reason, but he didn't much like her either. "Ye can dislike me all ye want, lass, but that does not change the fact that ye are my wife." Breckin stood and rounded the bed. He grabbed his tunic from the floor and pulled it over his head. "Best get rest because we leave at first light."

Eva turned to her side and faced away from him. Tears threatened to fall but she resisted and sniffled her heartache away. He hadn't hurt her, but truth be told, her heart ached with his uncaring words. She had hoped their joining would bring them closer or at least offer her an opportunity to find something about him that she found appealing or redeeming. She wanted to appreciate him even in an affectionate way. Everything about him overwhelmed her: his strong body, confidence, and handsomeness. If she was honest with herself, she might even admit that she liked being with him, and longed for his touches and kisses.

She drew a deep breath and decided that she would suffer through the ordeal when she needed to. Since she'd rarely be in his company, Eva suspected that it wouldn't be too difficult to feign acceptance. And perhaps one day, she might even hold the tiniest bit of fondness for him—when she was long in the tooth and grayer than a wild hare.

On the morrow, they would take her father home which would give her time to come up with an excuse to stay at her father's manor. Breckin certainly didn't want a wife and some-how, she had to convince him that he'd be better off without her.

CHAPTER SEVEN

B RECKIN WAS GLADDENED to finally leave Edinburgh. The journey to Eva's home took three long days of riding toward the border, which would usually take him a day or even two at the most. Eva had demanded that the horsemen ride slowly because of her father's ailment. He wanted to turn his horse and head in the opposite direction but alas, he'd agreed to escort her father home. Yet the closer he got to the border, the more he regretted his promise.

Eva barely spoke two words to him during the trek. Of course, she had opted to ride with her da in their carriage. He rode his horse ahead of Lord Scott's men-at-arms. To keep himself from thinking about their disastrous first night together, Breckin focused on the lane, sounds, and for possible foes.

Even though he tried not to consider the ramifications of their first coupling, his mind relived the night over repeatedly. He flinched and was thoroughly disappointed in himself. Breckin had never left a woman dissatisfied before but his body had a mind of its own. He disbelieved he'd lost control and gave way to his need before he brought his bonny wife to pleasure. Not that he professed to be a great lover, but he was adept at bringing a woman to completeness.

What was wrong with him? Had he gone addled? It sure seemed so.

Since their departure from Edinburgh, there had been no time to discuss with Eva what had happened between them. He wanted to apologize, not that he was versed in making such amends. Breckin seldom apologized to anyone, but he owed her that. She'd sworn that he hadn't hurt her, but he knew that he had acted without care of her tender feelings. She was a lass, young, and unknowing in the ways of sex and men. He should have taken more time to woo her. Breckin regretted it now and vowed to make amends for his boorish behavior at the soonest.

The lane rounded a grouping of trees ahead and the area was sparse in its woodland. He concentrated on his surroundings and listened to the tromping of the horses' hooves. Being near the border kept him on alert but the Scott men-at-arms appeared lax in their courtesy. One of the lord's men-at-arms whistled lightly and he stopped to find out what was happening. Breckin spotted no one ahead and heard no sounds from the meagerly wooded area around them.

"Laird Buchanan," a man unknown to him, almost completely covered with chainmail and a helmet, said, "Let us go ahead. Our watchmen shall see us and have the gate opened before our approach. They might be guarded if they spot you."

He wasn't the least bit insulted by the man's request. Those by the border were usually standoffish when a Highlander was in their midst—a Buchanan even more so. Their reputation for brutal force preceded them and that suited him well. He'd rather have men-at-arms fear him than welcome him with open arms.

Breckin signaled to his horse to move to the side to await Eva's carriage to pass. As he rode next to it, he tried to see her face. She looked pleased and wore a smile on her bonny face. Breckin wished she'd smile at him that way. The carriage rolled forward, past the extravagant golden gates, and continued until it reached a row of steps that led to the lord's home.

Breckin sat on his mount and tilted his head back. His eyes widened at the expanse of the heavily bricked manor home. He had never seen so many windows on an abode, and covered in glass, no less. The expense to build such a home must have cost a fortune.

Then his shoulders tensed when he realized that he could offer no such dwelling to Eva. Maybe the inside wasn't as grand and lacked the extravagance of the outside.

He dismounted and waited for Eva and her father to retreat from the carriage. She walked past without a word to him and held on to her da's arm.

"Let us get you settled, Da. You must be weary from the journey. Shall I have Luella fetch the healer for you?" Eva purposely ignored him as she assisted her father inside their home.

Breckin walked behind them and followed. He sighed heavily when he eyed the entry of the manor. Beyond the access, a hallway led to overlarge doors to which he suspected the great hall sat. On the walls were tapestries, and beneath were placed tables of wooden elegance. On the gleaming tops of the tables sat ceramic bowls, statuettes, and vases.

Torchlights were set in golden holders along the wall and brightened the expansive hallway. Breckin continued onward, impressed by their wealth and home. Even though he suspected he would never be able to furnish Eva with such luxury, he hoped she understood that they lived a simpler life in the Highlands. They didn't need shiny floorboards, expertly done tapestries, or artful bowls, statues, and vases.

In the great hall, she removed her cloak and set it over the top of an ornate chair. She helped her father settle in another chair and called forth a maid. "Luella, it is so good to see you. Can you bring a drink and some light fare?"

"Aye, Mistress." The maid bowed to them, eyed him curiously, and hastened away.

Breckin stood by the roaring fire in the hearth and waited for his wife to approach. But he suspected he'd wait until Hell froze over because she made no move to join him. She retrieved her trunk which he'd only just noticed inside the doorway of the hall.

"I will give you a dram of the tincture, Da. It shall help ease you and then we will put you to bed." Eva took care of her father and he found himself a wee bit envious of her care.

Finally, she glanced at him and he raised a brow. Breckin approached and stood next to her. Being close to her allowed him to take in her flowery scent, her beauty, and all that was Eva. He sighed and searched for the right words.

"We will not stay the night and must be on the road to the Highlands."

Her brown brows furrowed. "Now? You want to leave now? But it is too soon."

"Aye, what better time, lass? Ye know that I need to get home. We cannot afford to waste more time. Your da is home and settled now. We must go."

"Daughter," her father called. "You should not keep your husband waiting. Your new life awaits and I bid you to be a dutiful wife."

"But I wanted to collect my belongings. Surely, Laird Buchanan, you would allow me to bring my possessions."

"You may bring whatever fits in a small satchel." He nodded to her and tried to be amiable. Surely his acquiescence would please her.

She had the gall to test him further and make more demands. "But I...I can fit a good amount in the carriage."

Breckin chortled a laugh. "Lass, where we are going, no carriage can cross. Unless we take the long way around the hills and mountains, which will put me at least a fortnight behind. I will not be delayed further. Nay, ye can bring whatever fits in your satchel."

Eva flopped down into the chair adjacent to her father's. "Surely we can rest and leave on the morrow. And my belongings will not fit in a satchel, Breckin."

Her da chuckled. "I vow there are probably four or more carts already loaded with her goods. There will be plenty of items to keep you in comfort as you begin your life together."

"Four or more carts…" he said, aghast. "Ye must be jesting with me, Lord Scott. Eva, I have no time or patience for this. I care not about your possessions. Ye will not need such items where we are going. Bring some garments and something to keep ye warm. That is all ye need."

"I will not leave a single item behind." She folded her arms over her chest and her brows pulled together as she inserted her claim. "Why the haste? What lures you home so quickly?"

"War."

"War? You mean to go to war when we reach your home?" She seemed astounded by his simple explanation.

Breckin made no qualms about it. "Aye, war."

"Then perhaps you might consider leaving me here. Later, when the weather warms and you finish your war, you can return to retrieve me. By then, I can have my belongings packed tightly in the carts and ready to be transported." She appeared confident in her demand but he scoffed with a grunt at her forceful speech.

Breckin maintained a serious expression. "Where I go, ye shall go as ordered by the king himself. Nay, we will leave shortly with a small satchel of your possessions."

"Daughter," her father called. "You should concede to your husband's will. I shall see to it that your beloved possessions are packed in the carts and transported to you in the Highlands. My men will bear arms and protect it on the journey. Will that suffice, Laird Buchanan?"

"The carts will take an extra fortnight or longer to reach my holding, but aye, I suppose I can live with that. Presently, I cannot be delayed in my return."

"We understand," Lord Scott said. "Sprig, you need to go. Laird Buchanan will take good care of you. I promise to send a missive and you must write back to me to tell me how you fare."

She nodded but remained silent.

"Then I shall await ye outside, lass. Do not keep me waiting." Breckin bowed his head to Lord Scott and turned on his heel. He left the beautiful manor home and stood by his horse.

"Milord," a lad said as he rounded his horse. "I gave him a little bit of hay and water."

"My thanks, lad. Where is the stable?"

"'Tis behind the manor, Milord."

"Fetch a horse for Lady Eva."

The lad's mouth hung open. "Milady never rides horses. Are ye sure, Milord?"

"Aye, I am. Make sure the horse is sound. We have a good distance to ride." Breckin grabbed the reins of his warhorse and followed the lad to the side of the manor to ensure that Eva was given a proper mount, one sturdy enough to make it up the incline and hillier mounds.

Eva caught up to him and called out. He noticed her over-large satchel and eyed her skeptically but decided he would allow her to bring whatever she'd put in the baggage. His wife tested his patience but since she was leaving her home, he'd give in to her, if only to show her that he could be reasonable.

"Breckin, can my maid come? She has looked after me since I was young and I cannot do without her. Her name is Luella and she is—"

He shook his head.

"But why? Surely you will not refuse my need for a maid. Will you please cease shaking your head? Surely, a maid will not inconvenience you."

"Outsiders are not permitted on my land." It was all the answer he would give. Breckin busied himself with tying her packs to her horse, a cream-colored mount with brown speckles. The horse was unlike any he'd ever seen and its kind had to come from across the channel. But then, Lord Scott was a trader and probably had acquired the horse from a breeder. Its value must be high given its confirmation and coloring.

"I am an outsider," she said, softly. "Perhaps I should stay here and..."

Her words trailed off when he shook his head again. "Nay, Eva, ye are my wife, not an outsider. Now, here, take the reins of your horse. I hope to make good ground before it gets too dark to travel." Breckin handed her the horse's reins and mounted his own horse. He rode ahead and didn't look back. Once he was through the gate, he slowed his progress so she could catch up to him.

She kept a slow pace behind him and he gave a side glance to ensure she followed. Eva was irked, given the daggers in her eyes and the pout of her bonny lips. He felt the hotness of her stare on him and though he wanted to chuckle, he kept his expression devoid of his mirth. Breckin did not know how to abate her ire. She'd release her anger once they were well enough away from her home.

HIS WIFE WAS furious with him. Throughout the ride to the Highlands, she spoke not a word, not even to make a complaint. Breckin tried to make small talk with her, but she wasn't having it. When he asked her if she needed to rest, she'd either nod or shake her head. He hadn't heard her bonny voice for days. With a sigh, he stopped earlier that evening so they could rest and make an early start on the morrow. By nightfall next, they would reach his land and he was never so happy to be close to home. There, he'd part ways with his surly wife and allow her to be for a time. Sooner or later, she would accept her fate and then, perhaps, him.

He set a tartan on the ground in front of a large crag that would shelter them from the strong winds. The day grew chillier but at least it hadn't rained. As soon as he set the cover for her, she sat wearily upon it and rummaged through her satchel. She pulled out a small loaf of wheat bread and tore a piece off for herself. He could hope that she'd offer him some but he wouldn't hold his breath.

Breckin scrounged the area for small logs and twigs so he might light a fire. Even though they were on Stewart land, he wasn't too worried about being attacked. His relations with the Stewart clan wasn't close at the moment but there was no cause for them to attack him. He would have kept riding but Eva appeared tired and besides, he wanted to spend a little time with her before they arrived at his keep. Somehow, he would get her to talk to him…and then a notion came to him.

After he set the logs and kindling, he retrieved the flint from his satchel and within a moment, had the dried grass lit with flame. The fire took hold and brightened the area where they had made camp. She shifted closer to the warmth.

"There is a small stream yonder if ye wish to wash," he said and motioned in the direction of the water.

She knelt and then rose. "I do. Have you a flask? I will get us some water."

He handed her his empty flask and turned back to his horse. Breckin found a good spot where new grass sprouts covered a small area and began to hobble them so they'd stay close by. The horses immediately lowered their heads and nibbled on the shoots.

"If you want some bread, help yourself," she said over her shoulder as she walked away.

His head snapped around to watch her leave. Breckin grinned at hearing her voice. She *did* care about him and wouldn't let him go hungry. At least, there was hope for them yet. While he waited for her return, he retrieved his small bow and a handful of arrows. He'd do a little hunting and perhaps kill something for their supper.

She returned and sat down upon his tartan. With her eyes on him, she clasped her bent legs and held her knees. "Are you going to…"

He nodded, surmising what she was going to ask. "Aye, I will not go far. If ye need me, just call out. I hope to hunt something for our supper. Ye are hungry?"

Her chin bobbed slowly. "Then I will rest whilst you are gone. Is it safe here?"

"Aye, safe enough." Breckin left her and walked quickly toward a copse of trees in the distance, not too far away. As he crouched down in wait for a rabbit or small creature, he grinned to himself. She could not stay angry with him. Likewise, he couldn't stay angry with her. Somehow, Breckin needed to think of a way to make amends and call a truce betwixt them. He didn't want her anger, he wanted the coy and sweet gazes she'd given him on their wedding night.

A rabbit emerged from a thicket to nibble on grasses near the base of a tree. He quickly positioned an arrow and let it loose. The arrow pierced the animal and it fell where it had stood. The rabbit was large enough to feed him and Eva, so he decided to forego hunting and hastened back to camp. As he neared, the sound of a horse alerted him that riders approached, and as they crested the rise and emerged from the woods, Breckin looked to see that his wife was still sleeping under the rocky outcropping before he recognized his one-time ally.

"William, 'tis ye there," he greeted the leader of the Stewart clan.

"Breckin, my sentry reported riders and so I thought to ensure no marauders intended to attack us. Ye are usually surrounded by a sentry of Buchanan warriors. Do ye travel alone?" William removed his helmet and fanned back the strands of his brown hair.

Breckin shook his head and pointed at Eva who lay upon the cover. She seemed to be sleeping and had her eyes closed. He set down his kill and bow and walked to William.

"Who is she?" William asked when his dark eyes shifted to Eva.

"My wife." Breckin wasn't about to say more. "I will not linger on your land and will be gone early on the morrow. We are just passing through."

William dismounted from his horse and stood nearby. "Naught to worry about, my friend. It has been some time since we last met. I wanted to tell ye how sorry I was about Marian's death and should have attended her burial but clan matters kept me away. I still hurt from the loss, as I am sure ye do."

The loss? The man presumed to be his comrade but on the day of his sister's burial, he'd proved what a good friend he'd been. That he hadn't shown for her entombment told him all he needed to know about William Stewart.

"My clan continues to mourn her."

"As ye should." William settled his hands on his waist and peered at him.

Breckin kept his expression from showing his temper at the man's admission. His now-rival had been betrothed to his sister when she'd died. Reverently, he should have come to pay his respects to a woman he supposedly loved, but he hadn't. Apparently, William hadn't considered Marian important enough to forgo his duty to his clan. Now, Breckin had no wish to be neighborly and he certainly didn't want to talk about his sister.

William motioned to his men to stay back. "Whilst I have ye here, I should tell ye that I married Danella MacLaren. Her brother approached me about an alliance. Danella coveted the union and so we took our vows last year."

Breckin tried not to react to William's news. He'd married Breckin's former betrothed last year? The MacLarens had only just rescinded their pact when they made their offer to the Stewarts then. Rage shot through him like hot fire. Not that he begrudged the man any happiness, but Danella was supposed to have married him.

That her clan called off the marriage infuriated him because there had been no cause to do so. Even though, at the time, Breckin had considered the matter insignificant, it now made him wonder what caused the MacLarens to change their minds and why they'd offered Danella to William Stewart instead. Their alliance gave him a slight concern but really, the Buchanans could handle any hostility from either clan.

"I do not want animosity betwixt our clans, Breckin, which is why I tell ye of this now. I should have come sooner and met with ye and told ye long ago. Och, Danella wanted to keep the news quiet for a while. Laird MacLaren's son came to me with the offer and ye know that I needed to form an alliance. We are allied now but that does not mean that we are against ye."

Bollocks, Breckin thought. The day the MacLarens called off his betrothal to their daughter was the day they became rivals. And if the Stewarts thought the Buchanans feared them, William had to be dimwitted. The Buchanan warriors could easily crush their forces, both the Stewarts and the MacLarens. He certainly didn't need them as allies and wouldn't even consider such an offer if one was put to him.

William stepped toward him. "Ye say nothing and that makes me wonder if ye are angry with me. I have always held ye in esteem, Breckin."

"Felicitations, William," Breckin said hastily, not wanting to give his thoughts on the matters he'd spoken of, "...on your marriage. I too recently married and am pleased with my bride. Alexander himself offered her hand to me. We are just returning from Edinburgh."

William reached out and set his hand on his shoulder. "Gladdened, I am, Breckin, to hear your joyous news. I want no resentment amongst us. I offer my felicitations on your marriage as well. Stay as long as ye want on my land. There is no need to rush off on the morrow. And I am sorry for what happened to Marian." He bowed his head and turned toward his men.

Within a moment, the horses disappeared over a hillock and the sound of their hooves faded. He was gladdened to see the man's back. In time, he would deal with the MacLarens' traitorous deed and the Stewart's disrespect for his sister's death.

When he'd calmed enough from his go-between with William, Breckin retrieved the rabbit and withdrew his dagger from the sheath on his belt. He knelt next to the fire and situated some rocks to form a base. Nearby, he found a large enough stick to use for cooking the animal. After he banked the flames, the fire increased enough to warm him. He quickly skinned the rabbit, used the stick to skewer it, and set it over the rocks to cook.

Breckin cleaned his dagger with a cloth gotten from inside his tunic and used a little water from the flask to ensure no animal blood remained on the blade.

"Who was that?"

He glanced at Eva and found her watching him. Breckin moved to sit next to her, and used the cloth to dry the dagger. "A neighbor."

The meat sizzled over the flames and wafted its scent to them.

"Who is Marian?"

She'd heard their discussion. Breckin sighed heavily. He was reluctant to explain what happened to his sister and besmirch Marian's good name. "A betrothed."

"What happened to her?"

"She died." Without further explanation, he disregarded their conversation.

"I am sorry to hear that, Breckin," Eva said softly and set her hand on his arm.

"It was a long time ago and I wish not to discuss Marian." When she removed her hand, he released a dejected breath, hoping she didn't withdraw.

The sounds of the forest lent to the easiness of being with Eva. He stared into the flames of the fire, lost in his thoughts and she in hers. At least being with her wasn't uncomfortable and he need not fill the silence with senseless conversation. Still, being near her allowed him to smell her flowery scent and notice the creamy skin above her bodice. He doubted he'd ever tire of looking at her.

A while later, the rabbit appeared ready to eat and had cooked long enough. Breckin took the meat from the spit, cut it into pieces, and by the time he'd given her some, it had cooled. He sated his hunger and offered her more but she refused it with a shake of her head. After, he cleaned up the remnants and tossed the animal's bones into the fire. He ensured the horses were tethered tightly to the bushes near the stream's bank, grabbed a small pail he used when traveling, and untied it from his saddle. He filled the bucket, approached Eva, and set it next to her.

She sat quietly, and had placed another blanket on the ground. It would make for a soft place to sleep. He wasn't used to such comforts and usually slept against a tree with only his tartan as a cover. He returned to the horses to get his saddlebag and hurried back. Breckin untied his saddle bag and took out the small cloth he used to wash with when he traveled.

"Now, I have something I wish to share with ye." He took her hand and faced the palm upward. Her fingers still had a little greasiness on the tips and he used the cloth to wash her hands. She seemed shocked that he would do so and gasped lightly at his touch. "The Buchanans have a sacred ritual that we perform whenever we marry." He gripped her hand and used the dagger to cut a small slice in the center of her palm. She gasped and tried to retract her hand but he held fast until she got over his brashness. Blood pooled there and turned her skin crimson.

Then he did the same to his hand and his warm blood covered his palm. He clasped her hand and said, "Not only are we joined in God's eyes but we are now bound by blood. Our blood is forever joined, Eva, and nothing but our end will ever change that."

"How barbaric," she whispered.

Breckin took the small cloth and wrapped it around her wound. He poured water on his palm and wiped it on another cloth he retrieved from his saddlebag. "Not barbaric, Eva, symbolic. Ye are mine as I am yours, forever."

"I need not be reminded of that, Breckin."

They finished eating in silence, and after, she lay and faced away from him. Breckin shimmied close to her and used his body to shield her back. He set his arm around her and smiled to himself.

"What are you doing?"

"Holding ye."

"Why?"

He moaned softly at her objection. "Eva, I wanted to…to say that the first time we were together was…" Damnation, he couldn't form the words. "Was difficult for us both. I should have been more gentle and wooed ye as ye deserved."

"There is no need to apologize, Breckin. What's done is done. Now, should we not get some sleep?" She continued to face away from him.

He used his hand to caress her and send subtle messages to her body. "I find I am not tired."

"Me either." She shifted her body to the side and peered at him.

"Ye know what I want to do?"

"What?" she said breathlessly.

He grinned before he answered her, "Kiss ye."

CHAPTER EIGHT

H IS HARD BODY lured her touch. Eva shimmied closer to him and his tempting heat. She set her palm on his naked chest and pressed her lips on his because she wanted his kiss. Whatever had happened between them on their wedding night was forgotten. Eva couldn't help but be drawn to him; he was too attractive to deny. She longed to caress him, to feel him against her, to receive him with open arms.

Breckin cuddled her face with his hand and kissed her, his lips continually brushing against hers. Desire swarmed within her. Eva pulled back and shifted her gown from over her body. When she was about to remove her chemise, he stilled her hand.

"Keep it on. I find it appealing on ye."

His husky words made her grin. "Then I shall leave it."

Breckin removed his garments and left nothing on. He lay beside her and stared into her eyes. She liked the way his eyes smoldered when he wanted to kiss her. Eva held out her arms and he rolled to lean against her. His mouth found hers and they kissed with such passion that she moaned with delight. There was something about the way he kissed her that spurred her passion. Any hesitation she'd had scattered away with the breeze.

His hands roamed her body, teasing, caressing, and massaging her. She, in turn, glided her hands over his muscular arms, chest, and torso, until her fingers became entangled in the strands of his hair. He was well-bodied, and though she should fear the strength of him, she knew he wouldn't hurt her. Breckin eased her onto her back and he reached to touch her femininity.

With skillful touches, he teased her womanly nub until she rasped for breath. The sensations swarmed her and her body gave way to his desirous caresses. She closed her eyes and concentrated on the lightness of him sliding his fingers against her and the pleasure he created.

Eva didn't know what came over her but her body erupted in a mass of light and twinges as if she left herself. She kept herself from squealing in the delight of it, and yet, panted with desire. When her breath calmed and she could think again, she opened her eyes and stared at him. He flashed a quick grin at her.

"What did you just do to me?"

"What I should have done on our wedding night." Breckin chuckled and beamed pridefully. "I need ye to touch me, lass." He pressed her hand on his erection and groaned a sound of pleasure. With his eyes closed, he tilted his head back with abandon.

Eva was fascinated with the heat and hardness of his manhood. She clasped him and used her fingers to slide along his silky shaft. He moaned and seemed to enjoy her touch. His manly neck was on display and she kissed his skin, sliding her mouth over the softness of his throat under prickly whiskers which vibrated her lips with his groans.

Breckin shifted back and dislodged himself from her hold. "That is enough of that, lass. Ye make it too easy to lose control."

"Do you want to continue—" Eva wasn't sure if she should voice her question.

"Hell, aye, I do." Breckin leaned over her and pressed kisses on her face. "I vow to ye, lass, ye will not feel pain this time, only pleasure."

He eased into her and she gasped at the sensation of him there between her legs. Eva held him as he pressed onward. When he rocked against her, her mouth hung open in awe at the twinges permeating her body. Eva's muscles tingled and she couldn't get close enough to him. She wrapped her legs around his hips and met his thrusts. Soon, her breath came heavy as she panted with desire in unison with Breckin. The climax of their joining hit them at the same time and they groaned in surrender, their moans blended in euphoria for them both.

Eva lay lethargically beneath him until he shifted to her side. How had she been so wrong about joining with him? She could have laughed at her ignorance because she'd enjoyed every moment of their second encounter. Breckin lay back and ran his hands through his hair. He groaned and continued to breathe heavily. She kissed him and used her hands to caress his body, telling him that he'd pleased her.

The sensual act between them was over. Eva shivered as the evening air chilled her. She hurriedly retrieved her gown and pulled it over her. "'Tis cold this night."

He reached for his tartan and handed it to her. "It is always cold in the Highlands. Best get used to it. Keep this. It shall warm ye. Ye might want to get heavier garments when we reach home."

She grinned at the thought of having to purchase new, warmer gowns. Eva closed her eyes contently and sleepiness overtook her. She felt Breckin cuddle beside her and wrap his arm protectively around her waist. She felt safe and cared for and, with a soft moan, gave over to her need to dream.

A bang startled her awake in the morning. Groggily, Eva peered at Breckin who stood by the fire. He dropped a large log into the embers and the dried wood didn't take long to ignite. Flames licked the air and sent cherished heat to her.

"Sorry, lass, did I awaken ye? We should eat and be on our way. 'Tis only a few leagues until we reach my land." He turned his back to her and continued to attend to the fire and the meat—another rabbit—that cooked on the stick. As he knelt, the fabric of his tartan rose and she peered at the naked backs of his knees and lower thighs. Bulges of muscle met her eye and she smiled at the thought that she'd married a well-bodied man.

"Are ye going to continue to stare at me and laze about or rise?" He raised a brow as if he wanted her to get moving.

Eva groaned at the soreness of her body and throbbing aches. She stretched and rolled to her side. "Aye, I am getting there." After grabbing her cloak, she pulled it around her and folded Breckin's tartan. She approached and handed it to him. "Here, my thanks."

"Nay, lass, keep it. It will keep ye warm on the ride." He removed the meat and used his dagger to cut it into small pieces.

They ate in silence. She pulled the remaining bread from her satchel and offered him a piece. The awkwardness between them brought on a shyness. Eva was uncertain what to say, if anything, about what happened between them the night before. Instead, she collected her things and helped to gather his belongings while he kicked dirt onto the fire to ensure it was out.

She ambled like an old woman toward the horses. "Can we walk a little?"

"I would rather we make haste and leave Stewart land. 'Tis only a few leagues, lass, until we reach my border. We should reach it by mid-day."

Eva moaned at the thought. "My bottom is sore, which is why I always disliked riding horses." Her face heated at her admission.

"Are ye blushing, lass? If ye need to ride with me…"

"'Tis not because of last eve but from riding these past days. My muscles ache and I am not sure I can withstand another moment of riding, let alone until mid-day." She wanted badly to rub her aching backside and inner thighs but resisted.

"When we leave Stewart land, we can walk. Until then, ride with me." Breckin secured their belongings to her horse and then mounted his. He threw his hand down at her and she took it. With a yank, he propelled her upward and she shifted her body so that her legs were to one side. As she leaned against him, she relaxed.

As Eva swallowed, she noticed that her throat hurt. She

hoped she wasn't coming down with a malady. But throughout the morning, her condition worsened and she began to sneeze repeatedly, so much so that she needed to sniffle, and worse, her eyes watered. As she peered ahead at the view, she wiped at them to abate the filmy tears.

The Highlands were beautiful even if they were somewhat barren and blurry. Hills led from one to another with valleys between great mountains. A thick fog rolled over the top of a large mound, almost ethereal in its movement. She was enthralled with the sight of it.

"Behold, Buchanan land," he said in a whisper by her ear.

"Your land is beautiful, Breckin."

"Aye, 'tis and I am gladdened to be home. The air seems clearer here and the water pristine. Some fairy pools lie on our land and the waterfalls are breathtaking. When I have time, I shall take ye to see the beauty that is now your home." He tightened his hold on her when the horse pitched slightly as they rode down a hillside.

When they reached the bottom, ahead stretched as far as the eye could see were blackened tree trunks. Eva craned her neck so she could discern where the trees began and ended but they seemed to go on in a line that crossed the land. It was as if the tree trunks were warriors standing guard with outstretched swords that reached the sky.

"What happened here? Was there a fire? Was your land touched by a catastrophe?" she asked because it appeared the trees had suffered damage and were scorched to the bark.

Breckin shook his head. "Nay, lass, 'tis a warning."

"A warning for whom?" She was saddened to see the pines burned to their trunks. Blackened limbs rose in the air, seemingly reaching for the sky and the scent of burnt wood had long since dissipated. At least, she couldn't detect an odor now.

"A warning to whoever tries to cross our borders. We lit the trees on fire to blacken them on purpose to frighten those seeking to provoke us. It is a blunt warning that from that stretch of trees, lies Buchanan land. None cross it without retribution."

Eva moaned and closed her eyes against the unsightly view of the poor trees. That they hoped to instill fear in people who traveled the land saddened her. Did the Buchanans get along with anyone? Apparently not, and it seemed that they didn't want to.

She shook and a shiver overtook her body. "Breckin, I'm cold."

He slowed his horse and removed the tartan he wore around his shoulders, then reached behind him and held it in her direction with a light shake. "Here, put another tartan around ye. 'Tis not long now." Breckin helped her cover herself and then kissed her head. "Ye are hot. Are ye burning with fever?" He deliberately kept his lips on her forehead and pressed the back of his hand on her face. "Aye, ye are."

Eva swallowed. She'd thought she might be feverish. With a nod, she moaned. "I need to rest. Wake me when we reach your holding?"

"Aye, lass. Rest against me. We have only a league to go and should reach home soon."

She closed her eyes and moaned. What she wanted was a warm bed, a heavy blanket, and something warm to soothe her throat. She couldn't remember the last time she was ill but somehow she had come down with an illness on their trek. Perhaps at court, or perhaps from her foray into Edinburgh. It mattered not. The point was, she was ill.

Eva pressed herself against Breckin, hoping to feel some of his warmth. She kept her eyes closed and drifted to a lethargic slumber.

CHAPTER NINE

THE CLOSER BRECKIN got to home, the more concerned he was for Eva. She'd fallen asleep and hadn't awakened for the remainder of the ride. On the approach to the bridge, he passed by his sister's torch to ensure it had remained lit. Its flame was steady and bright.

The horses' hooves tromped over the wooden boards of the bridge and instead of riding to the stable which he'd normally do, Breckin continued and headed toward his aunt's home.

Gideon trotted toward him from down the lane and met him at the entrance of Clare's cottage. Breckin was about to dismount but with Eva in his hold, it was most difficult so he waited for his comrade to reach him.

"Ye are back. Who is the lass?" His friend scowled in wonder. "Did ye find a wee fairy in the woods on your journey?" Gideon chortled at his jest but ceased when Breckin glared at him.

"She is my wife."

Gideon bellowed a laugh and pressed his hand over his stomach. "Your wife? Ye jest, Breckin, because I recall ye saying ye wanted no wife. Ye were most adamant about it."

"I do not jest and that was before…" He closed his eyes briefly and ceased his explanation. "This is Eva, Lady Buchanan to ye," Breckin finally retorted testily. He wanted no banter from his friend because his utmost concern was getting Eva inside and tended to. "Here, take her for me."

Gideon stepped forward and accepted Eva from him. He held her in his arms and Eva continued to slumber. She hadn't woken even with the shift of her body. "Praised be, Breckin, she's a fair bonny lass. I want to hear how this came about. Married, why 'tis unthinkable. Did ye not profess before ye left that ye had no time for a wife? What caused this miracle?"

Breckin dismounted and took Eva back into his hold. She snuggled against him and set her head on his shoulder. Eased by her acceptance, he sighed. "There is no time for this discussion now. Will ye fetch Willa? My wife ails and needs medicine. She burns with fever."

Gideon gave a quick nod and sprinted away. Willa, his commander-in-arms' mother, was a skilled healer but she preferred to stay in her reclusive cottage on the other side of the bridge. His clan rarely called her forth and usually only for dire situations or on their return from war to patch up his soldiers.

Breckin reached the door and entered his aunt's cottage. It was after the mid-day meal. He'd thought his aunt would be there. She was always at the cottage in the later part of the day. And indeed she was, kneading bread at the table. She looked up as he entered the room and ceased her work.

"Breckin…ye have returned. What, ah, who is that?"

He continued past the kitchen area and reached the bedchamber he used. Awkwardly, he almost dropped Eva when he tried to push the door open. Inside the chamber, he ambled toward the bed and set her gently upon it. Eva still hadn't awakened. He set his hand on her head and sighed at the heat permeating from her. Heat emanated from her.

Eva moaned as she rousted and blinked her eyes. "Where are we?"

"We are home. Rest easy, lass, and I will fetch ye a cup of water. Ye must be thirsty." Breckin left the chamber and hurried to the kitchen.

His aunt followed him and mumbled under her breath, "Ye

cannot bring your woman here, Breckin. This is a moral household and God fearing. I will not have ye here fornicating with that woman—"

"She is my wife, Clare. Cease pestering me now. I must get her water." Breckin found a half-filled pitcher on the table. He snatched the cup next to it and retraced his steps back to the chamber. There, he poured a small amount of water for Eva and held it to her mouth. She groaned and took small sips.

"I am sorry…," she rasped.

"Our healer is on her way here, Eva. She will have ye feeling better in no time." But Breckin didn't believe what he'd told her. Concern furrowed his brows and he felt the pull between his eyes. With a long drawn-in breath, he tried to maintain calmness. But his parents had perished from just such a malady when fever ravaged them. Breckin admitted to himself that he didn't want to lose Eva too, just when they were getting along, and just when he was beginning to accept her.

"Sorry to…ruin your…homecoming," she said groggily.

Breckin pressed his hand to her face and shook his head. "Ye did not ruin it, lass."

Noise alerted him that Willa had finally arrived. The small chamber was suddenly filled with people: him, Eva, Clare, Gideon, and Willa. He explained her malady to the healer and waved her forward. "Will ye tend to her? She needs care."

"Go on with ye, Laird, and all of ye get out. I shall see to her," Willa said.

The aged woman wore a head covering over her brownish-red hair, streaked with a little gray. Her eyes had dulled to a steely blue but there was still a shine to them. With a smile, she shuffled all of them out of the room with flaps of her hands. "I cannot take care of the lass with ye all looking over my shoulder. Worry not, for she is in good hands."

Breckin stood by the door. "I will return shortly. She's been feverish since early this morn."

"All will be well, Laird. The willow bark shall cease the fever's hold on her, I can promise ye that. Before ye leave, light a fire in the hearth." Willa turned away from him and began her ministrations.

He did as she asked and placed logs in the small hearth. Then he set kindling in and found flint in a basket where the logs were kept and set the flame. Breckin was hesitant to leave because Eva wasn't quite aware of where she was or that Willa tended to her. She had fallen back to sleep before the healer arrived. Breckin would hurry about his tasks and return to ensure she was on the mend.

As he passed through the cottage, Clare stopped him. "Who is she? I will hear no tales, Breckin, and disbelieve that falsity about a wife. If ye think to keep your mistress here in my home—"

Gideon stopped next to his aunt and bellowed, "She is his wife if ye can believe that."

His aunt scoffed. "I never knew ye to be deceitful, Breckin. If ye were going to marry, ye would have told me, would ye not? Nay, Gideon, he must speak falsely."

Breckin grew wearisome of their incredulity and grunted before he explained, "Alexander bade me to marry her when I was in Edinburgh. Unfortunately, we owe the king a good amount of tax on our land and he was willing to forgo it if I married Eva."

"Oh, good Lord. Did ye not tell him that we paid Lord Lennox as agreed?" Clare asked.

"I did, but the king said that regardless of our agreement with Lennox, we still owed tax on the land to him, to our sovereignty, and hadn't paid it since we'd received the land from Lennox. Ye can imagine how it amounted as we have held these lands for years. As ye know, we do not have the coins to pay such an exuberant amount of tithe and I had no choice but to marry her."

"Well, I for one am gladdened," Gideon said and shoved his shoulder. "She's a bonny lass, Breckin. Ye are fortunate. I fear our soldiers will have a hard time focusing on their training if she passes by them." He whistled low. "I do not think I have ever seen a more beautiful woman."

Clare set her hands on her hips and glared at his commander. "I will be sure to tell your wife ye spoke such nonsense, Gideon."

Gideon snorted. "Och, go ahead, for she will not believe ye. But 'tis true enough because your wife, Laird, is breathtakingly beautiful."

"I would appreciate it if ye did not notice or say such things." He wanted to laugh but with Eva being ill, he kept his mien serious. "Now, tell me about the happenings whilst I was away."

At that moment, his brothers entered the cottage shouting his name. Breckin shushed them. "Quiet. Why must ye bellow?"

Connor pushed past Caden. "Is it true, Laird, that ye brought a woman home?"

"Aye, the men said they saw ye holding a woman," Caden said with awe, "...upon your horse."

"I married a lass in Edinburgh named Eva. Lady Buchanan, to all of you."

Breckin stepped outside and stood before the cottage. He needed air. The closeness of the cottage and the retelling of the events at the king's castle nearly suffocated him. But his family and commander followed and surrounded him. They seemed to want to question him further about his marriage.

Meanwhile, his younger brothers continued to snicker.

Conner said, "Why do ye need a wife, Breckin? Och, we do not need another to tell us what to do. We get enough of that from the elders."

He wanted to cuff his brother's head for such a comment but just shook his head. "I did not need a wife, but when the king demands ye accept one, ye do. And as for telling ye what to do, go on and see to my horse and my *wife's*. Bring our satchels and belongings back to Clare's."

"Breckin, the cottage is small. There's barely enough room for me and the lads."

"We shall only stay long enough for Eva to recover from her ailment." Breckin had given thought to where he would put Eva when they arrived. The only available lodging was his uncle's longhouse. No one had occupied it for a time, but he'd have his brethren make it habitable.

As he waited for Gideon to give his report, his aunt left them and ambled down the lane to speak to some of the women who stood in a group. He suspected they would gossip as women were likely to do.

"Tell me the happenings, Gideon. Did the men train hard?"

His commander nodded and pressed his hands over his tunic. "Aye, they practiced from sunup to sundown, Laird, and even the fledgling soldiers have improved. They are ready for any fracas and anticipate taking to arms."

"Good, because I saw William Stewart when I passed his land and he told me that he married Danella MacLaren."

"What say ye? He married your former betrothed? How did that come about? What a knavish traitor. I never trusted the Stewarts." Gideon practically kicked at the dirt beneath his feet.

Breckin agreed but his ire at the situation had lessened on his ride home. "He said the MacLarens approached him about the marriage. It matters not now because I would not have given thought to taking Danella in marriage, not after they retracted the betrothal. And I suppose that I am somewhat pleased with Eva. Still, William professed to want to gain an alliance with us. Not bloody likely."

"Nay, what a pile of cosh. The MacLarens are goddamned traitors and no alliance will change that. I suspect ye feel the same about the MacLarens," Gideon grunted and seemed to be as appalled as he was.

Breckin nodded. "Of course I do, but I have no time to deal with them now. In the future, it may become a matter of concern and if we war with them, believe me, I shall bloody my damned sword to the hilt."

Gideon scowled hard. "When that time comes, Breckin, we will rout them easily. They will rue the day they decided not to align with us. Ye need to consider what is more important..."

"What do ye mean, Gideon? Go on, ye can speak freely." Breckin scowled at his commander because it was obvious that he was annoyed with him.

"We waste our time battling for lesser, weakened clans. We should forgo aiding them. Let them fend for themselves. We have bigger fish to skewer, Laird, namely the MacLarens and now, the Stewarts. They affronted ye with their insult of retracting the betrothal. That ye allowed them to get away with it, has long perplexed me. We should have taken arms against them right off. The MacLarens probably deem us weaker now. Have ye thought of that?"

Breckin allowed Gideon to finish his tirade and when silence fell between them, he set a hand on his comrade's shoulder. "Ye know why we aid others. Until I find out the truth behind Marian's death, I will not desist. As to the MacLarens and Stewarts, Gideon, we will deal with them eventually. Be patient for now."

His commander sighed and with a nod, he drew away. "For now, Laird, but ye need to make a decision soon. Aid the weaker clans or become one ourselves."

Suddenly, Breckin noticed that Aymer, the gate watchman, was sprinting toward him. "Laird, ye received a missive from Laird MacNab earlier this day. Ye rode by so quickly, I did not have a chance to give it to ye." When he reached him, his soldier thrust the folded parchment at him.

"Damnation, I have no time for MacNab right now," Breckin gripped the parchment. He kept his gaze on his aunt's door in case Eva needed him.

Gideon took the missive from him and read it before he shoved it back. "He says that he must have our aid. Two of his soldiers were killed and he needs the protection of the Buchanans."

"This could not come at a worse time. I shouldn't leave Eva when she is ailing and newly arrived. Still, I suppose we should go. We promised them protection and the situation seems to warrant our arms." Breckin reopened the parchment and read the plea for himself.

"Your aunt will look after your wife until we return. And my ma is the best healer in these parts. Lady Buchanan shall fare well in due time. Are ye worried about her?" Gideon asked.

He was worried but wouldn't confess such a flaw to his commander. "I suppose we should head out then." Breckin was displeased at having to attend to his duty because he'd hoped to get Eva settled before he left his land. But he'd told her that he was often gone. Hopefully, Eva understood that he had a sworn duty to his allies and a war that called to him.

THE NORTH WAS rife with petty clan wars. Lesser armed clans didn't stand much of a chance against the many arms of larger clans. Breckin fought for the wee clans but had grown tired of supporting them. He wasn't obligated to battle against his ally's rivals. Unless the matter concerned the Buchanans directly, he shouldn't have involved his clan but it was too late for regrets now.

If not for his aim to give his sister salvation, he wouldn't have bothered and only did so to gain God's forgiveness. Now, immersed in battles that had no bearing on the Buchanans, he understood why his commander was also weary of it.

Soon, he would have to decide if he wanted to keep or end alliances. Now that he was married, Breckin considered that the time to end their participation approached. But what would he do if he wasn't warring? That question had kept him awake during the nights on the trek to the MacNab land. The answers taunted him with whispers of his parents' voices, telling him to strengthen the Buchanans, see to the needs of his people, and beget heirs to carry on their traditions and name.

Was he softening? Was the lure of having a family and finding joy more meaningful to him now? Breckin hadn't given much thought to having children. He had enough difficulty rearing his brothers. Yet the image of him holding a wee bairn in his arms, a babe that resembled the beauty of his wife, struck him. Could he find happiness with Eva? And that question nudged him to accept that he could. But could she be as happy with him? Such matters never concerned him before and now that they pressed on him, the weight of dejection made him utter a grunt.

"Bollocks," he muttered, but then his relationship with Eva wasn't completely hopeless. He'd find a way to get her to accept him.

"Och, what are ye ruminating about? I could guess by the look on your face." Gideon chortled as he rode next to him.

"Naught but simple thoughts. Let us make haste so we can see to this matter that concerns the MacNabs." Breckin urged his horse to a canter and rode ahead of his brethren.

At the border of MacNab land, Breckin spotted his ally lying in wait for him. He directed his men to take a rest until he questioned his ally. It had taken them two full days to reach Daniel's land and he was anxious to find out what had happened to the MacNab soldiers. Breckin marched forward and ignored the awed stares of the men who lazed about at various campfires. None spoke to him or stopped him. He reached the center of their encampment where one lone tent was erected and waited. None of the MacNab's men lit fires but stood about on guard. Within a moment, Daniel was alerted of his arrival. His comrade ducked beneath his tent's entry and gave a quick wave.

"Laird Buchanan, Breckin, what took ye so long?"

"Daniel, I received your message and came as soon as I could."

His comrade was dressed for war with chainmail on his torso and shoulders. A large sword hung from the belt on his hip. With a press of his short black beard, he grunted. "I did not deem ye'd come. Gladdened I am to see ye though. Come and I will tell ye what has happened."

Breckin followed Daniel inside his tent. He stood by a table that held a pitcher full of ale. His comrade poured him a drink and thrust it into his hand.

"Drink, ye must be thirsty. 'Tis terrible events. Two of my men were killed at the border of our land by the MacLarens. My sentry confronted them when they found them trespassing. Damned blighters. Arms were drawn and they made threats to bring their full army to my fief." Daniel motioned him further into the tent. "Do ye wish to rest?"

Breckin shook his head. "Nay, we will go now and find out what the MacLarens intend."

"I see ye brought a full regiment of Buchanan warriors. Gladdened, I am, because my army's numbers have dwindled in recent years and with MacLaren's threats… We do not have the arms to protect my clan, Breckin. I am grateful for your aid."

"Of course, Daniel, ye are my ally. I am sorry though, that I did not come sooner and was detained in Edinburgh. Do ye wish to join us on the excursion to meet with MacLaren?"

"If ye think that wise."

Breckin suspected that it would be better if he and his warriors confronted MacLaren without the MacNabs present. "Perhaps 'tis better that ye await us here."

"I can have some of my soldiers intermix with yours to give ye an extra arm or two," Daniel said. "We are not opposed to fighting our battles, och we need a wee bit of help though."

Breckin would have laughed but the seriousness of the situation called for a severe mien. "Nay, my soldiers are capable of handling this mission. My thanks though. Your men will just hold us up. I mean to get it done quickly because I need to return home hastily." What he wanted to add was that the Buchanan warriors would be insulted if he suggested adding to their numbers with men of such a lesser skill. They would probably have to use valuable time protecting MacNab's men instead of fighting off their foes.

"I shall stop on the way back and tell ye the news." Breckin chugged the ale and drained his cup then set it on a nearby table.

Daniel walked him to the tent's exit. "We shall await ye here then. I wish ye well. Och, I doubt ye shall need it."

Breckin hastily made his way back to his men who stood glaring at the MacNab soldiers. He mounted his horse and whistled to alert his men that they were on the move. Their progression south-easterly through Stewart land would afford them to reach MacLaren's holding just as the sky pitched. He rode swiftly, wanting to reach them in darkness which would give his men an even fiercer appearance.

"Laird, are we going to take arms against the MacLarens?" Gideon asked.

"If they instigate us, then aye. Och, I will find out why they took arms against my ally." Breckin was furious because the MacLarens dared to instigate the matter.

The sky pitched and they hadn't slowed their progress while they rode for MacLaren land. As their walls came into view, the Buchanan soldiers called their war cry 'Clar Innes' and bellowed with calls and whoops to alert the MacLarens that they had arrived.

Shadows of men appeared on the barbican above the wall and a man shouted to them. "What do ye here?"

"We are the Buchanans. Tell your laird Breckin is here."

Silence abounded after he told them who he was. A flapping of a pennon above the gate sounded, but all else stilled until the creaking of the gate came. A rider rode through with a handful of soldiers on foot behind him. The man rode daringly forward until he was a short distance from him and then dismounted.

Breckin recognized John MacLaren's wispy graying hair and beard. The man stood in front of his horse and shouted, "Buchanan, what do ye here?"

"Ye know why I have come. Tell me… Did ye dare to take arms against my ally, the MacNabs? We Buchanans take it as an insult, aye, and so we have come to ask ye directly."

"Since when do ye side with the MacNabs?"

"Since I no longer side with ye," he returned in a shout.

"Cosh, Breckin, there is no need for your hostility," John said. "'Tis not my fault that ye broke off the betrothal and forced us to consider ye a rival."

Breckin's shoulders tensed at the man's words. "It was not me who rescinded the betrothal, but ye. My da made the pact with ye and I would not have defied my father for any reason. I deem ye are muddleheaded, John. Have ye been long in your cups this day?"

John ambled closer. "You did not break the treaty? Do ye speak the truth?"

"Aye, why would I lie? We received word that ye no longer accepted the betrothal and that it was ended. At the time, my parents' death plagued me and I gave no care about the broken treaty betwixt our clans." Breckin shook his head, confounded by what John told him.

"Something is amiss here because I did not break the treaty. I was pleased that Danella was to marry ye and we coveted the union of our clans. Years of negotiations betwixt your da and my clan settled the matter finally. I wanted naught more than to align my clan with yours."

"If ye did not break it, then who did?" Breckin fisted his hands as ire overtook him and heated him from within.

"I recall that time and I was ailing, aye, and I'd taken to my bed for a good month. All thought me dead. Och, I wouldst not appease them. My son handled clan matters whilst I recovered and … It had to be my son John. I shall speak to him and find out the truth of the matter. 'Tis strange that he would go against me and negate the plan I put into motion. With the Buchanans as an ally, our clan would have prospered."

Breckin shook his head. "It matters not, John, because the treaty was broken and ye have raised arms against my ally. I cannot allow your insolence."

John stepped back and motioned to his soldiers.

Breckin continued, "If ye take arms against my ally, 'tis as if ye take arms against me. Ye killed the MacNab sentry on their land and I want to know why. Tell me why I should not stick my sword in ye, why my soldiers should not attack ye." Breckin slowly pulled his sword from its scabbard, provoking John to do the same.

"My son tells me that he did not know they were the MacNab soldiers and thought they were interlopers. And he definitely would not have taken arms against them if he knew they were your ally, which he did not."

"Your son is holding deceit, MacLaren. If there is anyone to blame for this atrocity, 'tis him. Mayhap ye should find out what he intends because if I get to him first, he shall exist no longer."

Breckin sheathed his sword, retreated to his soldiers that awaited him in the distance, well beyond the keep's high walls. He stood next to Gideon and recounted his conversation with John MacLaren. "I believe him not." He turned to his commander-at-arms. "Should we skewer them or let them be?"

"Ye know my answer to that, Laird." Gideon set his hand on the hilt of his sword at his waist and nodded as if all Breckin had to do was give word for a battle to commence. He chuckled lightly. "Still, I do not wish to bloody my garments, do ye?"

Gideon shook his head with a scoff. "I suppose not. Och, the men will be displeased, though, if we leave without shedding a wee bit of blood. We have come all this way."

"My thoughts exactly. Very well, Gideon, tell the men to draw their swords. We shall remind the MacLarens that we are to be feared. Och, no lives are to be taken. Let us give the MacLarens some wounds to lick, though."

"Damnation, Laird, the men will be disappointed to give them paltry nicks. I shall tell them to hold back. Ye are being a mite merciful."

Breckin wanted to laugh but nodded. "Perhaps I am, och I find I'm in a good-minded mood." He flashed a smile at his comrade and chuckled.

Gideon chortled. "I'd say, Laird, that marriage might be

agreeing with ye."

He bellowed then and slapped his commander on the shoulder. With a yank to his sword, he drew it from the sheath across his back. "Damn me, I believe it does agree with me, Gideon. I find my heart is not in it, this fight with the MacLarens, och I will give it my best effort."

Breckin waved on his men and marched beside them as they moved in to confront their enemy.

CHAPTER TEN

EVA AWAKENED WITH a clear mind and was free of fever. She shifted her legs to the side of the bed and sat for a moment, taking in the view of the room she was in. In the small bedchamber, there was enough room for a bed with plentiful comfort for one person. A little table sat beside the bed and there was a chest situated at the end. She peered at the decorative etchings of flowers and delicate scrolls that rimmed the edges of the wooden chest, surmising that it belonged to a woman.

No window afforded light and she was unsure whether it was morning or evening. She listened for sounds or voices and heard shouts of children somewhere in the cottage and then a bang. Eva was hesitant to leave the room, unsure of where she was, and hoped Breckin would come soon. She was ravenous and could eat a good helping of food.

Near the doorway, she spotted her bag. With a glance at her lap, she realized someone had removed her garments and put her in a nightdress. She found a cup on the side table filled with water and quickly drank it, alleviating the dryness of her throat.

Suddenly, the door opened and a woman appeared. "Oh, ye are finally awake. I am Clare, Laird Buchanan's aunt. This is my home where ye will stay, hopefully for a short time."

"Good day, Milady Clare," she said and offered a smile in greeting.

"Nay, lass, not milady at all. I am simply Clare. I suppose ye must be famished for ye have been asleep for nearly three days. The healer says ye shall recover from your malady."

"Three days? I am feeling much better." Eva felt oddly alert as if she had slept for a fortnight. "And, yes, I could use a bite to eat."

"'Tis Willa's cures which do wonders. I vow she has a talent for healing and ye be fortunate that she took care of ye. I shall fetch ye something to eat." Clare left her without a parting word.

While she waited for the woman's return, she found no basin to wash in. She quickly grabbed a clean gown from her things, donned it, and slid on her slippers. Rummaging through her satchel, she found a comb with which to detangle her hair. The door creaked open and she saw two lads with similar faces peeking in at her.

"Come in," she said.

The two lads couldn't be more than half a score in age. Neither spoke but stared at her with widened eyes.

"Who are you?" she asked.

The lads moved farther into the room. "I am Connor and this is my brother Caden."

"'Tis a pleasure to meet you both. Are you Clare's sons?" Though now that she thought about it, Clare appeared a mite too aged to be the lads' mother.

Connor shook his head. "Our mother is dead."

"Oh, I am sorry to hear that. Does Clare take care of you then?"

Caden nodded. "Aye, mostly…sometimes. Och, Breckin is responsible for us but he is mean and oft makes us do tiresome chores."

"Are you Breckin's sons then?" Eva tried to discern why he hadn't told her about the lads. Who were they and did they live with him? Though she should be angry with Breckin for withholding such information, she supposed they had much to learn about each other.

"Nay, Breckin is our elder brother. When our ma and da died, he took care of us."

That information appeased her a bit. Not that she was jealous, of course, but the thought of Breckin lying with another woman even before he'd married her caused a twinge of unrest in her heart. "Well, that was good of him. Do you know where your brother is?"

Connor answered, "Off to war. Aye, and I cannot wait to hear about it when they return," his voice rose with the enthusiasm of hearing the sordid details of battle.

"They?" Eva's heart tensed at hearing that Breckin had gone to war.

"All the Buchanan soldiers," Caden supplied. "One day we will join them but not until we master the skill at arms. Breckin says we have a few years afore we can join a regiment."

Clare arrived carrying a tray which she balanced on her hip. "Out, do ye two not have chores? The stable will not clean itself. Go on now with ye and leave the lady alone." She shooed the boys from the chamber as they scurried out. She watched them go with a frown before she turned to look at Eva with an exasperated expression. "I apologize, Milady, and hope they did not bother ye."

"No, they didn't bother me." Eva took the tray from her. "This smells delicious. My thanks for the food, and please, call me Eva."

Clare frowned at her as if she'd grown horns. "Ah, I cannot, Milady, for ye are our clan's lady and the laird's wife. We must call ye Milady or Lady Buchanan as the laird ordered."

She did not much appreciate the formality, especially since she hoped to befriend the woman. Given the staid expression on her face, Clare wasn't a friendly sort of person. She hadn't smiled once in her presence.

"Now eat and I shall return for the leftovers." Clare reached the door and pulled it closed behind her.

Eva used the spoon to try to distinguish what was in the

bowl. It appeared to be a stew of some sort with chunks of unknown meat in it. Still, it smelled good and her stomach grumbled. On the tray, there were two large pieces of bread. She dunked the bread in the stew's broth and once the bread was gone, quickly ate spoonful after spoonful. Finally sated and full, she had emptied the bowl.

She set the bowl back on the tray and then placed it on the bedside table. Eva was unsure if she should leave the room. Clare mentioned that she would return for the tray which indicated that she should wait. Eva paced beside the bed and it seemed as if an entire day passed. She needed to take care of her personal needs and hoped to bathe. Finally, footsteps sounded outside the bedchamber and Eva waited for the door to open.

Clare knocked and entered without being bid to. She collected the food tray and stopped at the doorway. "I am leaving the cottage, Milady, and shall return later this eve. If ye wish to make something for your supper, ye may use the kitchen. There is plenty of foodstuff."

Eva was unsure whether it was morning, midday, or evening. "Is there a place to wash or to see to my personal needs? I must launder my gowns. Is there a servant who can see to it for me?"

Clare snorted with laughter. "Do ye jest, Milady? Servant? We have no servants here and take care of our own needs. If ye need to wash your garments or yourself, ye will have to go to the stream or loch. Och, my wash is hanging on the lines so ye need to wait until the morrow."

"Oh." Eva nodded, her stomach sinking. "My thanks, Clare, for telling me. I shall wash my gowns then on the morrow at the loch. I shall go then to the stream to get clean."

The lady did not bid her farewell but left and closed the door behind her.

Eva allowed her shoulders to slump as she wondered if this was how her life would be—lonely, isolated, and leaving her to fend for herself.

FOR ALMOST A fortnight, Eva stayed in the bed chamber except for her brief jaunts to the stream to wash. She felt like a prisoner. Who knew how long it would take for Breckin to return? She'd go barking mad if she didn't get outside soon. When she lived at her father's manor, she often walked among the grounds even when the weather was frigid.

Finally, she decided to brave the unknown. She had to get outside. Instead of using her cloak, Eva grabbed the tartan Breckin had given her and wrapped it around her shoulders. She found a belt to one of her overdresses and tied it around her waist to keep the tartan secure. There, she'd be warm if the weather was chilly, and at least, she might look as though she belonged.

With her hand on the door handle, she called forth her gumption and yanked the door open. As she walked through the small cottage, she realized no one was inside. At the door, she hesitated but called on her courage to venture out. Brightness forced her to squint her eyes. As she adjusted to the light of day, she walked on the lane and smiled at the people she passed. They were as friendly as Clare and offered no greetings or smiles.

She passed a large building where a small group of men stood and assumed it was where the soldiers lived. They gawked at her and her cheeks brightened at their attention. Then she noticed the stable. Men stood atop the roof and worked at repairing it.

Near the bridge, she regarded the guardsman and hoped he didn't stop her. She wanted to see what was on the other side of the structure. The man seemed oblivious to her as he argued with another man about an overturned cart. Eva slipped by them easily.

Along the waterway, trees lined the bank and shaded her with their newly leafed branches. Spring sent a warmer breeze with sunshine and nary a cloud in the sky. Scattered amongst the trees were homes of various sizes, some small and some larger. The homes were made of stone and wood with thatched roofs, wooden doors, and window closures.

When several people glimpsed her, they either closed their doors or hastened away. The Buchanans definitely didn't appreciate outsiders. She was gladdened now that she hadn't brought Luella, for she would have been daunted by the clan's people. Still, she wouldn't be as lonely if Luella had come.

Ahead, a woman carrying a large basket walked along with a dog. She had pretty reddish-brown hair and a thick long braid hung over her shoulder. The woman's blue-gray eyes shone as she smiled. A simple overdress was covered with a draped tartan over her thin body and wrapped with another at her waist. The dog scampered toward Eva and barked but it wasn't an unfriendly greeting. Eva held her hand out for the dog to sniff.

"He's a beautiful dog," she said and gazed fondly at the canine. But the woman's pet was larger than any mutt she'd ever seen, and had the thickest black fur woven with light brown. Its coat was unlike any she'd ever seen on a dog. "Can I pet him?"

"She, my pet is a she. Aye, of course, ye may. Her name is Ise-Olcan."

Eva knelt and used both hands to pet the dog's head. Ise-Olcan whined and wagged its tail enthusiastically at her attention. "She has an unusual but pretty name. Does it mean something?"

"*She-wolf* in Gaelic, lass. Aye, she was a runt of a wolf litter and left for dead. I found her, nursed her back to health, and now she's kept me. I belong to her. How are ye feeling, Milady?"

Eva raised her brows as she wondered why the woman would ask her such a question. But then she thought perhaps the woman was familiar to her. "I apologize if we met and do not recall. I was ailing when I arrived but am much better now."

"Och, lass, I am the healer and the laird asked me to care for ye. The birch bark did the trick, aye, as I thought it would, and chased away your fever."

"My thanks for caring for me. I must have caught a chill on the journey here."

"Ye look like ye could use some company. Would ye like to walk along with me? I am just headed down the way. I am Willa, and mother to the laird's man-at-arms, Gideon."

"It is a pleasure to meet you, Willa. I am Eva. And pray, please call me such, not lady or milady." She reached out and took the basket from the woman. "Let me carry that for you. 'Tis the least I can do for the aid you gave me." The basket was heavy, but Eva used both hands to carry it in front of her.

"Well, Eva, I appreciate that." Willa snapped her fingers at the dog who immediately heeled beside her.

"What is in here? It is quite heavy."

Willa chuckled. "'Tis medicinals. I am taking it to the encampment yonder."

They walked in silence for a little way and then Eva spotted the smoke from the various campfires. Situated among the clearings between the trees sat cloaked people, shielding themselves from view, or perhaps they were cold. Fabric draped from one tree to another in an attempt to shelter them from the elements.

Willa took the basket from her and handed out small vials of medicinals to the people around the fires as they passed. "I wish I could have brought them bread or some food, alas, I have nothing to spare in my cupboard presently. Perhaps I can have Gideon hunt for meat for them when he returns."

"From war..." Eva assumed the commander-in-arms traveled with Breckin and they were on a mission. She felt sorrowful for the poor vagrants and that she was unable to help them too. With a glimpse at them, she lightly gasped at the large pox-like marks on their faces and hands. Cautiously and keeping a little distance, Eva walked around the small settlement and offered greetings. Among them were older men, women, and some younger people nearer to her age.

The healer spoke briefly to some of them and introduced her to a young woman named Harriet. "Drink the medicinal, Harriet. It shall ease ye a bit. Get some rest."

"We are hungry, Mistress. Have ye any food?" Harriet asked.

Willa shook her head. "Nay, I'm afeared I only have the medicinal. I shall try to bring food on the morrow or have the men bring ye meat when they return to the holding."

An older man approached but stopped a good distance in front of them. Eva gently grabbed Willa's arm to stop her and they turned to face the man. From what she could see beneath the hood of his cloak, his hair was long, scraggily, and practically white. His beard matched the color of his hair and his eyes were an unknown hue and appeared glossed over.

"Fret not, Willa, for I am going on a hunt later this eve. I shall feed this brood."

"I wish ye good hunting, Gareth. When the laird returns, I shall tell him of your plight here. Breckin will aid ye." Willa waved as she passed the people on the way back to the lane.

As they walked away, Eva lowered her head, despaired for them, and wished she had the means to give them food, shelter, or care. "Do they live out here alone and unprotected?"

"Aye, they do. The clan forbids them to live amongst the Buchanans. Och, do not despair, lass, because no one would risk getting close to them. All keep a distance."

She walked next to Willa and Ise-Olcan ran ahead but returned to them and repeated her jaunt. The Buchanans were unkind and unfriendly, she surmised, since they treated the people who ailed in the woods so horridly. "That saddens me; the poor condition of those people and that they are unwelcomed by the clan. What ails them?"

"'Tis unknown but some suspect their ailment is catching, which is why they stay here in the woods. Father Murphy has sent a description of their condition to his order in Edinburgh in hopes they might offer a cure or give suggestions on how to care for them." Willa reached her cottage and snapped her fingers for her dog. Ise-Olcan ran at breakneck speed until she reached the door of the cottage and whined to be let inside.

"Would you mind terribly if I visited you on the morrow? I

can help collect herbs or—"

"I would welcome the company, lass. Not many come out to visit me, even my daughter-in-law, Gideon's wife, Deena. She despises being on this side of the island."

Eva nodded. "Well then, expect me on the morrow and we shall have a nice visit."

"Until the morrow, lass." Willa disappeared inside her cottage with Ise-Olcan pushing to get ahead of her.

Eva continued her walk in the opposite direction of Willa's cottage. She kept going until she reached a beautiful church. It was a long building made of heavy stone with a thickly thatched roof. A heavy wooden cross hung above the double doors. She wondered if the church doors were unlocked and pulled at one. It opened and she entered. Inside, she walked between the wooden benches that lined the center lane until she reached a beautiful but crudely-made stone altar.

There didn't seem to be anyone inside the church. A smile tugged at her lips as she thought about singing. Her favorite cleric chant came to mind and she wanted to sing the words to Salve Regina. With none to tell her it was forbidden, she opened her mouth and let the song flow from her lips and heart:

Queen, Mother of Mercy:
Our life, sweetness, and hope, hail...

The door banged and she startled and turned. A man shuffled down the center lane. He was an older man with little gray hair on his head. Given his attire of all-black garments and a vestment edged with golden embroidered crosses, she discerned he was a priest. Eva tilted her head to him when he reached her.

"I hope you do not mind, Father, but I..." She wasn't sure what she should say.

"Good blessed day, lass. All are welcome here inside God's domain. I heard ye singing and how pleasing it was to my ears." His smile was infectious.

"I apologize, Father..."

"Aye, for what? Oh, forgive me, but I am Father Murphy, and who are ye? I have not seen ye hereabouts."

"Eva. Ah, I recently married Breckin Buchanan, the laird."

The priest bowed and bobbed his head. "Oh, Milady, I should have known who ye were right off because I heard that Laird Buchanan had taken a wife. 'Tis a pleasure, aye. Now tell me why ye would apologize for singing?"

"Where I lived, our clergymen forbade women from singing in church. I secretly had a brother teach me the songs because I loved to sing and the sounds of the words."

"God would not discourage anyone from singing in His house. Ye are welcome to sing anytime ye wish in our church, Milady." Father Murphy rounded her and reached the altar. He pressed a large volume open and peered down at the words then closed the book and lifted it. After he tucked it under his arm, he left the altar area. "I am preparing for Mass on the morrow and wanted to find the perfect scripture in the Good Book. I hope ye join us."

"I will be gladdened to, Father."

"Stay as long as ye like," he said and walked to the exit.

The door banged closed and Eva found herself alone again. She sat on the closest bench to the altar and her heart burst with happiness as she sang:

Queen, Mother of Mercy:
Our life, sweetness, and hope, hail.
To thee do we cry, poor banished children of Eve.
To you, we sigh, mourning and weeping in this valley of tears.
Turn then, our advocate, those merciful eyes toward us...

CHAPTER ELEVEN

"WHAT DO YE mean ye do not know where she is?" Breckin had returned to his holding and rushed to his aunt's cottage. He'd wanted to ensure that Eva had recovered from her illness but now that he'd arrived, she was nowhere in the cottage.

"She was here when I went to the river to do my laundry. When I got back, she was not here." Clare continued to fold her laundry as if it didn't matter that Eva was missing.

Breckin pressed at the throb of his head. "I will go in search of her. If she returns before I do, send someone to find me." He left the cottage with a slam of the door. His aunt was being uncaring which was unlike her. But then, he hadn't spent much time in her presence in the last year or so. She'd always been amiable toward him whenever he'd stayed at the cottage.

As he walked along, his clansmen tried to stop him but he waved them off. At the bridge, he peered across and wondered if that was where Eva had gone. He spotted Aymer talking with his brother, Alton, and approached. "Have ye seen my wife? She's not in Clare's cottage."

"Och, nay, Laird, but I just got on duty," Aymer replied. "She could have come this way."

Breckin scoffed with an expletive and crossed the bridge. At the other side, a group of his soldiers stood about. When he reached them, he saw his brothers. One appeared to be sitting on the wood rail of the bridge and the other stood next to him. When he got closer, he realized his brother was injured and a piece of splintered wood stuck through his brother's lower leg.

"Are ye going to weep like a lass, Conner?" Caden asked with a snicker of laughter. "Ye be bleeding like a stuck pig. Aye, ye are gushing."

Connor whimpered and huffed. "Cosh, it hurts! Get me off…!"

"Went straight through his leg, aye, that is going to hurt," one of his soldiers remarked, "when we pull it from him."

Breckin shoved back the soldier and knelt near his brother. "What did ye do to yourself?"

"I was…walking on the rail…and it broke," Connor said and whimpered.

"Stabbed him like a sword, Laird, aye, right through his leg," Caden said with excitement.

He didn't want to hurt his brother further but there was no getting out of it. Breckin noticed Gideon walking toward them. When he reached them, he peered at him with a silent message. His comrade understood. As Breckin took hold of his brother and lifted him, Gideon yanked out the splintered wood and tossed it into the water flowing beneath the bridge.

At once, one of his soldiers offered a cloth. Breckin wrapped it around Connor's leg and lifted him. "We will get ye to Willa's. She will tend to ye."

"Let me take him, Laird," Gideon offered.

"Aye, I am searching for Eva. She's not at Clare's cottage and has gone missing. Go with them, Caden, and try to be helpful. I shall come when I can."

Gideon carried his brother away and they set off toward his mother's cottage.

Breckin stood on the lane on the other side of the bridge and considered where Eva might have gone. Surely someone had to have seen her, unless she decided to walk back to the border. The nonsensical thought caused him to grunt because if that was what she'd done, he'd be furious.

Father Murphy walked toward him, holding a thick volume under his arm. The clergyman smiled widely and bowed to him when Breckin reached him.

"Good day, Father. Have ye seen my wife, Milady Eva?"

Father Murphy chuckled. "Oh, aye, indeed, Laird. I did see her."

"Where?" Breckin waited for the man to reply but he seemed flabbergasted. "Father, where did ye see her?"

"Oh, pardon me, Laird Buchanan. I saw her in the church. Be quiet when ye enter and ye shall be rewarded." Father Murphy bowed to him and hastened away.

Breckin peered after him, confounded as to what the man meant. Rewarded? But when he reached the door of the church, he pulled it gently open. Someone was singing and he stepped to the center of the aisle. His wife sat on the first bench before the altar and sang with all her heart.

He was astounded by the beauty of her voice and the ethereal sound. Breckin didn't want to interrupt her and waited for her to reach the end of her song. When she ceased singing, he marched forward and sat on the bench behind her.

Eva gasped and turned when she heard him. "Oh, Breckin, ye startled me."

"Apologies, lass. Ye sing like an angel."

"You heard me? Father Murphy told me that it was not forbidden so I…could not resist."

He felt the tugging of his lips and wanted to smile but instead, he bowed his head to her. "Why would it be forbidden?"

"At home, women are not allowed to sing in church. My father paid a brother to teach me the songs and how to sing them properly. It was a great pleasure of mine. So you have finally returned from your war?" Eva stood and a slight frown set betwixt her eyes.

"Aye, only just. I remind ye, Eva, this is now your home.

Things are far different here than they are by the border. Och, I went to see ye when I arrived but when I got to Clare's cottage, ye were gone. I worried for ye."

"Sincerely? Why in heaven's name would you worry for me? You cared not a whit about me when you left me here with strangers whilst I ailed. Surely you gave me no thought when you left and I see not why you would bother worrying about me now."

Breckin was appalled at her put down. "Ah…ye are angry. Well, I was called upon by our ally and had to go. I hoped ye would understand."

She clutched her hands together and continued to glare. "Oh, I understand, Breckin. Is war more important than your ailing wife? Do not answer because I am certain what your answer would be. I cannot speak to you right now." With that, she turned and fled from the church.

"Bollocks," Breckin uttered, taken aback by her forwardness. Rarely did anyone speak to him thusly but he supposed he should excuse her. He had left her but certainly not without thought. "Forgive me, God Almighty, for my blasphemy." He bowed before the altar, made the sign of the cross, and marched toward the exit, intent on finding and placating his wife. Being married was going to cause him much distraction and turmoil.

Outside, he saw her ahead on the lane but she was going in the wrong direction. When he caught up to her, he grabbed her arm to stop her. "Eva, ye are headed away from the bridge."

She yanked her arm from his grasp. "I know that, Breckin. Please, leave me be. I need to be alone."

"I want to speak to ye about what ye said in the church." He tried to step in front of her but she turned away. Breckin stood behind her and let her have her way as she faced the flowing waters below the bluff.

"I do not want you to see me weep. Ye shall think me weak or a coward. Go away."

Breckin sighed heavily because he'd caused her distress.

"Why are ye weeping? Because I was called away? Believe me, I wanted to stay to ensure ye fared well and that Willa healed ye. As laird, I am beholden to my duty. Many lives were at risk and I had to go to protect my ally. Ye should understand that, Eva. Was your father not often called away?"

She wiped at her eyes. "He was, but not because of war. My father traveled most of the year to other lands. I was left alone with servants but you left me with strangers... I awakened and was uncertain if I could even leave the bedchamber. Your aunt was not unkind, but she was not friendly either. I did not know what to do..." Eva stammered and sighed between words. Her distress further disgruntled him.

He stepped in front of her, pulled her into his embrace, and held her, saying nothing. With his chin resting on her head, he took a big breath through his nose and tried to settle himself. He felt like a heel for causing her dismay. As he stood with her in his arms in the center of the lane, he spotted Aymer approaching.

"Laird," Aymer called from afar.

Breckin continued to hold Eva and wanted to make amends but knew not how to even begin to make up for his affront. "Go away, Aymer."

"Och, Laird, I wanted to tell ye that—"

"Is it important? If not, go away and I shall find ye later." He'd spoken with a bite to his words, but that couldn't be helped.

His soldier lowered his head, turned on his heel, and trudged away.

Breckin pressed his hands over Eva's back, trying with all his heart to console her. He didn't like that she felt alone. It shouldn't matter to him, but her despair brought forth an empathy he'd never felt before. "Forgive me, lass, because I did not realize the predicament I put ye in. I should not have left ye but the matter was of great importance. Not that ye are not as important, 'tis just... Well, hell, I am making a muck of this."

Eva leaned into him and gently eased her arms around his body. Breckin sighed with relief at her acceptance.

"Come, we shall keep walking until ye feel ye are ready to return." He turned her and set his arm around her shoulder to guide her.

They progressed farther away from the bridge and reached the spot where the torch was mounted before the waters of Loch Lomond. Breckin stood in silence and he caressed her cheek with his thumb. He raked his eyes over her loveliness and couldn't fathom how a woman could appear so bonny. Her blue eyes brightened with unshed tears. The long locks of her brown hair hung in waves over her back. As if he saw her for the first time, Breckin's breath caught at the beauty before him, much like he had on that day in the market.

"'Tis beautiful here. Why is there a torch-lit?" She pulled away from him and stepped closer to the edge of the land.

"This place is special to me."

"I can see why," she said and continued to peer at the waters flowing rapidly below.

Breckin sidled next to her and took her hand. "Take care, lass, because the drop here is steep. This is where Marian died. The torch signifies our mourning of her death."

"Oh, then it is a sad place for you. Perhaps we should return." Eva dislodged from his hold and turned to walk back toward the bridge.

Breckin stepped quickly to follow her. As they walked along, he wondered if he should have divulged more about his sister's death. But Eva hadn't asked and he did not want to talk about it. Marian's death still hurt deeply and he wondered if there would come a day when he wouldn't mourn her or feel the intense pain that her passing caused.

"We need to stop at Willa's because my brother was injured. I want to see how he fares." Breckin took hold of her hand again and her touch somewhat lightened him. It was an odd sensation but he felt the squeeze of her fingers. Her acceptance brought forth the realization that he needed her—needed her solace, care, and affection.

A warrior should not concern himself with the needs of love, he realized. It was better to keep himself shielded against such tender-hearted measures. Breckin did not want to be hurt again and after losing so many who he cared about, like Marian and his parents, he wanted to keep himself from experiencing such sentiments.

At Willa's cottage, he opened the door for Eva and they entered the crowded, small confines of the healer's domain. Connor sat on a table with his leg outstretched. Willa plied a needle with string to his leg and sewed up his brother's wound.

"Oh, Connor, you hurt yourself," Eva said and rushed to his brother's side. She pressed a hand on his shoulder and then gripped his chin and lifted it. "We shall take good care of you."

"How do ye know he's Connor?" Breckin was astounded that she knew who his brother was by name. Most couldn't tell his brothers apart.

Eva flashed a wily smile. "Of course, I know he is Connor. Conner has a wider nose than Caden. Caden has a small scar above his eyebrow. Do you mean to say that you cannot tell them apart...your own brothers?" She chuckled.

"Bollocks, most times, nay." Breckin was dumbfounded that he hadn't ever made the distinction of differences between his brothers. He rounded the table and stood on the other side. "Are ye all right, Connor?" he asked.

"I gave him a wee dram to ease his pain. He shall be out like a candle in the breeze before long, Laird, aye, very soon. Then I shall try to assess his leg," Willa informed them. Whatever it was she'd given his brother, it appeared to be working. The lad wasn't struggling as she sewed along his wound. Breckin had never seen him be so still, and it was unsettling.

"Aye, Laird. Willa said it was a nasty gash to be sure." Connor seemed proud of his injury.

Caden scoffed as if he wished to be lying in Connor's place. "Ye were lucky and ye probably broke a bone too."

Breckin smirked at his brother. "How is he, Willa?"

"He shall take a wee bit to heal, for it appears his brother is correct. He might have broken a bone. I had to stitch both sides of his leg. He will have a good bit of pain and trouble walking for a spell, but alas, he shall walk again. I will bind him to keep his leg immobile." Willa disregarded them as she continued her ministration.

"Ye scared the hell out of me, Connor. I pray ye have learned your lesson. No more daring feats and senselessness, do ye hear? I will hear your pledge."

"I did not know the wood was weakened, Laird. Och, I vow to be more careful in the future," Connor said groggily.

Willa ambled around the table, took a clean cloth, and dipped it into a bucket of water. "Eva, fetch that balm there on the table. The small vessel at the end."

Breckin watched as Eva helped Willa by taking away the bloody cloths and returned with the medicinal the healer asked for. "Willa, Connor should stay here overnight. Will ye care for him? On the morrow, I will have him moved home."

"I agree, Laird. He might need pain tinctures and he needs to be watched for infection. Caden, ye can stay too. Ise-Olcan will need to be taken out whilst I see to your brother," Willa said.

"We shall leave ye then. Lads, listen to Willa. I will return for ye both on the morrow."

"I shall visit you on the morrow too. Rest, Connor, and allow Willa to tend to you," Eva said and pressed a hand on his brother's head.

Breckin led the way from the healer's cottage and Eva followed him. Across the bridge, several of his clansmen gathered. Their gazes stayed on Eva as they passed. Gideon's observation was astute because his men would have difficulty paying attention when she was within view. Her beauty was going to cause disruptions, he was certain of that, but he couldn't help but be pleased with her. Not only was she beautiful, but she was graceful and caring. Beckin wanted to learn everything about her.

Yet it might take time to win her trust.

Gideon approached with his wife Deena beside him. "Good day, Milady. I wanted to meet ye. I am Gideon, the commander of the laird's army. This is my wife, Deena." Both bowed to Eva, and Gideon's smile spread across his face.

"It is a pleasure to meet you both," Eva said and slightly curtseyed to them.

Deena said not a word and quickly left her husband's side. She walked away, down the lane, where she met with another woman. They seemed to whisper and used their hands to shield their mouths. Breckin did not appreciate the way his commander's wife failed to welcome Eva and he'd have to have a word about it with Gideon later.

"Milady, if ye need anything, anything at all, just say the word. I am happy to oblige. 'Tis good to see our laird happily married," Gideon said, still flashing his smile.

"Go on and get back to duty. I shall come and see ye later. Some matters need discussion," Brecken said.

Gideon tipped his head and marched off.

Breckin took hold of Eva's hand and led her toward his aunt's cottage. When they reached it, he stopped her from entering. "Eva, we will only stay here for a fortnight and then we will leave."

"And go where, Breckin? Are we leaving the land? Returning to the border, to my da's home?" Eva asked with eagerness.

His body tensed at her questions. She seemed too hopeful that he'd return her to her father's manor. "Nay, we are not leaving Buchanan land, lass, but will move to our home."

"Do you have a home of your own? Must we stay with your aunt? Even a fortnight will be difficult. I do not think she is fond of me, and likewise, the clanswomen are so unapproachable."

She sounded so overwrought. Given Deena's actions, he could understand why she felt that way. Still, he needed to try to help her understand it would take a while for her to gain acceptance. "Eva, I told ye, lass, that my clan is…"

"Leery of outsiders? I can understand that, but to be so cold and unfriendly…" She sighed and her shoulders slumped. "It matters not because I am used to keeping my own company," she said in a sorrowful tone.

He flinched because he should have taken the time to explain to his clan who she was and how important Eva was. Her sadness was his fault. "Truth be told, I am disappointed in them for not being accepting of ye. I should tell them to greet ye and befriend ye. Ye are now our clan's lady and deserve more respect than that."

She shook her head. "No, I do not want to force their friendships, Breckin. I want them to accept me in their own way. I want them to be my friends. Perhaps in time…"

"Well, I am fond of ye. Now, I have a surprise for ye. Come with me and mayhap it will put a smile on your bonny face." Breckin led her away from the cottage and walked onward. Toward the far end of the island, past thick-trunked pines and dense yew bushes, the lane shaded and darkened. The walk didn't take them long.

Situated beyond a copse of trees stood his uncle's home. Isolated from most of the buildings on the island, the home would afford them privacy.

"Why have you brought me here?"

"Because this is where we shall live. It might look worse for wear now but 'tis old…an ancient building that was erected by our ancestors many, many years ago. My uncle lived here his entire life."

Her eyes darted from the worn edifice to the dilapidated thatch, to the holes in the wooden walls, to the crumbling stone of the chimney. "We are to live with your uncle then?"

Breckin chuckled. "Nay, my uncle left on a pilgrimage years ago and I doubt he shall return any time soon. He will not mind if I take over the abode. We shall make repairs to it and make it a worthy home. I know ye are used to grandness… Your da's manor was extensive and beyond in its elegance. We live a simpler life here in the Highlands and do not need such grand homes. I hope ye understand that."

She reached out and grabbed his hand and wrapped her fingers around his. "I do, Breckin, but soon my belongings will arrive and I shall have our home looking as grand as my da's."

For her sake, he hoped that was true. "Come, let us go inside."

Breckin stepped on the wooden rundle and it cracked beneath his weight. Eva skipped over the step and climbed until they stood together on the small landing before the door. He pressed it open and the creak of the iron hinges pierced the air. With care, he crept inside and tested the floorboards to ensure they did not give way under his weight. Eva stood beside him and she gaped with her mouth open slightly at the deplorable condition of the inside.

Breckin couldn't blame her, but tried to sound confident as he said, "Needs some fixing but I have a skilled group of builders who will see to the task. Before we know it, they shall have this place repaired and readied to live in."

"It shall take more than a fortnight for skilled builders to fix this place." She jumped and bumped him when a bird fluttered its wings and left its perch on an overhead beam.

"Nay, my builders are good at what they do. I promise ye, our home will be ready. I only ask that ye be patient until then."

"I shall try, Breckin. But I want another promise from you."

He held her face and gazed at her. "And that is?"

"You will not leave again without telling me. Because if you do, I shall be alone and will perish." Her gaze told him that she spoke truthfully.

His hands shifted to her shoulders and he scowled at her words. "Perish? Surely, ye jest."

"No, I do not jest. You might not have realized this but I… I cannot light a fire…have never done so in my life. I do not know where to begin to start a fire. And I cannot cook or clean. I am afraid that I lack the necessary skills to care for myself, or you, as a wife should. Servants cared for me all my life and I never had to learn such tasks. Clare told me there are no servants here. There, 'tis a sad admission but the truth."

Breckin almost bent over and laughed from the absurdity of her passionate speech. It seemed to be important to her and he nodded. "I will not let ye perish, Eva. Aye, and I give ye my vow not to leave again without telling ye. 'Tis true that we have no servants but I might be able to persuade a woman or two to come and help ye. Now, let us return to Clare's. I am famished and want to enjoy a good supper."

She flapped her arm and shrieked. "Is that a…SPIDER? Sweet Mary, get it off, get it off!"

Breckin chuckled. "'Tis but a wee spider." He flicked it off her arm and grinned.

"One more promise," she said breathlessly as she pressed herself against him. "Make sure all the spiders are removed before we take residence."

Breckin couldn't resist and leaned toward her. He set a light kiss on her lips and then pulled her into his arms. As he peered down at her bonny face, he said, "Aye, any more promises?"

"One more…" she said as she wrapped her arms around his body and sensually kissed him.

He could stand there in the dilapidated longhouse with Eva kissing him without care of time. Her sweet lips lured his with desire. Breckin pulled back, took her hand, and hastily led her from their future home, intent on giving her the "one more" unspoken promise that she'd hoped for.

CHAPTER TWELVE

A WARM MOUTH pressed against the delicate skin of her throat and Eva moaned softly at being awakened in such a desirous way. She stretched against Breckin and his hard body kept her from shifting to his side of the bed. His hand caressed her torso as he pulled her closer.

"'Tis pleasant to have someone next to ye, to wake up to," Breckin said as he nuzzled her neck with his lips, his bearded scruff brushing her skin.

Eva sighed in delight as Breckin continued to kiss and caress her. Her one more promise that she demanded of him, was that he fill her with desire. He'd done more than that twice during the night. She could get used to having him there, beside her, doing all the wicked and marvelously sinful things to her.

Morning arrived, and still, he seemed content to stay beside her. She did not even mind the small bed that they shared or that he took up most of the room. It meant that she could snuggle closer to him, reap the benefit of his warm body, and feel his masculine, hard muscles pressed against the soft curves of her body.

Breckin kissed her hard one more time and when he drew away, he flung his legs over the side of the bed. "Bollocks, I wish I could stay here all morn. Och, I forgot that I was supposed to meet Gideon on the training field at sunrise. He wants me to raise the morale of the soldiers."

"You sound as though that will be difficult." Eva almost laughed at the sour expression on his handsome face. Her husband, she realized, was a man of little words.

"Nay, I am a great motivator. 'Tis just... I must incite the soldiers to train hard because..." his words trailed off when he turned back to her.

"Because you mean to go to war again and soon?" She wasn't fond of the fact that Breckin sought to go to war but he was the leader of the Buchanans and she supposed she should get used to him leaving her. Yet, he'd only just returned and she hoped to spend a little time with him.

"Perhaps, and the weather warms so war is expected. I shall see ye later, lass." He leaned over her and pressed a kiss on her head. "Do not laze about in bed all day. Get out and find something to do. Ye might want to check on the progress of the longhouse later. I mean to meet with the builder this morn after I leave the training field. Oh, and I need to bring Connor home before the end of the day. If ye want, meet me there near supper time." Breckin finally drew himself away and lingered by the door as if he was hesitant to leave.

"He will be gladdened to come home." Eva waved him away.

He dressed and left. As soon as he'd closed the door behind him, she flung the covers from over her and began her morning rituals. When she finished dressing and taking care of her needs, she hurriedly tidied up the bed chamber and reminded herself to fetch clean water for the basin she'd had Clare put in the room.

In the main area of the cottage, she found a trencher full of cut fruit, slices of bread, and two kinds of spreads. She poured herself a little mead and ate her morning fare. Fortunately, Clare was nowhere in sight and must have already left the cottage.

After she ate, Eva retrieved her cloak and the tartan that Breckin gave her and used it to cover herself as she left the cottage. Outside, the air was a bit chilly but not cold. She liked the land and being on the other side of the bridge and so she ambled there. Groups of people seemed to be headed toward the church and so she followed them. Eva entered the church and realized that Mass would soon take place. She sat on the last pew and listened to Father Murphy preach about acceptance.

Sweet Mary, the Buchanans could use a lecture or two on that topic.

After Mass, most people didn't linger. She waited and thanked the priest for the service. Then she set off to Willa's and as she approached, Ise-Olcan met her with enthusiastic barks.

"Good morn, Ise-Olcan, you beautiful dog." She petted the scraggly mutt and rounded her to get to the door. Eva knocked and awaited someone to answer. Caden yanked the door open.

"Milady, ye are here," he said with a big grin. "Conner is being a wee bairn this morn."

She entered the cottage and glanced at Connor who sat on a chair with his leg elevated. "How are you, Connor? Feeling better?"

"Pfft," he muttered. "Not bloody likely. I am not allowed out of my chair. Oh, I should not speak so, not in front of a lady… I apologize, Milady, for being surly."

She smiled because she'd probably be in the same mood, being stuck in a chair, and most likely in pain. Eva found Willa mixing herbs at a small table near her kitchen area. "Can I help?"

"Oh, Milady… I did not hear ye come in. I was so focused on this mixture…" Willa waved her forward. "Ye can keep me company for a bit. The lads had their morning fare and want to go but Connor's wound needs to be watched. 'Tis beginning to fester. I should probably keep him here for another day or two until I am certain he is out of danger."

"Breckin has gone to the training field. I shall tell him if I see him but he said he would come by later near supper." Eva motioned to a small bowl and nodded to her. "Shall I crush these leaves?"

"Aye, please." Willa mixed water with the concoction she was mixing. "The day is a wee bit chilly. What are ye about?"

She pressed the pestle against the greenery in the bowl and

crushed it until the leaves were unrecognizable. The scent of it was alluring and she wondered what it was. There were no flowers on the stems, and yet it smelled sweet. "What is this?

"'Tis just lemon balm, and aye, it has a wonderful scent, does it not?"

"Yes, it's wonderful," she agreed. And then she said, "I thought to walk about and take in the air. Is there a market nearby? I thought to perhaps bring Connor a treat, maybe some sweetened bread or jellied tarts."

"Oh, aye, there's a small marketplace beyond the kirk toward the east. 'Tis about a league or so toward the southeast. Just follow the lane and ye cannot miss it. Ye should be safe enough for the market is on Buchanan land and none would bother ye. I am afraid that I cannot leave the lad here without someone watching him. Are ye certain ye wish to go on your own?"

Eva doubted anyone would miss her. "I shall be well enough on my own. My thanks, Willa. I shall stop by on my return."

She finished her task of mixing the herbs and handed the small bowl to Willa. After, she said farewell to the lads and exited the cottage. With Willa's direction in mind, she headed south on the lane. Ise-Olcan followed and she shooed the dog but it heeled beside her as if it was intent to take the journey with her. "Go on, go home." The dog ignored her and walked lively next to her. "Well then, I suppose I could use the company."

Buchanan land differed from the land near her home. There was a beauty about the barren stretch between the lane and the market. Rolling green and brown hillsides swept away from the lane and the beginning of purple buds sprouted on the stems that reached her knees. Her home was mostly green shrubs and trees, and not as enthralling as the Highlands.

The walk to the small village where the market was held lay ahead, given the view of tents and stalls. Eva was as excited as Ise-Olcan whose tail wagged haphazardly. She hadn't been able to attend a market since she'd been in Edinburgh. With the anticipation of what she would find, she hastened her steps and reached the stalls in a short time.

As she meandered along the lane, she stopped and pulled out her coin pouch which she always kept tied to the inside of her cloak. Ise-Olcan stayed near her. She purchased sweetened bread for the lads, one small meat pie for the dog, and two tarts for herself and Breckin. She had a soft spot for tarts and would enjoy them after supper. She wondered if Breckin liked sweets. There was so much she didn't know about him and that saddened her a little.

The baker wrapped all but the dog's item in a thin cloth. As she turned away from the stall, she tossed the dog's treat to her and Ise-Olcan caught it in mid-air. Eva ruffled the hair on the dog's head and smiled. Ise-Olcan whimpered for more treats.

A man whose oversized woolen cap fell to just above his brows stood nearby. With watchful eyes, he regarded her and she realized he was the stall's owner.

The burly man bent his head. "Good day, Milady."

"Sir." She perused his goods, mostly furniture made of good quality wood, and various other items that were obviously previously used, given their wear. "You have a good amount of items."

"Aye, Milady. We take on items for people and when we sell them, we take a portion of the profits and give the rest to them. If ye have anything ye would like to sell, I would be pleased to take it off your hands. Otherwise, be ye free to browse."

She shook her head and eyed a chair that might be a good addition to the longhouse once it was completed and liveable—if that ever happened. "Good day." With a snap of her fingers, she called to the dog and turned but the man stopped her.

"My name is Amos, Milady, if I can ever be of service to ye."

"I shall remember, Amos. My thanks." Eva walked away, ensured the dog followed, and carried her purchase of bread and tarts in her arms. She hurried to return and the walk heated her. By the time she reached Willa's, she longed to take off her cloak. The day had warmed and even the sun shone between the thick white clouds.

At the cottage, the dog sprinted past her through the open door and flopped down near the cooking fire. Eva entered and found the lads grumpily teasing one another. "I brought you some sweet bread. Eat it, for it shall cheer you."

"I detest being in this chair, Milady," Conner said sullenly. "There is naught to do."

She pressed her hands over his light blond strands of hair and nodded. "I would detest it too. Willa, can Conner be moved outside? He could at least see those about the lane and get some air."

Willa wiped her hands on a cloth and nodded. "I do not see why he couldn't. But we should have Laird Buchanan move him. The lad is too heavy for us to lift and we do not want to injure him further."

"We shall ask Breckin to help ye later when he comes," she told Connor. "Perhaps I can find some sort of entertainment for you whilst you are recovering. I shall think about it and return with Breckin later this eve to visit you. And I want you lads to call me Eva."

The lads' mouths were full of bread but they happily nodded.

Eva waved to Willa and left. On her return to the other side of the bridge, she found a group of women sitting at a table situated about knee-high from the ground. On the table were heaping piles of fleece. Some of the women grabbed portions of it while another poured water over the fleece. They began singing a melody as they washed the woolen. How lovely they sounded as they sang. She wished she knew the words so she might join in but they eyed her warily and ceased singing as they noticed her watching them, as if she intruded on their privacy.

With a nod of apology, she continued onward, saddened that the women in the Buchanan clan shunned her. She had to wonder why. Was something wrong with her? No, that was absurd, she thought, because she was friendly, likable, and kind. Surely that mattered to the Buchanan women. But perhaps not. That they didn't appreciate outsiders made her ponder how long it would take for them to consider her one of them.

She kept walking along the lane and glanced at the river that flowed next to the land. Eva found a spot where vines wrapped the lower trunks of trees. The vines gave her an idea of a use for them. Eva tugged and collected a score of thick green climbers and had to yank hard to loosen them enough to free them.

She'd make rings of them for the lads to use in a game of entertainment. Her brothers had taught her how to make them and when they were young, they often spent time in the woods when her brothers were not at their lessons. But she had to figure out what they could toss them at. Connor would be able to participate even if he was restricted to a chair.

Eva continued and reached the end of the island where the longhouse sat. Banging came from inside, but she stood still and viewed the repairs done so far. The holes in the walls were patched up with pieces of wood and there were bales of straw sitting beside the longhouse, ready to be raised to the roof to cover it.

"Milady, can I help ye?" A tall, brawny man exited the house and stepped off the landing. He wore his hair shorn to his head but it appeared light brown. His eyes were a soft brown and his smile becoming.

"No, I was just checking on the progress. Breckin asked me to stop by…" She did not know what else to say.

"Aye, ye must be the laird's wife. Why do ye not come inside and we can talk about what ye would like us to do? I am Lawrence, milady, the Buchanan builder. We will make sure your new home is exactly how ye wish it to be." He waved at her.

Eva followed him inside, still holding the collection of vines in her arms. "You have accomplished much for only a short time."

"Aye, we work quick and are skilled. There were no major repairs needed, milady, only minor fixes of the walls and roof. Now, we will be situating the kitchen there," he said and pointed to the left of the house. "There is a flue already there for a small oven and we will strengthen the floor boards afore we set the stone of the hearth."

She nodded even though she had never used an oven before.

"We shall put in a new hearth and I have already sent my men to collect stones and slate." He rambled on, listing all the things he would provide in the kitchen area.

Eva could have laughed because she was not knowledgeable about what she'd need for the cooking area. Hopefully, she would learn to utilize the hearth and oven. "Will you close in the sleeping area?" She wanted some privacy within the longhouse and the ability to close a door would also enable her to relax without watchful eyes in a quiet place.

"It was not planned, Milady. Och, if ye wish us to close it off, we can do that."

"I would appreciate that. And if you would make at least two more closed-off sleeping areas for Breckin's brothers and guests." Eva hadn't asked Breckin if his brothers would live with them, but she hoped so. They needed their elder brother and she needed them, if only to be accepted as family.

"What is that area back there?" As she stepped toward the end of the overlarge longhouse, she reached the limit where there was no wall but a fenced area that led to the dirt ground.

"Oh, that is where ye can keep your animals, Milady. Longhouses were made to shelter both people and animals." Lawrence stopped before the dropoff where the fence secured the area.

"We do not plan to have animals in our home. Can you close this off with a wall? We shall use the outside area for something else and shall figure it out later," she explained.

"Aye, certainly." Lawrence bowed to her and turned away. He returned to his task.

Eva exited the building and rounded it. When she got to the back where animals were previously kept, she wondered what she might utilize in the place. Maybe Breckin could keep his horse there or maybe a small garrison of arms. He was, after all, the leader of a fierce army.

She left the longhouse with the vines in her hold and meandered back on the lane. Before she reached Clare's cottage, someone shouted. Eva stopped and stepped aside as carts rolled by.

A man whistled and shouted, "Halt." He reached her and bowed. "Milady, I do not know if ye remember me but I am Aymer, the gate watch. These carts arrived for ye. Apparently, the sentry intercepted them and had them come directly to the holding. What do ye want us to do with them? There are five carts and beyond, a group of six horses."

Eva couldn't withhold her smile. Her precious belongings had at last arrived! She looked at the carts with affection because she knew what was beneath the tarps—the thing she held most dear.

"Milady? Where do ye want me to put them? This amount of belongings surely will not fit in Clare's cottage. She's likely to have a fit if ye try to bring in your items."

"No, you are right, Aymer. Clare would definitely not appreciate me bringing in my belongings." She thought about where she might store the items until the longhouse was ready and then an idea sparked. "Have them continue to the longhouse. There is an area there, at the back, where we can store the carts until I can unpack them."

"What about the horses, Milady?" Aymer waved to the men on the carts and the wheels turned, taking them farther along on the island.

"I have no use for horses and wonder why my da sent them. Why do you not take them to where they keep the soldiers' horses? I am sure Breckin will figure out what to do with them." Eva wasn't fond of horses or riding them which was why she preferred to ride in the carriage when she'd traveled to Edinburgh.

Aymer bowed to her and marched off toward the back of the procession.

Eva was excited and could not wait to unpack her possessions. Now that she had a place to put them, she would make good use of whatever her father had sent her. She followed the carts to the longhouse and as they untethered the horses, the men pushed the carts into the sheltered area.

One of her father's men approached. "My Lady Eva, 'tis good to see you."

"And you, Donald."

"Are you well? I am sure your father will ask after you if we can return."

Eva surmised his tone was somewhat fearful. "What do you mean...if?"

"The Buchanan sentry, My Lady... they took our weapons and forced us by the points of their blades as we traveled here. They found us at the blackened trees and threatened to do away with us until we professed that we belonged to you."

She was dismayed by his explanation. "I apologize, Donald, for the horrid treatment by the Buchanan soldiers. You have my thanks for being so brave. I shall speak to their laird about their behavior and ensure your safety whilst you are here."

Donald scoffed. "Their laird was there. It was he who told his men to take our weapons. They even searched us for daggers and short swords. The Buchanans said they would allow our entry upon their land but they would decide if they'd allow us to leave."

Eva drew in a shocked gasp. "Breckin took your weapons? I will make sure he returns them, Donald, before you leave. And I promise that you shall be free to leave and return home. I appreciate you coming all this way." How she would enact such an achievement, Eva wasn't sure, but she would use every wile in her armory to ensure Breckin treated her father's soldiers with more reverence.

"Do you want to go with us, my lady? If you do, maybe we can sneak away. It would have to be in darkness, though...and there could be danger." His gaze shifted about as if he feared he'd been overheard.

"I cannot leave, Donald. No, I am destined to remain here

with my husband." How dreadful that sounded to her own ears. A little bit of homesickness entered her heart and she pressed her hand against her chest in sorrow.

He eyed the longhouse. "Is this where you live?" Donald sounded aghast at the thought of her living there.

"This will be my home, once the men make repairs. Worry not for me. I am now married, Donald, and must make the most of it." She tried to sound enthusiastic but failed miserably.

"Your home was as grand as any and now you have to live in a shack in the woods. You are a courageous woman, my lady." Donald turned then, when one of the men called to him.

Eva's chest tightened at Donald's judgment. For some reason, shame and its sorrowful mien overtook her. She pressed her hands on her cheeks and shook her head, though she had nothing to be shameful about. The Buchanans didn't need a grand manor home. They were content with what they had—which was next to nothing in the way of possessions or luxurious homes. Breckin had said they lived a simpler life and he wasn't mistaken about that.

The men departed and headed for the bridge. Eva followed in their wake, hopeful that she would cross paths with Breckin on the way. At the bridge, Aymer whistled at them to stop.

"Aymer, is Breckin here?"

The man nodded. "He is probably training with the men."

"Fetch him for me, please." Eva folded her arms across her chest, sweeping the vines that she still held across her face, and glared. The curt tone of her voice sent the man running.

It did not take long for Breckin to arrive. When he did, he appeared flummoxed to see her ireful expression. Eva couldn't hold back her anger at the treatment of her father's soldiers. She walked to stand away from everyone so no one could overhear them. "Breckin—"

"Are ye pleased? Your da sent your belongings. Where are they?"

"I had them taken to the longhouse. We should discuss—"

"The longhouse? I would have thought ye would want to keep your belongings with ye." Breckin thumbed the strap of his sword's sheath that crossed his chest, looking so handsome but she couldn't let that detract from her intent to reproach him.

"There is no room for my belongings at Clare's. Now, I want to talk about—"

"I have no time for this, lass. My men await and we have much to do before darkness comes." Breckin shifted his eyes toward her father's soldiers and his men standing beyond them.

Eva stepped in front of him to block his view and to keep him from leaving. "A moment, Breckin, of your valuable time. I understand that you took my father's men's arms and that you told them they were permitted on Buchanan land but that you might not allow them to leave. Is this true?"

Breckin scrunched his eyes and he appeared taken aback by her question. "It might be."

"Did you or did you not take their swords?"

He nodded and said, "Aye."

"Did you threaten to disallow them from leaving? And what, pray tell, were you going to do to them? Do not, if you considered harming them, speak of it."

"Then I shall not," he said low.

"Those men traveled all the way here to bring me my things. The least we can do is to return their weapons so they can protect themselves on their journey home, which they should be graciously afforded to do." Eva hadn't raised her voice but the pitch of her tone was well noted by her gruff and now ornery husband.

"Damnation, I suppose we shall have to let them go then."

"Yes, you must," she said with determination. Behind her, a rush of laughter ensued from the Buchanan soldiers, effectively telling her that all had heard their discussion. Her face heated with embarrassment.

"We only meant to intimidate them, lass, and I was going to let them leave but without their weapons." Breckin bowed his head to Aymer who shouted out orders to return the men's arms.

"Tell your sentry to escort them to Buchanan's border. And if one man is injured with even a thistle prickle, I shall be more wrathful than any woman you have ever seen." She hastened past him and marched with vigor toward Willa's cottage, crossing the bridge and down the lane. By the time she reached it, her anger had lessened considerably.

Willa was exiting her cottage and smiled. "Oh, you have returned, Eva. The lads are about to have their supper if ye wish to join them."

"I shall. My thanks, Willa. Where are you off to?"

"I need to take a remedy to Gideon's wife, for she ails and cannot keep anything down. 'Tis the truth, I think I know what troubles her but neither my son or daughter-in-law wish to accept that she is with child again."

"I will stay here with the lads then until you return." Eva watched the healer start down the path before she entered her dwelling and closed the door.

The cottage was warm and the lads were quiet. She was grateful for the peace because she was certain that once Breckin caught up to her, she'd hear his rebuke. At least she could enjoy the solitude for now. "There you two are. How are you feeling, Connor?"

"Ye should have seen it, Milady... Willa had to cut my leg open and all this pus oozed out. It was a relief, though," Connor said with pride.

"Aye, it was gross," Caden said with shining eyes.

Eva chuckled. The strangest things fascinated lads. "I wanted to tell you that I have thought of a game. I shall use these vines to make rings and we will toss them onto something, a target. Maybe you can help me think of something to use for the target."

"That will help, Milady, and keep me from thinking about my injury," Connor said.

"And since I have your attention, I was hoping..." Eva wanted to win the lads' friendship. She smiled and then continued,

"Have you trained at all in arms?"

Caden nodded. "Aye, but the soldiers say we are troublesome and we are only allowed on the training field when Gideon or Breckin is there to observe us. But we already surpassed many of our friends in our skills so it matters not."

"Good. I want you to teach me how to fight."

Caden bellowed with laughter. "Ye, Milady, a lass…fight?"

"Aye, me, a lass. I want to learn how to defend myself too."

"Why would ye want to, Milady?" Caden asked with widened eyes.

"Because, Caden, I never had to defend myself, but if ever I need to, I want to be prepared. Just because I am a woman does not mean that I am incapable. I will learn what I can from you."

"That is admirable, Milady," Connor said.

"I trust you to keep this quiet and between us." Eva hid her smile. In getting them to teach her defensive tactics, she'd keep them busy and out of trouble. There was also the benefit that she might learn something valuable. Being a Buchanan now, she surmised that she should know how to protect herself.

Chapter Thirteen

Breckin stood shocked by Eva's chastisement and watched her march off. By his faith, though, she was even more alluring when she scolded him. Maybe he appreciated her feistiness or maybe he was impressed that she dared to admonish him in front of his warriors—no one else dared to challenge him.

"Laird, we are ready to escort Milady's father's soldiers to the border. Do ye want to come with us?" Aymer asked.

"Have the sentry see to it. I would rather ye keep to your post. I must see to something..." Breckin didn't give him time to respond and crossed the bridge, intent to find his obstinate wife.

Father Murphy met him midway across the bridge and smiled. "Good day, Laird."

"Is it, Father?"

The man bobbed his head. "Aye, for there's no rain. Any day there's no rain is a good day."

"If ye say so, Father. I am off to seek my wife. By God, the woman needs to have her bottom thrashed." He squeezed his hands closed and drew in a resigned breath.

Father Murphy leaned toward a bush and broke off a good switch. "Here, Laird, use this. But do not break that tender, sweet lass's skin."

He accepted the switch from the priest and marched onward. But as he progressed, Breckin scoffed to himself and tossed the switch into the nearby thicket, knowing Father Murphy was jesting with him. Besides, he would never harm a single hair on his wife's head, let alone beat her with a damned switch. With a long stride and a bit of vigor pushing him, he'd reach Willa's cottage in a short time. He supposed that was where Eva had gone. En route, he saw Willa walking toward him.

"Laird, I am gladdened that I came across ye. Connor will need to stay another day or two. I am afeared an infection has beset his leg. I had to open his wound. I shall tend to him but wanted to let you know." Willa waited for him to say something.

Breckin half-listened until she repeated what she'd said. "My thanks, Willa, for your care of Connor. Did ye see Eva?"

"Aye, she came to the cottage and is there now with the lads. I need to go to Gideon's but should not be gone too long." She quickly walked off and disappeared beyond the trees on the lane.

He continued until he reached the cottage. Instead of knocking and giving warning of his arrival, he thrust open the door and stepped inside. Three gasps met him. He peered at his brothers but shook his head, and gave the signal that he did not wish to be spoken to. Within several steps, he reached Eva, clasped her hand, and gently pulled her from the cottage.

She huffed and tried to dislodge her hand from his but he held fast. "Breckin… What are you doing? If you mean to punish me—"

"Shhh…await." He kept walking until he was far enough away from the cottage and stopped. "I was wondering where that lass was—the one who chastised me at the market in Edinburgh for trying to rescue her—and here ye are. What I want to know is why ye have been so reserved. And why ye now found your gumption to chide me so?" He folded his arms across his chest and waited for her answers.

"Breckin, I… Well, you were going to harm my father's soldiers and I couldn't have that when they only came here to aid me. It has been difficult being here. No one talks to me, the women, that is, except for Willa, but she's always busy. I do not belong. At least at home, I had the servants to talk to. I have been crushed beneath the feet of tyranny." She sighed deeply. "I am not used to such isolation."

He stepped close to her, set his hands on her shoulders, and peered into her eyes. "Eva, forget not, lass, that ye are now a Buchanan. We allow naught or no one to crush us."

"Except another Buchanan," she countered.

"Ye are a lioness, not a weak mouse. Never allow anyone to crush ye, not even me. When ye need to conquer, ye shall do so with all the strength of a Buchanan."

"That is absurd because I do not feel like a Buchanan. Besides, Breckin, I want to fit in, not conquer." She lowered her face but he wouldn't allow her to hide her gaze from him and lifted her chin.

"Ye already conquered me, lass, the rest will follow easily. I vow to ye that it will be so." He leaned in to give her a wee peck on the lips but heard Gideon shout. With a groan, he pulled back. "Next time ye wish to rebuke me, Eva, wait until we are alone."

"I am sorry, Breckin, that I embarrassed you. I did not mean to and did not think—"

"Me either, lass. I had not realized how my treatment of your father's soldiers would affect ye. I must remember that ye care too much for others. I should go." Breckin's frustration tightened his fists when he turned and walked away from the sweet minx. He hastened his steps as he left the cottage, and soon he reached the bridge where Gideon awaited him.

"What goes?"

"We received a message from Colin Campbell. He says he is going to take arms against the MacDoughalls and calls upon us as his ally to support him."

"Damnation," Breckin muttered. "I did not want to leave our land but I suppose I must. Gather as many of our soldiers as possible, och leave a score of them behind to protect the clan."

Gideon bowed his head, turned, and marched off.

Breckin returned to Eva and found her tying vines together. He thought it strange but didn't remark on it or ask what she was doing. "I must leave the holding and am not sure when I will return."

She hurriedly stood when he'd entered, dislodging the flora from her lap, and nodded. "My thanks for telling me."

"I shall try to return with haste," he said as a sort of peace offering.

"You are off to war, are you not? Just return in one piece and unharmed."

He grinned because it seemed she too wanted peace betwixt them. "Is that an order?"

She smiled with shining eyes. "No, simply a request."

"Sounds to me, lass, that ye might be beginning to care for me." Breckin pulled her against him and gave her a longing kiss. Lord, he did not want to leave her but his obligation to the Campbells couldn't be ignored.

His brothers snickered with laughter and made gagging noises. When he pulled away from Eva, Breckin glared at them. He pressed his hand on her face and dallied in leaving because her sweet lips were rosy from his kiss and her face flushed.

"Perhaps I care for you a little but I shall think more about it whilst you are gone."

Breckin chortled to himself as he left Willa's cottage. By the time he reached the stables, his men had assembled. Gideon had retrieved his sword, armor, and satchel that he used when he went to war.

As they rode out, he kept thinking about Eva and how she'd been miserable. He should have done something to make her feel more welcomed but with his duty to his clan, he had no time to deal with such matters. When he returned, he'd find a way to show her that she was now part of his clan and that she mattered.

Along the route to the Campbell land, they passed through hostile territory of the MacFarlanes. His regiment of soldiers knew how to be quiet to bypass the MacFarlanes' sentry.

The weather remained fair with a slight breeze but no rain. Over the barren hills, crossing the waterways, and riding past the stretched-out meadows throughout the day exhausted their horses and made his soldiers sullen. Breckin called a halt and for all to make camp. He sent two men to Campbell to alert him of his arrival.

Nearly three days passed as they waited on the border of Campbell land. Throughout the day, Breckin paced between two trees, knowing that his ally wouldn't have called for him unless there was a good reason. Night pressed onward and lent to the duskiness of the sky, and his men lit fires, hunted for small game, and took the time to rest.

As the sky pitched, his impatience wore on him and he was growing testy. None of his men approached him or spoke to him. Finally, several men on horses rode through the wooded area in the distance.

When Campbell dismounted his horse, Breckin hastened to his comrade and greeted him. "Colin, ye called us. We came."

Colin slid from his mount and reached him. He shoved his chest in greeting and his blue eyes shone with mirth. The man always wore his long light locks pulled back from his face. Breckin regarded his comrade and grunted.

"What say ye? Are we to war?"

"Aye, at break of dawn. My men encamp close by. We will take to arms, and at last, route the MacDoughalls." Colin's words came hard and with more than a touch of ire.

"What did they do to merit a thrashing from the Campbells?"

Colin chortled. "Need they do anything? Still, their misdeed calls forth my army and I will meet their call. They set fire to my storage sheds and encroached on my land. I am through being lenient toward them. 'Tis time I show them that I will not stand for their insolence."

"Aye, come and join me by the fire. We will discuss the battle plan."

THE MACDOUGHALLS MUST have gotten wind of their forthcoming attack because when they approached their fief two days later, most of the soldiers were gone. Only women, children, and elders hid in the recesses of walls, and behind barred cottage doors. They peered through windows.

On the return to the border situated between the two clans, they met up with a regiment of MacDoughall soldiers and Colin called his war cry. The Campbells led the attack and Breckin commanded his men to follow closely behind them. Scores of soldiers raised their swords and ran into the breach.

During the fracas, Breckin cut down at least two MacDoughalls. He searched for another foe but it appeared the cowardly MacDoughalls tucked tail, fled, and retreated into the nearby woods. Breckin detested such a cowardly act. Yet he supposed the men were only intent on saving themselves from being injured or even killed.

After the fight, Breckin was invited back to the Campbells' fief. "Ye be welcome to rest a wee bit before ye head home," Colin said.

Breckin begged off. "I need to get back to my land, och my thanks for the offer." He wanted to get settled in the longhouse. A new life would begin when he and Eva took residence. He envisioned a calmer, more enriched life with his wife. Lord, he hoped that would be the result, especially if he rejected the call of his allies in the future.

"My thanks, Breckin, for coming all this way. It was not a complete waste of time because the MacDoughalls will think twice before they intend to encroach again." Colin shoved his shoulder in a parting farewell and bellowed laughter as he marched away.

Breckin called his men to assemble and his commander stood by his horse and handed him the reins. "Find out if anyone needs aid. We are headed home, Gideon. Direct the men."

His commander shouted orders as he strode off. When Gideon returned, he reported, "We suffered minor injuries, Laird.

Only two men needed to be stitched and one a wee bit more serious. He's been tied to the horse for transport home."

"My thanks. Let us head out then. We will make camp when it gets dark and we are closer to home." Breckin mounted his horse and rode ahead of his men.

Behind him, a trail of soldiers rode on their steeds, eagerly talking about the melee. They headed easterly toward Buchanan land. The day wasn't completely gone and the late afternoon sun shone with a glorious glow. It made the ride more enjoyable. Breckin hoped to reach their land before it got too dark to continue.

The blackened trees were silhouetted in the dusky sky in the distance. Breckin heard the sound of riders approaching them from behind and raised his arm to alert his men. As the riders neared, he recognized William Stewart who had a handful of men with him. Stewart stopped his horse but did not dismount.

"Breckin, I was hoping to run into ye." William bowed his head, respectfully greeting him.

He wasn't about to appease him and do the same. "Why are ye here?"

"I was asked to come by Laird MacLaren. He wants a meeting to discuss the troubles betwixt ye and seeks peace. He says he has news that will remedy the situation of his clan calling off your betrothal to his daughter."

"Ye mean your now wife?" Breckin grunted. The two clans were in cahoots, he reckoned, and he wasn't about to placate either of them.

"Are ye surly because I wed her? I told ye that she coveted the marriage and at the time, I needed to marry," William said.

"Aye? Marian was but an afterthought? She told me that she coveted the union betwixt you and her. That ye cared so little about her after she died tells me that I am gladdened she was unable to marry ye. Ye damned did not even have the bollocks to mourn her as she deserved."

"So, ye do hold hostility. I understand, och do not take it out on the MacLarens. And I tell ye, Laird Buchanan, I did mourn the lass. I was devastated when I learned she had died."

Breckin scoffed and gripped his horse's reins so tightly his knuckles turned white. "Go back to MacLaren and tell him that there will never be peace betwixt us. Warn John that I am not finished with him. Whilst ye are at it, be sure to kiss your father-in-law's arse." He nudged his horse to turn away and rode hastily toward the blackened trees.

Before he could cross the landmark, a lone horseman rode toward them. It was a Buchanan messenger, Banny, an elder man who all but retired from taking to arms.

"Laird, Aymer sent me with an urgent message," Banny said and handed him a scrap of parchment. He turned his horse and headed back through the row of blackened trees.

Breckin unsealed it and read the one line. *MacNab needs your aid. He bids ye to come.*

"Damnation," he uttered. "I just want to get home and… Gideon, turn around. We need to head to MacNab's. He's called for us."

"What does he want?" Gideon said grumpily.

Breckin shrugged. "Who the hell knows? Let us get there. We shall return home on the morrow." He was in a foul temperment now—as far from amiable as could be. God help whoever instigated his wrath because he would use his sword with the full measure of his strength behind it.

After riding hell-bent to the MacNabs with a league to go, Breckin had to slow their progression. Their horses were winded and needed rest. The last thing he wanted to do was to delay his return, but he couldn't risk harming or exhausting their already spent horses further.

"We will take rest here. If we are fortunate, the MacNab sentry will see us and send Daniel to us and we needn't ride further." Breckin dismounted and led his horse to a small stream. His soldiers did likewise. They settled down to take a rest and the night, even though it was a bonny one, did little to allay them.

He settled down on a bedroll next to Gideon, who handed him a flask of ale. Breckin took a swig and handed it back. "I am filthy, by God, and do not think I shall be able to wash away the stench of MacDoughall's blood."

Gideon laughed. "Aye? I know what ye mean, for I detest when they bleed on me." His commander handed him a helping of whey bread which he'd broken into two pieces. "Eat something. It might make ye less disagreeable."

Breckin raised a brow at his comrade. "Disagreeable? I tell ye if the MacNabs are being attacked again by the MacLarens, disagreeable will be as mild as I shall be."

"Aye, aye. Ye want to take arms against them and now have a wee bit of bloodlust in ye. About bloody time, because they deserve it, not only for attacking our ally but also because they reneged on a promise. Och, Laird, ye should be gladdened ye did not marry Danella. She cannot hold a candle to Lady Eva's beauty or spirit."

"Ye are so right, Gideon. I probably should thank the MacLarens for saving me from a deplorable fate. Honest to God, though, I tire of these petty wars, the needy clans, and the alliances. Have I not given more than I should to such causes? I think a change is in order. When I can obtain vengeance for Marian, if need be, then I can ensure our clan's prosperity."

"What do ye mean? Are ye going to retract our alliances?"

"Nay, but I need to make our allies understand that I am not at their beck and call. They will also need to support us. We will no longer be their only support. Changes are coming, my friend. I can smell it in the air."

"Good. 'Tis about damned time. Och, but I tell ye this, sometimes seeking vengeance costs more than what ye are willing to give." Gideon stood. "Someone comes."

Breckin got to his feet and surveyed the riders coming at them. The MacNabs rode hastily toward them and barely stopped their horses before dismounting.

"Daniel, I received your message. What is the trouble?"

Breckin asked.

The MacNab laird scoffed. "What message? I sent ye no message. My sentry reported men on our land and I came to find out who ye were."

"Ye sent no message?"

"Nay," Daniel said with angst. "Did I not just say that? We have had no troubles since ye handled that matter for us. Why?"

"We were given a message saying ye needed aid." Breckin gave a glance to Gideon and then signaled to his men. "We must leave, Daniel. I fear that we have been lured away from our land and our home might be attacked. We must make haste." Without a farewell, Breckin retrieved his horse and mounted. He rode in the direction of the blackened trees, followed by the Buchanan soldiers.

On the ride toward his home, apprehension filled him. He worried that his family, Eva, and his clan's men and women were in jeopardy. If one person was harmed, there would be hell to pay. Breckin was in the mood to slaughter a field full of his enemies.

CHAPTER FOURTEEN

WITH BRECKIN GONE, Eva decided to keep herself busy. Now that she'd gotten the lay of the land and her bearings, she would make progress with the longhouse, befriending some of the clan's women, and taking care of Breckin's brothers.

She arose early that morn and groaned because most of her life, she'd been a late riser. Since she'd arrived in the Highlands, she had begun to awaken earlier, which she supposed was a good thing. She had much to accomplish before Breckin returned, all in hopes of winning his heart. Somehow, she would prove her worthiness.

She hurried through her morning tasks and rushed to the main area of Clare's cottage. Through the small window casement, she realized the sun had not risen yet. It was earlier than she'd thought. Eva found Clare setting a large pot over the fire in the kitchen's hearth. When she reached the table, she sighed and hoped her conversation with the woman was successful.

"Good morn, Clare. Will you join me? I hope to discuss something with you."

Clare pulled out a loaf of bread that she'd wrapped in a thin cloth and set it on the table. "Aye, ye can talk to me whilst I eat my morning fare." She sliced the bread and smeared a jellied sauce on it. "This is a busy day, for the shearing of the sheep will be at its busiest and I promised to aid the women who wash the wool."

"I suspect that you have your hands full with Breckin's brothers too." Eva took a piece of bread and poured herself a little mead in an empty cup. "Now that they have returned from Willa's cottage."

"Ye do not speak a falsity there. Those lads are tough to keep track of, and to be honest, I am getting a mite old to be running after them. I tire of it."

"I thought so, *ah,* not that you are too old to run after them but that they are hard to keep track of. I have a proposition for you..." Eva wasn't sure if the woman would agree so she rambled. "If you teach me how to cook, I shall take the lads off your hands. They can live with me and Breckin when we move to the end of the island. The longhouse should be finished soon and I was going to start getting it ready. There is plenty of room for us and a place for the lads to sleep."

Silence.

Eva's shoulders tensed as she waited for Clare's answer. She needed to learn how to cook and the only person who spoke to her besides Willa was Clare. There was much to be said in learning new things and she wasn't against doing something for herself—she'd just never had to—until she reached the Highlands.

"Ye mean to say that I shall be free of them completely?" Clare raised her eyes and intently stared at her.

"If that is what you want, then yes. Breckin is their brother and should be responsible for them, and being his wife, I am related to them now. The chore of watching them should not fall solely upon you. I will be gladdened to keep watch on them until Breckin returns. You will have your cottage to yourself and perhaps a little peace."

Clare continued to stare hard at her and then her chin bobbed slightly. "'Tis been some time since I have had the cottage to myself. I agree, Eva, and shall be pleased to show ye how to cook. When will they stay with ye? Because ever since they returned from Willa's, Connor has been a bear, and with his brother recovering, Caden has been pacing about with nothing to do."

Eva chuckled. "Connor is just cross because he cannot walk on his leg yet. I shall put Caden to work and find something to keep him occupied. Are the lads still sleeping?"

"Connor is in their room and Caden went to visit Aymer."

"Are you making stew for supper?" She peered at the pot.

"I am. Since ye want to learn, ye shall prepare it this day. I will tell ye what to do."

Eva spent most of the morning following Clare's directions. She made a rabbit stew and learned how to make basic bread. Cooking was much easier than she'd thought it would be and, she decided, it might even be fun. After she'd taken the bread out of the small oven, she set it on the table to cool. Clare had been patient with her and didn't rush her through the tasks which helped Eva to remember all that she'd spoken and the order of the tasks.

"That is how ye can prepare supper. Stew is the easiest to make. Och, there are other meals too. On the morrow, I will show ye how to make a delicious pottage for the morning fare," Clare said as she cleaned up the kitchen area. "A hearty meal is best to begin the day. We shall meet early in the morn before all rise."

Eva nodded. "My thanks, Clare, for your help and for showing me how to cook. I look forward to learning more from you. I need to go now. I do not want to be late for Mass."

"Father Murphy usually begins about midday, so aye, ye should get going."

Eva helped to clean up the table. "Are you attending Mass?"

"I would. Och, I promised to help the washerwomen. This day will be busy enough with the sheep shearing. I am sure God will understand my absence." Clare waved to her and headed for her bedchamber.

The day was warm, so Eva forwent her cloak but grabbed her tartan in case the wind picked up. She walked to the bridge with a spring in her step. On the other side, she ambled to the church. Several people were entering, though some lingered outside. Eva entered and reached the first pew before the altar where she genuflected toward the altar before she sat next to an elderly man. She bowed her head in prayer, asking that Breckin return unharmed and soon, because though she was loath to admit it, she missed him. The church was such a place of solace, she felt serenity steal over her.

Soon, Father Murphy entered and approached the altar. He stood and gazed at the people who had attended the midday mass and smiled before he began his liturgy and spoke at good length about sins, forgiveness, and kindness. Then he peered at her for some reason and motioned to her. Eva was astounded that he'd purposely chosen her for whatever he had in mind. She rose and walked to the altar, then stood by the side.

"Good folks, we shall now hear a psalm from our beloved lady, Lady Buchanan."

Eva felt the heat overtake her face. "Oh, nay, Father, I cannot sing in front of so many," she whispered low, hoping no one would hear her.

"But ye must, lass. Come now, sing a psalm for us. Your voice is bonny and the clan needs to hear ye sing. Send your voice to the heavens. Will ye withhold God's blessing from them?" The priest winked at her and his grin widened, spreading across his face.

She thought she'd fall over as utter panic set in. But Father Murphy waved her onward and cajoled her to sing. "How about ye sing *Dies Irae*, Milady? If ye need to, face the altar when ye sing. Our ears will rejoice at the bonny song."

Eva's embarrassment trembled through her but she nodded and faced the altar. She kept her gaze on the wooden cross that sat on a table behind the altar. *"Nay, Lord, not thus! White lilies in the spring, Sad olive-groves, or silver-breasted dove, Teach me more*

clearly of Thy life and love, Than terrors of red flame and thundering…"
Her voice echoed in the church and when she finished the song,
silence met her.

With a deep breath, she bowed her head to the priest and
returned to her seat on the first bench. When she turned, all eyes
bore into her as if the parishioners were stunned. Eva sat and
clenched her shaking hands. When Mass ended, she hurried out
of the church and weaved her way through the exiting people.

Outside, she took gulps of air, and as she walked onward, her
body ceased its trembles and nervousness. She couldn't believe
Father Murphy had made her sing in front of everyone. Eva had
never had an audience before. She only sang because she loved
the songs and the beautiful words.

As she stood there trying to calm herself, she spotted Aymer
walking toward her. He didn't appear jovial but had an unsettled
look on his face, evidenced by the purse of his lips and pull of his
brows.

"There ye be, Milady," Aymer, the gate watchman said when
he reached her on the lane. "I was looking for ye."

"Good day, Aymer. Why were you looking for me?"

"I hoped ye would find the lad Caden and keep him busy.
Aye, for he is intent on pulling pranks on the clan this day. By
God, he has done some tomfoolery. Usually, the lads do such
deeds on Hunt the Gowk day, aye, but alas, they were being
punished then and had no time to attend to such antics. Caden
has told every person that he'd crossed this day that someone was
searching for them and to find whoever it was… He told the
same falsehood to at least ten people. Och, no one is searching for
anyone. The lad has our clansmen and women scampering
around for naught."

Eva withheld the urge to giggle at such a folly because the
gate watchman seemed angered by what Caden had done. "Hunt
the Gowk? I never heard of such a thing."

"'Tis usually done on the first day of April, but as I said the
laird punished the lads because one of them fell through the

stable roof. Hunt the Gowk means 'hunt the cuckoo' or foolish person because that's what they are for falling for such a prank." Aymer pressed back the tangled mane of his hair and chortled.

"I would help you but I am headed to the market. When I return, I will find Caden and keep him busy and out of trouble." Eva was about to march on but turned back to Aymer. "I wanted to ask… The horses my da sent… Are they still in the stable? Breckin has not given them away yet, has he?"

"Oh, Gracious God, I plum forgot to tell him about them. My brother, Alton, took them and I suppose they are still in the stables. I can ask him. Why, Milady?"

"I wish to give Caden and Connor each their own horse and I changed my mind. I will keep one of them for myself, the horse I used during my trek here." Eva smiled at the man who seemed confused by her request but then he nodded and seemed to accept her order.

"I shall tell my brother Alton to pick the horses for ye."

"My thanks, Aymer. I shall return soon." Eva waved to Aymer and continued onward on the lane. Ahead, she saw Ise-Olcan who barked in greeting. "Go home." But the dog wouldn't heed her command and followed instead. Eva didn't mind so much that the dog trailed her.

As she passed the encampment of the ailing, she lowered her head sorrowfully because she hadn't anything to give them. None of the sick greeted her or waved but hunched over and seemed unaware of her presence. Many of them covered themselves with tattered cloth, even over their faces. She suspected they did so to hide the bumps and atrocious evidence of their infirmity. Eva pulled her tartan tightly around her and hurried past, almost sprinting ahead. She reached the market and had a single purpose for attending but now, another thought came to her.

She stopped by Master Amos's building, commanded that Ise-Olcan stay outside the door, and stepped inside. He was speaking with someone so she didn't interrupt him. While she waited for him, she perused the section that seemed to be where the kitchen items were stored. There were a good many items and she didn't know where to begin in selecting a pot or other needed objects.

He finished with the person on whom he was waiting, before he turned to her. "Milady Buchanan, 'tis good to see ye again. Can I help ye?"

She explained her dilemma and sighed heavily when she finished. "I need to purchase items for my kitchen but I do not know where to begin… What is needed for cooking and such?"

"Oh, 'tis easy enough, Milady. Ye need a good cooking pot, and some good spoons with long handles. Maybe a long spit to cook meat on. I shall show ye." Amos walked toward a section of his stall and motioned to items stacked in crates.

"I am going to have a good many items to offer for sale, Master Amos. Can we do a trade or perhaps barter for what I need?"

"Aye, of course, Milady. I can pull some items that will be useful to ye and hold them aside until ye bring your trade."

"There is another matter… Any items that you sell, I want you to use my share of the coins to buy foodstuff and clothing for the people in the encampment down the lane. Can you do that for me?"

Amos's bushy eyebrows rose in awe. He shook his head and cleared his throat. "Ye want me to buy foodstuff and take it to them, Milady? I fear no one will go near enough to them, even me because we know not what ails them. 'Tis risky what ye ask."

"I do and before you reject my offer, I hope that you will do your good Christian duty to those poor people. All I ask is that you buy bread and food items for them. They can use warm blankets and garments too. You can take the items and leave them close by if you do not want to get near them. And if you do, I wish them not to know who gave them the alms. Will you do that for me?"

Amos pressed his hands over his dusty tunic and nodded. "Very well, Milady, but only because ye are the laird's wife and I cannot refuse to do your bidding. I will buy the items and have them delivered to the needy as ye requested but shall leave them nearby where they can find them."

"Good. I will be going through my things in the next day or so and shall have them delivered to you for the trade. I shall send a list of the items that I wish to sell and expect an accounting when next I see you. Once I repay for the cooking items, all other coins should go toward the food and items for the ailing. My thanks, Master Amos."

He bowed. "'Tis a pleasure, Milady, doing business with ye. I will have my lad bring the kitchen items ye asked for after I receive the goods from ye."

"Wonderful, have them delivered to the longhouse on the island. 'Tis the farthest abode there and cannot be missed. Or ask Aymer, he shall direct you," she said and gave a quick wave.

Back outside, Ise-Olcan barked and seemingly skipped beside her as she made her way back to the bridge. Halfway along the lane, the dog took off, and Eva assumed she was going home.

When she crossed the bridge, she saw Aymer speaking to Caden. The poor lad had his head lowered and it was apparent he was being reprimanded for his earlier jest. Eva stopped near them and waited for Aymer to cease his tirade. "Aymer, I will see to Caden now. I need you to fetch Connor for me and bring him to the longhouse. We shall spend some time there this afternoon."

"Aye, Milady," he said and walked away ahead of her.

She fixed her gaze on the boy. He had an expression of chagrin on his face and wouldn't meet her gaze until she lifted his chin with her fingertips. "I heard what you did earlier." She kept herself from laughing but, truly, it was somewhat humorous. She was sure her mirth shone in her eyes. "Let us keep you out of trouble. I need some help at the longhouse and there is something that I want to talk to you and Connor about. Come along." Eva walked next to him and Caden was oddly quiet. Of the two brothers, he was the talker and Connor was the silent, pensive one.

But then he surprised her when he said, "Am I in trouble, Eva?"

"Oh, no, not at all. I am going to be setting up the longhouse and want to bring some of my things inside. I need a strong lad like you to help me." She smiled now to show that she wasn't disappointed with him.

Caden tugged the neckline of his tunic and nodded. "Aye, I can help ye. What about Connor? He is testy because he has naught to do."

"Well then, we shall find something for him to do too." They reached the longhouse and Eva opened the door. "Lawrence said the house was finished. There's a remarkable difference on the outside. Come and see the inside."

The boy peeked his head in the door and peered around before stepping in. She thought, perhaps, he was searching for spiders. It had taken her a bit of time to feel confident enough that she wasn't about to find another one crawling on her, but Lawrence and the other workers had cleared them all out when they'd fixed the roof and walls. Now Caden said, "Aye, ye should have seen it when our uncle lived here."

She smiled at Caden and meandered through the home. She couldn't stop looking at all the changes. It was like a different house.

Now, the kitchen area was fitted with a nice-sized hearth and worktable. The floorboards were swept and cleaned, and a wall had been erected to give all of them privacy in the sleeping areas.

Before she got to the additional rooms she'd requested of Lawrence, Aymer entered with Connor on his back. He lowered the lad to the ground and helped him sit on the floor.

"Oh, I am gladdened you are here, Connor. My thanks, Aymer, for bringing him."

Aymer gave a wave and left the house.

Eva grabbed Caden's arm and motioned for him to sit next to his brother. Then she sat on the floor and faced them. "Whilst we are here, I wanted to talk to you about possibly living here with me and Breckin. I already spoke to Clare about it and if you want to…"

Both lads appeared pleased by her news and they smiled.

"Ye mean it, Eva? Ye want us to stay here?" Caden asked.

"I do, but you must promise not to pull pranks on me. You must do your best not to cause trouble for your brother. If you want to be part of our family, you must act like good family members." She paused, letting her words take effect before continuing.

The boys nodded eagerly.

"And I have one more gift for you… My da sent horses, and at first, I did not want them, but I changed my mind. I asked Aymer to arrange to select a horse for each of you and one for me. Perhaps when we are bored, you can teach me to ride properly. Do you know how to ride?"

"Aye, we have ridden but not a lot because Breckin says we must earn it," Connor said.

"Then I sadly must agree with him. You will earn the privilege of riding the horses by doing good and not getting into trouble. And, of course, you will need to each care for your horse. Make sure it's fed, watered, groomed and…whatever else you do with horses. I'm not sure. But you will have to be." She chuckled lightly. "Now, whilst we are here, Caden, will you help me bring in some items from outside?"

He nodded. "But what will Connor do?"

She turned to his brother. "Can you hop outside? You can keep us company while we go through the carts."

"Aye, Milady." He grinned.

"Eva. Call me Eva." She helped him rise and kept hold of his arm as they made their way outside. At the back of the longhouse where the carts were stored, she settled him nearby on a grassy spot.

"I want to go through the carts, look at every item, and figure out what I want to keep." Eva whipped the tarp from over the first cart. Dust streamed through the air around her. She blinked and sneezed. The boys giggled and she tossed them a grin before she peered at her belongings.

Fond memories came as she went through the objects. Her dear da had sent many household effects: a dissembled table, two long benches, and a rolled carpet from the small solar next to the great hall. There were at least ten candle holders but she only kept five. The rest she put in a pile for Master Amos.

There were also two oil lamps and a container that held the olive oil used to keep them alight, chamber pots, small crates of candles, ornate jars and jugs, and various other household items that dear Luella must have included for the keeping of her home.

The second cart held her bed and a few small tables, all of which had been disassembled and needed to be put back together. She hoped with all her heart that the bed fit in her and Breckin's bedchamber. There were sacks stuffed with blankets, embroidered tablecloths, small supper cloths, and other material items. She'd have to go through those later when she had time to sort them.

She and Caden moved all the items to Conner. She found a few cloths in one of the wagons for him to use to clean the road dust from things before they were moved into the house. He set to work and she and Caden moved all the bigger pieces she wanted to keep into the house. She placed them where she thought they should go. Even with disassembled tables and beds, the longhouse was beginning to look like a home.

They tired themselves with all the activity and the heat of the day had them overtaxed. She brushed her hands together to wipe off the dust and swiped the sweat from her forehead before setting her hands on her hips and looking at the boys. Exhausted, for once they were still. But they deserved a reward.

"I think that is enough work for this day. Why do we not go to the loch and cool off?"

"How are we going to get Conner there?" Caden asked.

"We shall find him a good walking stick. I will help him too." Eva gave her hand to him and pulled him to stand. "We shall take it slow, Connor. If it hurts too much, I shall have Aymer come and fetch you."

She supported Connor on one side and Caden supported him on the other. He seemed capable of hopping along. When they reached the guardhouse, Aymer ceased speaking to the man he stood with and rushed forward.

"Milady, why did ye not send Caden for me? I would have come and got Connor."

"We are headed to the loch."

Aymer knelt on his knee and Connor got on his shoulders. "'Tis a good day to be by the loch and many have sojourned there. This has to be the hottest day but fret not, for the heat shall not last long."

They walked together toward the opposite end of the island where a stream met the mouth of the loch. Some of the clan's people had had the same idea and swam in the shallow areas by the bank. The lads pulled off their tunics and belted tartans at their hips. Caden ran in a sprint into the water, splashing with force all those nearby. Eva laughed when he fell and sank beneath the surface.

Aymer carried Connor into the water. "Go easy now, lad, and do not reinjure yourself."

Eva set the tartan she'd wrapped around her waist earlier on the ground and slipped off her slippers. She already felt cooler but still hastened to the water. She was glad that she'd worn one of her less-fancy gowns now because this one was about to get wet. She hoped it didn't get ruined. But it was still long and kept her from rushing into the water like Caden. With slow steps, she moved until the water finally reached her waist. Then she ducked down and thoroughly doused herself.

"Oh, this is pleasant."

Aymer laughed from the water's bank. "I need to get back to my duty, Milady."

When Eva turned back to him, Aymer was gone.

"Now is a good time to practice, Milady. I will show ye some defensive movements," Caden said and swam toward her. "It will not hurt as much if ye fall in the water."

"Oh? You think you can make me fall?" She teased him and he chortled loudly. Eva wanted to learn and Caden seemed enthusiastic about teaching her.

"Ye need to come at me like this," Caden said and showed her how to sneak attack him. "Try to capture my arms." As she went for him, he grabbed her and tossed her to the side and she fell into the water. Repeatedly, they performed the tactic, and still, she was unable to thwart him. But Eva wouldn't give up and tried again. "Ye are getting it, Milady. Have another go."

Suddenly, she heard Breckin's voice. He ran into the water, gripped Caden's arm with force, and flung him away from her, then he grabbed his arm again to keep him from fleeing. His face reflected his ire and Caden cried out.

"Sweet Mary! What are ye doing, Breckin? Why are ye attacking Caden? Release him at once!" Eva stood with her hair dripping on her face and her hands set on her hips. Her glare surely let him know that she was displeased with his abrupt arrival.

CHAPTER FIFTEEN

"RELEASE HIM! I'LL bloody well thrash him." Breckin let go of his brother and turned his scowl on Eva. "He was hurting ye." When he saw firsthand how forceful his brother was being, Breckin had only wanted to aid her. It seemed that he wasn't privy to whatever it was that they were doing and now he felt foolish.

"I asked your brothers to teach me how to protect and defend myself," Eva scoffed and marched with vigor from the water. But then she turned back and helped Connor to the bank. He hobbled next to her and she set him gently on the slope at the water's edge.

Breckin hurried after her and stood on the beach of the loch with consternation. "Why in God's good name do ye need to protect yourself? Is someone threatening ye? Tell me and I'll—"

She shook her head vehemently. "No, no one is browbeating me, Breckin. I asked your brothers to show me defensive tactics for no other reason but because I am a Buchanan."

He stared at her as if she'd gone addled. "Because ye are a Buchanan? Explain what ye mean by that, lass. Why do ye need to protect yourself?"

"You probably have many enemies, what with all the warring you do. Just look at you, covered with blood and Lord knows what else... I thought I should learn how to defend and protect myself in the event that your enemies make it past the blackened trees. Most of the women in your clan probably know how to fight and I thought…" She seemed to sink in front of his eyes as her shoulders slumped. "Never mind, Breckin, it matters not and it was a foolish notion. Come, lads, we will go to Clare's cottage and have our supper." She helped Connor to rise, assisted him by supporting his body, and walked away before he could respond.

His jaw twitched as he kept quiet. Breckin watched her leave, unsure if he should go after her or give her time to get over her pique. He chose the latter, discarded his garments, and left them in a pile on the bank. Then he sprinted into the water and swam a good distance from land, and enjoyed the coolness that took the heat from his body.

As he floated just below the surface of the water, Breckin closed his eyes and tried to release the tension of his mad dash home. When he'd arrived, there was no threat as he'd suspected. Aymer reported that a scrappy lad had delivered the message but he'd hailed off before he could get his name. Whoever sent that message had some intent, but what? Why would they say MacNab wanted a meeting but hadn't? If they wanted him away from his holding, what purpose would it have served if they'd done nothing? He was perplexed by the event and needed to find out if he had another enemy to put to the blade.

On his arrival, he'd expected to find cottages burned, his brethren killed, and his home desecrated. But nothing was amiss. All the buildings were intact, his clansmen and women were secure, and his holding as it had been when he'd left. When he crossed the bridge, he'd assured himself that all was well. Then he commanded that triple the sentry be sent out to secure his land in case the threat remained. If there was foulness afoot, he'd be ready for it. Once he'd been certain his clan was safe, he went in search of his wife. That was a terrible mistake. He should have bathed and met with Aymer for his report—anything but confront Eva.

He chuckled now at the absurdity of his action. He should

have known his brother would never hurt Eva. He was a lad, after all, and certainly not capable of really harming her. Caden had yet to learn to put aside his emotions when tarrying or when he wielded weapons. That was something he needed to work on with his brother. Connor, on the other hand, didn't allow emotions to rule him when he practiced arms.

No matter what their faults as individuals, collectively the two needed training and he'd been remiss in guiding them.

When he finished bathing, he redressed and instead of going to Clare's as he'd intended, he sauntered toward the barracks. The barracks were crowded since most of the men had recently returned from the excursion with him, except for the score of men sent on sentry duty. Some rested, some caroused, and some sat quietly eating their late meal. Breckin greeted the men as he passed, and near the back, he discarded his garments in the laundry pile and opened a trunk that held a little of his belongings. Within, he kept a dagger that had belonged to his father, a kerchief of his mother's, and an ornate hair comb that had belonged to Marian.

Breckin cherished these items and kept them as a reminder of what he'd lost. With a shake of his head, he placed the items back in, pulled out a tan tunic, and pulled it over his head. Then he wrapped a clean tartan at his waist, belted it, but forwent strapping his sword to himself. Being home afforded the protection of his brethren so he left it on the bunk he usually used.

He was now ready to face Eva. With hurried steps, he walked the lane toward his aunt's cottage. Since he'd been gone longer than a fortnight, he wondered what his wife had been up to whilst he'd been away.

At the cottage, he pulled the door open and entered. His family sat around the table eating their supper. Without a word, Breckin joined them at the table and pulled a trencher toward him. He then piled it on with vegetables, bread, cheese, and pieces of ham. His stomach rumbled at the sight of the meal because he didn't eat so lavishly while on the trail.

No one spoke to him when he joined them and as soon as his brothers finished their meal, they hastened from the table and retreated to their bed chamber. Connor was somewhat slower than Caden in leaving, but he hobbled away and appeared not to want to be left behind.

Clare must've sensed the hostility in the air because she ate quickly too. But she didn't leave the cottage and busied herself with cleaning up after the meal. Breckin finished his meal and when he looked up, Eva rose and, without a word to him, walked toward their bedchamber. Damnation, he mistook what was happening at the loch. Surely she should understand that and give him a chance to explain. With that thought in mind, he set his trencher atop the others in the pile for discarding and reached the chamber he shared with Eva.

He found her sitting on the bed. "Eva?"

She peered down at her folded hands on her lap. "I should go and ensure the lads are settled for the night." She made to get up.

"Await. I…reacted poorly, did I not? When I saw Caden hurting ye, I saw naught but the need to protect ye. Och, I am gladdened to know that ye take defending yourself seriously. My ire was unaccountable."

She stood and he stepped near her. "It is not me you should be apologizing to."

Breckin sighed because he'd meant to make amends for his show of force. "I will speak to Caden later. Right now, I just want to kiss ye." He leaned close and took hold of her face. She seemed so delicate and perhaps fragile in his hands, and yet, she'd taken to practicing defensive tactics. His wife surprised him at every turn. Breckin set his mouth on hers and the slightest touch caused his blood to heat.

Eva pulled away and stepped back, out of his embrace. "I am gladdened you are finally home and that you appear to have suffered no injuries."

"I am well enough. And ye, how did ye fare whilst I was

gone? Did ye miss me?" He flashed a grin at her but she maintained a serious mien.

"Since you are the only person who speaks to me here, well, besides your brothers, Willa, Father Murphy, and some of the men who direct me... None of the women, though. I suppose I did miss you because it has been a wee bit lonely. I should go and make sure the lads understand that you are not angry with them. You might not realize this, Breckin, but they revere you and only want your attentiveness, just as I do."

Before she could flee, he grabbed her arm. "Eva, what do ye mean by that? No one talks to ye? Has my clan been unkind or mean-spirited? Tell me and I will speak to them."

She stepped backward until she reached the bed, and sat. "I shall never belong here and understand that now. Your clanspeople are wary of outsiders and are guarded even though I have been here for some time. Surely, they know that I am your wife but... Perhaps the women in your clan are just unfriendly."

Breckin was disheartened at the tone in her voice and sadness in her eyes. He should have done more to gain her acceptance by his clan's men and women. "'Tis my fault, lass. I thought I made myself clear when I discussed with them that ye are my wife and they should honor ye."

"It does not matter, Breckin, whether they befriend me or not. I really must go."

Breckin sat back on the small bed they shared and sighed wearily. He thought he'd confront an attack on his land upon his homecoming, instead, he was challenged with an even greater force—his wife's ire.

He left the cottage and made the rounds of checking in with the watch, gaining any reports from Aymer whilst he was gone, ensuring the training regimen was in place for the next day with Gideon, and taking in the night air. The walk about the island brought forth a calming mood.

By the time he returned to Clare's cottage, his bonny wife was asleep. He wasn't too pleased because he'd missed her, her body, and her touch, in the time he'd been gone. He refrained from awakening her, however. He might have been daft this day when he thought his young brother was attacking Eva, but he wasn't as dimwitted as to wake her because he wanted to seek pleasure.

He settled next to her and closed his eyes, content at least to be home, lying beside her.

In the morning, he awakened to find his lovely wife gone, her side of the bed cold, and an uncomfortable silence within the cottage. Breckin was well chagrined with himself of late. Eva hadn't asked to be put in such a position where his clan's men and women ignored her. It wasn't right and he knew that he was to blame.

Not only was Eva's acceptance into his clan troublesome, but he'd also neglected his brothers. It was time to remedy both situations. He nodded firmly at his thoughts and hastened from the room, intent to find her and his brothers.

Clare met him before he could leave the cottage. "Breckin, 'tis gladdened we are that ye are home. We should speak about your wife…"

"We should? Why?" He sat at the table and poured himself a small helping of mead. "What kept her occupied whilst I was gone?"

"Eva is resourceful, I shall give her that. She made an agreement with me…to teach her how to cook. She's a quick learner, I must say, and I am sorry that I was so—"

"Sorry for what?"

Clare sat across from him. "I was distant when she came but I see the worthiness in her and I am gladdened ye married her. She shall be good for you and ye deserve happiness, Breckin. Aye, Eva will help abate the pain that has had a hold of your heart. Afore ye get angry with me, ye should know that the clan is beginning to accept her."

"She does not know that."

Clare absently smoothed her hands over the tabletop, collecting the crumbs that had scattered about from the morning fare. "I am not one to talk behind anyone's back. Och, whilst ye were gone, Father Murphy made her sing before the congregation. All those at Mass were taken aback by her beautiful singing. Since then, most have attended Mass now in hopes that she will sing again. And then there is the arrangement she made with Amos, the merchant."

He frowned sternly, wondering what arrangement his wife could have made with the cantankerous man. "And that is?"

"Well, she wanted to fill your home and so she trades with him for items she wants or needs, like the kitchen items and furniture."

Breckin raised his brows at that. "Seems she has been busy."

"Aye, indeed she has. There is more. Och, I should let her tell ye about it."

He nodded. "I wish she would have told me all this. She should be the one telling me about her accomplishments. Och, I deem her to be humble and free of vanity. She does not realize how beautiful she is or how kindhearted." Breckin chuckled to himself.

"Perhaps that is why many of the women here have kept their distance—because of her beauty. She might be unassuming but the women are envious of her and fear their husbands might stray if she shows any interest in them. We both know that she wouldst not betray ye like that, though, because she seems devoted to ye. Besides that, ye will have some decent meals for I showed her how to make your favorite foodstuff."

He recalled her saying that she didn't know how to cook or light a fire. The lengths that she went to in order to please him, brought forth a heavy sigh. He didn't know how to begin to thank her. "Did ye teach her to light a fire too?"

"Nay, but I think Lawrence might have, or perhaps it was Aymer. She has spent the afternoons at the longhouse and kept busy whilst ye were away and kept to herself. Your brothers sometimes attend to her, otherwise, she's been alone." Clare rose and busied herself tidying the kitchen. "Eva told me to tell ye to meet her at the longhouse later."

Breckin nodded to his aunt, muttered a farewell, and left.

On his walk to the longhouse, he wondered what she'd done to it. It was time they began their life together as man and wife, in their own home. This night, he planned to spend it with Eva so he could show her how much he'd missed her, appreciated her efforts, and how much he cared. Admittedly, in the short time she'd been part of his life, he couldn't see himself without her.

The closer he got to the cottage, the quicker his pace. On the approach, he noticed the new wood that covered the walls, the new thatch on the roof, and the solid steps leading to the door. Other than early morning insect sounds, it was quiet. He opened the door and stepped inside. Breckin stopped short at seeing the hearth, where she'd placed an elegant carpet on the floor, chairs, and tables. Near the kitchen sat a work table and a smaller dining table with benches on each side. There was a useful porcelain pitcher in the center with cups situated around it.

He ambled closer and smiled at the hominess of the abode. Eva had worked hard and made the place a home for them. Upon entering, he found the openness of the longhouse had been sectioned off and doors led to private chambers. As he made his way through the longhouse, he stopped at a closed door and opened it. Inside the room were what appeared to be parts of furniture that hadn't been put together. Breckin wondered if the items had belonged to Eva, and surmised they did.

A knock came and he turned to find Gideon standing in the opening of the doorway. "Laird, I thought I would find ye here." He took a step inside and looked around. "The place looks good."

"Aye. Can ye believe she accomplished all this whilst I was away?"

"Women can be skillful when they set their minds to it." Gideon chortled. "Aye, and it looks like Eva certainly put her skills to use."

"Come and help me..." Breckin returned to the bedchamber

and gestured to the pile of wooden furniture pieces. "I want to put this together."

"What is it?" Gideon asked, gazing at the various pieces of wood scattered on the floorboards.

"'Tis a bed. At least, that is what I think it to be." Breckin found the dowels that held the wood together and with Gideon's help, pieced the parts until they made the platform for the mattress which was rolled up in the corner, waiting to be filled with feathers or straw. "Help me get that filled. This night, I shall sleep in a comfortable bed. I only hope my wife is not too irked with me and joins me."

His comrade laughed. "Aye, all heard that she was miffed with ye because those that were at the loch spread the tale. Is she still irked with ye over your mishap with Caden?"

"I think she might be, 'tis likely," Breckin said testily.

"Well, she cannot be irked with ye when she sees what ye are doing here. Come, there's a large wardrobe in the hallway, shall we bring it in for her?"

Breckin helped Gideon carry the over-large piece of furniture inside the bed chamber. "'Tis hard to imagine that all this fits on the carts. She has some good pieces."

"Ye be fortunate that she furnished the longhouse and ye need not spend your coin to do so."

A noise came from the front of the longhouse and he left the bedroom to meet Eva as she entered. She set down a pail of water on the table she must've just retrieved. Without a word, Gideon gave a wave and departed. His brothers were nowhere to be seen and he wondered if they'd returned to his aunt's cottage.

"Ye came. Clare said ye wanted me to meet ye here but I thought ye still might be ireful with me and would not come."

"No, I understand that you were only concerned for me."

"Where have ye been all day?" He ambled toward the kitchen area and snatched the pitcher from the table. Breckin retrieved cups and dunked one in the pail of clean water on the worktable. "Are ye thirsty? The day has grown warm."

She nodded and accepted the cup that he offered. "Just walking about and visiting Willa but she's often busy."

"Eva, the longhouse is…looks homey. Well, ye made it a home. I have not had a home since my parents passed… What ye have done here is remarkable…" His voice pitched with emotion because he hadn't anticipated to have such a place or even what it would mean to him. It was a place he hadn't ever expected to have—a place which could be filled with his family, a sanctuary of sorts that offered privacy from his needful clan.

"I hope you do not mind, but I used some of my belongings to furnish it." Eva set her cup down on the table and meandered through the longhouse.

Breckin followed her and she entered the sleeping chamber. "Of course, I did not mind, Eva. I hoped ye would make use of your possessions because this is your home too." He stood back watching her reaction. "I put together the bed with Gideon's help."

"Oh, you even put up the canopy. I had thought not to use it but it looks elegant, does it not? It might be out of place and too much for the size of the room. Perhaps we should remove it." She left the room and returned with a sack filled with fabrics. "I shall make the bedding up after I have it restuffed with fresh straw and feathers."

"I will have Aymer handle that for ye." He helped her to place the coverings and blankets, fluffed the pillows, and smoothed the wrinkles. "This night, we shall sleep in our chamber and be together as we should be…"

Outside, Breckin heard his brother Caden shout, and frowned.

Eva cleared her throat. "You want to stay here this night? I told the lads that we would return to Clare's. They're probably here now, looking for me. But…there is something that I should tell you…" Eva sat on the bedside and looked down at her hands, which she clasped on her lap. "I am not sure if you will be angry."

Breckin sat beside her and took her hand. "What could ye

have done to anger me?"

"I arranged with Clare and told her that if she taught me how to cook, your brothers could live with us. I realize now that I should have spoken to you about it before I made such an arrangement with her. But she seems not to want the lads there."

"She is getting on in age and she is short-tempered." He pressed his hands on his knees and shifted his gaze to the doorway when his brother's footsteps pounded on the floor in the front of the longhouse, followed by the *thump whump shuffle* of Connor's limping steps. "Eva, if ye want the lads to stay here, then of course I agree. I probably would have suggested it once I spoke to Clare about it."

Her shoulders rose and then fell with her deep sigh. "My thanks for that. The lads need your guidance more than ever now. Being here will help them more than you know. They need family…us."

He didn't have time to respond, because Caden entered the room. "There ye are," he said. "Aunt Clare sent me to find ye. She said supper is on the table and ye should come and eat."

Breckin stood and took her hand, lifting her to stand. "Then let us onward to supper." He guided Eva from the longhouse and they walked toward his aunt's cottage. Caden sprinted ahead. "We will eat with them and then spend the night here by ourselves. We deserve at least one night alone."

Eva nodded. "One night, that is more than I could hope for."

CHAPTER SIXTEEN

AFTER THEIR MEAL, on their walk back to the longhouse, Eva kept quiet. She was gladdened that Breckin had returned even though he'd been somewhat high-handed with Caden at the loch. Still, that he was concerned for her also lightened her heart. It had taken most of the afternoon for her to understand why he'd reacted the way he had, and then she reproached herself for being so harsh toward him.

The night sounds came, that of insects and birds making their way home to their nests. Breckin captured her hand and held it as they meandered on the lane toward the end of the island. The solitude and being with him relaxed her, and yet, she could not wait to be in his arms.

When they reached the longhouse, she stepped through the threshold and pulled her tartan away from her shoulders. She dropped it on a chair as they passed by the hearth and made their way to the sleeping chamber. Eva opened the door and sighed at the sight of their private space. There, they would be as close as they could be. Nothing could interfere in their relations when they were inside their room, except, of course, their most guarded thoughts.

That made her consider the fact that Breckin had shared very little of himself with her. She didn't know what happened between him and his betrothed, why he kept a torch lit for her, how he'd lost his parents, and why he sought to war with just about every clan in the Highlands. One day, she might gain answers but for now, she had to be patient because he was a warrior and such men were reticent about their thoughts.

"Ye are quiet," he said as he discarded his garments. Breckin lit the few candles she'd placed within the room. Shadows danced in the corners of their chamber as they readied for bed.

When Eva turned around, she found him unclothed, completely unabashed at displaying his body. Words got caught in her throat as she peered at the manliness before her. His muscular torso shone in the candlelight, sinewy bulges of his arms and legs braced as he stood staring at her. She was uncertain whether she should go to him or await him by the bed. Or *in* bed.

"There will be no coyness betwixt us, lass."

Eva stepped closer to him and held out her arms. "True enough, Breckin. 'Tis just… We have not been together for some time and I am taken aback by your handsomeness."

"As I am with ye. Ye are a bonny lass, Eva, och your beauty is but a small part of the reason I find I'm utterly taken with ye."

A smile tugged at her lips. His words filled her heart with hope that someday he might be more than taken with her. Perhaps he might come to love her—dare she dream? "Do you mean that?"

"Of course I do. I never say anything that I do not mean. Now, can I kiss ye the way I have longed to all day…since my return?" He pulled her against him and settled his mouth on hers.

Eva kept her lips against his and the fervor of their passion sent desire through her. She turned her mouth over his as passion took hold. Nothing mattered at that moment: not her inane thoughts or his secretiveness—only the intense urges his caresses invoked. She stroked his bare, warm abdomen and chest, effectively kissing him and letting him know her need.

Breckin groaned and pulled back. "Ye make me burn for ye, lass." He scooped her in his arms and set her gently upon their bed. His hooded eyes seemed to darken. He joined her and pressed his hard body against hers, set his mouth back on hers, and used his hands to heighten her desire, knowing where to touch. He shifted his lips to her neck and said, "I love this part of you. Ye do not know how bonny ye are."

Her breath hastened when he pressed her womanhood with touches to excite her. Eva moaned softly as twinges flowed through her body, knowing what would come. He cupped her breast as his tongue explored her mouth and his other hand continued to caress her. She settled her hands on his shoulders and returned his sensual kisses. When he dislodged his mouth, he leaned back and smiled.

"I cannot cease looking at your lovely body," he said with a deep gruff tone. "But, aye, ye excite me and I cannot wait to be inside ye."

She gasped lightly as she peered back at him; his skin shone with the flickering candlelight, making him appear fierce, strong, and desirous. Breckin glided his hands along her body until they rested on either side of her neck. With gentle kisses, he slid his nose along her cheek and as he did so, he reached for her center again. When his fingers slid inside her, she drew an awed gasp, certain she would expire sooner than she hoped. He teased her with caresses to incite her undoing.

Eva was overwhelmed with the heat of their encounter and the feeling of his nakedness against her. As if she'd succumb if he didn't join with her, she pulled at his arms, wishing he would make her his. Breckin didn't seem to be in a hurry and shifted his head lower even though he'd alluded to wanting to join with her. He took the tip of her nipple into his mouth and used his warm tongue to spur its reaction. She could barely breathe as each touch, lick, and caress further lured her to plead with him to end her torment.

With her fingers spread in his soft locks of hair, she tugged at him. His hair fell forward as he dipped his head once again to her breasts. She continued to comb her fingers through his hair as he lavished his attention on her bosom.

Breckin groaned lightly and pulled away. "I vow, lass, ye weaken me to a state of… I have not the strength to resist ye and am filled with my need to take ye."

"This is…incredible, Breckin, but please… I cannot bear…to wait."

As his mouth retook hers, he shifted his body and entered her. She writhed her body beneath his, aiding him in filling her. She gasped with pleasure at the sensation of his hardness and the feeling of him so intimately inside her. As Breckin rocked against her, his breath came heavier. Each thrust sent her reeling, knowing she was edging closer to her culmination.

He groaned and the vibration of it against her fingers on his chest caused her to moan in response. Eva continued to pet him, to make desirous sounds of pleasure, and kissed his skin, wherever her mouth could reach.

"Hell, lass, ye best make haste because I cannot last much longer."

His deep voice and plea gripped her. She focused on the pleasurable sensations building within her. Chaotic twinges thronged her womanhood and she couldn't control her movements. Her legs shook with such force when his hard staff drove into her as he held onto her body. Eva's breath rasped and she practically squealed his name when pangs of ecstasy exploded within her. She called his name repeatedly and squeezed her eyes closed as her body acted of its own accord.

Breckin's movements became frenzied then as he thrust within her, set kisses on her face, and fanned her neck with his heavy breath. Eva gripped his biceps as his body crashed against hers. Within a moment, he fell against her, his moans rising to the ceiling. He tensed and stilled. Breckin became even more appealing at that moment, when he was vulnerable, depleted of everything he was, and became completely hers.

She peered at his handsome face, taut cheeks, tensed jaw, and his closed eyes. She pressed her hand to the side of his neck and caressed him, hoping to ease him. When he recovered, he opened his eyes and peered at her as if he wanted to say something but he stayed quiet. Breckin gently pulled away from her and settled beside her. After a bit of time, his heaving breath slowed and he shifted his hand, reaching for hers. She clutched his hand as he squeezed her fingers, saying without words what his heart wouldn't admit.

The chamber was quiet as if the world did not exist beyond their bedchamber door. She sighed contentedly but then heard him say, "Each time with ye, lass, is more pleasurable than the last."

To tease him, she uttered. "You need not woo me with your sweetened words, Breckin."

"Aye, and yet, I should...do."

They settled to sleep and Eva cuddled next to his warm body. She closed her eyes and dreamt of him saying the words she longed to hear. *I love you.* Those small words beheld such a tremendous meaning for her and she hoped he might be beginning to care for her as she was for him. Her dreams were filled with visions of happiness of being with Breckin.

She opened her eyes with a flutter and realized morning had come and Breckin was still lying beside her. She remained still. She appreciated that he wasn't a snorer and he practically made no noise whilst he slept. Eva considered his vulnerability while he slept and decided it made him even more handsome. He was only her husband in those moments, when nothing of the fearsome warrior showed.

Gently, she eased from the bed, hurried about her morning routine. She was getting used to caring for herself, but still, she missed having a maidservant to take care of the little things. After tidying the chamber, taking care of the chamber pot, and folding the garments in the basket by the door, she left and headed to the kitchen. Eva decided to light a fire, but had trouble with the flint. She didn't give up and finally got it to spark. The kindling lit quickly, and before long, a good fire built up beneath the small cauldron. She grabbed a jug of mead from the sideboard for her and Breckin, uncovered half a loaf of bread she'd made the day before, and cut it into slices. She crushed two plums, added a bit of spice to them for a spread, and set the small vessel on the table.

After she ate, Eva left the longhouse, intent on letting Breckin catch up on his sleep. She strolled along the lane, waved to Aymer before she crossed the bridge, and entered the church. It was early and no one was within the sanctuary. Eva said her prayers quickly before she left and retook the lane toward Willa's. When she reached her home, it appeared the woman was not inside so she continued and neared the encampment of the ailing.

On the stretch of lane before the camp, she heard the sound of a growl and a fierce squeal that sounded like one of the hogs the clan raised. It was odd to hear it here, away from the pens. But then she heard a shout and a young lad burst from the brush lining the path. He sprinted toward her with his eyes wide and a look of terror on his face.

"Run, Milady!" he called out.

She waited for him to reach her. What had him so afraid?

"A tree, Milady. We must climb a tree!" She took his hand, and together they sprinted to a nearby copse of trees. Only one branch was climbable and she boosted the lad upward until he reached a heavy enough branch. Then she pulled herself up and sat next to him, grateful she'd been adventurous enough as a girl to learn to climb trees.

This one shook now as a boar emerged from the thicket and threw himself against the trunk with a fierce squeal.

"Hang on, Milady!" The boy said. "Don't fall!"

She peered down at the beast. The distance to the ground was well over a man's height.

"Sweet Mary! I detest boars. They stink to high heaven and are one of God's crankiest creatures. My thanks, for the warning." Eva peered down at the brownish, coarse-haired animal. "Go away!" she shouted, hoping he'd run off but the boar continued to thrash the tree trunk.

The lad swung his legs as if he had no cares, but his voice

trembled when he said, "'Tis I that should thank ye, Milady. Ye saved me. Aye, I was not sure where to run. It would've run me down, aye."

"Let us hope the animal tires and leaves us. I wish I had something to fling at it and scare it away," Eva said, gripping the tree branch. "What is your name? I have not seen you before."

"I am called Hamish."

"Someone should come along soon, Hamish, hopefully."

Hamish dug inside the tartan tied around his body and revealed a small sling. "I have this, Milady, och only two rocks so our aim must be true." He handed it to her. "Ye have a better view of it. Go on…" He pressed the object into her hand.

Eva took the sling from him and set the rock. It was a good-sized stone, about half the size of her palm. She set it in the center of the leather pouch, pulled back, and released it. The rock missed its target but not by much. "Sweet Mary, this is harder than it looks. I shall try again."

Hamish handed her the other rock and she set it. "Aim true, Milady. Do not rush."

She took a calming breath, aimed the center of the sling at the horrid beast, and pulled back. When the tension was as far as it would go from the sling, she released it. The rock hit the boar square on its head. The creature squealed loudly and spun around, then ran off.

Eva almost shouted at the triumph. "We should wait a little to make sure it is gone."

"Ye did it, Milady. I could not even do that." He grinned and excitement shone in his eyes.

After a good bit of time passed, Eva eased herself down the tree and helped Hamish from the branch. "Should I walk you home?"

Hamish shook his head. "Nay, Milady, I am just going down the lane a wee bit."

"Be careful and keep watch."

She waved to Hamish and continued. When she reached the

encampment of the ailing, she noticed the foodstuff being shared with those around the fire. Seeing their hunger abated pleased her. She took an empty pot, retreated to the stream nearby, and filled it. After she returned, she set the pot on the fire to heat the water.

The young woman she'd met in her previous visit to the encampment drew near. She said, "Milady, it is kind of ye to visit." She pulled her cloak around her and sat on the other side of the fire.

"I wanted to check on you and see if you now had food."

"Aye, someone brings us food daily now and sets it in yonder basket. Do ye deem the laird helps us?" The young maiden dipped her chin.

"Perhaps he does," Eva said but wouldn't give herself away and wasn't the least bit disappointed to give Breckin the credit for her generosity. She was happy to help the ailing but she didn't want them to make a fuss over her aid.

Someone nearby strummed a stringed instrument and the ailing people seemed much more gleeful than they had the last time she'd visited. It made her happy too; Eva couldn't help herself and sang the words of a sweet song she'd learned from Brother Abrams. When she ceased singing, she rose.

"Ye are blessed by our Lord's Mother, Eva, and must come again to sing for us," Harriet said and smiled.

"I shall come again soon, Harriet. Take care of each other." Eva waved, walked off, and was pleased to see her efforts made a small difference in their lives. Even if no one could cure them of their ailment, at least they were no longer hungry.

She hurried along the trail and crossed the bridge, watchful still for the boar. But it didn't reappear.

When she saw Aymer, she waved at him, then stopped to warn him about the animal lest anyone else be attacked. He thanked her and volunteered to escort her the rest of the way, but she told him to stay at his post and continued onward until she reached the longhouse.

She heard Breckin speaking with someone inside, so she ambled around the back and decided to go through another cart. Only two remained unpacked as yet and she wanted to get the chore done so she could have Aymer take it to the market like the others.

Eva uncovered one of the carts and smiled when she spotted the basket that held all sorts of sewing items. She'd tried to learn how to sew when she was younger, but couldn't make a straight seam to save her life. She had spent many hours trying to perfect the skill, and yet, she'd never achieved the ability. But she would continue to try. She put the basket in the "keep" pile. Then she reached for a large silver bowl; it was heavier than she expected, and awkward to lift, and she dropped it. It clanged when it hit a small pile of other silver bowls still inside the cart.

"Eva? Are ye out here?" Breckin came through the door that led to the back.

The builders had put in a set of wooden steps as a way to get down from the rise. She turned hastily toward him and reached for the bowl, setting it next to the basket of sewing items that she wanted to keep. "I am sorry and did not mean to disturb you. I dropped a bowl and it made such a racket."

"I am gladdened ye are here. Where did ye hail off to this morn? Ye were gone when I awakened." He reached her and leaned against the cart.

"I took a walk, went to church, and visited the ailing on the other side of the bridge."

He visibly sighed. "I wish ye would not go near those people. Until Father Murphy hears from his order, we know not if they are contagious or what ails them. Best ye protect yourself."

"I do not get close enough to catch whatever they have. There is much to go through here and I wish to get it done this day." She reached for an ornate box that had burned etchings of a scroll over the top of the wooden box. It was a beautiful object, one which she hadn't seen before. She wondered if it was put with her belongings by mistake. With a press of her fingers, she let them linger over the bumpy design of the wood and smiled.

"What is that?"

She shrugged. "I know not and have never seen it before but 'tis heavy. Should I open it? It does not belong to me."

"Your da sent it to ye, so I say open it."

She did so and on the very top was a folded parchment. Eva retrieved it and held it, her heart heavy because she was uncertain what she would find written on it. She handed it to Breckin and peered at the coffer, filled with coins. "Read it for me?"

Breckin held it and, with a nod, opened the parchment. He read:

Dearest sprig, since you were a young lass, I never could explain the heartache I suffered when we lost your dear ma. Before she passed, she made me promise to love you as much as I could, along with your brothers. I fear I might have lacked a little on that pledge because I traveled and sought to win your affection by giving you your heart's desire.

I tucked away a bit of coin for you when you married. Since the king betrothed you, I thought no reason to give the coin to Alexander or your future husband. I bid you to use the wealth for whatever needs arise in your life. It should be more than enough to see you through. With deep sorrow, I am afraid that I will not likely peer upon your lovely face again. Be well, my sprig, love life, and all that comes. ~Da

Eva gently pressed her fingertips over the coldness of the silver coins. There was a good many in the coffer—likely a bloody fortune. Her father had never told her about his gift and she hadn't expected that he would give her riches upon her marriage. She was lost in thoughts of her life, how when her father left on his travels, she'd spent many a day by herself with only the servants to see to her needs. Her brothers had all gone off, seeking their lives, albeit in war, religion, or other manly pursuits. If she could have traded this wealth for his company, she would have done so in a heartbeat. Living simply with Breckin and his clan had taught her that things were nice to have, but not important. Or necessary.

"Eva?" Breckin handed her the parchment.

Sadness welled in her eyes as she accepted it from him. "I cannot believe he gave this to me. Should I give it to you? I know not what to do with such a vast amount of coin and have no need of it now, do I?" She tried to lift the heavy box to press into Breckin's hands, but he shook his head, so she set it in the "keep" pile.

"I told ye, lass, we do not need that kind of wealth here in the Highlands. Och, we have what we need and 'tis given to us by the land. Keep your coins. In fact, come with me. I have another surprise for ye." Breckin took her hand and guided her into the longhouse.

She trailed along, curious about where he was taking her. At their bedchamber, he opened the door and guided her inside. Eva entered and turned to face him. "'Tis not the time to seek pleasure, Breckin. Surely, you can await the night." She giggled lightly.

"Though that sounds like a winsome notion, I wanted to give you this." He motioned to a chest that sat at the end of the bed.

It was the same beautiful chest that was at his aunt's home, the one with the beautiful flowers etched along the trim—the one she'd thought belonged to a woman. In fact, it was probably his betrothed's.

She couldn't breathe as the weight of his thoughtless gift reminded her that he had once loved another. Eva did not want what belonged to his former betrothed; instead, she wanted to burn the beautiful, wretched chest. "I thank you for thinking of me...but I do not want it." Eva turned and hastened from the room.

Without considering where she was going, she crossed the bridge, passed the church, and kept walking until she reached the summit where the lit torch stuck in the ground. She ambled close to the edge of the land and peered down the cliff's depth. The beauty of the spot was not lost on her. There was a ruggedness about the land, but a sereneness too, and a sense of calmness overtook her.

"Wait!" She heard Breckin call, and turned to see him rushing toward her. Before she could move, he reached her, wrapped his arms around her waist, and pulled her back from the edge of the land. "If ye jump, I jump."

"Have you gone addled? Why would I jump?" Eva pulled away from him and dislodged his hold. As she turned to peer at him, she saw his face and realized he was seriously afraid. Even now, he was reaching to tug her back from the edge. Realization dawned. "Oh, was it…? It was how she…died. Breckin! Fear not! I was not going to jump."

His eyebrows furrowed and he tilted his head to the side. The fear on his face drained away as he studied her, and he dropped his arms by his side. "Ye were not? I thought ye were going to…Well, ye are my wife and… Eva, what is bothering ye? Care to explain why ye fled and why ye were distraught about the chest?" Breckin stood beside her but he made no move to touch her again.

"I will not accept what belonged to another… The trunk…you should leave it at Clare's—"

Breckin cut her off as he folded his arms across his chest and stared hard at her. "I thought ye might want to use it and one day give it to our daughter."

She gasped. "You want me to *use* it? I find it dispiriting, Breckin, that you want me to give your heartless gift to our daughter too. But I refuse to use your former betrothed's trunk and need not be reminded that you once gave your heart to another." Eva's body tensed as she admitted such jealousy.

His brows furrowed even lower before they rose in surprise. He stared at her with his brilliant green eyes wide. "Former betrotheds? I deem there is something amiss here, lass. That chest belonged to my sister Marian."

His sister? Her heart rose with joy, then plummeted as she realized she'd probably brought her warrior more pain, making him relive the death of his sister and then talk about it. *Oh no.* "Marian is your...sister? You told me she was a former betrothed."

He shook his head. "When ye asked, I thought ye meant who she was to William Stewart. My sister was *his* betrothed before she...died."

She'd been so mistaken. This was terrible! "Oh. So then... you were not betrothed?"

"I was betrothed a long time ago, to the woman who is now William Stewart's current wife... Danella was supposed to marry me but her family called an end to our treaty and she married Willian right after my sister passed."

"Oh..." She shook her head as she tried to put together the relationships. "So Marian was intended for William but when she died, he married Danella, your former betrothed? I see." Eva stepped closer to the torch and admired the carved wood of the holder. He'd obviously had it made; that he kept it burning for his sister showed how very much he'd loved her. "I'm so sorry, Breckin," she said softly, then turned to look at him. "I want to know...if you can tell me...how did Marian die? Did she jump? If so," she said and pressed her hands to her chest, "that saddens me."

Breckin rounded the torch and stood on the other side. "Nay, she did not jump. We had just buried our parents not more than half a year before... I was attending to matters of the clan and had taken over the duty as laird, as well as raising my brothers and seeing to Marian's well-being... I fear I paid little attention to what was happening in her life. Now that I think back on it, she must have been quite melancholy to take her life."

"She took her life?" Eva hadn't meant to sound so shocked but she couldn't fathom anyone going to such lengths for any reason. Ending your life was a sin and poor Marian would've condemned her soul to the very depths of Hell. It meant she could not be given a mass at her death, and no prayers could be offered up for her in church. It meant she couldn't be buried in consecrated ground. The thought of it brought tears to her eyes.

It also meant her family could be held in ill-regard by the rest of the community, unjustly stained by her sin. She supposed since Breckin was the Buchanan laird, his clansmen and women couldn't shun him or his family.

"Aye, Willa said she drank poison, a potion, for she smelled it in the cup found near my sister's body and also on her lips. Marian did not jump but was found here, on this spot which is why I erected this torch. I doubt my sister would take her life and I vow to find out what really happened to her. In honor of her life, I keep the torch lit, and only when I find out the truth shall I douse the flame."

"Oh, Breckin, I am sorry. That is all so disheartening and it saddens me that you lost her in such a way."

"I fight many other clans' battles to try to win favor with God so he will accept Marian in Heaven." He lowered his gaze to the ground and she couldn't see his eyes.

Eva stepped toward him and took his arm until she was able to clasp his hand. "Breckin, that is commendable of you to care for your sister's soul. But she is gone now and you should not fear for her or yourself. I understand that you have suffered loss and your heart is despaired."

"I fear nothing, Eva, and my heart is intact. One day, I shall prove that Marian did not take her life but until then, I must seek to appease God."

She sighed and felt the pain he must be suffering in the deepest part of her heart. "So now you shield yourself and your heart because you have lost those you cared about and you hope to gain solace by making promises to God?"

He nodded slightly but enough for her to see his chin move. "Just my promises to God, not the rest."

Eva wrapped her hands around his torso and settled her cheek against his chest. "Unshield your heart now, Breckin, because there is naught you can do about the past. There is no reason to hold guilt or responsibility for what happened. But you are too bull-headed to realize that, yes?"

Breckin closed his eyes and settled his head next to hers. "Aye, perhaps I am."

"Then your future might be damned," she said with all seriousness.

"Aye, 'tis, if ye will not cease harping on me about it. Do not be so sullen or ireful with me, lass. What happened before… I cannot let it go and will not." He continued to hold on to her even though she tried to pull away.

After a quiet moment between them, he shifted his face until his lips met hers. He kissed her gently and continued to hold her. She would get him to soften his heart toward her, and somehow, she would take away the pain of his losses.

CHAPTER SEVENTEEN

Clangs of metal rang in the air as a field full of warriors practiced arms. Breckin ambled past the sparring partners and began to give feedback on their methods when his commander whistled to him from the far end of the field. With haste, he marched forward and met Gideon.

"What goes?"

Gideon appeared put out about something and glared across the field. "Ye see them... I vow to the heavens that they do not intend to follow the rules."

Breckin squinted his eyes and found his brothers sparring a wee distance from them. "I see naught amiss. They are training..."

Gideon shook his head. "Nay, they are supposed to be by the quintains this morn, not grappling on the ground with the other lads. If I did not know better, I'd say they instigated the brawl betwixt them and the others."

Breckin whistled loudly and called his brothers' attention. They walked toward him, each shoving the other, seemingly in a dispute about their fracas. Connor ambled along with a slight limp but seemed to be healing. His brother had only been given a reprieve from convalescing the day before and since then had remained outside except for sleep.

When they reached him, Breckin settled his fisted hands on

his hips and glared. "Do ye mind telling me what ye were doing?"

Caden bobbed his head. "'Tis naught but a wee disagreement, Laird."

"Oh? A disagreement about what?"

Connor pulled Caden back and stepped forward. "One of the lads made fun of Milady and so I walloped him. Aye, blackened his eye but good because he deserved it."

"Made fun of how?" Breckin motioned to the other lads to stay where they were.

"They said unbecoming things, Breckin, and we would not stand for it." Caden spat on the ground and pulled his brother back. "One of them said that she was too bonny to be married to ye and that she probably was addled or lacked an intelligent thought."

"Another made some crass remark about her bosoms. Aye, so we walloped them," Connor added.

"I appreciate ye sticking up for Eva, lads, but ye need not. I will speak with them. If ye hear more unbecoming things about my wife, ye will tell me or Gideon. Ye will not take your fists to your brethren. Understand?" Somehow Breckin managed to show patience on the outside while he gave the instructions to his brothers, but inside, he was furious.

His brothers nodded.

"Perhaps a wee bit of time in the stables will do ye both good. The paddocks need cleaning. Ye will groom your horses and Eva's as well. Then exercise the horses for they're growing fat. That'll keep ye busy for a time. When ye finish with those chores, return to the longhouse. Eva could probably use your help. She is still going through the carts." Breckin watched them sprint off and then he turned to his commander.

"That punishment is but a reward, Laird. Aye, did ye see their smiles as they scampered away?" Gideon chortled.

"What do ye mean? Why would they be pleased with having to muck out the stalls?" Breckin was perplexed by his comrade's observation.

"Alton has a hard time keeping the lads out of the stables. Ever since they found out the horses were theirs, they tend to them throughout the day. They're anxious to begin riding, och Alton will not let them, not without permission from ye."

Breckin could've laughed. Indeed, he'd rewarded his brothers instead of punishing them. "I am gladdened they found something to keep them occupied and out of trouble. Perhaps on the morrow, I will allow them to ride their horses. This business with the other lads... I am uncertain how to handle it," he said, daunted.

"Ye see... I knew the lass would be a distraction but oh, what a bonny one she is." His comrade snickered with laughter.

"'Tis unbecoming, Gideon, to gaze overlong at my wife or to notice her beauty."

"I apologize, Laird, och I cannot help it and neither can the men or lads. I suppose I should punish them and have them do some heavy lifting so their lips will stay firmly shut." He motioned toward the opposite end of the field where she was passing. As she did, all of the soldiers ceased sparring and stood staring, some surreptitiously, others openly. "Can a man not enjoy a moment of pleasure?"

Breckin shoved his comrade's shoulder. "Nay, he cannot, not when the pleasure is my own wife. I wish she was not so bonny sometimes..."

Gideon guffawed. "Aye? We should all be so misguided. Och, the woman is modest. Mayhap ye should give her a looking glass so she can understand why the women resist befriending her."

He pressed his hands over his face and groaned softly. "Do ye mean to tell me that none of the women in our clan has befriended her because she is too *bonny*?"

"Aye, at least that is what Deena said. If ye want my advice, my friend, I wouldst not get involved in womanly matters. They will work it out. It could take a bit of time but och, eventually the women will get used to your wife." Gideon removed his dagger from his belt loop and used it to clean his fingernails whilst he spoke to him.

"I am concerned about Eva but not addled enough to speak of matters of women. But I vow, Gideon, my wife confounds me," Breckin said testily. "One minute I want to kiss her and the next I want to wring her bonny neck."

Gideon chuckled. "Aye. 'Tis the way of a married man." He grinned and looked up from his nails. "What's she done now?"

"She insists that I let go of the past and... Sometimes she scares me because 'tis like she can tell what I am thinking." Breckin never shared his innermost thoughts with anyone but Gideon and had been that way since they'd been lads.

That he could not confess to his worries or the sadness that welled whenever he visited the torch with Eva, disheartened him. She wanted him to give her what he was unwilling or unable to give—his shielded emotions. A warrior kept that part of himself hidden and he refused to unfetter that part of himself.

"Well, Laird, my grandda once told me that if your wife does not scare the hell out of ye then she is not the one for ye. Maybe ye should talk to her more about what happened...when your parents died and your sister...and your broken betrothal."

Breckin scoffed at his comrade. "I am getting past all of it. There is no sense in dwelling over it and I will not be speaking my feelings in a way akin to a grubby-faced lad. Nay, I have important matters to see to and should get back to it." Though Breckin tried to sound determined, he took a heavy breath to release the tension that had overtaken him with his discussion with Gideon. "I suggest ye get back to your duties as well."

Gideon bellowed with laughter as he walked away.

He let out an expletive at his comrade's gall and then marched toward the fields. After spending some of the afternoon training with the men, Breckin decided to call it a day. He stopped at the loch to wash and clean up before heading home.

When he reached the longhouse, he rounded it until he got to the back where he now found Eva, handing Caden an item for him to load in the cart. He hadn't expected to see the lads back at the longhouse but they must've finished their chores with haste.

"Still at it? What are ye doing putting that back in the cart?"

Eva jumped at his intrusion. "You startled me, Breckin. Can you not give a warning when you are approaching?"

He shrugged in answer. "Caden, Conner… On the morrow, we will meet at first light at the stables. Your horses need to be exercised and I want to accompany ye. We might even do a spot of hunting whilst we are at it." The lads grinned from ear to ear. "Go and wash up for supper."

His brothers shot off, whooping and cheering at his suggestion. Breckin found himself smiling at their excitement.

"I made a good hearty stew and it should be hot enough now to eat. Come inside. The lads said you were at the training fields and I saw you on my return from the church. Did you get your duties finished?" Eva ambled around him and up the small set of steps that led to the inside.

Breckin followed her. He sat at the table and appreciated how attentive she was being. She set a bowl of stew before him, sliced a piece of bread, shifted a small bowl of spread toward him, and handed him a spoon.

The lads entered and sat at the table. Eva placed bowls of stew before each of them and smiled. Caden said, "We cannot wait until the morrow, Laird, to go hunting with ye."

Connor nodded and said, "Aye, and we get to ride the horses."

"I wanted to spend some time with you," Breckin said. "Aye, and if ye stay out of trouble, ye can ride your horses more frequently."

The lads continued to spoon in their stew but acknowledged him with nods to their heads.

Eva gazed at them affectionately and said, "Breckin, must be famished because you left so early this morning."

With his mouth full, he just nodded. She sat with him while he ate and, after he finished the meal, he used a cloth to wipe his mouth and hands and wasn't in much of a hurry to get back to his duties. "Where did ye put all your things? There is hardly anything about the longhouse... I would have thought ye would have filled it with your belongings."

She took his empty bowl and stood, then busied herself with washing his utensils in the washpan. "I, uh...am only bringing inside what I find useful right now. Perhaps we shall need the other things later."

Connor said, "Can we go outside now?"

"We finished our supper," Caden said.

He gave them and nod and the lads left the table and headed to the back of the longhouse.

Breckin raised a brow. She was being evasive, though how he could tell this, he knew not. Perhaps it was just that she'd worked long at the carts and several of them stood empty. Where were the items her father had sent?

Eva cherished her belongings and, because she didn't want to bring them inside, told him something was amiss. "Ye can bring in whatever ye wish, Eva. This is your home now. I do not mind if ye clutter it up with your trinkets."

"Trinkets? No, I am happy with the items that I have inside now and will keep the others stored."

Breckin made to retort but suddenly became aware of the sharp scent of something burning. He pushed to his feet, praying it wasn't one of the cottages with their thatched roofs; a single spark from an unchecked fire could cause the entire keep to become engulfed.

"Do ye smell that?"

Eva turned toward him and raised her chin. "It smells like smoke."

They both hastened to the back of the longhouse and retreated through the back door. Breckin jumped off the steps and rushed towards his brothers who appeared to be stomping the ground. "What are ye two doing?"

"Naught, och Connor accidentally lit the grass aflame."

"I did not. Ye did." Connor put the final stomp on the ground and put out what flame remained.

"Go on now and get back to the training field. I will hear of no further scuffles with the other lads. Ye will spar together and with no others until I say otherwise. Gideon wanted ye to use the quintains this day, get to it. I will test your ability when I return to the field. I might reconsider taking ye hunting on the morrow if ye do not do as I say."

His brothers set off and he turned back to Eva who stood looking disheveled by her morning chores and from worry by the ruckus his brothers caused. With little effort, he scooped her into his arms and grinned.

"What in the name of Mary are you doing?"

"I just want a wee kiss," he said and leaned his head toward her but she pulled back.

"Honestly, Breckin, there is too much to do this day to fool around."

"Aye, hurry up then and kiss me because my back is hurting."

She gave him a quick peck and giggled. "You can put me down now."

"The hell I will," he said and pressed his mouth against hers. Breckin wanted to be alone with her and now that the lads hailed off to the training field...

"Laird! Breckin!"

Someone shouted for him and he dislodged his mouth from Eva's and allowed her to slide against his body until she got her footing. "Damnation. I should go, I suppose, even though I would rather stay here kissing ye until I make ye shake with need."

Eva continued to clutch him. "Yes, you should go."

Aymer whistled and called, "Laird, are ye here?"

"Aye, inside." Breckin took hold of her hands and slid them slowly from his body, disappointed that he wouldn't spend the afternoon as he'd wanted.

"Oh, there ye be." Aymer appeared around the side of the longhouse and spotted them in the back. Now he waved a missive in the air. "This just came for ye from a Campbell messenger."

Breckin sighed and took it from him. He opened the message and gave it a hasty read. Would it never end? He barely had time to take care of the people of his own clan. He turned to Eva. "Colin calls me to aid him. He is having trouble with his neighbor, the MacNaughtons."

She frowned but didn't say anything.

"Aymer, tell Gideon to ready a regimen of soldiers with haste. We will leave shortly."

"Aye, will do, Laird." Aymer bowed to Eva and said, "Good day, Milady." He left on his quest to ready the men.

"I will be gone for a wee bit. Ye will fare well?" He detested leaving her when he'd only just returned. Breckin pulled her into his embrace and kissed her head. "Do not overwork yourself. The longhouse is fine as it is."

"There is plenty more for me to do. Go on about your war. I shall be busy enough without you here. But Breckin," she said and stopped him by taking his hand. "Be careful."

"Worry not because I always am. I will return soon." He hurried away then, walking along quickly on the lane toward the stable. Though he certainly wished to stay, he had to answer the call of his fiercest ally. That the MacNaughtons caused the Campbells grief concerned him. Breckin wondered if the matter was of importance or if Colin called him for naught.

SUMMER WAS BEGINNING to wane, although it was still warm. Well, as warm as it could be. Soon Autumn's bluster would roll over the hills and settle once again in the valleys. Breckin didn't much mind the cold season because that meant he got to spend more time at home. Now with Eva there, he hoped to put off any travel come the late autumn and winter.

His men lingered in the loch, carousing, and carrying on.

Their bellows echoed from the heavy bluffs that surrounded the loch. After the brief scuffle with the MacNaughtons, they retrieved the missing cattle the Campbells had claimed as theirs. Since the MacNaughtons did not protest much, Breckin took it as their guilt. Their rivals took to the woods and absconded before they could decrease their numbers. The few bloodied MacNaughton soldiers that remained behind were not long for the ground. He commanded that his brethren dig a large enough hole to bury them in.

Colin Campbell scoffed when he heard him. "Why in Heaven's name wouldst ye give them a place of honor?"

Breckin chortled and paced along the row of men digging the ditch. "Colin, these men were sent by their laird to steal your cattle and were only following orders. I will not leave such dedicated men lying in the woods to rot. Nay, we will bury them not because we care about them but because we respect their loyalty."

Colin whistled to his clansmen who stood nearby. "Assist the Buchanan warriors." His men retrieved shovels and some used their hands to scoop the earthen away from the trench.

When the hole was large enough, they worked to collect the five or so men who needed a final resting place. When all was finished, Breckin turned toward his horse but said over his shoulder, "I will not be able to come and aid ye for some time, Colin, so best ye call up your other allies or strengthen your soldiers' ability when ye come to trouble."

His comrade's brows drew together. "Why? Have ye troubles of your own? 'Tis unlike ye not to give aid."

"I need to spend time at home and I cannot do that if I am out riding through the Highlands aiding every clan that begs for help." He hadn't meant to affront Colin, but it appeared he had. "I mean no disrespect, Colin, och I have been remiss in my duties toward my clan. I need to remedy that and I cannot do that if I am aiding others."

"Perhaps it is time for me to get my men better trained. I

understand, Breckin, and wish ye well then." Colin gave the order for his soldiers to return to their land.

Breckin directed his soldiers to take a rest on Campbell's land overnight. Near a smaller loch by the border of Campbell land, they set up camp and some hunted for the late day meal. Once they rested, they'd get a good early start on the morrow.

Gideon leaned against a tree and took swigs of his flask. He held it out to him but Breckin shook his head, rejecting his offer.

"If the horses did not need rest, I'd be halfway home by now."

"Aye, aye, and back to marital bliss," Gideon said with a chuckle.

"Cease being an arse, Gideon. Married life is new…different…and I am navigating it as best I can." But that wasn't necessarily true because he avoided what was on his mind and in his heart.

"Cosh, look at them… Nothing like seeing the shining arses of a bunch of Highlanders after a good brawl. Shame the MacNaughtons did little to entertain us. Och, the heat though…'tis good to cool off in the loch. We should join them." Gideon set his flask aside and ran in a sprint, discarding his tartan and tunic on the way.

Breckin soon joined them and had to admit the water was refreshing, cooled him, and even allayed his sullen mood. He was much more agreeable and as he rested in the camp that night, he peered above at the star-speckled sky.

Gideon lay on his side and used his arm as a pillow. His comrade appeared relaxed and untroubled with thoughts. "We shall soon be adding to our family, Deena and I. Maybe we will give Hamish a brother. Aye, for we will have a bairn come late winter."

"That is good news, my friend. I know that ye were hoping to have more children." Breckin reached for his cup beside him and raised it in a silent cheers to his comrade.

Gideon lifted his head in response and nodded. "We had

given up hope, och, God has blessed us. Deena is pleased by it, for she will now have another child to care for. Are ye thinking of having children soon? Now that ye are married and plan to be home more oft?"

"I have not spoken to Eva about having children. 'Tis the truth, I would welcome a bairn or two. But the clan has made life difficult for Eva and I have not made it easier," Breckin said without much deliberation of his words. "Sometimes, I deem I am not worthy of her. She received a fortune in coins from her da and he bade her to use them for her life. Yet she was willing to give them to me. Of course, I refused them."

Gideon frowned at him. "What say ye? Ye turned down a fortune in coins?" He swatted his arm. "What in God's name is wrong with ye?"

"I told her that we did not need coins, only what we are given from the land."

His comrade chortled. "What a load of cosh that is. Ye know that next year the king will demand the tax and we have no measures to amass the forfeiture. Just because the king allowed ye a respite from what ye owed does not mean he will not seek to receive it going forward."

"There is that. And I was hoping that since we will pull back from aiding other clans, we might expand our crops and cattle. Maybe even purchase additional sheep. 'Tis time to progress and make our land profitable." Breckin had overheard his da when he'd been alive and the dreams that he'd had for the land that his grandfather had been given. Cultivating land and animals took time and resources, and sometimes hard times hindered them. Now with the coinage given from Eva's da, he might be able to make some progress.

"'Tis time indeed that we consider the Buchanans before others, Laird. We should meet and make a plan when we reach home."

"Aye, that is a fair idea. I also want to build Eva a manor home. If ye saw the home she lived in... The longhouse is but a shack compared to the luxury of her da's home. I want to give her a better life."

"Seems to me ye are coming to care for the lass."

"Aye, maybe more than care, Gideon. I am not one to speak about how I feel but Eva deserves much more than I have given her."

"Ye will rectify that, Breckin, and I have faith that she will appreciate it. She's a kind lass, even if she was somewhat spoiled by her rich father."

"That is the thing… Even though she had wealth, she has never used it nefariously. When I met her, she tried to aid a lad in Edinburgh who intended to thieve from her. I could not believe that she would go and search him out to help him but she did. She is unlike any woman I have ever met."

"And ye are gladdened now that ye were forced to marry her?" Gideon flashed a wide smile and nodded.

"Aye, I certainly am." Breckin lay upon his bedroll and quieted. He thought about how blessed he'd been to be called forth by King Alexander and forced to take Eva's hand. At the time, he recalled being filled with angst about it, but now, he realized his good fortune.

In the morning, he opened his eyes to find most of his men moving about the camp and readying for their departure. He hastened to the nearby stream and washed. Once back at the meeting place, he took the reins of his horse from Gideon.

"Let us make haste and get home." Breckin mounted his horse and nudged the beast forward.

Throughout the ride, he couldn't help but recall the words he'd spoken to Gideon the night before. Breckin was determined to make changes upon his return home. Before the cold season came on, he wanted to send a missive to his allies letting them know that he would not be taking to travel until the spring. If they needed aid, they'd be on their own.

Then he would meet with his clan and begin making plans for the spring planting, buying sheep and cattle, and expanding on the wealth of their land with, of course, Eva's coin, if she was amiable. But he was certain that she would be pleased to help the Buchanans since she was now the lady of the clan.

As they passed the blackened treeline, he let his guard down, happy to be home. He'd only been gone for a fortnight but it felt much longer. He missed being home, his wife, and even his wild brothers. When he broke through the trees and saw the cottages speckled about, his chest tightened with pride. His clansmen and women had been busy the days he was gone, preparing for the first sign of winter's arrival.

Roofs were rethatched, repaired, and wood replaced on some cottages. Shutters now protected homes and were already closed. Though it wasn't too cold yet, it would be, soon enough. Bales of hay and sacks of grasses, clovers, legumes, and alfalfa were stacked in the stable for winter fodder for the horses. A great wood pile lined the wall with enough to keep most hearths blazing.

Before he crossed the bridge, he thought to stop by the torch to ensure it had remained burning. He redirected his horse and rode in that direction. There, the flame rose steadily, motionless. On the return to the bridge, he peered down the lane in the direction of the market and noted the denseness of the air and haziness. Something wasn't right and then he smelled the faint scent of smoke. As he drew nearer, the pungent smell increased and haziness in the air irritated his eyes and made them tear up.

He rode speedily by Willa's, past the ailing encampment, and finally reached the market. A stall was heavily encumbered with flame, its harrowing growl burning the wood and all the contents inside. Breckin dismounted and noticed his brothers standing amid a group of onlookers. A group of older men held buckets and dipped them into a barrel to fill and toss at the flames. Eventually, his soldiers reached the calamity and joined the line of men putting out the fire.

"What happened? How did the tailor's stall become lit?"

Connor lowered his head as did Caden. Neither would answer.

"I shall tell ye, Laird, these two thought by playing at burning stuff on the ground entertainment. Aye, for they lit the ground near my stall and my hut went up like a campfire." The tailor accused as he threw his hands in the air and marched off.

"Does he speak the truth? Did ye set his hut on fire?" Breckin didn't have to await their answer because guilt set in their eyes and plainly on their faces. "We shall walk back to the longhouse and ye will tell me what happened." He turned to Master James. "I apologize if my brothers had anything to do with this destruction. Be assured that I will see to reparations."

"My thanks, Laird," James said and dunked a bucket into a barrel that had been delivered to aid in putting out the fire.

Along the lane, Breckin didn't speak. He waited for his brothers to offer their excuses.

Caden spoke first, "Breckin, brother… Laird, we did not mean to set fire to the tailor's hut."

"We had a piece of glass that we found in Milady's belongings and we took it. She does not know that we have it. We used it to burn things and—"

"Ye know it was wrong of ye to take something that does not belong to ye."

Both his brothers nodded.

"We did not realize the fire would catch so quickly, and well, there was fabric on the floor inside his hut that caught before we could stomp it out," Connor offered.

"I am highly disappointed in both of ye, so much so that I cannot even find an acceptable punishment. In time, I shall think of something. Meanwhile, ye will be forbidden to leave the longhouse and ye will not be permitted to ride your horses. I will not see ye outside until I decide what to do with ye." Breckin had reached the bridge. "What were ye doing at the market?"

Caden answered, "We were awaiting Milady."

"Eva was there? I did not see her." Breckin thought to return to find her, but since he was already at the bridge, he decided to get his horse settled, check in with the watch, and gain a report from Aymer.

"Before ye flee, I want ye to understand something. The reason I forbid ye to train fully is that ye have not proved yourself yet. Instead of playing at this silliness, ye should be practicing your swordsmanship. Neither of ye are proficient yet with the sword, bow, or daggers. Ye need to put your hearts into it. Unless ye do not want to be a Buchanan soldier?" Breckin posed his question to them and stared hard, waiting for one of them to speak.

"We do, Laird, we want to be akin to ye, and be fierce and strong," Caden said.

"There is much more to warring, brothers, than being proficient with the sword and such. But it helps to keep ye from being killed. Ye have never stepped foot on a field soaked with the blood of your brethren, ever had to carry your comrade's bloody body home, witness limbs being torn from one's body. Ye learn, brothers, not to let death enter your heart. Until ye mature enough to handle such atrocities, ye must train and be ready to face the hardships of war. On the morrow, ye will work with me and I shall get ye readied."

Both his brothers smiled widely.

"Before da passed, he made me vow to make ye into warriors like him…like me, and ye have yet to show such ability. Show me that I can trust ye and that ye are mature enough to be Buchanan warriors."

"We will, Breckin, we will show ye and prove we are worthy," Connor said.

"Go on and get back to the longhouse. Ye will not leave it until I permit ye to do so. And tell Eva that I will come as soon as I am able. I must handle some clan matters." Breckin waved them away.

He sighed wearily because that talk had been long in coming. Now, he had to make good on his promise to his brothers. It was time that he ceased ignoring them and forgoing the promises made to his da. He needed to be better at guiding his brothers and making them what his father had made of him—an honorable, but fierce Buchanan warrior.

CHAPTER EIGHTEEN

THROUGHOUT THE MORNING, Eva kept busy doing her chores. She rummaged through the sacks of clothing from the carts. Within the sacks were chemises, fur-trimmed overdresses and mantles, headdresses, shoes, belts, capes, and cloaks. There were also small boxes that held brooches, chains, and rings.

Now that she knew the trunk belonged to Breckin's sister, she intended to put her clothing in it, and one day, give it to her daughter. Hopefully, by then, Breckin would be able to talk about his sister and tell their children about their aunt.

She only kept two more elaborate dresses for special occasions and the rest were more suitable for daily wear. Being in the Highlands, she suspected that she'd get more use of her daily wear overdresses than anything ornate or embellished.

She knelt in front of the trunk and opened it. It was empty, save for a small bulge in the silk (?) lining on the right side. Eva used her fingers to open the slit of the fabric and pulled out two folded pieces of parchment. Her curiosity spurred her to open the first piece of parchment which appeared to have been torn from a volume, and she read:

Soon I will be a married woman. My heart belongs to William and I cannot wait to be his wife. Yet a distressing situation has arisen because I have spoken to Danella. She claims that she has

always been intended for William and that my betrothal to him is but a way to thwart the Buchanans. When I asked William about it, he declared it to be true. He'd been betrothed to Danella when he was born. He professes to love me still but I fear he does not. I must warn Breckin of the possible danger but I intend to question Danella further to find out what she meant.
~M.B.

Eva's mouth hung open as she perused the lines again. The page must have been torn from a personal volume of Marian's. Why would Marian hide the parchment in her trunk? Perhaps she didn't want Breckin to find it before she might speak to him of the matter. Eva pressed the parchment against her chest and was saddened at the thought that Marian took her life because she could not marry William. The lass had a broken heart. Had Marian discovered that Danella was right and that William also coveted a marriage with Danella? There were more questions than answers, and Eva sighed, suspecting the answers may never come.

The second parchment was written by Breckin's mother and was directed to Conner and Caden. In it, she praised them and bade them to follow their brother's lead and become great Buchanan warriors.

Eva stared at the lines written in her husband's mother's hand. It brought a sense of melancholy for the lads because she too missed having a mother. Unlike the lads, though, she had never met her mother or had memories to hold on to. She had to wonder if Marian had put the message in the trunk before she died and had not ever given it to the lads.

With a sniffle and wipe of her eye, she folded the parchments and tucked both parchments in the seam of her overdress for safekeeping. She would show them to Breckin when he returned. Apparently, he'd never opened the trunk and seen the missives. Or perhaps he had; she had no way to tell until she spoke with him. But she was sure the lads would like to have the message from their mother and would give it to them that night.

When she finished setting the garments inside the trunk, she closed the lid and headed to the kitchen area. She found the lads sitting at the table. They were unusually quiet and still.

"What has your tongues this day?" She smiled to offer sincerity, but they squirmed in their seats and didn't look at her; instead, they appeared most severe. She tried again. "Why are you inside? 'Tis a fine day to be outside. I'd think you would be out causing havoc—"

"Connor and me…Well, when we left earlier and visited the market, we took a piece of your looking glass. Ye were busy with Master Amos and we used the glass to light the grass."

Caden held his head with his hands and muttered, "It caught a seller's stall alight. We are being punished and are not allowed to leave the longhouse. We have not been the best of brothers to Breckin. When he left us, he was mightily disappointed in us."

Eva took the bench across from them and peered at their distraught faces. "Breckin returned? When?"

"Aye, he returned a short time ago," Connor supplied. "He told us to tell ye that he would come after he took care of clan matters."

Eva thought that he should have come straight to the longhouse. He'd been gone for almost a fortnight and she was still the last thing on his mind. With a discontented sigh, she shook away the trepidation. "You should not have used the glass to light the grass but I am sorry you got in trouble. Maybe your punishment will not be so severe." Eva took a slice of bread from the basket in the center of the table.

"He took away our horses," Connor said woefully. "We're not allowed to ride until he gives his permission."

"Yes. And Breckin vowed to take our training more seriously." Caden pushed the bowl with a spread toward her.

She used a supper dagger to smear it on the bread. "That is good to hear, Caden. I know that Breckin is concerned for you both, as am I." She paused, and put down the bread, then reached into the seam in her dress for the parchment. "You know, your ma wanted you to do well in your training as well. When I was cleaning, I found a message written by her for you." She set the piece of parchment on the table and slid it toward Conner.

Conner peered at it but made no move to take the parchment.

"Do you not want to read it? I am certain it would be nice to have words from your mother, written in her hand."

"Did ye read it, Milady?"

She nodded.

Conner pushed the parchment back to her. "We know not how to read. Will ye tell us what it says?" He swiped his tunic sleeve over his tear-streaked and sooty face and nudged his brother. "We will listen."

Eva stared at them, shocked. "You cannot read?"

Both lads shook their heads.

She took a deep breath, assailed by memories. "When I was a young girl, I was forbidden to learn like my brothers. They had several monks and brothers come to teach them all sorts of lessons, from languages to history and mathematics to reading and writing. I was so envious of their learning."

"Aye, most lassies do not read, Milady," Connor said.

"Och, ye do though?" Caden asked with a wondering tone.

"I most certainly do. I learned because it was forbidden. But I sat at the table when they had their lessons and pretended to be occupied with sewing so I could see what they were learning. My brothers used to tease me and say girls could not learn, except for my middle brother, Stephen. He gave me parchments and ink so I could practice and he used to help me when I had trouble with a word or language. We learned Latin, French, Gaelic, and English. I had hoped to learn Italian too but my brothers outgrew their lessons and the monks and brothers ceased coming." Eva sighed, disheartened at the memories that overtook her of those times. She missed her brothers even though they often teased her and ignored her. Still, she cared about them and hoped they had good lives.

"Mayhap ye could teach us, Milady?" Caden asked.

"I would be happy to, Caden. We will begin after suppers when 'tis quiet and we can focus. Now that you will be taking to your training, by the evening you will appreciate a little peaceful learning time."

Connor pushed the parchment toward her again. "Will ye read it to us?"

Eva took the parchment and opened it. She read:

Dearest Connor and Caden, My heart is heavy writing this as it appears your da and me may not survive this dreadful illness. Before I am unable to, I wanted to tell ye both that I am proud of ye. I shall always look out for ye even from Heaven. Be strong, lads, and follow Breckin's lead. He shall see to your training and ensure ye become fierce Buchanan warriors to rival your ancestors. Be not sad or dispirited by our departure, for one day, we shall meet again. ~Your loving ma.

Eva's voice cracked on the last words and she lowered her face so the lads couldn't see the tears in her eyes. But when she raised her chin, she saw tears in theirs. "I am sorry that you lost her, your mother. She loved you."

"Our ma would have liked ye, Milady, and would've thought ye good for our brother."

Caden nodded at his brother's sentiment. "Aye, he has changed since he returned with ye as his wife—for the better, Milady."

Eva wondered how true this was. Had he changed? What did they see that she didn't? "You are both so kind and I am grateful that you accept me. Now, let us leave this melancholy here at the table and we shall go outside. We have a few warm days remaining before it becomes cold. If you need something to do, you can help me. I intend to finish sorting through the items that I want to give to Master Amos."

Eva didn't bother to clean up the trenchers and foodstuff from their midday fare. She'd see to it later when she prepared the late meal. She hurried to the back of the longhouse and approached the last cart that needed to be emptied.

Connor jumped atop the cart with her help when she boosted him. He pulled the tarp from over the items. "What are ye doing with the empty cart?"

"I was going to ask Aymer to give the last one to the Buchanan farmers. They probably could use another to carry crops and such. I do not need it." She wondered if the farmers made good use of the other carts she had sent but Aymer hadn't told her if he had even delivered them.

"Let me and Caden do that for ye, Milady," Connor said. "Och, Breckin told us not to leave the longhouse since we are being punished."

"I am certain he would understand that I sent you on the errand. And I see how excited you are to take the cart but you must promise, though, to return after you deliver it. You shall not dally or get distracted."

Both lads nodded enthusiastically.

She absently perused the rest of the items until she came across another coffer. Eva was almost afraid to open it because she didn't want more coins from her father. Breckin hadn't accepted the first coffer and she'd put it in their bed chamber where it remained untouched. Once, she would have coveted having such wealth but now, the coins were useless to her. She had no need of exquisite garments or items for her home. She sighed at the memory of the joy it had once brought her—visiting the markets.

"What is that?" Caden asked and approached.

Eva opened it and peered into the deep wooden box. There was a layer of loose gemstones. She fingered the red, blue, and clear jewels in awe of their beauty. "I wonder how these got in here. My da often traded and must have received these in exchange for goods."

"I have never seen so many gems, Milady. 'Tis a fortune there…" Connor said with admiration as he eyed them.

"Perhaps. I shall put these in a safe place until I can return them to my father."

Caden scoffed. "Why would ye want to return them?"

"I do not really need gems here… No, I shall return them." Eva tucked the small coffer beneath her arm. "I think that's all there is. We shall take this last load to Master Amos and then you can ask Aymer where to take the cart."

"I will drive the cart," Connor said and hurried to attach the horse's harness to the cart's hitch. His leg must have continued to bother him, for he limped a little.

Caden groused and shoved his brother. "Och, ye drove the last one. 'Tis my turn."

"Why do you not both drive it and take turns holding the reins? Now, come along and I shall walk ahead." Eva didn't wait for them to agree and hurried on the lane. She wanted to get the chore done and return before she had to ready supper.

Eva walked nimbly past the bridge and didn't see Breckin on her trek. She passed the encampment of the ailing and reached the market in a short time. There, she found Master Amos and he greeted her with a grunt.

"Milady, I have barely any room left for all your items are taking up all the space. Ye bring more. Where shall I put it?"

She bowed slightly to him. "I apologize, Amos, but I do not need these items. This is the last of them, I promise. I will take some items off your hands, though, to make room. Do you have a few trunks? I mean to give each of the lads their own. And I need more chairs or benches."

He scoffed. "Ye already took all the chairs that I had. Och, if any come in, I shall set them aside for ye. Come, lads, and help me unload the cart."

"Amos, you have continued to keep your bargain?"

"Oh, aye, Milady, of course, and each morn when the market opens, I have one of my lads take a basket of foodstuff to the sick. The coins are all accounted for, Milady, and set aside for the purpose. Do ye wish me to send ye the coins?"

"No, no…keep them here. My thanks, Amos, for your help. Lads, find Aymer when you are finished here and return to the longhouse for supper." Eva waved to the boys and walked at a slower pace back toward the bridge, enjoying the solitude and quiet.

The encampment was silent when she reached it. A crowd gathered near a tarp-covered area and she approached to stand with Harriet. "What has happened?"

The young woman lowered her head. "Gareth is on his deathbed and shall meet his maker soon. Father Murphy has not come to give him last rites yet."

"Oh, no. I am sorry, Harriet. I know he was your friend."

Eva prayed for the poor man's ascension to Heaven. How she wished that Father Murphy received word on how to help the sick. There had to be a cure for their ailment but as yet no word reached them on how they might help or treat them. After a while, Eva decided to leave to give Gareth's friends privacy for their mourning.

She hurried along and waved to Willa when she reached her cottage. "Good day, Willa."

Ise-Olcan sprinted toward her and jumped up. Willa shouted for the dog to get down but the dog's tongue lapped at her and Eva petted her head.

"She is just excited to see me. I am gladdened someone is." She could've laughed at her pitiful remark because her husband still was nowhere to be seen and obviously not eager to see her.

"Oh, that reminds me," Willa said and ambled toward her. "My daughter-in-law told me that you saved her lad, my grandson, Hamish."

"Hamish is your grandson? We were chased by a dastardly boar. But it was he who saved me and not the other way around."

Willa shook her head. "The way he tells it is that ye saved him. Hamish's parents are mighty grateful for your aid to him. I am sure Deena shall tell ye so when next she sees ye."

Eva smiled but doubted that. Gideon's wife all but ignored

her whenever she saw her on the other side of the bridge.

She decided to change the subject; she wasn't interested in talking about herself. She was here about more important things. "I just visited the encampment and learned that Gareth is on his deathbed. The poor man. All the sick gather around him. Father Murphy has not yet arrived but has been called for."

"Oh, nay, not Gareth." Willa lowered her head with despair. When she raised it, a shimmer of tears set in her eyes. "I shall go and see him before he passes. My thanks for telling me."

Eva clasped her hand. "I am sorry, Willa, for the loss of your friend. I shall see you later." With that, she walked on and entered the church.

Inside, a group of women sat on the benches before the altar. They sang a beautiful melody. Eva was envious of their camaraderie and wished she had friends with whom to sing. In an almost unheard voice, she sang along, knowing the words to the song. When the song ended, without being seen, Eva snuck out of the church and strolled along until she reached the area where the torch was erected. She wondered that if Marian had lived, would she have befriended her?

Eva shook away the sorrowful, woeful mood and viewed her surroundings. Yet as she took in the beauty of the land and waters, the height was treacherous. She wondered why Marian drank poison rather than having just jumped from the ledge. It seemed strange to her but then, she did not know Marian and perhaps the woman wanted to enjoy the view in her last moments.

She stepped back to a nearby tree and sat on the ground. With her hands clasped around her knees, she sighed at the beauty of the place. The sky seemed vast in its pinkish, blueish hues to the bilious clouds that spotted the distance. Eva closed her eyes and prayed for Marian's salvation, for her father's good health, for the lad's patience, and that one day the Buchanans would accept her. One day, she would belong.

CHAPTER NINETEEN

BRECKIN FINISHED SETTLING his horse, speaking with some of the soldiers, and searched for Aymer to gain his report, but the soldier was taking rest. Aymer, according to his brother, Alton, had been on night duty so Breckin decided to find him later.

He walked hastily toward the end of the island and entered the longhouse. He expected to find his brothers inside. They were gone, as was Eva. Silence met him. Breckin gazed about and noted the cleanliness of the floors, the sweet smell of beeswax that shone on the floorboards, and the gleaming table by the kitchen area. Eva had been busy.

He quickly changed his garments and stood in the bedchamber, feeling oddly welcomed. He hadn't felt so eased but the coziness of the room with the Buchanan tartan covering the large bed, to the sight of items belonging to Eva, assured him that he was home. She even made use of his sister's trunk which pleased him. Then he remembered that she'd thought the trunk belonged to his betrothed, that Marian was pledged to him. He smiled at her ireful response because that meant she might be beginning to care for him.

He retreated to the outside, intending to find his wife. His first thought was to kiss her until she was breathless because he'd missed her, his second was to find out how she'd fared whilst he was gone. Then he'd search for his brothers. He was somewhat irate that they had disobeyed and hadn't stayed in the longhouse as he'd bade. Now his punishment for them would be harsher. If only he could come up with a reprimand that expressed the seriousness of their misconduct. He would think of something—he usually did.

As he walked about the island, he greeted his clan's people. They seemed remarkably cheerful, a strange occurrence because they were not the cheery sort. Nevertheless, he ambled onward and when he got to the bridge, he stopped to talk to Aymer who'd returned to his post.

"Welcome home, Laird." Aymer closed the gate to a small corral where three horses nibbled at the grass.

"Ye were on duty late? When I returned, ye were asleep so I thought I would catch up with ye… I assume there is naught to report?"

"Nay, Laird, all was well when ye were away. We had no troubles and even your brothers were somewhat be-haved…except for the mishap with the tailor's hut earlier. Still, they being lads, they did not know they'd light it up. I hope ye went easy on them."

He gave a firm nod and agreed. His brothers needed to be reminded of the dangers of fire before they lit another building aflame. "I spoke with them. They were supposed to be in the longhouse but were not inside. Have ye seen them?"

Aymer fingered his beard and chuckled. "Oh, aye, they went on a mission for Milady and should be back soon."

Breckin leaned against the fence post of the small corral as he spoke to his guardsman. "What mission?"

"Milady is giving her cart to Old Thom. The lads are taking it to him as we speak and should return soon," Aymer said.

"Old Thom, the farmer? Why did she send the cart to him?"

Aymer bobbed his head. "She told the lads to have me send the carts to farmers who might be in need. Aye, she gave away all the carts. This be the last one."

Breckin hadn't realized that she had given the carts away and hadn't noticed any missing. "So she emptied them all. I wonder where she put all her belongings. There wasn't much inside the longhouse and there was little left in the store area."

"She made a pact with the merchant…Amos. He will sell her possessions and in return, well, he keeps the coins and uses them to buy food for the ailing in the woods. Milady has a kind heart."

Breckin had forgotten that Amos told him about their arrangement. After Clare had spoken to him about her learning to cook, he'd gone and spoken with the merchant. Astounded, he wanted to broach the subject with her but then he had been called away.

"Och, I guess ye have not heard about Hamish…" Aymer leaned his folded arms on the fence and grinned. "Well, now, the way I heard it was… Gideon's lad was going to his gran's and was being chased by a boar. Milady helped him up a tree and then she used the lad's sling to scare it away. Deena says Milady saved her lad's life."

"Eva was fortunate that she was not killed herself. That she put herself in peril…" He groaned at the thought of her being attacked by a boar, but Breckin was glad she was able to save the lad. He should have warned her that there were wild creatures in the woods on the other side of the bridge. Then he was crestfallen because he should have given her a dagger or something to use for her protection when she went on her walks.

"Father Murphy says he hopes ye stop by because he wants to speak with ye about something." Aymer waved to his brother who held the reins of a horse he was putting in the pen.

"I will speak to the father later. Right now, I want to find my wife. Have ye seen her?"

Aymer chuckled. "She gets around, Laird, och the guards told me that she crossed the bridge earlier. I have been on duty since and have not seen her return."

Breckin waved to him as he turned and left. When he got to the other side of the bridge, he saw Father Murphy leaving the church. "Good day, Father."

"Laird, for some 'tis, but earlier I gave last rites to Gareth. I am on my way to get him put in the ground." The priest blessed himself and raised his face to the sky.

"Gareth died? I am sorry to hear that, Father. My thanks for seeing to him. Have ye not heard back yet from your order? Surely they must know of a cure or what ails them."

Father Murphy shook his head with dejection. "Not as yet but I am going to write again and urge them to send a response. I should be off."

"Have ye seen Lady Buchanan?" Breckin trudged forward and peered along the lane in both directions.

"I saw her earlier. She headed that way," Father Murphy said and pointed toward the area where the torch sat. "I would speak with ye about her if ye have a moment."

"If it can wait, Father. I have not yet seen my wife since my return and long to greet her. We will meet later, and my thanks for the news." Breckin marched off, determined to find Eva before the sun set. On his approach to the torch area, he spotted her sitting on the ground at the base of a tree with her eyes closed. *Much like Marian when she…* Immediate panic tensed his chest and he sprinted forth. When he reached her, he grabbed hold of her shoulders and forcibly shook her.

He shouted, "Eva! Eva…"

She opened her eyes and tried to pull back from his hold, alarmed. "What is the matter? What is it, Breckin?"

Breckin fell to his knees before her. "God Almighty, I thought ye were…dead."

"I am well, Breckin, I promise. Why would you think I was dead?" Eva grabbed his hand and held it in her attempt to placate him.

Her touch mollified him and he sighed with relief. "I…well, I found Marian here by this tree in the same position. I thought that you… 'Tis absurd and I apologize if I frightened ye." He shifted to sit next to her.

"Oh, I did not know that you found her…Marian. I wanted to rest here before I headed back to the longhouse. You returned earlier but I understand that you were busy."

"I had to gain reports and check in with the men. So ye were busy, aye, whilst I was away. I saw the longhouse. Looks akin to a home now. Where are all your belongings? I would have thought every inch of the house would be filled. I told ye to bring them inside." Breckin knew where her items went but he wanted her to tell him.

"I only kept a small amount of the items, what I thought was needed."

He squeezed her hand a little. "Where is the rest of it?"

"I gave it to Master Amos, the merchant, to sell."

He had to keep himself from smiling. "Oh? And what will ye do with the coins ye make from it?" Breckin hoped she'd be more forthcoming but she was being evasive.

"What do you mean? Do you need coins? I told you to keep the coins my father sent. Oh, and there is a small coffer of jewels, too, that I found with my belongings. I really should send them back. Surely my father did not mean to send them."

He released her hand and drew in a heavy breath. "There was no message?"

"No. As to the coins that I receive from Master Amos, I am afraid that I have given them away." She kept her gaze on the far reaches of land in the distance, avoiding his gaze.

Breckin couldn't withhold his humor at the situation. He chuckled and drew her furrowed brows. "Master Amos told me and that ye directed him to buy foodstuff for the ailing. Ye are tenderhearted, lass."

"Someone should look out for them, Breckin, the ailing. They believe you are their benefactor and I did not correct them when they told me they thought you most kind to give them food."

His shoulders sagged at that. "I should have thought of it, och ye did a kindness for them and me. Is there anything else ye have not told me?"

She shifted her head in small shakes but he disbelieved her. He was sure on the morrow, he'd find out something more about his bonny wife and the care she'd dealt out to his clan.

"Can we stay here for a little while longer?"

He nodded and moved closer to her. Breckin wrapped his arms around her and pulled her against him. With his drawn-in breath, he smelled her sweet fragrance. She always smelled of flowers. Holding her close, he eased and stroked the softness of her arm until he reached the underside of her breast.

"I missed ye, lass. Will ye give me a welcome home kiss?"

"If you wanted a kiss, you should have found me right off instead of gallivanting around the island." She giggled after a moment of quiet. "I jest, Breckin." Eva pressed her mouth on his.

Breckin allowed her to lead the kiss but he became impatient. Passion overrode his good sense and he used his tongue to spur her to respond. The motions of their mouths sent him to groan and to an unsatiable state. It had been some time since he'd been with her and now that he had her in his arms, he wanted nothing more than to enjoy her body.

Eva pulled away from him and tried to get up but he pulled her back onto his lap. Breckin didn't speak but found her mouth again and kissed her longingly. When he was satisfied with his welcome home kiss, he drew away.

"Lord, I missed ye. Come, we should return to the house. This night, we should seek our bed a wee bit earlier," he said teasingly. Breckin helped her to stand and took her hands in his.

Eva gasped and peered at the sky. "Oh, look. The sky is beautiful this eve."

He turned and glanced at the duskiness of the sky but it was entwined with various shades of green, red, and purple. The colors weaved in a remarkable pattern that often held him spellbound. "Ye know, lass, that most believe the lights in the night sky predict a bad omen. Och, I do not agree."

She held on to his arm but kept her gaze on the sky. "What do you believe?"

"Others say it is a sign from the spirits of the dead."

"Like ghosts?"

Breckin shrugged. "I deem it is a sign from God sending his blessings to us. Aye, because I was most fortunate when Alexander forced me to marry ye."

Eva laughed with a scoff. "Forced you to marry me? Hah, I think he forced me to marry you. That seems so long ago, does it not? I find that I am not as displeased as I thought I would be."

"I was blessed that day and every day since. Aye, 'tis gladdened I am that ye are not displeased, Eva, because I thought ye would have a difficult time adjusting to the Highland way of life." He kissed her lightly on her cheek.

"There are days when it is difficult, especially when I have no one to talk to. But now that you are home, I find I am most content."

Breckin wrapped his arm around her waist and guided her back toward the bridge. "This night, ye can show me just how content ye are." He hooted a light laugh when she smirked. Breckin pressed his hand on her face and a smoldering yearning came. He needed her more than she knew.

She leaned her face against his palm and smiled. "Perhaps you should show me how much you missed me."

He stopped in the center of the lane, holding her face in the palms of his hands. With a serious gaze, he stared hard at her. "If it means anything to ye, I thought of ye often when I was away. I missed ye more than ye know. Ye have no notion what ye do to me, lass."

CHAPTER TWENTY

A PLEASURABLE SIGH came when she was roused by Breckin's hand caressing her thigh. His hand meandered to her center and his fingers magically awakened her desire. Eva got swept up by his enthusiastic love play. She wanted to caress him in return, but he pulled her back against him and held her in place. His breath was a promise in her ear of what was to come.

A knock came at their bedchamber door, stopping them momentarily.

Breckin gritted out, "Bloody hell, this better be important."

"Laird, ye received a message, and 'tis of some import," came Aymer's voice.

He rolled away from her and glared at the door. "We will never have privacy or peace. I should go, though. Och, I make this vow, lass, that we will pick this up when I come to bed this eve."

Eva rolled onto her back and watched him garb himself. Looking at his brawny body made her pout with disappointment. She had hoped to be pleasured and wanted to make him as desirous as she could. Nevertheless, it was time to rise and begin her day.

"I will find out what the message is and return for our morning fare." He turned and gave a quick wave before disappearing behind the door.

Eva threw her legs over the side of the bed and sat up. There was a chill in the air and she hastened to close the shutters to the window casement. After, she rummaged through her garments and chose a heavier underdress and then pulled over it a blue gown. Once she'd finished her morning routine, she hurried to the kitchen area.

Breckin's brothers sat at the table and snickered. She wondered what they were up to, but it didn't take long for her to figure out what. Their cheeks puffed out and it appeared they had something in their mouths.

"Tell me you did not eat that entire basket of blackberries." She glared at them but they gave her innocent looks with blackberry juice staining their teeth until she groaned at their affront. Then they gave her guilty looks and their gazes lowered.

Eva waggled a finger at them. "How could you? I had intended to make a blackberry pie for after supper. Well, now, you will go with me this day and help me fill that basket again. And maybe we can get in a little practice. I want to learn how to wield a dagger."

The lads' eyes widened.

Connor chortled, "Och, Milady, ye might get hurt and then..."

"Breckin will blame us," Caden finished.

"I shall not. I promise to take care but I need to be able to protect myself when I go for walks on the other side of the bridge. There are boars there and they are dangerous creatures. Now, have you eaten anything else for your morning fare or just all my blackberries?" Eva tidied up the kitchen area and ate a quick bite of bread.

"We had the leftover pottage from yestereve's supper, Milady," Caden said.

"It was good," Connor said.

"Well then, let us get outside and find those blackberries. And then we will practice. Can you bring an extra dagger or two?" She grabbed the empty basket and then retrieved another. Maybe she could make more than one pie if they were fortunate to find more than one berry bush. With the colder season coming, the bushes were full with an abundance of berries.

The lads hastened from the kitchen area and when they returned, they had covered themselves with a heavier tartan and Caden was shoving daggers inside a pouch that he'd wrapped around his waist.

Eva pulled her cloak around her shoulders, certain she would need it because the day, it seemed, was much colder than the previous days. Autumn was close, so much so that the days grew shorter and the sun sank earlier.

Outside, the air was misted with a fine bit of fog but it was early, and hopefully, it would wear off as the day progressed. Eva followed the lads across the bridge and they foraged the woodland for the berry bushes.

"Let us make a contest of it. Whoever wins shall forgo their chores on the morrow." She laughed when they each approached her and snagged a basket for their collection. They hurried away, running through the thickets and jumping over the shorter yew bushes.

She heard their shouts of triumph and moseyed along in the woods, enjoying the peacefulness of the outdoors and the lad's enthusiasm. How many times had she taken such walks at home but without company? It suddenly struck her that she hadn't thought much of her home lately. She didn't miss the loneliness even though she had few friends here on Buchanan land. With the lads' company, Clare's, Breckin's, and some of the other clansmen, she was beginning to think of the Highlands as home.

"I filled my basket," Connor said with glee as he bounded from behind a large pine.

"Not fair," Caden bellowed. "He cheated."

"Let us see what you have found." She took Connor's basket and nodded. Then she took Caden's and glanced at it forlornly. Caden had only filled his halfway whereas Connor's basket was almost overflowing. To appease them, she nodded. "I deem you both can forgo your chores on the morrow, except I shall still need you to fetch water in the morning. Then you can have the rest of the day to yourselves."

"Breckin has yet to give us our punishment and we might be stuck inside," Connor said.

Caden grumbled. "Do ye think, Milady, that he forgot?"

Eva was certain Breckin had not forgotten but she didn't want to spoil their afternoon with thoughts of what he'd make them do. She shook her head and waved them onward. "Whatever it is, you would do well to be thankful he cares enough to punish you. If you are stuck inside, you can always use the rings I made for target practice. Come along."

"I know the perfect spot where we can practice dagger throwing." Connor walked ahead and she followed.

They passed the bridge and continued. At the headland where a large copse of trees prevented them from seeing the edge, they stopped. It was close to the place where the lit torch that memorialized Marian stood. She thought to perhaps visit that spot when they finished their dagger practice and place some flowers if she could find any.

Connor took the berries from Caden and set the baskets on the ground. He then handed them each a blade. "Milady, ye take the blade and pinch it with your fingers. Take aim, pull back your arm, and then release with all your might." He let go and the dagger sailed through the air. It hit a spot on a pine that had lost many of its lower branches.

Her shoulders sagged as she realized she probably would be no good at throwing a dagger. But she would give it her best.

Caden was next. He said nothing as he took the spot vacated by Connor, took aim, and released his dagger. The dagger sailed through the air, making a swoosh sound. His target was above Connor's and in the exact center of the tree trunk. She was impressed by his talent.

"That was incredible, Caden," she said as she took his spot. "I doubt that I shall even come close." Eva held the dagger the way

Connor showed her and took aim. She pulled back her arm and threw it with all her strength. It missed the tree by a mark and she sighed. "Sweet Mary, this is difficult. Maybe we should forget about this."

"Try again, Milady," Caden said. "Ye will get it. It takes a wee bit of practice."

She reached the tree, grabbed the dagger from the ground, and held it. "I will do better this time—" Eva turned abruptly when she heard a woman's shout. "Did you hear that?"

She raced toward where she'd heard the noise come from and the lads followed. On the approach to where Marian's torch stood, she spotted Breckin standing with a woman. The dark-haired woman spoke but she couldn't hear her words.

The stranger lifted a flask hanging from her belt and appeared to consider taking a drink. Then she offered it to Breckin. He took a sip and then—at the woman's apparent prompting—a larger quaff.

Eva wondered what the flask contained, especially when she saw that he returned it to the woman. Then she pressed the cork back into the spout without taking a drink herself, but instead let it drop to hang by her hip.

The lads stopped behind her and crouched down, likewise watching quietly.

"Who is she? Do you know her?" Eva didn't see a horse near-by and suspected the woman must have walked to their meeting place.

"'Tis Danella," Caden said as he knelt beside her.

Eva's heart sank. "His former betrothed?" *The woman he loved?*

"Aye, but she's married to William Stewart now," Conner said.

"We should leave," Eva said then, but she couldn't draw herself away. Instead, she stayed partially hidden by the thicket as her heart thudded in her chest so loudly, she was certain the lads—if not Breckin himself—could hear it.

Eva was overcome by a sense of betrayal as a range of emotions swarmed her—shock, anger, and extreme sadness. How could he be with another woman when he'd enjoyed being with her? Whatever they'd shared, which had seemed so monumental to her, must have been trivial for him.

Now the lads stood silently next to her as they too watched their brother's boorish behavior. It was as if an arrow pierced her heart. Why had she been so trusting? Unwilling to see any more, she made to leave. She'd return to the longhouse and there, she would decide her next course of action.

But then a movement and the woman's laugh made her turn back. She watched as Breckin's knees seemed to buckle, and the strong warrior fell back and landed on the ground without trying to stop himself from falling. He lay still, without moving. Her breath caught in her throat at the sight of him lying there.

Then a stream of sunlight pierced through the morning mist and Eva saw the glint of a blade in the woman's hand. Eva gasped, pressed her hands on the lads' shoulders, and shifted them away.

"Both of you, go and fetch Gideon and Willa. Your brother is in danger." The lads didn't question her and ran off. Eva ran toward her husband, ignoring the woman. When she reached him, she saw blood staining the front of his tunic. "Breckin!" She bent to reach for him but then the woman grabbed her arm, preventing her from touching him.

"Who are you?" She still held the dagger, stained with Breckin's blood. Now she pointed it at Eva.

Eva held up her hand and said, "Who am I? I am his wife. What have you done?"

The woman's eyes were darkened with anger and she peered at her as if she intended to harm her as well. "He needed to be stopped and I had to… Ye are his wife? I did not know Breckin had married."

"Who are you?" Eva hid the practice dagger she'd forgotten to return to Caden, held in the folds of her gown. She was afraid to look away from the woman, thinking she might attack her but she was more concerned for Breckin. He still had not moved since he'd fallen.

"I am Danella."

"Danella. Why would you harm him?" Eva pressed forward, knowing she had to put herself between the woman and Breckin. Somehow she had to protect him until Gideon arrived. She had no time to wonder why Breckin's former betrothed would want to kill him. Yet, she would do everything to prevent her from doing so.

"He was going to war with my family and would murder everyone in my clan. Aye, we heard that he vowed to make war against us for what I had done. I could not let that happen." Danella shuffled closer to Breckin's body but made no further move to strike him again.

"What did you do?" Eva had to keep the woman talking. She took a glance at Breckin and noticed his eyes fluttering slightly. He was not dead, at least not yet.

"I called off our betrothal. Ye see, I did not want to marry the fiercest warrior in the land. I wanted to marry William and Buchanan stood in my way."

"William? Do you mean William Stewart? But he was betrothed to Marian." Eva shook her head, confounded by the woman's reasoning.

"Aye, 'tis why I had to do what I did because Buchanan could not know that I wanted him not. He would have been wrathful at the time and sent his army to kill us." Danella paced the area before Breckin, hardly giving him any notice now. She seemed caught in memories of her purpose.

"What you did? Did you do something to Marian?" Eva stepped closer to her. "Why would Breckin want to kill your clan? Much time has passed."

Danella's steps increased as she paced before her, holding the dagger in a threatening manner. "I had to get rid of her…Marian. William was in love with her and unless she was gone, he would not have accepted my clan's offer. So I did what I had to do—sent her to the hereafter. It was not difficult because she did not suspect what I was going to do. We were good friends, aye, and she easily took the poisoned drink from me just as Buchanan did now. And so, once she was under the potion's spell, I just had to wait for her to take her last breath."

"If that is so, then why did you stab Breckin?" Eva's heart hurt knowing he was in danger, that his life hung in the balance whilst she stood there talking. But how else could she keep the woman from striking him again?

"The poison would only subdue a man of his strength so I had to seize the moment. I struck him true in the chest, in his overzealous heart, aye, for he'd professed to love me and I could not have that." She looked down at him and waved her hand dismissively. "He shall perish soon. 'Tis time for me to seek my leave."

Eva couldn't let her go and stepped in front of her. "You are not going anywhere. Did you think you could strike down the laird of the Buchanans and walk away?" She rushed at her and grabbed her arm with her free hand, the one not holding Caden's dagger.

"Let go of me," Danella yelled. She yanked her arm and tried to get Eva to release her.

"Not on your bloody life." Eva struggled against the woman and hoped to get her to stop fighting but the woman cocked her arm to strike her with her knife. Eva tried to dodge but moved too slowly.

A sting spread over her shoulder and she drew in a shocked breath. She pushed at Danella, but the wound made her unable to grip the practice dagger and she dropped it. It fell to the ground with a thud; now her chance to protect herself was too far from her reach.

The two of them grappled. Eva saw that they were nearing the edge of the cliff. She tried to move away from the precipice but Danella reached out, grasping at Eva's hair and yanking at it. Eva yelled from the searing pain at her scalp and reached out to strike at her tormentor, trying to escape as stars sparkled in her eyes, punching out. She landed a blow to the woman's midsection. With a grunt, Danella let go of Eva's hair to clutch at her belly and as Eva watched, she stepped backward and away.

Time seemed to stand still as Danella lost her footing at the edge of the cliff. Eva tried to grab hold of her garments. The woman had possibly killed Breckin and tried to kill her as well, but that didn't mean she wanted her to die. Now Danella flapped her arms, trying to regain her balance. Her eyes widened and her mouth rounded in surprise as she fell back. And then she disappeared over the ledge with a shriek that faded as she fell, and then the shriek stopped abruptly.

There was silence. Not even birds sang. Eva dropped to the ground and crawled backward, scrambling to get away from the ledge, and get to Breckin.

When she reached him, she pressed her hand on his face and called his name repeatedly. His eyes didn't flutter now. His skin was pale and his lips had taken on a bluish hue. He'd succumbed to his wound, and the poison he'd swallowed.

Eva's heart thrashed in her chest and tears welled in her eyes. "Breckin, you cannot leave me now…now that I know that I love you. Do not dare to leave me. You cannot, do you hear? Please answer me. I love you…love you…" Distraught, heartache overtook her as tears blurred her sight. She sniffled her tears and tried not to shudder as the fear of losing him took control and sobs began to wrack her body.

"Milady, move back. Let me see what the laird did to himself…" Willa called from behind her. She knelt next to Breckin, shouldering Eva gently aside.

"She poisoned him…" Eva's voice came out in a whisper. Her voice was trapped in her throat, in a thick ball of tears and anguish. "I smell it on him, Milady, the Devil's Nightshade. 'Tis a nasty poison that renders one immobile whilst they still are aware of what is happening. Now that it has taken effect, the laird shall sleep, which is a blessing. Worry not, for I shall care for him, och, ye must let us take him."

Eva wouldn't move, though. She took hold of Breckin's hand. Willa rounded Breckin's body and assessed him from the other side. She cut away his tunic and leaned in to take a whiff of him. While she did so, Eva called him and tried to get him to respond.

Willa rose and waved; suddenly, Gideon and a group of Breckin's men moved forward. They must have arrived with Willa, Eva realized. And the lads! They were there too, seeing their brother still and covered in blood. She tried to compose herself for their sakes as Willa ordered, "Gideon, have the men take him to my cottage. I might have a remedy and we shall see what the dagger's damage is." The healer took hold of Eva, who couldn't stand yet. She was suddenly shaking too hard. Too much had happened, in such a short time. Now all Eva could do was watch through blurred vision as they carried Breckin away. *Breckin!*

"Oh, Milady, ye are covered with blood. Lads, take Milady home so she can get cleaned up. I shall see to the laird. He will be fine, Milady. All will be well. Come once ye can." Willa hurried off.

As if in a dream, Eva followed Connor and Caden until they reached the longhouse. Along the way, many of the clan's men and women lined the path. No one spoke to her and all lowered their heads as she passed. News of the laird's attack had spread faster than a blowing storm. I should speak to them, she thought, but it was too difficult to find the proper words right now. It was getting harder and harder to keep up with the lads. Her feet were too hard to lift and her shoulders too heavy to hold straight, and everything seemed to be behind a thick curtain of sorrow that she could barely see through.

Finally, they reached the longhouse. Without feeling the familiar comfort of her carefully decorated and cleaned home, Eva entered her room and pulled her garments from her body, dropping them to the floor as if she still had servants to care for them.

She couldn't bring herself to care about that. But when she looked, the torn garments were stained with blood. Breckin's? She looked down at her own torso. Her skin was also covered in blood. Bright red, fresh blood. Thick, not thinly smeared, still dripping. Hers? *How?* Then she remembered. Danella had stabbed her. It *was* her blood. The sight of it instantly made her dizzy and she fell back upon the bed.

A knock came and then Clare entered. "Eva, are ye ready to go to Willa's—"

Eva panted and tried to sit up but found it difficult. Finally, she managed to roll to the edge of the bed and push herself upright. "I…I seem to be… She stabbed…me."

"Oh my, Milady. Let me help ye." Clare retrieved a cleaning cloth from the basin and wiped the blood from Eva's body. Once she had her cleaned up, she used a dry cloth and pressed it against her wound. "We need to bind this cloth to ye until we can get ye to Willa's, to stop the bleeding. I'm afraid she'll have to stitch you up." She tore a strip of cloth from one of her underdresses and then used the swath of material to tie the cloth to her body. Then she helped her to dress and covered her with a tartan.

"My t-t-thanks," Eva said with a shiver of shock.

Clare put her arm around her and helped her to stand. "Come, let us get ye to Willa's. She will have ye patched up right quick."

Eva stumbled along until she reached the outside where they ran into Gideon. She heard the muffled words between Clare and Gideon but her head spun and she wobbled on her feet. Gideon marched toward her and snatched her up into his arms and cradled her like she was a child. She rested in his arms with her cheek against his chest.

He wasn't Breckin. He didn't smell like Breckin, or feel like Breckin. Breckin was…she bit back a sob. *Sweet Mary*, was Breckin dead?

"Milady, easy now. I will take ye to Willa's. Rest easy."

Eva closed her eyes. Everything seemed to be getting farther and farther away. Suddenly, the words of her favorite hymn rose unbidden to her mind and she held on to them as Gideon walked quickly to the house of the healer.

It seemed like only moments and yet, an eternity before he entered the dwelling. She opened her eyes as he set her in a chair. Eva peered around and saw Breckin lying still and still bloody on the healer's table. She lowered her gaze to shield her sorrow.

"Milady, are ye well enough to wait a few moments?" Willa asked.

Eva nodded. Their words were muffled in her ears and she tried to pay attention. While she waited for Willa's attendance, she prayed for Breckin. *Mother Mary, to thee do we cry, poor banished children of Eve. Turn then, our advocate, your merciful eyes toward us...*

"Gideon, I need ye to hold down the laird so I can bind his wound. He was fortunate the blade did not pierce his heart, for he was struck just beneath his underarm and the damage was minimal."

"Why then has he not awakened?" Gideon asked.

"I am afeared he's been poisoned with nightshade. There is no antidote. I was able to get him to expel the contents of his stomach so hopefully the effects of the poison will wear off soon. We shall care for his symptoms, for he will likely be confused and might have hallucinations. But my herbal calming mixture shall ease him readily. We must ensure he continues to receive water, so after I stitch him up, Gideon, ye shall pour a drop or two of water in his mouth every so often. We shall keep observing him to ensure the treatment works."

"Is he going to die?" Eva could barely form the words as she asked that question.

"I cannot say, Milady, och we will do our best to aid him."

As Willa continued her remedies, Eva closed her eyes and replayed the event at the torch site in her mind. Her body shook as coldness swarmed her.

Men's voices sounded and she opened her eyes to find two

Buchanan soldiers standing near Gideon. He nodded to them and sent them off.

"Milady, will ye speak to me and tell me what happened? The men found Danella's body at the bottom of the ravine. She perished in the fall."

"I...I did not mean to kill her."

Gideon flashed a smile at her. "Nay? Och, we are mightily gladdened ye did."

She shook her head. "Breckin will be ireful when he learns of this."

"Why would he be ireful, Milady?"

"Because... Oh, sweet Mary, she was his betrothed."

"Tell me what happened," Gideon demanded with a little vigor in his tone.

"The lads and I were gathering berries and then we decided to practice dagger throwing. Ye see, they... Well, they were teaching me because I... This matters not, but as we were practicing, I heard a woman's shout. We went to where we thought she was, and when we arrived, we saw Breckin with her. I was about to leave because I thought..."

Gideon shook his head. "Ye thought your husband was cavorting with her?"

"I might have, until he fell. And then I saw she had a blade...He did not get back up and I realized she had stabbed him. I approached her and she admitted to me that she'd killed Marian, and that she intended to kill Breckin too because she said he was coming after her clan."

Gideon frowned and his voice came out like a growl. "What happened then, Milady?"

"We tussled and when she stabbed me and pulled my hair and I—I punched her in the stomach. She stepped back. I don't think she realized she was so close to the edge. She floundered and fell back and then...I tried to grab her, to pull her back up, but...she disappeared over the ledge." Eva's stomach rose to her mouth and she gagged. With an effort, she swallowed hard and worked to steady herself. Finally, she managed to whisper, "I did not mean to kill her. You mustn't tell Breckin that I did because he has had enough misery of late." Eva couldn't hold back the distress in her tone.

She was unsure if Breckin cared about Danella. Would that change once he learned that she'd murdered his sister? Still, Eva did not want to cause him further grief.

"I cannot keep such an important matter from my laird, Milady."

"I beg you to reconsider."

But Gideon wouldn't appease her and shook his head. Eva lowered her face in defeat, suspecting that Breckin would be distressed to learn that it was her fault that his former betrothed had died, even if she deserved it.

CHAPTER TWENTY-ONE

B RECKIN OPENED HIS eyes and moaned as he peered at the ceiling above. He recalled being stabbed by Danella and seeing Eva there by the torch. Little else remained in his memory. He tried to sense the pain, knowing it was there but he felt nothing. Maybe he'd passed to the hereafter. Maybe he was gone from his world. If that was so, where was he?

"Och, so ye finally awaken?" Gideon's voice came.

Breckin turned his head a little to see his comrade. "Thirsty."

Gideon held a cup to his mouth. "Not too much for the nightshade still weighs heavily upon ye. 'Tis a miracle ye survived it."

"Nightshade?

"Aye, ye were given a potion with nightshade in it. Do ye not remember what happened?"

Breckin pressed his hand over his face, hoping to alleviate the muddled sense that stayed with him. If he'd been given the poison, he suspected that was why he felt no pain. The dulling aura of the nightshade disallowed him to feel the discomfort. "I was injured and yet I feel no effects."

"Aye, and fortunately for ye, she did not do too much damage. She struck your chest, just above your heart. A wee bit lower and ye would be at a glorious feast in the afterlife." Gideon waggled his brows and smiled.

"Bollocks. There would be no celebration for me in the here-after."

Gideon chortled. "Mayhap not, but in the underground, ye would be most celebrated and welcomed."

His comrade's banter forced a scoff from him. "Eva?" Breckin tried to shift from the bed which he now knew to be in Willa's healing cottage. "Is she...? Was Eva harmed? I recall her being there..."

His comrade pressed him back. "Ye are in no condition to go seeking your wife. Best lay back and let the awful potion wear off completely. Eva was harmed, och she is back at the longhouse, resting. Willa is tending to her with Clare's aid. I am afeared that her wound became infected and she is under the spell of a fever. At least that was as it was yestereve."

"I need to see her." Breckin's voice rasped and he motioned for more drink.

Gideon appeased him and allowed him more than a few drops of water. "I was commanded to see to it that ye stay abed for now. Your legs will not support ye, Breckin, so do not argue with me. And I promise ye, I will not be carrying ye."

His breath came heavier as he considered what happened between him and Danella. He remembered receiving the missive from her asking to meet him by the torch. She'd wanted to discuss his war on the MacLaren Clan and hoped to get him to abate. When he refused to back down, she became agitated and spoke harshly. Though now, he couldn't recall what she'd said. Her demeanor at the time, though, certainly alluded to the fact that she was the cause of the troubles then and now.

Breckin closed his eyes and tried to shut out the memories of that day and prayed that Eva survived. He refused to lose her and needed to get to her. But sleep weighed heavily upon him; he struggled but eventually it claimed him.

When he awakened from slumber, he peered into the darkened room. Willa wasn't there, and he could hear no sounds within. His stomach grumbled with hunger and so he shifted his legs aside and sat on the edge of the cot. With a press of his face, he decreased the rest of the grogginess that held him restrained. He wondered briefly how long he'd lain there.

"Willa?" No response came.

He stood on his feet and was a little unsteady. Trudging through the cottage, he made it to the small kitchen area and found half a loaf of hardened bread. Nearby sat a pitcher of warm ale. He poured himself a helping, dunked the bread into it, and took a bite.

Breckin needed to regain some strength and once he filled his stomach, he felt much better. Although his stomach twinged and he thought he'd lose the battle, he took slow breaths until he recovered. He searched around for his garments but there was nothing wearable in the small cottage. His tartan lay across the bottom of the cot and he reached for it. He wrapped it around his body and grabbed his belt to secure it. Once he was modest enough, he yanked the door open.

Darkness set the sky in a dismal aura of a brisk chill. Breckin ignored the cold and walked toward the bridge and crossed it. Aymer stood in the center of the lane on the other side.

"Laird, good to see ye about."

"Aymer, all is well?"

His guardsman nodded. "Aye, Gideon went on sentry duty with a group of soldiers. He will not return until the morrow. Do ye need me for anything?"

"Aye, has Danella's body been retrieved from the ravine?" Breckin wanted to get her off Buchanan land at the soonest.

"She has, Laird, and was wrapped and put in the cold shack until ye told us what to do with her. Should I have her returned to the MacLarens or the Stewarts?"

He took a brief moment to consider the ramifications of both situations. If he sent her back to the Stewarts, William would probably come seeking answers for his wife's death. If he sent her back to the MacLarens, they were sure to take up arms against them. The latter was preferable since he wanted to confront the

MacLarens and end their scuffle. War was inevitable with either of the clans, if not both.

"Await Gideon's return and have him come see me. She will be returned after I speak with him." Breckin nodded firmly to his comrade and set off down the lane toward the longhouse. The closer he got, the more he grew concerned for Eva.

At the door, he hesitated a moment, took a deep breath, and then entered. Inside, a fire crackled in the kitchen hearth. He found Clare pouring heated water into a bowl.

"How is she?"

His aunt glanced up but continued her task. "She sleeps. Her fever abated and the infection has lessened with Willa's tender care. Eva shall live, Breckin. Worry not for her."

Relief washed over him in a wave that would have brought him to his knees were he not a strong and stubborn warrior. "That is good news, Clare, and I thank ye for all ye did for her."

"We Buchanans should be thanking her. For if she had not come to your aid, ye would be dead. She saved our laird and we are grateful." Clare set the pot on the table. "We will ensure Eva knows how important she is to us."

"Aye, she is that…most important, especially to me," he said in a soft voice as emotion snuck into his retort. Though he was a fierce warrior, he didn't usually express such tender-hearted feelings, even to his aunt. With that, he turned toward the bedchamber and entered. Using a gentle hand, he closed the door, making no sound. On the approach to the bed, his heart thrummed slowly, seeing his bonny wife lying so still and in such a wretched condition.

Breckin peered down at her. Eva's face was pale and her bonny brown locks were in tangles. He eased the bedcovering from over her shoulder and hissed at the sight of the stitched, unbound wound there. Her skin was reddened, puffed, and looked sore. The poor lass. What she'd done to save him, how she'd endangered herself, and what she'd endured, all pained him.

"Oh, lass, ye should not have put yourself in danger," he

muttered to her.

Eva's eyes opened and she stared up at him. Then her lips spread in a slight smile and she reached toward him.

Breckin took her hand and held it tenderly. "Ye are awake." He kissed her fingers.

"I worried for you. No one would tell me what befell you. They only said that you survived. I feared the worst, Breckin, but I am pleased to see you," she said in a weak voice.

He grabbed the cup on the sidetable. It was half-full of water. He held it to her mouth. "Drink, lass, ye sound hoarse."

She took the cup from him and downed the contents. When she finished, she handed the cup back to him. "Breckin... I am sorry."

"For what, sweetheart? For saving me? Och, now ye are stuck with me. If it takes me the rest of my life, I will repay ye for it." He let loose a small chuckle at his jest.

"No, for killing her, your betrothed. You cared for her, did you not? And I killed her."

Breckin felt the pull of his brows as he heard her words. "Aye, she cannot hurt us again. Do not hold guilt because ye were protecting yourself."

"You are not angry with me? I tried to get her away from you after she stabbed you and I realized that you were under some spell. We struggled and she stabbed me too. She lost her footing and I tried to keep her from going over the edge but I fell back and she disappeared. She was your betrothed and intended to be your wife, yet I..."

He drew in a deep sigh because Eva misunderstood. "Eva, of course, I am not angry with ye. Aye, she was my betrothed at one time, but I never professed to care for her. Marriage was nothing but a means to strengthen the ties betwixt my clan and hers. Nothing more. I never loved her as I..."

"As you what?" Her grip on his hand tightened.

"As I love you." Breckin grinned. "There, lass, ye heard that aright? I said that 'I love ye' and I mean it." He sat back in surprise as tears rose to Eva's eyes. "Nay, lass, do not weep—"

"I'm crying because you told me you love me, Breckin. And I love you too. More than you could ever know. When I thought you were dead, I—"

"*Wheesht*, now, lass. I'm not dead, and I'm not planning to be for a very long time." He kissed the backs of her fingers again, then stroked them with his thumb. His brave, selfless wife. "Danella sent me a message to meet her and I thought she wanted to discuss a means to end the discord between our clans. We spoke about old times, old friends, my sister. She seemed to have no harm in her, and when she offered me a drink from her flask, I took it as a peace offering. Aye, aye, I was dimwitted to do so, but I thought she was being honorable. When I finished the drink, my head spun and I told her that I would never accept a treaty with the MacLarens and that was when she stabbed me."

"Oh, Breckin, I am sorry she was not to be trusted."

He nodded. "The potion rendered me unable to move but I understood everything that was happening. My mind was clear. I heard your scuffle with her and heard Danella's cry as she went over the cliff. I also heard ye profess to love me."

"I did. I was so afraid of losing you."

Breckin leaned over her and pressed a kiss on her forehead. "Imagine hearing that and not being able to reply. Aye, I wanted to tell you that since the moment I met ye, ye have won me over with your sweet, giving nature."

She waved his comment away, in her usual selfless way. She didn't want to talk about herself, obviously. "Are the lads well? I have not seen them." Fresh tears brought a new shine to her eyes and she smiled.

"I have not seen them. I came to you immediately upon waking. But I will go and search for them now. Whilst I do so, I bid ye to rest, lass. On the morrow, I will have Danella removed from Buchanan land for good. That will be the end of it."

"Will it? I do not mean to question you but... I suppose you probably want to take vengeance on her clan for what she did."

"For what *she* did?" Breckin was uncertain of what she spoke. "If ye mean that she tried to kill us both, then aye, mayhap vengeance is in order."

"When we talked before she went over the cliff, she admitted to killing Marian. Did you hear her say that? She told me that she had to get rid of Marian because she wanted to marry William but he was betrothed to your sister and so she poisoned her. Your sister did not take her own life. She was murdered."

He didn't recall hearing that discussion and surmised that perhaps his worry for Eva must have overtaken him. "I did not hear her confession but believe ye."

"I also found a piece of parchment in the trunk you gave me. Read it, Breckin. Marian wrote something and left it in the lining." She pointed to her trunk that sat across the room.

Breckin chuckled. "I remember when our da taught her to read and write. My da told me once that he valued the time he spent with Marian. She boasted about it too for months as she learned… Lord, I miss her. She had the best banter and enjoyed baiting me."

He found the parchment atop his sister's old trunk and grabbed it, then returned to sit beside Eva on the bed. He realized he didn't want to have any distance from her. Not anymore. Breathless, he opened the parchment and stared down at Marian's fine writing. He blinked back tears as he read the words she'd written.

When he was done, he worked hard to compose himself before turning to Eva. "Ye found this in her trunk?"

"Yes, it was stuck in a seam inside. I forgot to tell you about it. We have not seen each other much and something always distracted me… What are you going to do?" Eva kept him from moving away when she grabbed his arm.

"Naught, love, och I thank ye for giving this to me. Now, get some rest and I will go and find the lads. They shall come on the morrow to see ye."

"That would please me. Will I see you on the morrow too?"

"I am unsure because there are some duties that I must see to and I might be detained. But I promise to return to ye as soon as I am able. I want a vow from ye, Eva… Vow that ye will recover because I wouldst be lost without ye."

She reached to cradle his face with both her hands and promised, "I vow, Breckin, that I shall recover. Now go and see to your duties. When you return to me, I want you to join me here so you can hold me." Her softly spoken declaration reached her eyes with a smile.

"There is naught I want more." Breckin kissed her lips. "When I think of how close I came to losing ye…"

When she'd finally seemed to fall asleep, he retreated from the bedchamber and left the longhouse. Outside, he stood upon the small landing at the door and peered at the sky through the branches of trees, where he noted shining stars. Autumn embraced the Highlands now, and soon, winter would have them in its grip. With that thought in mind, Breckin knew time was essential now. He needed to end his battle with the MacLarens.

For the rest of the night, he settled his brothers and assured them he was well. He gained their promise to look in on Eva and keep her company while he was away. When dawn streaked the sky, he left the longhouse and searched for Gideon.

At the bridge, by the guardhouse, he stood with Aymer in wait for the sentry's return. "Go and tell Alton to have the horses readied. I mean to leave soon after Gideon arrives. Have him get the men rousted and readied."

"For what, Laird?"

"War." Breckin noted the horsemen who rode toward the bridge. The sentry had finally returned. In the lead, his commander-in-arms rode ahead but when he saw him, Gideon slowed his mount and slid from its back.

"Laird, ye be up and about. Gladdened I am to see ye whole and of good health," he said as he approached.

Breckin nodded. But the time for greetings was past. Now was the time for battle, and not for one of his allies, but for the good of his own Buchanan clan. "Gideon, I ordered Alton to ready the horses and gather the men."

His comrade stopped in front of him. "What goes?"

"We will return Danella's body this day and then..." Breckin wanted to form the words properly.

"And then what?"

"And then, we use our arms to seek retribution. Aye, for the death of my dear sister, for the attack on me and my wife, for the lies and deceit enacted by their clan when they pulled out of the treaty, and because I bloody well detest them."

"Many good reasons, Laird. 'Tis time the MacLarens understand they cannot go against a Buchanan and not suffer for it."

Breckin wanted them to suffer and once he saw to the MacLarens, he'd deal with the Stewarts. Before the cold weather crept in, he was determined they'd be at peace. "Nay, they cannot. We will bring them to heel or end them completely."

CHAPTER TWENTY-TWO

S MOKE EMANATED FROM the spires atop the MacLaren holding. Breckin sat upon his warhorse on the hilltop with his men, awaiting his allies. Not that he needed additional forces. He could well take the MacLarens with the two scores of men he'd brought. Yet he wasn't about to disappoint the MacNabs or Campbells. They'd want in on the fight and he would allow them to right several wrongs done to them by the MacLarens.

"'Tis time to go forth, Laird," Gideon said as he sidled his horse next to his.

"Not yet. I am awaiting Daniel and Colin. They should be here soon if our messengers rode like hell. Besides, the MacLarens are unaware that we sit here waiting to attack."

"My sword arm is tense with anticipation. What gets me is that they sent a woman to do their foulness."

He shook his head. "I am uncertain that they did and deem Danella might have acted on her own. Och, I would not put it past John to send his daughter to try to murder me. We shall find out when we breach their holding."

"Good thing Milady pushed her over the edge and saved us from having to murder a woman. Her act warranted a killing, Laird, and we would have done our duty," Gideon said.

Breckin raised a brow at his comrade's summation. The Buchanans might be a bit coarse but they were certainly not murderers of women or weakened people. That was what he'd done these past years: aided those who could not defend themselves. But Danella MacLaren needed no one to save her from her own peril. She gambled against the Buchanans and lost.

"Here comes Colin now." Breckin turned on his mount and faced his comrade.

Colin looked ready for war. He wore more chainmail and leather than usual and he had not one but two swords strapped to his back. As he approached, he called out, "Breckin, tell me your message is true. Do I get to cut down a few MacLarens this day?"

"Aye, ye do."

Colin grinned. "Well then, 'tis a bonny day to be sure."

Daniel MacNabb approached with several of his followers. "Laird Buchanan…Breckin, 'tis good to see ye this fine day. Are we to war?"

"We certainly are," Breckin said with a lilt of humor in his tone. "We will surround the fief and attack from all sides. I will go with Gideon and gain entry to find John MacLaren. He has some questions to answer before he meets his maker. I am through with being patient. No one goes against the Buchanans and then sends a woman to do their dirty work."

Daniel twitched his finger. "What do ye speak of? What happened?"

Breckin filled Daniel and Colin in on the attack at his home and how his sweet wife had to defend herself and save him—and herself—from the horrid woman. "I seek vengeance now. We will take it and by day's end, will be satisfied with our reward." He patted his horse's neck and nodded. "Go on, take your men, and begin the besiegement. MacLaren protects his walls and has a good amount of men within but not enough to thwart us. We will prevail."

"What are we going to do?" Gideon asked.

"Breach the gate and find John MacLaren. He will tell me to my face that he intended for his daughter to murder me and then…"

"Then?" Gideon said and yanked his sword free.

"Then retribution will be mine." Breckin rode through a mass of footsoldiers but stopped when the gates opened and a rider appeared, heading straight toward him. He recognized William Stewart and was about to shout out his war cry when the man had the nerve to wave a white piece of cloth above his head. He called for a parlay and Breckin wasn't sure he was willing to give it. Yet, he would hear what the man had to say.

"Buchanan, ye are attacking my ally. What goes?" William stopped his horse near his and grimaced.

"What goes, William? Your wife is dead. She attacked me and my wife and she fell off the cliffside to her end. Her body is yonder. I was going to bring her to ye once I handled the MacLarens and their demise. Were ye in league with them, William? Tell me true."

William scratched his head and then shook it. "Nay, I was not. Ye killed Danella?"

"Nay, she stabbed me and my wife. Eva and she struggled, but then she stepped too close to the edge of a cliff during the scuffle and fell to her death. 'Tis no one's fault but her own, for she tried to murder us." Breckin shifted his horse closer. "I tell ye this, though, if she had not fallen, we would have sought justice for her action."

"Why would Danella attack ye? It makes no sense. Och, she acted alone, though, because I know that John never would have gone against ye. The MacLarens had no involvement in what Danella did. I vouch for him. He is a good man, Breckin."

The fact that the man showed no emotion or care about the death of his wife said much about him, and his marriage. Breckin would have felt pity for Danella, had she not shown such hatred toward his sister, him, and Eva. She had been a cold and calculating woman, and had died because of her own treachery. "So ye say, och I disbelieve ye. Why would she try to kill me then, if not for her clan's directive? Her father sent her to murder me and I mean to make him pay for it."

William scoffed. "Nay, he would not do that. Neither did I, Breckin, and know not what the woman intended. Talk to her da and he shall tell ye that neither of us instigated her. Ye know that I wouldst never raise arms against ye. John wouldst not either. He was a good friend to your da and coveted the union betwixt your clans, as do I."

Breckin was unsure whether to believe William but he nodded and motioned to him. "Come then, ye will question the MacLaren laird with me and we will get to the bottom of this." He nudged his horse forward, past the men who took up defensive arms. It wouldn't take much incitement for his men or his allies' men to seek vengeance. Especially after what the Buchanans lost in the wake of the MacLaren's despicable deeds. Breckin forged on toward the main fief.

Gideon held his sword aimed at William Stewart and nodded to him, giving the silent notion that if William was up to no good, he'd protect his back.

At the fief, Breckin dismounted and marched forward. Gideon pressed William Stewart on with his blade at his back. "Go on, follow… And do not try anything because my sword is thirsty for some blood."

William remained silent as they entered the fief.

Breckin continued until he reached the great hall. The hall was dark with a handful of candles lit and a fire brightening the hearth. He found John MacLaren standing with his son near the blazing warmth. Breckin did not bother to announce himself but listened to their discussion. They seemed oblivious to their presence.

"Tell me why my walls are being breached." John MacLaren grabbed his son's tunic, fisted the fabric, and shook his son. "What in bloody hell have ye done?"

"I did naught, Father. 'Tis not me that draws them to our walls. Best ask them."

"If ye had anything to do with this, I vow I will scuddle ye." John slapped his son's head and turned with a glare. "Well, it appears we have company. Buchanan, mind telling me why ye breached my walls and ye and your allies have drawn your arms?"

"Aye, I will." Breckin stepped closer but kept a little distance between him and his enemy. He reiterated what Danella had done and how she met her demise. "Why would ye send your daughter to murder me? Ye said that ye wanted an alliance and did not call off the betrothal—"

John grunted and continued to hold on to his son's arm. "I did not. Ye know that we set in place a covenant to join our clans." He turned a scornful gaze to his son. "Did ye have anything to do with this? If ye intended to have your sister murder the Buchanan laird, I swear by God, ye will pay for it. Tell me now."

"Da," his son cried out when John gripped him tighter. "Nay, I did not. Danella told me naught about what she was up to."

"I disbelieve ye because ye were always doing her bidding. Ye never wanted us to form an alliance with the Buchanans, och we needed to so we could survive. Many clans go against us now. Did ye go against my wishes?" Laird MacLaren shouted each word and his voice thundered through the hall. His son tried to gain his release but was unable to and then his father grabbed his throat and squeezed. "Ye will tell me the truth now."

Breckin was astounded by their interaction. It appeared the elder had no regard for the younger and the younger had no respect for the elder. Stunned, he could do nothing but wait to see what would happen. It only took a brief moment before the son cried out.

"Aye, aye, it was me. I broke the almighty covenant that ye sought. I had to because we do not have to be at the Buchanan's mercy. We can make our way and have always done so. Besides, Danella did not want to marry Breckin and begged me to help her out of it. She wanted to marry William and she pleaded with me to try to persuade Marian to accept me, but I could not. Marian suspected our treachery and told me so. Danella and I...we formed a plan."

John MacLaren shoved his son and he fell on his backside,

staring up at his father. The younger MacLaren said, "Danella came the other day and said that the Buchanans intended to infiltrate our clan and sought war with us. With our recent fracases, our soldiers' numbers are depleted and I told Danella that we might not be able to withstand a battle."

John bellowed, "So ye sent your sister to murder the Buchanan laird?"

"Nay, nay, I told her to go and speak to Breckin…that he might take her word that she wanted to marry William, not him, and that maybe he would understand," the younger MacLaren shouted.

"This recent event, Breckin, might be down to me. I might've said something about your angst about her taking me for her husband and that it might cause a war." William approached John MacLaren. "Breckin is my comrade and I never would have gone against him if I had known that ye did not break the betrothal. This has all been deceitfully designed by your children. I am no longer aligned with ye, MacLaren. Your daughter's corpse is outside the walls. She died because of her and your son's own duplicity. I refuse to tend to her as I would a true wife." William spat on the floor in front of John MacLaren, then turned to Breckin. "Buchanan, when ye wish, come and see me. We will talk about a possible alliance." With that, William left the hall.

Breckin stood with his arms folded over his chest. He wasn't sure what to say. The MacLaren children caused the strife and he did not want to bring trouble to MacLaren. Not really. Not if he had no hand in the attacks that had nearly killed him and Eva. Now that his daughter was dead, it seemed Marian's death had been revenged; both of them had lost beloved women. Beyond that, John had been a close comrade to his father which was why the betrothal had been created in the first place.

John paced before the fire and glared at his son. "I know not how to make amends for this. In time, I shall make recompense for your understanding and for bringing my daughter's body home. Though she does not deserve it, we shall bury her with her mother. As to my son, he shall be stripped of any authority."

"I want no further trouble, John. If I let ye be, I expect the same."

"Ye will have no trouble from me."

"Let that then be the end of this." Breckin nodded to him and turned away. His body tensed with the pressure of the situation but when he reached the outside, he gulped air. It was done. Now he knew why Danella attacked him, why her brother had broken the betrothal, and especially knew that their father had been completely unaware of their traitorous acts.

"Laird, are we done here?" Gideon asked.

"Aye, we are finished. Call the men to retreat and let us head home." He had promised his wife he would return to her quickly, and he intended to make good on that vow. Perhaps, now that he knew his sister's soul resided in Heaven and didn't need his sacrifice to be released from Hell, he might even be able to promise that he'd stay home for good.

CHAPTER TWENTY-THREE

FOR NEARLY A sennight, Eva rested, ruminated about what happened at the torch with Danella, and prayed that Breckin didn't hold extreme wrath against his enemies. Or they, him.

Surely, after all their losses, it was best not to add to others' despair or even their own. The thought of others being killed because of a woman's selfish acts clutched at her heart.

Now, somewhat healed and definitely stronger, Eva retrieved a tartan to wrap around herself. She wanted to get outside for a short spell. She'd decided that she'd been cooped up long enough. Now that she was on the mend, she needed to get back to her routine—which somewhat baffled her. In truth, she had no responsibilities to keep her to task. The longhouse had been tidied by Clara after the lads spent most mornings in the kitchen area learning how to make meals. She smiled to herself at their folly but was impressed that they cared enough to learn to cook.

Outside, she walked aimlessly toward the bridge but then stopped at the stable to see Alton. Inside the stable, the darkened lane led her to her horse's stall. Eva had yet to name the mare, but she was a beautiful honey-colored shire mare with white specks on her coat. "What shall we call you, hmm?" She petted the soft hair on the horse's nose.

"Milady, good day. She's a fine mare, there… Ye having trouble naming her?"

"I was thinking of naming her Starlight because of her speckles. I shall think about it some more. Where are the horses kept for Connor and Caden?"

Alton waved his hand toward the exit of the stable. "They be occupied in the pen outside."

She smiled and looked to see the lads in the paddocks beyond. Caden was cantering his horse barebacked, while Connor was sitting backward on his horse and watching his brother with enthusiasm while his horse munched, disinterested and unconcerned, on some hay. "I'm hoping that soon they will teach me to ride, now that I am healed." She sighed. "I suppose Breckin has not returned?"

"Nay, I am sorry, Milady. None of the soldiers have returned as yet."

"I shall go then and visit Willa. Maybe she could use a hand." Eva smiled at the man as she passed him and left the stable.

By the time she reached Willa's cottage, Eva's stride had quickened. Being outside agreed with her and made her feel strong. Before long, she would be back to her usual walks. Now she approached the healer's door and knocked, then waited for the woman to answer.

Willa opened the door and smiled. "Good day, Milady. Come inside. I just heated a good batch of mead and welcome the company. We shall partake of it together. I should check your wound too and ensure ye are healing properly."

She stepped through the threshold and breathed deeply. "It smells so good in here."

"'Tis the sweetened honey, aye, for it is ripe and ready. This is my best batch of mead in a good long time. Sit." While Eva did so, Willa set cups on the table and took a cloth to take hold of the warm pitcher. She poured them each a helping and rounded the table. With gentleness, she shifted the material of her overdress and inspected Eva's shoulder.

"How is it? Does it look ghastly?" Eva drew in a resigned breath, hoping that the wound wasn't gruesome.

"'Tis healing nicely, lass. Take care not to reinjure yourself or open the wound, though. What are ye about this day? Have ye naught more important to do than to visit this old lady?"

"You certainly are not old, Willa. I thought to give you company and I… Well, I wanted to thank you for your aid. You have been so kind to me since I arrived at the Buchanan holding, even on that first day when I ailed. Then you cared for me again when that woman struck me. I want you to know how grateful I am." She paused and drew a breath. For courage. "There was something that I wanted to ask…"

Willa took a sip of mead and set her cup before her. "Ye seem to hesitate, lass. Whatever it is ye wish, I shall be delighted to help if I can."

"I have not talked to Breckin yet but want to discuss having children. There is a matter that concerns me, though. My mother died whilst birthing me. I never knew her. None ever spoke how or why she'd died but only that she had perished after she bore me. I am frightened because…" Eva lowered her head, unable to speak her fears.

"Ah, I understand. Ye are afeared to get with child because ye think ye will die?"

She nodded.

"We know not what God has planned for us, och I will tell ye that I have aided many women in birthing their bairns. My son's wife had a difficult birth but we were able to save her lad, Hamish. As you know yourself, my grandson thrives now." Willa smiled and Eva knew she was thinking again of how Eva had sat in a tree with him and used Hamish's slingshot to chase away that boar. But then Willa sobered and said, "There have been easy births and difficult ones. My skill precedes me, it seems, because most of the clan's women seek my aid. So ye should not hold back because of your fears, lass. We shall confront any difficulties when and if we must. Until then, dream and hold to your heart the joys of motherhood."

"I want to give Breckin children and I want to be happy about it," Eva confessed.

"Then ye shall do so. Now cease your fretting, lass. All will be well and I shall be with ye. When ye find out ye are carrying, come and see me and we will form a plan." Willa set her hand atop hers and patted it.

"My thanks, Willa, for your kindness and for aiding me."

The two women sat, chatting. How easy it was now, for Eva, to talk to Willa. Truly, the healer had become a friend. After she finished her cup of mead, Eva bid her farewell and left her cottage.

On the way toward the bridge, she smiled to herself and wondered what Breckin would think of her announcement that she was ready to enlarge their family.

The short distance to the bridge lay ahead. Before she reached it, a handful of riders tromped over it. Aymer stood in the center of the lane and held up his hand.

Words were spoken, but she couldn't discern what it was until she got closer, and Aymer began to yell. "Och, Milady," he called. "Ye have company."

The horsemen parted and Eva was surprised to see Chamberlain Edmund riding through. When he reached her, he dismounted and smiled. "Milady Buchanan, 'tis good to see ye."

"Edmund? What are you doing here? Oh, sweet Mary, there is no bad news about her grace?" Eva hoped Queen Margaret had no difficulty with the birth of her baby.

"Her grace has borne us a new princess, one who the entire court dotes on, and who promises to be as strong as her father and her mother. But nay, that is not why I am here, Milady. I...ah, perhaps we can go somewhere quieter, more private."

Eva bowed to him. "Forgive me, Edmund. You must be tired and ravenous from your journey. Come, and I shall see to your needs." She walked toward the longhouse and the man followed. She said nothing along the way, completely caught up in thoughts of why he was there and what news he brought.

When she reached the longhouse, she opened the door for

him. He stepped through the threshold and made his way toward the hearth. Eva hurried to it and added a log. There was a small flame there, and hopefully, the additional log would ignite and send warmth to the man. Surely, he needed warmth from his tiresome journey from Edinburgh.

She then went to the kitchen area and fetched a cup of ale for him. On her return, she handed him the cup. "Please, Edmund, be seated and tell me why you have come all this way."

Edmund lifted the cup and took a sip of the drink before he set it on the table in front of him. Briefly, he considered the fire before turning his gaze on her. His eyes were saddened. "I am afraid my news is most dire, Milady. Is Laird Buchanan here?"

"No, he is off," Eva ceased her words because she didn't want to impart that her husband was off warring. "He should return soon if you wish to wait…"

"'Tis not he whom I have come to see. My news is troubling and I know not how to tell ye this, other than to just say it." He took a deep breath. "Milady, your dear father has departed."

Eva's breath hitched as she listened to him. *Departed?* "Edmund, are you saying that my father has…died?"

"Aye, Milady. I received word from your brother Richard. He tells me that your father's ailment was difficult and that he never recovered from it upon returning from Edinburgh, after your marriage. He died early in the summer. Richard heard that I was headed this way, for I intended to visit others in the area, and he wanted me to tell you because he did not want you to hear the news from others. I am sorry, Milady, to be the bearer of such unfortunate news."

Eva suppressed the urge to weep. She pressed her eyes so they would not tear. "I suspected his ailment was perilous. I deem he tried to tell me so and sent me a missive before he passed."

"Aye. For he was a good man, your father, Milady. The king has received many missives from those with whom your father did business with across the channel, proclaiming their sympathies. Our nation shall long mourn for him." He bowed his head.

"I am sorry for your loss."

"My thanks, Edmund, for making the journey and coming to tell me." Eva pressed her hands against her chest, trying to abate the tremble that overtook her. But her sadness still crept through her and she had to will herself not to cry.

"It was no trouble."

Eva leaned on her knees and wanted to flee to her bed chamber so she might weep in private, but the man made no move to leave. "Do you need a place to rest this night, Edmund? I can have a room ready for you if you would like to stay."

"Oh, nay, I must be on my way. The king's emissary will not await me for long. We must be on our return to Edinburgh. I just wanted to impart my news and... Will you give my regards to Laird Buchanan?"

"I will. Shall I walk you back to the bridge?"

"There is no need. I hope to see you in Edinburgh in the future, Milady, along with your husband. I am sure the king and queen will welcome a visit." Edmund bowed to her.

"Take care, Edmund." Eva walked him to the door. Once it was closed, she leaned against it and felt coldness wash over her. "Oh, Da, I should have been there...should have been able to say farewell." She wiped at her eyes and shivered, overcome with the despair of losing her father. But Eva wasn't one to dwell with emotion. After a long moment, she gathered herself, opened the door and stepped outside.

A good long walk would ease her and she ambled on the lane until she reached the bridge. By the time she got there, the chamberlain and his men were gone. She crossed the bridge and strode toward the torch. The flame danced in the breeze, reminding her of how fleeting life was, flickering like a flame. At least her father had lived a good, long life. Others, like Marian, were not so fortunate and only survived a score of years.

She sat near the tree where Breckin had been attacked, where Marian had died, saddened by thoughts of those who departed from them. But soon, her solitude was broken as noises came down the lane. She recognized the tromping of hooves, horses' snorts, the squeak of saddles and the clank of armor. Eva readied to get to her feet as she spotted Breckin.

He dismounted from his horse before it came to a full stop. With a quick stride, he reached her and took her into his arms. Neither spoke but only embraced in the dimming light of the evening.

After a short time, Breckin pulled back and gazed at her. "I am sorry, love, about your da. Aymer told me that Edmund came to relate the news."

"My da knew that he was going to die and he tried to tell me. I am just sad that I could not be there with him in his final moments." Eva pressed herself against him and sighed.

"It was how he wanted it. That's why he sent ye the missive and the coins. Do not blame yourself, lass, because there was naught ye could do to help him." Breckin's large hand caressed her back, solacing her with his touch.

"You should not hold guilt either."

"Aye? I should not, och I do because…" He lowered his head and ceased his words.

She cradled his face with her hands and lifted it. "Neither of us were responsible for what happened to our families. We will honor them, though, and shall never forget them."

"I deem it is time to douse the flame and have the torch removed." Breckin tried to pull away from her and reached for the torch.

Eva shook her head and kept hold of him. "No, I think we should keep the torch here and add other torches for those who have passed…my da, your parents… We shall only light them, though, on special feast days or days to remember them."

"That is a fair idea, love. Come, 'tis getting cold. We should return to the house. All were worried about ye." Breckin held out his arm for her to take.

Eva linked her arm to his and together they walked along quietly. "I think we should perhaps talk about starting our family."

Breckin stopped short. "Ye want to have a bairn?"

"I do." Eva gave him a smile. "Children will bring us joy. We need joy, Breckin."

He flashed a big smile. "Aye, we do need joy. Do ye know what would make me happy?"

She shook her head and giggled as she considered his answer. They crossed the bridge and several clansmen and women passed, offering greetings.

Breckin stopped in the center of the lane and pulled her against him. "Having ye naked in my arms again. Aye, for it has been too long since I was given such joy."

Eva set her mouth on his and kissed him longingly before she pulled away from him and sprinted toward the longhouse. Breckin followed her with a joyful shout, and when they got inside their home, she hurried to their bedchamber, thankful that the lads were still outside at the stable. Breckin closed the door with a thud and marched to her.

She couldn't disrobe fast enough. As soon as her garments were shed, she helped Breckin remove his tunic, belt, and tartan. His muscular chest beckoned to her hand and as she pressed her palm to his body, she gasped at the warmth of his skin.

"I am yours, Breckin, always."

A MARVELOUS EROTIC sensation awakened her from a deep slumber. She found Breckin between her legs pressing his silky tongue against her womanhood. Eva moaned as pleasure swarmed every part of her.

"What are you doing?" she asked breathlessly.

"Ye wanted to make a bairn," he said as he slid his nose over her torso and continued onward until his lips were but a breath from hers. "That is what I am doing. We will make one this day, this moment." Breckin slid into her and sent more rivets of pleasure to her womanhood.

Eva succumbed to the exquisite torment and squealed as twinges of pleasure took her to an unknown place, in an aura of intense desire. When she recovered, she pressed her hands on Breckin's chest and kept herself from being shifted. His thrusts were forceful, and she loved how he moved against her with unabashed passion. With the pad of her thumb, she caressed the manly curve below his neck and felt the vibration of his moan.

Breckin fell against her, his breath rasping, his body tense, and his smile wide. "Lord, what ye do to me. Ye are the sweetest, most winsome woman I have ever beheld."

She caressed the long strands of his blond hair and held him close. Eva didn't want the encounter to end but he fell next to her and set his head in the crook of her neck.

After a long moment, well after their recovery, she gently turned his face to look at her. "You never did tell me what happened."

"What happened where?"

"At the MacLaren holding. Did you war with them? Did you seek vengeance? I fear many were killed." Her heart tensed because as much as she understood why her warrior husband wanted retribution, sometimes there was more benefit to diplomacy.

Breckin leaned upward. "Laird MacLaren had nothing to do with what happened. Apparently, Danella wanted William Stewart and she was willing to kill Marian to have him. She convinced her brother to go along with her plan. When she thought I'd show my wrath against her father's people, she came to kill me first."

"What a woman would do for love." Eva almost groaned because she might have done the same if she was in a similar situation. "I wish she had not fallen over the ledge. We could have remedied the situation and talked to her, made her understand..."

He shook his head. "Nay, it was too late for understanding.

She'd already murdered my sister and put her clan in jeopardy. When she tried to do away with us, she probably knew she was in danger of losing her life. Justice prevailed."

"Aye, justice that took from many those who were loved. It is so sad, Breckin."

"Aye. My sister trusted Danella and that her friend murdered her... I cannot even think about it. Marian's final moments must've been torturous for her."

Eva smoothed a hand over his shoulder and scooted down to lie closer. "We shall keep Marian in our hearts and be contented that surely God welcomed her in Heaven. She does not despair in Purgatory, or worse, in Hell. But so, I presume you did not go on a murderous rampage then?"

Breckin scoffed, then sobered. "Lord, I wanted to. It took great will to withhold my sword but some died by my ally's hand and that of my men's. That could not be helped."

"Then we should go to Mass this morning to give thanks to God for intervening and pray for the lost men. Surely God played a hand in the MacLaren's protection." Eva scooted from the bed and went about starting her morning ritual of cleaning herself, tidying the chamber, and pulling out clean garments for them both. "Are you going to leave our bed this day?"

He flashed a grin. "I would rather not, och, I suppose I should see to my duties." Breckin stood, and quickly dressed then waited for her as she pulled a heavy tartan around her shoulders.

"I wonder where the lads got to," Breckin said when they entered the kitchen area.

"'Tis quiet. They probably left the house. Come or we shall be late for Mass." Eva smiled when he took her hand and held it on the walk to the bridge.

Aymer called out to them as they approached. "Good day, Laird and Milady."

Breckin nodded to him. "Have ye seen my brothers?"

"Indeed. They rousted early this day and went to the training field afore the sun rose."

"Did they? Tell Gideon to keep them there. I will join them later," Breckin said.

"Tell 'em yourself, Laird. He is standing yonder." Aymer tilted his head in the direction where Gideon stood awaiting him.

Eva walked ahead of Breckin and on the other side of the bridge, she stopped.

Greetings for the day came from the women they passed and she returned the courtesy even though she was surprised by their kindness. When they reached Gideon, she moved to stand next to Breckin. The commander's wife was not fond of her and Eva did not wish for awkwardness so she kept quiet.

"Milady Buchanan," Deena said and leaned to the side to see her. "I want to thank ye for your aid of our lad Hamish. I understand ye saved him from that wretched boar in the woods near my ma's home."

Eva shook her head. "No thanks are necessary. In truth, he saved me just as much as I aided him. He's a smart boy. If he hadn't had the slingshot and some rocks, I think we'd still be up that tree." She smiled at Deena, and was surprised to see her smiling back. Her heart rose. Usually the woman was staid and taciturn.

Then she surprised Eva even further. "Will ye and our laird join us for supper on the morrow? I am making a large meal and wish to thank ye properly."

Eva blinked. "I...yes, if Breckin..." She turned to her husband, hoping he agreed with her.

"We would be honored to join you," Breckin said and nodded to Gideon. Then he eased her away by wrapping his arm around her back and guiding her onward. As they walked, he murmured, "Seems to me that you have won another heart. Deena is not one to make friends, but I think you have won her over."

"Aye," she agreed, and leaned her head against him as they walked.

Across the bridge, near the church, groups of people waited to enter. Most smiled at them as they passed by. Eva entered the church and meandered to the front, near the altar. She crossed herself and genuflected towards the altar, then slid into the pew, making room for Breckin to sit next to her. Many followed, entering and filling the church. Father Murphy arrived at the side entrance and began to sing a hymn. Everyone rose and took up the hymn as he proceeded to stand in front of the altar. As usual, Eva joined in the singing, and she smiled up at Breckin as she did. He began to sing as well.

The hymn ended and Father Murphy raised his hands to the congregation. "What a glorious day, Clan Buchanan. 'Tis joyful to see ye here this day in God's house." He made the sign of the cross over them. "Let us pray."

FATHER MURPHY PERFORMED a delightful mass and after the last prayers were spoken, all began to exit the church. Eva smiled at the clergyman before she too left. Outside, she found Breckin waiting for her near a group of women. She took his hand and waited for him to move on, but he tilted his head at the women as if to give her a silent suggestion to speak to them. His encouragement gave her the mettle to do so.

She gave him a smile and turned back to the women.

Deena stepped toward her. "Eva, the women asked me to ask ye… Would ye be kind enough to join us on the morrow? We take singing practice just after the noon meal at my cottage."

"I would love that. You all sing so lovely."

As she and Breckin continued on the path, he kept his gaze ahead and said, "Ye see, lass, ye are well-liked here amongst your clan and well-loved by me."

Eva couldn't hold back the joy that came to her heart at hearing him say such. She smiled and leaned into him because that was all she had ever hoped for—to be loved, liked, and cherished. *My clan, my family, and my friends.*

CHAPTER TWENTY-FOUR

THE HARVEST CELEBRATION took place at the beginning of October. They had been late in planning it for several reasons. Fortunately, the women of the clan stepped in and handled most of the harvest and storing of the crops. Since it was stored away for the oncoming winter months, thanks to the aid of Eva's carts, the gathering could go forth.

With the possible war with the MacLarens, they hadn't considered getting started on planning a clan gathering because most of the soldiers were busy attending to arms. The MacLarens kept to their lands, likely licking their wounds from their traitorous acts against the Buchanans and others.

With the weather growing colder by the day, Breckin wanted to celebrate before it became too chilly to be outside. Throughout the morning, he met with his clansmen and had them assist in putting up streaming banners, building firepits along the lanes, and helping to hunt for the feast they would partake in before dusk set the sky that day. Fires now lit the pits and sent warmth to those who stood around the short, enclosed walls.

As he ambled along the lane and ran into Gideon. "Laird, all is readied. The children seem delighted and the younger soldiers set up games for them. There shall be competitions of fete this day. Why did we not have a harvest celebration before...? 'Tis good to bring the clan together."

"My ma and da did years ago but then I suppose it was forgotten. We will hold it every year going forward och much earlier in the season, for 'tis too damned cold."

"I am looking forward to the cold months and being inside and bloody warm."

Breckin stopped him from leaving when he asked, "Are the men repairing the tailor's hut as I bid? I promised James that we would rebuild it."

Gideon bobbed his chin. "They started yestereve and should finish this day. Lawrence put all his builders on it so they might finish before the celebration begins."

"Good. I certainly hope my brothers have learned their lesson about lighting fires. At least they seemed to have." Breckin turned but then his comrade stopped him by taking his arm.

"Oh, here, before I forget," Gideon said and pulled out a creature from inside his tunic. "This wee lad was keeping me warm. Ye wanted a kitten for Milady. Master Amos had a litter of them at his stall yestereve and I snagged one for ye." Gideon chortled and handed him the pet, a red-haired tabby that was a good size. He pounded his back with force and walked away.

Breckin held the kitten gently in the crook of his arm and walked hastily to the longhouse as the tiny creature mewed and made small hissing noises as it dug its claws into his sleeve. "Wheesht, cat," he soothed. "You'll be home afore long."

As he entered the longhouse, he saw Eva in the kitchen area making bread. She had a smattering of flour on the bodice of her overdress and a little on her nose. He kissed it away when he reached her.

"I have a gift for ye." He pressed the kitten in her hand. "My ancestors used to give kittens to their brides. It was thought to honor the Goddess of Love and bring joy to the bride. Or perhaps that was because her larder would then be free of vermin."

Her eyes rounded, then softened as she lifted the small feline to eye level. "Oh, what a sweet little thing," she cooed. And then she turned to him. "Thank you, Breckin. I shall love it, just as I love you."

"Perhaps ye can love me a wee bit more?" He laughed when she pinched his arm.

"Of course. You are the only man I love and far more important to me than a mere cat." She set the kitten on the floor and it scurried off to hide beneath a table.

"Come with me. There is another surprise for ye." Breckin led her from the longhouse and continued on the well-worn path.

Alton stood with his brother Aymer at the gatehouse. He stopped to greet his clansmen. Both glared and seemed disgruntled about something but that wasn't unusual because his brethren were known to be cantankerous.

"What is amiss?" he asked them. "Oh, nay, does this have something to do with my brothers? Have they caused some mishap or commotion? Tell me now so I might think of a suitable punishment."

Aymer chuckled under his breath. "I saw your brothers early this morn when they'd finished their rides and headed to the training field with Gideon. They wore serious miens, Laird, and I expect the commander is setting a hefty schedule for them."

"I saw Gideon earlier and he did not mention my brothers attending to their training. Mayhap that is good news. What then is the trouble?"

Alton set his fisted hands on his hips. "Seems Hamish was seen leaving the stables a short time ago. When I entered, I found all the reins in the stable had been tied together in knots. It will take me most of the day to unfurl them. Bollocks, no one has time for that this day. The lad pulled a prank worthy of your brothers' renown."

Breckin bellowed a laugh; Eva joined in with her soft, feminine chuckle. "For once my brothers aren't the cause of the clan's troubles," he told her, and she nodded, appearing pleased.

Although he wanted to head to the training fields right away to rub in Gideon's face the trouble his son had caused, he had something more important to do.

He clasped Eva's hand and smiled at the shine in her eyes, and they continued to walk.

They passed the bridge, the church, and the torch area until they could go no further. At the end of the lane in an open area of land before the waters of the river, sat a piece of land he'd always appreciated.

"It is beautiful here. How have I not been here before? Have you hid this from me?"

Breckin shrugged. "I kept this area to myself because… I liked the privacy and solitude of this place. 'Tis where I would come when I had thinking to do. But I deem this would make a good spot for a large manor home. I might even make it a tower with walls to protect us. What think ye of that?"

Eva walked forward and seemed to be taking in the beauty of the land. She turned and shook her head. "Breckin, I do not need a large manor home or castle. The longhouse is perfect because we are safe there and amongst our clan."

This is not the response he'd expected. Breckin frowned. "If it's the expense that worries ye, we have a plentiful amount of coin to build it. I want to give you a home that is befitting you, akin to your da's."

She reached him and took both his hands in hers. "My da's home was elegant…but it was also a solemn place. I would rather use the coin to build a shelter for the ailing in the woods. They need it more than we need a manor. Besides, I have come to love our home. It is where I want to raise our children."

"If that is what ye wish, then I will see to it. 'Tis shameful that Father Murphy received word that there is no cure for those that sickened. Father said that they need to remain isolated to impede the spread of the disease. A physician is being assigned to them from Edinburgh and Father's order. He deems that prayer and perhaps a pilgrimage might offer a cure, but aye, we will build them a structure to keep them protected."

"I wish there was more we could do. My heart aches for them."

Breckin pulled her soft body against his and set his head on hers. "Ye know, lass, I should have known that I would love ye that day I met ye in the market in Edinburgh. Aye, how could I not love a lass who reprimanded me for trying to save her?"

"You remember that day?"

"Of course I do. I recall thinking how brave ye were to yell at me and then hail off to save that lad from himself. Ye have a tender heart, wife." Breckin scoffed. "The queen told me a riddle before I was forced to accept ye. It took me a long time to understand what she meant."

"*Forced* to accept me?" Eva feigned affrontery with a gasp and a hand to her chest. Then she smiled. "I wanted to hate you that day, the day of our wedding. You were taking me away from my home, my da, everything I knew. But I lived a lonely existence then. Now, I have you and am finding my way here. I am happy, Breckin."

"As am I. Even though the king bade us to fight for the lassies' hands, it was the women who made their choice, aye. The queen's interference served me well and I will make no complaint. I remember exactly what Margaret said that day...the riddle... 'A dragon sits on a high cliff with her bright shimmering scales for all to see.' That is ye, all bonny and shining with glorious beauty. She said, 'All bask in her beauty and she appeals to all but most fear to get too near.' I suppose that is true because ye intimidated the hell out of me. Then she said, 'on the outside, she might seem unapproachable, but being a renowned warrior, I am sure that you have the intelligence to uncover the beauty within.' She saw the goodness in ye and bade me to do the same. I admit it might have taken me a wee bit more time to see it, och ye are kindness wrapped in beauty."

"Keep with those compliments and I shall let it go to my head," Eva scoffed.

Breckin bellowed a laugh when she then eyed him coyly. "Ye know, lass, that ye do sometimes resemble a dragon. I am not faulting ye because it takes a strong-willed lass to stand up to a Buchanan."

"You, Breckin Buchanan, are exasperating. Why did the king force you to marry? I never asked and you never spoke of it."

"There were several reasons. He professed that I owed him a good amount of coin in unpaid taxes. Alexander dangled the brawl with the other lairds before me and knew I would want to partake in the battles. Then when I saw ye… I never laid eyes on a more bonny woman. I thought ye haughty, but once ye showed your true self, there was no denying that ye have a pure heart. My clan reveres ye as do I, Eva, for ye won our hearts and they are yours to keep."

"I will do my best to hold them close." She paused and lifted her head, apparently taking in the beauty around her. "At least you do not need to worry about paying coin to the king now, for you have plenty to keep our clan debt-free."

"Aye, but there was one other thing he demanded… He bade me to join him when he confronts Norway to take the northern lands from Haakon. We will soon go to war and must go to give our arms when the king calls upon us."

"Oh, no. I thought we might have a little peace before you start fighting again."

"There is no end, lass, in fighting here in the north, especially when my life is dedicated to being a warrior. We have a saying within our clan: *Henceforth forward, the honor shall grow ever brighter*. I will never allow my clan to back down from its duty to our sovereign."

She wrapped her arms around his body and nuzzled her face against his chest. "Are you certain you wouldn't want to do something else? I really think farming suits you better."

Breckin laughed because in all his life, he never envisioned being a farmer. He also never envisioned loving a beautiful woman such as Eva and finding happiness. But he'd done that and more. Because of Eva, the Buchanans would prosper and he'd have an enriched life. He'd always be a warrior in his heart but now he was more: a husband, future father, brother, and laird.

EPILOGUE

Firth of the River Clyde, Largs, Scotland
October 2, 1263

THE ARMIES OF the clans rode forth in battle formations. On the last leg of the journey toward the coast, a storm battered the land and sea. None of the Highlanders and Scotsmen minded the pelting rain or brisk winds, for they were intent to win victory for their king. As they waited for the Norwegian vessels to reach land, they watched with awed reverence as Haakon's cavalry battled to salvage their vessels from the choppiness of the water.

Once on the ground, their enemy's boots stomped ever courageously forward to meet them. Arms were drawn, and the infantry and cavalry of the Scottish forces confronted the contingent sent by Haakon to secure his lands. It wasn't to be because their men were easily divided between the beach and a mound. The Norwegians sprinted to rejoin their men in the battle but the second group thought they were retreating and returned to their ships.

Those who remained had no choice but to raise their swords in defense of their army and nation. Bodies littered the beach, and after a day's long battle, the Scots took up position by the mound and secured it. But their enemy returned, and the Scots withdrew. When the sun rose, the Norwegians returned to collect their dead. Victory was on the Scots' side and though most wanted to cheer, they were too dog-tired. Norway's fleets fled back to their lands to nurse their wounds and bury their dead, thereby abdicating the land in the hands of Scotland.

Four men marched from the encampments that sat beyond the mound. Each intended to bid farewell to their king now that their duty was done.

Inside his tent, Alexander stood warming his hands by a fire on the ground in the center of the high-pitched ceiling. When he saw the men enter, he grinned slightly because they had helped him achieve what he'd set out to do—stretch his lands to the reaches of the northern part of the island.

"Welcome, come, warm yourselves." Alexander twitched a finger at the page who hurried forth to give each man a cup of ale.

"Cameron, Buchanan, MacKendrick, and Mackintosh, you are now standing on Scottish soil. I give you my thanks, for I could not have done this without you and your brethren."

"Ye gave us no choice, sire," Breckin said with a lilt of humor in his voice.

"Aye, och we would have come to support ye without ye forcing us to take a bride," Magnus said. "We shall always stand with Scotland regardless of the reward."

"You cannot tell me that you are displeased with your brides. From what Edmund tells me…" Alexander chortled a laugh and rolled his eyes slightly. "He says that ye are all well pleased as are the women."

The men broke out in laughter.

Alexander raised his cup. "To the winsome brides."

The men lifted their cups and clanked them together.

"This gives me an idea," Alexander said. "When I bound you to your brides, I wanted to gain your alliance, and in giving you each a bonny lass for a wife, your lives have been enriched."

"Mine certainly has," Magnus said. "Before I married Kendra, I only cared about my clan. Now I have a family. We are expecting another bairn."

The men offered their congratulations by raising their cups

and said in unison, "Slàinte."

After downing the ale in his cup, Shaw said, "Peace has come to the Mackintoshes thanks to Sorsha. We are planning to wed our lass to one of the Cameron lads. We will keep alliances with steadfast marriages."

"Alliances are spreading, sire, because of your forthright deeds," Breckin said. "Eva is expecting a bairn this spring and we shall consider his or her betrothed most carefully. Our clan rejoices."

Declan chortled. "Our congratulations, Breckin. Are ye not a farmer now? I heard tell that ye have given up being a warrior. Or will, now that this battle is won."

Breckin grinned before he answered, "Ye saw the effects of me being a warrior there on the beach. We will continue to test our arms, och many of my clansmen want to farm. Why not prosper our fields and farms when our arms are not needed?" He raised his sword in the air, sending a shimmer of colors on the tent fabric above from the jewels in the hilt that now embellished it.

Alexander bobbed his head. "Too true."

"What was your idea, sire?" Magnus asked.

"Well, now that the brides brought you fine Highlanders to heel and strengthened Scotland as I had hoped, I just might send a bride to Haakon. He has a son in need of the guiding hand of a sweet Scottish lass."

The page hurried forward and refilled their cups. When he finished, he stepped back into the shadows and kept himself unseen.

"To the maid of Scotland, may she bring Norway to its heels and give Haakon's son strong sons," Alexander said and raised his cup.

A bride was exactly what was needed to join the two nations and perhaps bring about long needed peace to the region.

The End

Author's Note

The Maid of Scotland, Margaret's daughter named the same, became Queen of Norway and was crowned by the Archbishop of Nidaros in Bergen. Margaret tried to cultivate her husband by teaching him languages, manners, and fashion, but she was met with hostility by her mother-in-law who dominated her position, husband, and the court. (We married women have all been there, haven't we?) Unfortunately, Margaret died in childbirth while giving Norway its Maid, her daughter and namesake, also named Margaret.

The song Eva sings is called *Salve Regina*. Originally composed in the Middle Ages, this was written in Latin, the primary language of the time, in honor of the Virgin Mary. This song is regarded as anonymous by most musicologists, but is also referenced back to a German monk in the eleventh-century.

My favorite rendition can be found here, if you want to give it a listen. https://youtu.be/f0YWKLNhTvE?si=2aIsma98xm0ESQhY

I hope you enjoyed these loving and emotional Highland tales. Thank you for reading, readers.

Fondly,
Kara Griffin

About the Author

Read a Scottish or Medieval Historical Romance book by Kara Griffin and transport yourself to the mystical enchanting realms of the Scottish Highlands and Medieval Britain. Stories of noble swoon-worthy warriors and strong but sweet heroines will have you rooting for them as they encounter dastardly villains, political upheaval, and family dysfunction. Be romanced with sweeping tales of love and honor.

Kara Griffin has always had a vivid imagination and has been an avid romance reader since her early years. Inspired by her grandfather's heritage, she loves all things Scottish. From the captivating land to the ancient mysticism, all inspire her to write tales that make you sigh. With heroes, heroines, villains, and romance, there's always a Happily-Ever-After in her stories.

When Kara is not writing, she enjoys family life with her husband of 34 years, daughters, and five grandchildren. Living in the Pinelands of New Jersey, she spends a lot of time at a nearby lake, the Jersey Shore, and wooded areas of the Pine Barrons. She and her family are huge sports fans and cheer on the teams of the city of Philadelphia.

Website – karagrif66.wixsite.com / authorkaragriffin
Facebook – facebook.com / AuthorKaraGriffin
BookBub – bookbub.com / authors / kara-griffin
Amazon – amazon.com / stores / Kara-
Griffin / author / B006ZCH4PG
Goodreads – goodreads.com / author / show / 1428371.Kara_Griffin
IG – authorkaragriffin

www.ingramcontent.com/pod-product-compliance
Lightning Source LLC
Chambersburg PA
CBHW071248300726
48975CB00002B/600